PLANS

BY
VICTORIA J.M. HOFFBECK

PLANS

BY

VICTORIA J. M. HOFFBECK
©2017

Cover Art: Watercolor by Elaine Frederickson

"For I know the plans I have for you,"
declares the Lord,
"plans to prosper you
and not to harm you,
plans to give you hope and a future..."

–Jeremiah 29:11

PROLOGUE

Two massive peacock-blue doors opened and white sunlight poured into the room. It streamed across the marble tiles and danced among the thousand prisms of the chandelier and enveloped the tall, dark figure waiting inside the threshold.

"Dr. Weisman," the man called. "Please, follow me."

Standing with a cup in one hand, Dr. Abraham Weisman looked at the expressionless face of the man standing there.

"Yes," Dr. Weisman replied. He set the delicate bone china cup on the table beside him and followed the man through the doors.

"You have an appointment at eleven o'clock this morning. I will do my best to make certain you are not late," the man said, as they walked down the corridor. The doctor noted a hint of tenderness in his voice and looked at the secretary's lean face.

"Thank you, Jonas," Dr. Weisman said. Jonas acknowledged him with a slight nod and opened the doors in front of him.

"Dr. Weisman," the secretary announced. During the short walk, the sun had hidden itself behind a bank of ominous gray clouds. The room was dark except for the light of one small lamp that sat on top of the polished mahogany desk. The door latch snapped shut behind him and the doctor looked at the two people before him. Katherine stood in the corner of the large office, gazing out the window while slowly twirling a cord of satin trim between her fingertips. She turned to the doctor and feigned a smile. William sat behind his desk holding a newspaper. His eyes were dark and sunken with deep circles of sleepless nights painted into his face. For a long, uncomfortable moment no one spoke.

William's jaw shifted from side to side as he ground his teeth. He dropped the newspaper onto the desk, and his chiseled granite features sharpened, then planed as he came to his feet.

"Abraham, thank you for coming today. You have probably guessed why I have called you here," William said, looking into the doctor's eyes. The doctor looked down at the floor and felt the muscles in the back of his neck tighten and an aching throb stiffen his shoulder. He stepped forward and looked directly at William, cupping his hands behind his back as he waited for him to continue.

William's mouth opened without uttering a sound and then closed again. He hesitated and then with new resolve he leaned forward and rested his white knuckles on the top of his desk. The tooled leather pad sunk under the pressure of his fists. "Abraham, we value your friendship and you know what respect we have for you and for what you have done for the University," he said, as his eyes gravitated back to the newspaper. The bold black letters of the headline taunted him, prodding him to read on. He tried to turn away only to read it again and again silently to himself. He took a long, deep breath and exhaled slowly as he listened to the drops of icy rain spattering against the windows.

"We are grateful and very pleased with the work you have done," William said without looking up from the paper. "I hope we have not interrupted your schedule." He rubbed his wrinkled brow as Katherine drew to her husband's side and clutched his arm, her eyes darting to his and then to Abraham's.

"Abraham, it's just that we are so anxious to hear the news," she said. "Has Marcus been accepted? We try not to interfere but Jacob has already heard from the medical school board and we just thought that perhaps this could be the answer. He wants this so badly, Abraham, and we hoped that being with you he might...." Katherine stumbled over her words, until at a loss, she resigned herself to silence.

"We have tried everything!" William said. He stood up paced the floor, his hands reaching out in question. "Why should this make a difference?"

"Hope," Katherine replied quietly.

"Hope! With much or little, he is the same." William turned to Abraham. "He has attended the finest schools, we made him serve in the military, I even sent him to Greenland for survival training with nothing for six months. And in everything he excels. But this...this rebellion, this recklessness of his, he shames our house," William said, his eyes burning as brightly as blue flames. "Ever since he was a boy he has been like this. It is as if I have watched him again and again walk, no, run up to the very edge of a cliff and dance on it, as if he were challenging God, testing Him, even daring Him! I tell you Abraham, I am at my end," William cried in anger. "My patience is exhausted, my efforts are fruitless, and now I fear my heart is growing cold to my own son."

"William John!" Katherine said as tears welled up in her eyes. "Do not say such a thing!"

A small quake of thunder rumbled in the drifting clouds and quieted as it passed by. "I'm sorry, Katherine. I'm tired. I'm tired of a lot of things," he said, rubbing his brow. Dr. Weisman focused on the small statue on William's desk, a bronze statue of children playing by a stream.

"He does excel," Abraham said quietly, still looking at the statue. "Marcus' grades are exceptional, his test scores are strong and his training and experience are superb." He looked up at them. "He is intuitive, direct and confident, all characteristics I look for in a new student."

"But,..." William said.

Abraham glanced at the small statue again, noticing the little girl in pigtails bending down to dip her finger into the stream. "Healing is not just a science or just an art," he said slowly. "It is an act of love." A trace of sunlight pierced the skies and entered into the sullen office, brightening the room. "William, I have heard you say on occasion, that for a person to be their very best they must have a right heart. I agree and perhaps this is even more true for a physician. The body and the spirit live so closely together that to neglect one is to neglect the other. It is not enough to have knowledge and it is not enough to feel. You must have both."

"We understand," Katherine said in a whisper.

William sat down and rested his elbows on the edge of his desk and looked down at the morning newspaper. His son's face looked back at him from a black and white photograph. He was in the middle of a crowded room holding a half empty bottle of liquor in one hand and a gaudy, over made-up woman in his other.

"He doesn't have an evil heart, William, it's just a lost heart looking for answers," Abraham said. "But I'm not the answer he is looking for."

"But Abraham,…" Katherine pleaded.

"The board has made their decision then?" William sighed.

"No," Abraham said looking down at the floor and then at William. "The board has left this decision up to me."

"And you have made your decision?" William asked. Katherine looked on anxiously with begging tears in her eyes. Abraham took a deep breath.

"No, I have not," Abraham said. "I have been waiting."

"For what?" William asked, puzzled.

"For this moment," Abraham said.

"Why? I don't understand."

"If I decide to accept Marcus, it will be on my terms. I will have it no other way," Abraham said, feeling his neck twinge with pain. "You must promise me that for the next four years there will be no interference from this house. Marcus will do exactly as I say, as do all the other students in my care. There will be no special treatment," Abraham went on. "For the first two years he will eat, sleep and work with the other students, no exception. If he fails, he will be expelled. If he takes special privileges, he will be expelled. If there is any attempt by this house to circumvent my rules in any way," he said looking at Katherine, "I will submit my resignation. If I am to do this, I must be in full control."

William's tired eyes glistened. "Abraham my friend, you have my word."

"Katherine? Do I have your word also?" Abraham asked. Katherine's soft pink lips quivered and pouted as she forced herself to look at the kindly doctor.

"You will take care of him, won't you, Abraham?" she asked. William took her hand and held it close to his side.

"Katherine," William chided, "Marcus is going to school, not on an arctic expedition with General Krovic! Although, he might earn himself a ticket on that little adventure after I speak with him," he said, picking up the newspaper and then dropping it back down on the desk.

"It will be a shock," Abraham said, "but I haven't lost a student yet."

William's intercom buzzed and he pushed the button with one finger still holding onto Katherine's hand. "Sir, I am sorry to interrupt but Dr. Weisman has an appointment at eleven o'clock this morning."

"Thank you, Jonas," William said with a ring of cheer that made him smile back at his own voice.

"I must be going," Abraham said. "Your cousin, Beatrice, is still having trouble with her knee."

"Is she still blaming me for that?" William asked. Katherine rolled her eyes as she dabbed a tear from her cheek and shook her head at William's denial. "I had to defend the net," he said, looking at his wife.

"Tennis isn't your game," Abraham said, holding onto the brass door handle to exit the office.

"And who won our last match?" William asked.

"It isn't my game either," Abraham said as he opened the door. He stopped and looked back at the couple. The clouds had disappeared from the sky and the morning sun was beaming through the windows again, sparkling on the drops of rain that clung to the panes of glass on either side of them. Katherine's hand rested on William's shoulder as he sat in his chair, not unlike the pose of the portrait that hung behind them, except that Katherine was closer to him, caressing him. William reached for her hand and covered it with his own and then leaned comfortably into her side.

"You know, Marcus did do fairly well on his entrance exam," Abraham said.

"He did?" Katherine asked eagerly. "He never mentioned it."

"How well?" William asked.

"Second," Abraham said. William raised his eyebrows.

"That *is* good."

"Very good."

"To Jacob," Katherine guessed. "He placed second to Jacob." Abraham nodded his head reluctantly. "A right heart," she whispered.

"Yes, Your Highness," Abraham said. With a slight bow and nod of his head he opened the door. "Good day, Your Majesties," he said, and closed the doors behind him.

CHAPTER 1

Megan Buchanan stopped to admire the magnificent backdrop of snow-capped mountains in the distance. The morning air was crisp and cold as she walked along the avenue. She took a deep breath of the early autumn air and exhaled slowly.

How did I get here, she wondered, gazing at the watercolor-blue sky. She tucked her scarf closer to her neck, laughed, and pulled her hat further down on her head.

"You don't have to answer that, Lord," she said aloud. "I know how I got here - a crazy uncle and a fleeting moment of insanity." The sound of the steady, hollow clomping of her boots on the cobblestone walkway slowed and then stopped. She looked again at the mountains in the distance and then at a glimmering spiral of frost that caught her eye. The frost had wrapped itself around the wrought iron fence like a Christmas garland. The untarnished black railing that separated her from the vacant avenue was an elaborate pattern of swirls and scrolls that mimicked the pristine village that she would call home for the next three years. Looking past the fence to the unfamiliar narrow streets of stone and brick buildings, an unsettling chill permeated her body and tingled through her fingertips and toes.

One day you're at home and the next day you're halfway around the world, she thought. It's not the *how did I get here* that befuddles me so much, Lord, Megan prayed silently, *it's the why*. Life was finally starting to go as planned.

In the still of the morning, her mind drifted back home. She turned to the west, thinking for a moment, that if she just looked back she would be able to see Minnesota in the distance. The weight of disappointment held her in her place. In her sight was another row of three- and four-story brick buildings wedged together forming an impenetrable wall. "It was all going as planned," she murmured aloud.

Her thoughts swept back in time: finishing college, walking up to the podium to receive her master's degree and running to the mailbox to find that she had been accepted into medical school in the fall. Everything was in order until Professor Joseph Buchanan summoned her into his office.

* * *

"I knew you had talent! I just knew it!" he said, pacing the floor and holding a bundle of ruffled papers in his hand. "You did it Megan! You did it!" the gangly professor said with a mighty yelp.

"Did what? What did I do?" Megan asked, mocking his enthusiasm with an excited giddiness. The professor paced the floor and then he sat down behind his desk, stacked high with reams of stapled and sorted papers and color-coordinated file folders. He sat staring at the papers clutched in his hand. Megan's eyes narrowed as she shut the door.

"Okay, Uncle Joe, what exactly did I do?" Megan asked, as she watched her uncle run his fingers through his flowing shoulder-length dark hair. "Better yet, what have you been up to?"

"Sit down Megan, sit down," he said, trying unsuccessfully to settle into his usual calm demeanor. She slowly sat down in the big leather chair he'd brought with him from the ranch in Texas; the room held many of his Texas artifacts, including the Mexican blankets and rugs scattered about the room and the bony steer head hanging on the wall that Aunt Julie refused to have in the house.

"Megan, you won the Scolengard. You won the scholarship!" he said, his face beaming and his eyes glazed with tears.

"That's impossible," Megan said with a laugh. "I never applied. Besides, I'd never have a chance at something like that. They have applicants from all over the world. Thousands of them."

"You did it Megan. You did it." The papers in his hand trembled as he held them out to her.

"How could that be?" Megan asked. "I'm telling you Uncle Joe, I never applied. There's no way I could have won. There must be some mistake."

"I applied for you," her uncle spat out the words at lightning speed.

"You what?" Megan said, jumping to her feet. "How? How could you? You'd need my transcripts and my records and...."

"We automatically enter the top three students and since I'm your advisor I entered for you."

"Without asking me?" she sputtered, with hands on her hips and eyebrows furrowed into knots.

"Now Megan, don't be angry," he begged and came around to her from behind his desk. "I know how you are about these things. You'd never do it on your own. You no more than admitted to it just now," he said and gripped her shoulders. His mournful brown eyes always exacted pity from her but she wondered if it was deserved this time.

"Oh, Megan you did it! You won. You did what your dad and I couldn't do," he whispered and gave her a hug that took her breath away. "You won the highest honor at the best institution in the world. You're going to be a doctor and not just any doctor, you're going to be a doctor from Dreiholm University! After you have completed your education there, you will be able to choose your assignments and research anywhere in the world!"

Megan stared at her uncle, unable to reflect his joy or his tears.

"I want to be a physician, not a research scientist," Megan protested. "I've already been accepted here. I want to stay here and if you don't mind me saying so, I think we have the best medical institution in the world and that's what I want to be, a physician. People come from all over to..."

"I know, Megan, I know," her uncle said. "But this is an opportunity of a lifetime. It was your parents' dream, my dream and then it was our dream for you and now, now it has come true. Megan, think!"

"Dreiholm," Megan whispered. Her eyes began to fill with tears. "I don't think I can. With all that has happened, I just want to stay home."

The professor sat on the edge of his desk, still hanging onto the papers in his hand. Megan had fallen back into his tattered, leather chair. "I know how difficult these past few years have been for you, but Megan, I wouldn't be doing my duty if I didn't try to convince you to do this. Only one person in the world is chosen for this honor and this year it's you. You have a gift, Megan. Don't let this blessing slip away."

"I don't even know where Dreiholm is," Megan protested.

"It's a small country," her uncle said with a hint of renewed enthusiasm. "It's tucked in the middle of a mountain range in Europe, a beautiful little country, an old country with a long history. I know you'd like it. Your aunt and I loved it. We were there before you were born."

"What would I be doing there?" Megan asked.

"They want you to carry on with the research you have started here," her uncle said hesitantly.

"But I have plans," Megan protested.

The professor pushed back his hair. "Plans," he said gently. "You planned on graduating with your high school class until you got mono and ended up graduating before them, remember? You planned on going away to college until your parents became ill. You planned on going right on to medical school until this research came up. Megan, we all have plans," he said with a tender smile. "And God has His."

The clock on the wall thumped as its hands labored around its face. Megan took the papers from her uncle's hand. The fine ivory stationary was damp with his imprints. She read the letter slowly and her uncle watched as she closed her eyes. A tear fell from her cheek and onto the letter.

"Your research, your parent's research is important, Megan, more important now than ever before. It could save lives, many lives," he said softly. "You'll be part of the Black Box program. Only I and a very few others will know, you understand." Megan nodded her head.

"Megan, I believe this is part of your plan."

"So, I'm on an adventure then?" Megan said with a forced smile.

"Of a lifetime," her uncle said.

* * *

Megan could still hear his words as she shook herself alert to the present, and the quaint university village outside Hebl, Dreiholm. A cold gust of air rushed across her face, nipping her nose. She burrowed her hands into the pockets of her red coat and forced herself to look away from the brick barrier and turned toward the mountains and the blue skies above. Buck up, Megan, she said to herself. You're here now and that's that. There's work to be done.

CHAPTER 2

The mission of the day was to find an apartment close to the university. Since her arrival, the activities had been nonstop and ran late into the evening hours. Megan had attended countless dinners and was given tours of the university, the city and the outlying villages. She met with faculty and was assigned advisors, classrooms, a laboratory for her research, and a dormitory room to live in. It was all very impressive and modern within the walls of the old buildings, except for the dorm room where she was to stay while she was in Dreiholm.

The small cement block room was painted a light prison-like gray. It had a large closet in the corner of the room and was furnished with a small wooden desk and chair, a gray metal lamp and a twin bed with steel springs and a black and white tic mattress. When she entered the room, the mattress was tied into a roll with a piece of frayed rope and leaned against the cement wall. Megan pulled back the curtain to the only window in the room, hoping for the best and found that it faced a brick wall with a series of rusted drain pipes attached to it.

The dormitory director, a motherly German woman with a gigantic smile and a mound of graying blonde hair pinned to the top of her head, handed her two keys. "Other students are not here until the fifteenth," she said, her blue eyes bright. "The yellow key is to the big door downstairs and blue key is for your room." The sturdy woman went to the end of the room, picked up the mattress and flung it on the bedsprings. The rope snapped and the mattress flopped open. The director pulled out the rope from underneath the mattress and opened the window. "The bathroom is down the hall. Enjoy now, in two weeks the other girls will come," she said, rolling her eyes as if she dreaded the day. "The noise!" she sighed. "If you need me, I will be in the office downstairs."

"Excuse me," Megan said, standing in the middle of the room. "Before you leave, how many girls are on this floor?"

"Twenty, twenty-five," the woman said.

"Twenty-five!" Megan said incredulously. "And how many bathrooms are there?"

"One."

"One?" Megan asked.

"Enjoy now," the director said as she went down the hallway to the stairs.

"Thank you," Megan called. She pulled out the chair from the small desk and sat down. Gazing around at the bleak surroundings once again, she picked up her purse and dug through it for her calendar. "I have ten days before my boxes arrive," she said. "Ten days to find an apartment."

If her need for an apartment wasn't so urgent, Megan could have easily spent her first day alone away from the campus investigating the shops and exploring the cubbies that made up the university village. The quiet streets were a relief from the bustling business district of Hebl on her arrival, Megan thought, as she walked down the avenue. The business district was like most big cities, a stunning glitter at night but an intimidating circus of activity by day. But around the university village there were prim townhomes and cottages adorned with window boxes filled with yellow edelweiss, violet primrose, and blue gentian. Not far down the block she could see an outdoor market about to open. It was an enchanting mix of old and new: the latest automobiles and scooters traveling on the aged, cobblestone streets; shop owners and street vendors chatting with customers and neighbors as they peddled their wares over the constant hum of cash registers; the fairytale castle-like buildings at the university full of state-of-the-art technology that she would soon enjoy.

Megan was relieved to find that most of the Dreiholmians spoke English and were willing to exercise their skill with a struggling guest like herself. "It is beautiful," she thought aloud as she kept her eyes on the mountains. Like an enormous white, blue, and gray picket fence, the mountains encircled the entire country. These rugged and dangerous mountains, she read before coming to Dreiholm, protected this small country through two world wars. Dreiholm was virtually untouched by invading forces and in its peace, the people immersed themselves in engineering and research.

Megan stopped at the address marker and checked the slip of paper she pulled from the pocket of her coat. She looked up at the building in front of her. So far, so good, she thought, stuffing the clipping back into her pocket. It was a three-story brick building with black shutters. A large, decorative streetlamp sat at the bottom of the stairway and gleamed with a fresh coat of black paint. Megan ran up the steps, and entering the first set of doors, pushed the red button that she assumed was the manager's doorbell. A thin man dressed in paint-splattered overalls and a cap answered the door. "I'm inquiring about the apartment for rent," Megan said. The man looked perplexed until Megan retrieved the newspaper clipping in her pocket and held it up for him to see.

"Come," the man said with a smile, and beckoned her to follow him down the hall and down a short flight of stairs to an open door. "I'm painting the apartment now." He stopped in front of the door. "I am Han Grutner, owner," he said in broken English.

"I'm Megan Buchanan," she said, "nice to meet you." Megan looked at the plank floor and carved wooden doors. "How old is this building, Mr. Grutner?"

"My father had it before me and his father before him...very old but, I fixed up new, new furnace, new windows, new roof, paint," he said as he opened up the apartment door. "Student?" he asked.

"Yes," Megan said, as she looked around the room.

"Six blocks to the university. Nice walk in the morning," he said as he set down the paint can on some old newspapers lying in the foyer of the apartment. He meticulously wiped the can and then twisted on its plastic lid.

The freshly white-washed rooms were quaint but cramped, Megan thought. The bedroom was just big enough for a twin bed and the living space and kitchen would only hold one small table and two chairs. Perhaps it was the dark brown carpeting or the half windows at the street level that reminded her of her bleak dorm room. "How much is it?" Megan asked.

"Three hundred schulen a month with heat."

Megan scanned her conversion chart and followed the row over to American dollars. "Well, that's within my budget," she said. She tapped the chart on the palm of her hand and looked around the room once more. "Are there any other rooms?"

"Top floor, but apartment will not be ready for one more week," Mr. Grutner said as he walked out to the hallway.

"Could I see it?" Megan asked. He nodded and closed the apartment's door and then thought better of it and opened it again while the paint dried. He led Megan up the three flights of stairs and opened the only door on the third floor. The apartment was one large room. At one end was a wall of windows looking out over the street and in the corner, by the windows, was an open kitchen with a large island to cook and eat at. At the opposite end of the room was a stone fireplace with two doors on either side. "Right door closet," Mr. Grutner said pointing to the doors, "left door lavatory." He hurried to the opposite end of the room, opened the doors and then pulled on a loop that stuck out from the wall. "Bed," he said, as he carefully set it down on the wood floor.

"Perfect!" Megan said, clasping her hands together. "How much is it?"

Mr. Grutner held his finger up to his lips and calculated Megan's eager question. "Six hundred and fifty," he said firmly.

"Oh," Megan said, and closed the kitchen cabinet door. "I know I can't afford that."

"Six hundred," Mr. Grutner countered.

"I can really only afford five hundred," Megan said.

"Five hundred and fifty is the lowest I go, no less," Mr. Grutner insisted.

"With heat?" Megan winced, hoping for at least that much.

"Heat, electricity, water and garbage," Mr. Grutner said, standing a bit taller than before. Megan opened and closed doors and looked around the room once again and began to imagine how she could arrange the few pieces of furniture she had coming from home. "I'd only need to buy a couch and maybe a chair," Megan said excitedly.

She turned. "Deal!" she said holding out her hand to a puzzled Mr. Grutner. "I'll take it for five hundred and fifty schulen a month." With that Mr. Grutner smiled back and shook her hand. He locked the door as they left and led her back down the stairway.

"You are American?" he asked.

"Yes," Megan said, "does it show?"

"American man rented this apartment before. He liked the open space," Mr. Grutner replied.

"Where the deer and the antelope play," Megan laughed.

He looked at her, puzzled, then shrugged. After all, she too was American. "Apartment will be ready in one week, one month rent deposit and first month rent now. You must rent apartment for full year," Mr. Grutner said, and opened a door in the hallway at the bottom of the stairs. He pulled out a copy of a lease, among neat stacks of paper on two shelves.

"That will be fine," Megan said and signed the lease. "I don't have a bank here yet. Would you take a check from my bank in the United States?"

"Credit card?" he asked.

Megan nodded and pulled out a credit card. Mr. Grutner opened the door again and to the side was an automated credit card system.

I should have known, Megan thought smiling. Mr. Grutner ran the plastic card through the scanner and in a moment he handed her a receipt. "Now that that's taken care of," Megan said happily, "I'll see you in a week."

"Yes," he said holding the door open for her. "One week."

Megan walked briskly down the street thinking of her new home. The sun had warmed the air and now the welcome breeze rustled the tops of the pines in the park across the street. "Maybe forest green curtains," she said to herself, then stopped abruptly. "What have I done? I have to buy books and I have fees. I can't afford this each month." She sat down on a bench and recalculated her expenses, subtracting out any luxury she could think of and she still came up short. I'll just have to get a part-time job, Megan thought. She walked to town and sent an e-mail to her uncle from a coffee shop.

Uncle Joe:

All is well, except that my expenses will be exceeding my means. Can you point me to possible part-time work? Give my love to Aunt Julie. I'll call soon.

Meg

Megan was asleep in her dorm room when the telephone rang. The old, black telephone had a thunderous ring that made her jump from her deep, dreamless sleep. She wrapped her pillow around her ears as she grappled for the receiver. "Hello."

"Megan? Megan is that you?"

"Uncle Joe?" Megan asked. She pulled the pillow off her head and squinted in the darkness to see the red glowing alarm clock sitting on the desk across the room, "Uncle Joe, do you know that it's two o'clock in the morning here? Is everything all right?"

"Yes, yes. Everything is fine," he said. Megan curled back down underneath the blankets and put the pillow back on top of her head. "I called as soon as I got your message. I figured crazy people didn't sleep so I thought it was safe to call."

Megan wrinkled her nose. "Very funny."

"What's this about a job? You have a job. You have your studying and your research."

"Before you get started," she said with her eyes closed, "I want you to know that at this very moment I'm sleeping in a dormitory that could pass for a penitentiary and that in less than ten days I will be sharing a bathroom, one bathroom mind you, with twenty-five other very young women, let me emphasize young women, who will only be one floor above twenty-six very young men." There was silence on the other end of the line. "They don't have housing for old folks like me and I really don't want to be a den mother to fifty-one very excited freshmen, nor do I care to share a bathroom with any of them, especially on Friday night, if you get my drift."

"Okay, okay. I get the picture. How much is the apartment?" Uncle Joe asked.

"Five hundred and fifty schulen a month," she said.

"Five hundred and fifty! Why, they're taking you to the cleaners. I knew I should have gone over with you and got you settled. Three hundred should get you a nice room close to campus."

"If I cut back on my expenses and use the money I'm given for living expenses in this dorm toward my apartment, I'm only short about two hundred schulen a month. And it already has a bed so I won't have to buy one."

"Megan, I don't think you realize how busy you're going to be once school starts and your research project begins. They're expecting a lot from you and you won't have time for any type of job."

"I know I can do it. I've done it before and if you'll remember my grades and research results have always been better when I was working part-time."

"Nice try," Joe said. "This is serious business, Megan."

"I know," Megan said, pulling the pillow off her head and tucking it underneath her neck, "but I really love it."

"Love what?" he asked.

"The apartment."

"You'll get over it."

"I signed a lease," Megan said.

"Megan!"

"I figured it out. I'll only need a few hours a week to make up the difference."

"Your aunt and I will pick up the rest," Joe said without hesitation.

"No, I can't let you do that. I'll take it out of what Mom and Dad left me if I need to."

"Megan, what your parents left you was for your future, a home, your retirement or an emergency, not for a better place to crack a book while you're at school. No, we'll send you the money."

"How about a job?"

"You don't have a work permit and besides I think you're missing the point. You're going to be busy. You won't have time for a job."

"There are plenty of American companies here and they can get me a permit. I would only need a few hours a week."

"I'll send you a few dollars a month," he said.

Megan sighed. "I love you for offering...and for everything...but I know I can do it. The distraction will be good for me. Do you know anyone who could use a helping hand?"

"You're an obstinate child," her uncle said in a low drawn-out drawl. Megan smiled knowing she had won the battle. "I have a friend who owns a pharmaceutical company in Hebl. I'll call him and see what he has to say."

"Okay then," Megan said.

"I'll call tomorrow and let you know what I find out."

"Say hi to Aunt Julie. And Uncle Joe,..."

"Yes, Megan," Joe said, as if he were patiently waiting on a demanding child.

"I love you," she said. The silence was so long she thought she lost the connection or he had already hung up.

"We love you too," he reassured her. "I'll call tomorrow. Good night, darlin'."

" 'Night."

"Megan?"

"Yeah?"

"Where is this apartment?"

"It's about six blocks to the university. The bus stops right at the corner."

"It's not on the first floor, is it?"

"No, it's on the third floor and it has a good bright street light at the entrance and has two locks on the apartment door," Megan said. "You'll like it. I promise."

"Good night, child."

" 'Night."

CHAPTER 3

Mr. Charles Payton was in Dreiholm for an extended stay and agreed to meet Megan the following Monday morning. Brier Pharmaceuticals wasn't located in the fashionable business district of Hebl where Megan expected it to be but near the university, only minutes away from her assigned laboratory. It was a foreboding building with no windows on its outside walls, only stone shadows of windows where they should be. Inside the fortress stood a tower that loomed above the gray walls and it peaked at the top like a castle turret.

Goodness, Megan thought as she approached the only entrance to the building. The glass doors parted automatically and as she passed a second set of doors she noticed a security guard waiting for her at the entry.

"Could I see your identification?" he asked in his native tongue.

"Do you speak English?" Megan asked timidly.

"Could I see your identification?" he asked again in English. Megan handed him her passport. He looked it over and then looked at the picture twice before handing it back to her.

"Miss Boocannon," he started.

"Buchanan," Megan corrected him politely.

"Ms. Buchanan?" a woman's voice called. "You're right on time. Mr. Payton is expecting you. I'm Rose Hanson, Mr. Payton's assistant. You can follow me." Rose was as radiant as her name. Confined to a wheelchair, her bright pink suit dulled in comparison to her smile and immediate warmth.

"It's a pleasure to meet you," Megan said, shaking her hand.

"Frank, I'll take it from here," Rose said cheerfully to the security guard.

Megan followed Rose through another set of security doors and to the second set of elevators in the marble hallway. Around the corner

Megan saw a profusion of light and heard the sound of falling water and the cackling of tropical birds.

"Our courtyard," Rose said, noticing Megan looking toward the light. Rose inserted a magnetic card into the elevator keypad and the door immediately opened. "I'll bring you by on our way out. The only windows we have are on the top two floors, the rest of the folks have courtside views. It's like having a bit of summer year round with the palms and birds flying around our little park."

"How nice," Megan said. She followed Rose into the elevator. Megan looked at her own reflection in the polished silver walls and as if she could hear her mother's voice in her ear, she straightened her suit coat and pushed her shoulders back and tried to smile.

"How do you like Dreiholm so far?" Rose asked.

"Oh, it's lovely," Megan said promptly.

"But, pretty far from home?" Rose asked, as the elevator swiftly accelerated up the tower.

Megan nodded.

"I've been here fifteen years next month. Green Bay, Wisconsin will always be my home but I love this place. I'm sure you will too." The elevator slowed to a smooth stop and the doors opened to a lavish cherry wood office. Rose wheeled herself behind her desk, put her card into a drawer and knocked on the door behind her. She motioned for Megan to come to the door as she turned to open it. "Chuck, Ms. Buchanan to see you." He didn't look up from his desk, but motioned to Megan to come forward. Megan followed Rose on what seemed like an endless journey to his desk. Rose gestured to a chair and Megan sat down, scanning the many family photographs that hung on the walls and were displayed in the curio cabinet that sat behind Mr. Payton's chair.

"Rose," Mr. Payton said, as he took off his reading glasses. "Rose, would you send these to O'Brien?" He stuffed some papers he had been looking at into a manila envelope and handed them to her.

"Certainly, do you need anything else before I go?" Rose asked. Mr. Payton looked at Megan and paused. "No, I'm just going to have a little visit here with Miss Buchanan," he said as he picked up his reading glasses and began to rock them by their bow. His steady, unflinching gaze made Megan uneasy, as if she had met up with a cat wagging its tail, but not knowing if it was making friends or readying itself to bite. "Rose, tell Jones I won't be able to make lunch today. Schedule it for tomorrow."

"Cancel Jones?" Rose asked. She looked at Megan and then at Mr. Payton who was still staring at her.

"Hum?" Mr. Payton said turning to Rose, "Yes, go ahead and cancel."

"Okay, then." Rose said. She put the papers on her lap and slowly turned her chair to leave. A moment later Megan heard the door close behind her. Mr. Payton's completely white hair and light blue eyes were a contrast to the rich, warm colors that surrounded him. The private office, with the massive desk and floor-to-ceiling windows looking out over the company's properties and the university's park, gave Megan the impression that she was not just about to talk to another of her uncle's eccentric laboratory soul mates.

"I understand you're the recipient of the Scolengard Scholarship," Mr. Payton said.

"Yes," Megan said, shifting the portfolio she brought with her between her hands. Mr. Payton held on to his reading glasses and continued to rock them as he leaned back in his chair.

"Joe gave you grand reviews."

"Uncles have a way of doing that," Megan said, forcing a nervous grin.

"Oh, it's not without merit," Mr. Payton said as he took a faxed copy from his desk and read from the letter. "You have two undergraduate degrees, one in chemistry and another in biochemistry, you have a master's in physics and a minor in mathematics, all with honors and not without your share of hardship, I might add. You have been published not once but twice in the *Beacon Scientific Journal* for your research in molecular biology and nano-technology, and now you have won the Scolengard. Quite impressive for such a young person," Mr. Payton said, and put the paper back down on his desk.

"Now tell me, why would you want to be employed when you have the scholarship? It's a tough road and I guarantee you will be busier than you can ever imagine."

"I leased an apartment that is more than I expected," Megan said. She could feel her face turn red after she said it and immediately wished she hadn't.

"Perhaps it would be easier to find a less expensive apartment."

"Mr. Payton, I'm terribly sorry. I didn't mean to put you in an awkward situation," Megan said, as she stood to leave. "I know that my uncle called and probably asked you to try to discourage me from getting a job and then if that didn't work, he most likely asked you to give me a job that wouldn't hinder my work at the university. I'm sorry that we wasted your time on something that I am sure was a nuisance and that is completely unfair to you and this corporation."

Mr. Payton laughed and set his reading glasses on his desk. "Sit down, Miss Buchanan, please," he said. "You're right about your uncle. He isn't happy about your going to work while you're at the university and I have to agree with him. You see we, you and I, we both have something in common. Many years ago, I received the Scolengard." Megan felt her way back to the chair and sat down. "And you'll have to forgive me for staring at you. It's just that you look so much like your mother."

"You knew my mother?" Megan asked.

"Your father and your mother," Mr. Payton said. "A long time ago. I was very sorry to hear about their passing."

"How did you know my parents?" Megan asked.

"We all went to school together. Your father and I were roommates in college and your mother, well, we met her our first year at school," Mr. Payton said. "Your uncle and I met years later when we both were at a conference in the States. We hit it off and through the years we've kept in contact."

"My parents never mentioned you."

Mr. Payton clasped his hands together. "Well, it's been years."

"Maybe it is because I miss them so much or because of their work but I long to hear about them, as much as I can."

Mr. Payton scratched the back of his left ear and then folded his hands and rested them on the top of his desk. He kept his eyes on his hands, sighed, and then looked up at Megan. "Back then, like today, competition was fierce," he said and rested back into his leather chair. His eyes shifted to a blue glass paperweight as if he were drifting back in time. "Your father and I studied and researched endlessly. We had big ideas. We wanted to find the cure to every cancer and run the Mayo

Clinic in our spare time," he expounded with a delightful whimsy that made Megan laugh. "But we were going about it all the wrong way. Now don't get me wrong, it's not that we didn't work hard, we did. It's just that if we saw a loophole we leapt through it or if anyone asked for volunteers we did it, if we thought it would help us get to the top of the class somehow. I'm ashamed to admit that once, before I knew what I opened my mouth for, I had volunteered to take one of my professor's daughters out to the opera. Turns out she wasn't interested in the opera but had a fetish for motorcycles. The only good thing that happened that night is that she took first prize in the motocross," Mr. Payton said as he looked at Megan biting her lip to keep from laughing.

"Go ahead, your father got a good laugh out of it too," Mr. Payton chuckled. "Your dad and I were quite the pair in school." He got up out of his chair and stood beside the window, put his hands in his pockets and looked out over the landscape. "Your mother, she was a different story. We both noticed her the first day. She was a beauty. Those eyes, just like yours," he said, looking back at Megan, "And she always had a pencil stuck her hair. I pulled it out once and her hair tumbled down in long curls," Mr. Payton said smiling. "Well, there she was, never having an unkind word for anyone. She didn't join groups or the clubs like we did, she didn't hobnob with the faculty, she didn't even study like we did and yet there she was at the top of the class. We couldn't understand it. Of course your father and I thought it was in our best interest to get to know this unusual woman dressed in overalls, and the more we were around her, the more I realized what it was."

Megan waited on his next words.

"She had a gift."

"A gift?" Megan asked.

"It's like a great concert pianist or a gold medal athlete. It isn't all practice. The greatest of the great are given a gift," Mr. Payton said, "and she had it."

"What happened?" Megan asked, relishing the story.

"Well, your father saw something else besides her outstanding intellect," he said, and Megan smiled. "It wasn't long and they began to date. Your father fell in love immediately, and we all marched on to the finish for the scholarship."

"And you won," Megan said.

"No," Mr. Payton said solemnly, "your mother did."

"What?" Megan asked. "No, she would have told me. She couldn't have."

"Things were different back then," he said bitterly. "Women were allowed in schools to be nurses, teachers or secretaries, but not scientists or doctors. And when your mother came too close to winning the scholarship, the school threw a wrench into the whole thing."

"What do you mean?" Megan asked.

"Your father and I were at a student-faculty gathering when we overheard the dean talking to one of our professors about your mother. 'It would be an embarrassment,' he said, 'to have a woman representing the school.'" Just remembering it made Mr. Payton's eyes narrow as he looked down at his shoes. "Exams were the next week, and it was no surprise to your father and I that your mother's grade from that very professor was substantially lower than her others. Then her papers weren't published and her application for the Scolengard was mysteriously lost for weeks."

"Didn't she do anything about it?"

"Your father and I went to the dean, told him what we had heard. We threatened and screamed. We convinced your mother to go to an attorney. But in the end, there was very little we could do. We didn't have enough proof, other than we just knew."

"So, she never had a chance," Megan said.

"No. Not really. On the same day I had received word that I had received the Scolengard, your mother received a personal letter from the chair of the scholarship committee. It said that her application had arrived late, that she was the finest candidate that they had ever reviewed, and he requested that she resubmit the following year."

Megan thought of her parents and their home on the river.

"You know the rest," he said, and turned back to Megan. "Your parents married and went back home to Minnesota. Your dad and I kept in contact for the first year or so and then after you came along and their jobs and my being here, sadly, we drifted apart."

Megan sat for a long moment absorbing the insights and memories of her parents.

"No regrets," Megan murmured in a dream-like memory. Mr.

Payton was watching her from the window with an inquisitive look on his face. "Before my mother died she told me she had no regrets. Mom loved her work at the hospital. And Dad, well, I never saw anyone as happy in the lab at the university as he was. We were blessed. We had a very good life together."

"I wish I could have said goodbye," he said, and sat back down at his desk. "I guess I can't change that but let's see what I can do for you."

"You don't have to feel obligated," Megan said. "Just finding out more about my parents was more than I expected."

"Nonsense," he said. "If you're determined to go through with this getting a job thing then how can I pass up a Scolengard recipient. Besides, your uncle asked if I would keep an eye on you while you're here and I told him that I would."

"My uncle still thinks I need looking after," Megan said, shaking her head.

"We all do now and then," Mr. Payton said, resting his reading glasses at the end of his nose. "I have vast experience. I have four children and ten grandchildren and one more due in March," he said, handing her a picture from his desk. It was a family portrait of his children and their spouses and grandchildren all laughing at a picnic, with one rambunctious, playful imp trying to climb on top of Mr. Payton's head.

"It looks like you have your hands full," Megan said with a broad smile.

"Like my wife says, 'What's one more?' You just let me help you here."

"What I would really like is a job for about ten hours a week. I'm not particular," Megan added quickly. "Besides my research ability, I'm fairly capable on a number of computer programs, or I'm willing to try something totally new."

"I'm sure we have something, and if we don't, we'll make something up."

"Can you do that?" Megan asked. Mr. Payton laughed out loud.

"I may not have cured cancer or run the Mayo Clinic but I do own this company."

CHAPTER 4

The first semester at the university had begun on an unusually warm autumn day. The sun was sparkling in the morning sky and Megan couldn't help feeling the excitement and hopeful anticipation. Each new year was a fresh page waiting to be filled, she thought, as she strolled down the avenue. However, opening the door to her first class and then another and another, she began to realize that this year she would be consumed in a walloping book, an encyclopedia of facts and findings with footnotes in tiny script that needed to be internalized, memorized and utilized in the ample confines of her laboratory. As days and weeks wore on, stacks of assignments, books, papers and research began to accumulate on her dining room table and then began to mount into disheveled, but ordered piles against her apartment wall. When one pile diminished, another emerged, leaving her feeling anxious and tired. Megan sighed as she thought of the heaps of data waiting for her at home.

"Bad day?" Ostride asked. Megan glanced up and over two black laboratory tables and the menagerie of glass beakers, microscopes, and glass slides to see her lab partner, Ostride Reynolds. A tall, thin young woman, Ostride's blonde hair reached down to the small of her back. Megan thought she could easily have been mistaken for a cover girl rather than an aspiring Canadian epidemiologist.

"Just tired," Megan answered.

"You could quit your job you know. Believe me, no one would think less of you," Ostride offered.

"Are you kidding? When I go there it's like a vacation. I don't have to read or study or test another sample," Megan said as she rinsed a glass slide. "I just sit in my cozy little room, snuggle into my comfortable chair and call the States to update existing orders. How much better could that be?" Megan asked as she took off her rubber gloves and dropped them into the trashcan. "No stress, no fuss, just simple, brainless work and once in a while I even get to talk to another human being about the weather or a Twins game." She added, "No thank you, I'll keep my job. Besides, I need the money."

"You're going to have to find some time to relax," Ostride said. "It'll all be here tomorrow."

"That's what I'm worried about. Tomorrow," Megan said, as she washed her hands.

"Last year when I came here I woke up at five, ate, studied, went to school at seven, worked all day in the lab till eight and then went home, ate, slept and started it all over again the next morning," Ostride said. "I went home every break just to get away from this place. I don't think I even knew what was around the block from my apartment until the middle of the year when I ran out of shampoo," she admitted. "This year it's going to be different. I'm not going to make the same mistake twice. Last year I never rested and my results weren't even close to my work at home. This year I'm going to make some time for a movie or I might even try going out dancing on a Saturday night, and you should too."

"Yeah, I'll keep that in mind," Megan said looking back at a stack of Petri dishes. "But, tonight, I'll spend a fun-filled evening with Dr. Schmidt."

"You have a date?" Ostride asked, jumping up from her stool.

"Date?" Megan asked. "Dr. Wilhelm Schmidt, the lecture tonight. I thought you said you were going."

"Immune systems, yeah, yeah, I'm going," Ostride said, sitting back down on the metal stool. She began to fidget with her security pass that hung around her neck from a red string. She kept her eye on Megan, shifting away as she tugged at her pass and stretching the red cord to its limit.

"Okay, spill it," Megan said. "You've been dancing around here all day with the glow of Tinker Bell and the disposition of a tom cat in a room full of rocking chairs. What is it?"

"What do you think about going on a blind date? A double date," Ostride blurted out.

"So, I need some rest and relaxation?" Megan asked, shaking her head and holding on to the table. "I need to be refreshed. I need to go to a movie or a little dancing?"

Ostride tried to contain a smile by puckering her mouth and biting the inside of her cheek.

"I've got news for you, my friend," Megan railed. "Going on a blind date is no way to unwind."

"Meg, you have to," Ostride pleaded and winced as if she were in pain. "For me?"

Megan looked at her faint reflection in a sludge filled beaker perched high on Ostride's table. She rubbed her pale cheek and then put her cool hands over her strained eyes. She turned again and looked at the mountain of dishes and slides waiting for her in the cooler. "I don't know...."

"Please?" Ostride begged.

"But, I just went out last weekend."

"You did?"

"Mr. Payton's grandson. After supper on Sunday he asked me to go see a movie."

"Meg, he's twelve years old!"

"Hey, it's the best offer I've had in weeks!"

"What about someone man-sized?" Ostride asked, drumming her fingers on the black laboratory counter. "Hum?" She raised an eyebrow.

"Who is the poor soul?" Megan asked.

"I don't know," Ostride said, again biting her bottom lip in a crooked smile.

"Excuse me?"

"Jacob Gustavson asked me out and he wanted to know if I knew of someone that one of his friends could go out with."

"Jacob Gustavson! Now the big picture is starting to come together."

"I know, I know. But Megan...."

"Don't even finish that sentence," Megan said, "I know you're crazy about him."

"Infatuated," Ostride said.

"Whatever," Megan said. "I've heard about this guy for weeks now. So, he finally got around to asking you out?"

"But he wants..."

"I know. He has a friend."

"Yes," Ostride said. If her big blue eyes could have looked any more pathetic they would have belonged to a Labrador puppy, Megan thought. Megan looked back at her reflection in the beaker glass. Her dark hair was a mass of untidy curls and her face looked drawn and ashen. She tried pulling her hair up like her mother did but it just fell down around her shoulders again.

"I give up," she said and then looked into Ostride's anxious and sad eyes. "When are we supposed to be going out?"

Ostride leapt off her stool and gave Megan a hug. "Saturday! We're going out Saturday. We'll pick you up at seven," Ostride said bouncing up and down. Her perfectly straight and brilliant white teeth gleamed as she smiled.

Megan looked back at her dim reflection and smiled broadly. "I don't remember even brushing my teeth this morning," she said. "I have to get some sleep. I'm going to clean up and then go to the lounge and catch a few. Could you wake me up before you leave?"

"Sure. Anything you want. Get some sleep. I'll be done here in about half an hour," Ostride said. "Go. Go on, I'll wake you up."

Megan went to the door and pushed the button. She turned, "You don't know anything about the guy I'm supposed to be going out with?" she asked.

"No. But if he is anything like Jacob, I know you'll..."

"I know, I'll just be crazy about him."

CHAPTER 5

On Saturday Megan walked home after work, turned the key to her apartment, dropped her purse inside the door and grabbed a leftover cookie from the plate on the kitchen table. She then curled up on her couch and pulled an afghan over her legs. While nibbling on the cookie she made a mental list of the things she had to do over the weekend. Buy some groceries, call home, file my report.... A crumb of chocolate fell on her blouse and when she tried to pick it up it smudged on the pocket. "Go to the Laundromat,..." she said aloud.

With more and more errands being added to the list, Megan sunk farther and farther down into the couch. She could feel her eyelids getting heavier with every breath. Finally, she surrendered to the warmth of the blanket and drifted off to sleep.

Her eyes opened to a dark room. Suddenly a thought flashed into her mind.

"Date! What time is it?" She scrambled to find the light switch to look at the clock on the kitchen wall.

"Oh no! Ostride is going to kill me!" She ran to her closet, pulled out her robe, and ran to the bathroom and turned on the shower. While she waited for the hot water, Megan raced through the house picking up scraps of paper, books and her cookie dish, and stuffed them all into an empty cupboard behind the kitchen counter.

Please Lord, let them be late, Megan prayed. Once out of the shower, she splashed on some makeup and put her long hair into a knot, letting the unfastened waves of curls fall around her brow and face. As she hopped about putting on her nylons, she pulled out the only pressed blouse in her closet, a double-breasted cream blouse with a crocheted lace collar.

"Perfect, unless we're going to a hockey game. I should have asked where we were going. Skirt, skirt, skirt," Megan mumbled as she dug frantically through the closet. She pulled out a dark suede skirt and tall boots and then rummaged through her jewelry and found a pair of gold earrings. The door buzzed and she ran to the door, sliding on the wood floor halfway to the intercom. One of her nylons snagged on a splinter of wood, ripping a hole in the toe.

"Nuts!" she yelled. "I'm wearing boots. Okay, no big deal." As soon as she heard Ostride's voice, Megan released the electronic security door and quickly unlatched her apartment door lock and flew back to the bathroom at the other end of the apartment. Within a minute Megan had buttoned her blouse, zipped her skirt and was putting on her boots when there was a knock at the door.

"Come in," she yelled. She heard footsteps come into the room. "I'll be just a minute, I'm running late. Go ahead and have something to drink. There's pop in the fridge."

"What an unusual place," Jacob said, looking up to the high ceiling and around the room. "And what is 'pop'?"

"I love it," Ostride said as she walked into the kitchen. "It's so open and comfortable." She opened the refrigerator and found a bottle of water. "Pop is what Megan calls soda. I think it's a Minnesota thing. Do you want a soda or some water, coffee?" Ostride asked the men.

"I'll wait," Jacob said, still looking around the apartment.

"Marcus?" Ostride asked.

"No thank you," Marcus said, searching for clues about his mystery date. How did Jacob talk me into this? I feel like a fool, he thought. He took off his black leather gloves and put them in his overcoat pockets and began his investigation as Jacob and Ostride chatted. Simple, he thought, but tasteful. A nubby rug was spread out in front of an overstuffed burgundy couch; an old wooden rocker sat by the fireplace and on the opposite side was a large tapestry chair and ottoman. A small table was piled high with papers pressing up against a lamp. The windowsills hosted a number of plants, but no pictures. Marcus spotted a book on a long, narrow table that sat against the back of the couch. It had a worn leather cover and multiple scraps of paper sticking out of its top. As he approached he noticed scribbling on the scraps of paper. Marcus picked it up and read the title, *The Holy Bible*.

Megan was still fastening an earring when she walked out from the bathroom. "You must be Jacob Gustavson," she said, looking at the tall man with sweeping dark brown hair who was standing beside Ostride.

"Yes," he said with a stunning and satisfied grin. "And you must be Megan Buchanan." He looked at Marcus who was watching Megan walk across the room.

"You know, Ostride gave me a magazine the other day and in it there was an article about a Gustavson. It was an old picture, but the man in the photograph looked so much like you. I think he was a missionary to the West Indies," Megan said.

"My great-grandparents were missionaries," Jacob said proudly.

"That was your great-grandfather?" Ostride asked.

"Most likely," Jacob said to Ostride. "They served in the Indies for twenty years."

Feeling a bit awkward, Megan turned to her blind date. "Hi, I'm Megan Buchanan," she said, extending her hand to the puzzling character before her. Her date was a picture of fashionable European culture, she thought. His black cashmere overcoat sculpted his broad shoulders, draped flawlessly on his frame and tied effortlessly at his waist. As he reached out to take her hand, she saw the glimmer of gold, blue and green mosaic cufflinks slipping out from underneath the sleeve of his dark suit, but she was perplexed by the fedora hat and the dark sunglasses that wrapped tightly to his temples.

"Hello," Marcus said, taking her hand.

Ostride broke away from her conversation with Jacob. "I'm sorry Meg, I haven't introduced you to Marcus." Marcus took off his hat and sunglasses revealing his mane of blond hair and his deep blue eyes.

"Good to meet you, Marcus," Megan said, wondering if she appeared as nervous as she felt. "I'll just get my purse and we can be on our way," she said and brushed by him to get to the coat rack by the door.

Jacob looked at Megan and then Ostride incredulously and then at Marcus, who seemed to be sizing up the two women. "You don't know,..." Jacob began.

"You really don't know much about me, do you?" Marcus interrupted.

"Not a thing," Ostride interjected. "Jacob only told me that he had invited his best friend and roommate."

"In fact, Ostride couldn't even tell me your name until this moment," Megan said, as she opened her purse to search for her apartment keys.

"My name is Marcus Holcombe, and I've lived in Dreiholm all my life," he said with a smile. He gave Jacob a quick glance and walked to Megan's side.

"We'll have plenty to talk about then," Megan said. "I'm American, from Minnesota, and I've lived there all my life, so everything here is completely new to me."

"Wonderful," Marcus said. He noticed Jacob scowl at him as Megan reached one hand down to the bottom of her bag. "I will be able to tell you anything you want to know. What are you interested in?" Marcus asked, helping Megan with her coat.

"Finding my key would be nice. This always seems to happen to me at the least opportune times," Megan said, slipping her arm into one sleeve of her coat while still looking in her purse. Marcus stood at her side watching her. Her long dark eyelashes knitted together at the corner of her eyes, a dark contrast to the hint of pink on the ivory palette of her childlike face.

"Eureka!" she exclaimed as she pulled out a set of keys. "What am I interested in? I guess I'm interested in everything; the culture here, music, art, the government, politics...." Jacob laughed heartily as they filed out of the apartment to leave. Marcus gestured to him to be silent.

"Am I making a fool of myself already?" Megan asked as she locked the door. "You're not from the department of tourism, are you? Or a professor of Dreiholmian history?"

"Jacob and Marcus are both in their last year of medical training. They're residents at the university hospital," Ostride said.

"Thank goodness," Megan said. "I've made so many mistakes since I've been here. When I first arrived, I thought I was asking a policeman for directions. It turned out that the man was a bellhop at the hotel. He was a Czechoslovakian who couldn't speak English and I was an American who couldn't speak Dreiholmian or Czech. He was confused, I was embarrassed, and neither one of us was the better for it."

"You made it here," Jacob said with a chuckle. He held Ostride's arm as they walked down the stairs. "That is all that matters."

"Yes," Megan said, "thanks to a very patient rail master at the station."

"I made reservations at Albert's for eight o'clock," Marcus said and looked at his watch.

"Albert's?" Ostride asked.

"It's in the old part of the village," Jacob said.

"We'll have to hurry if we are going to make it there on time, then," Ostride said.

"They'll wait," Jacob said confidently. He opened the door for Ostride and a breath of the night air slipped into the apartment house. It was crisp and fresh and clean, and it reminded Megan of the hint of winter that she felt so often at home, and for a moment she was homesick, lonely, and scared. Marcus held the door open for her and she looked down the steps.

"Oh my!" Megan said as she looked down at the dazzling black Mercedes-Benz parked in front of her apartment.

"You like cars?" Marcus asked, opening the car door for her.

"It's very nice," Megan said, not knowing what else to say. He shut the door after she got in and he stood outside for a moment, pulling on his gloves. He's probably wondering the same thing I am, Megan thought, why in the world did we do this? Megan turned to Ostride for solace but Jacob had already captured her complete attention. There was no use trying to talk to them now, she thought. She wiggled into the warm leather seats and tried to relax.

"I understand American women are impressed by expensive automobiles," Marcus said as he started the engine.

"Who told you that?" Megan asked. "Frankly, I was more impressed that you opened the car door for me. I haven't received that kind of chivalry since, well, well I can't remember when. The car is very nice though," Megan said, patting the armrest.

"Thank you," Marcus said with a smile. He seemed to relax as he shifted the car into gear.

Megan looked back at Ostride and Jacob who were still engrossed in their conversation.

"Do you like cars?' Megan asked.

"Some," Marcus said.

"Any favorites?"

"No favorites," he said, "But I did have an American car once. A Viper. Do you own one?"

"No," Megan smiled. "They're a little pricey for me. You had a Viper. Why did you get rid of it?"

"I needed a change," Marcus said. "How about you?"

"What?" Megan asked.

"Any favorite cars?"

"No, not really. I'm one of those 'happy if it gets me around town without any problems' type of girl," Megan said. "No rust though, I don't like rust," she said. Marcus laughed. He had set his hat and glasses aside and Megan looked at his face. His thick, coarse hair feathered at the sides and glistened in the evening lights like spun gold. And when he laughed, deep lines creased the corners of his eyes on his tan skin.

"Any cars that have impressed you?" he asked.

"You mean other than this one?"

"Yes," Marcus said, "other than this one."

"Let me think." Megan listened to the gentle rumble of the car as it made its way over the smooth stone back roads. "There's one," she said. "But it was more about what the car meant to me than the car itself that impressed me."

"And,..." Marcus said, prompting her to go on with her story as he turned the corner.

"There was a man at home, a neighbor, who asked me on a date. When he came to pick me up he came in a candy-apple red Corvette convertible. It was beautiful from its crest to its spoiler. Do you have any Corvettes here?" Megan asked.

"Yes," Jacob said, popping into the conversation. "But very few American cars make it to Dreiholm. They are costly to transport overseas."

"But what made that car so impressive?" Marcus asked.

"It was his brother's car," Megan said.

"You liked the brother?" Ostride asked.

"No, I just knew this family. And David, the man who asked me out, was in college and working at the time but his brother Bill was older and in the military and a car enthusiast. And I know Bill. He was tough as nails. He must have made David pay dearly to be able to drive that car for that one night," Megan recalled.

"You like sports cars?" Marcus asked.

"Not particularly, although my father was thrilled with the

Corvette. He took one look at the bucket seats, the stick shift, and the tiny back seat where you couldn't fit an oversized Schnauzer, and declared that all young men should have one."

"I agree," Jacob said as they all laughed. "Your father is a wise man."

Marcus turned into a narrow, deserted alley and parked the car.

"So where is Albert's?" Ostride asked, looking out the window.

"Look up," Jacob said. At the top of the small brick building was a large picture window outlined in white lights. The name Albert's was written in the middle of the window in gold and black letters.

"Will they let you park here?" Megan asked.

"Yes, after five it is allowed," Marcus said. Jacob wagged his head and narrowed his eyes as the two men got out and looked at each other over the black hood of the car. Marcus cheerfully ignored him as he walked around to meet Megan.

"It's a ways up there isn't it?" Megan said, looking up the side of the building.

"We can enter here," Marcus said, and opened an unmarked, plain beige steel door underneath the painted sign.

"Shouldn't we go to the front?" Ostride asked.

"This is faster," Jacob said, drawing her to the stairway. At the top was a dimly lit room aglow with the amber light of a steadily burning fire. Copper ornaments displayed on the walls reflected the quiet flames, and the exquisite woodcarvings, common to Dreiholm, decorated the walls. Waiting behind a podium was Albert, a stout, balding man with dark eyes and round, red full cheeks.

"Your name sir?" Albert asked. Jacob stopped and looked at Albert with surprise. Ostride stood in front as Jacob helped to remove her coat.

"Marcus Holcombe," Marcus said, and casually handed his and Megan's coat to a man dressed in a black tuxedo. Albert checked Marcus' name off the reservation sheet as Jacob stood holding on to Ostride's coat until the man in the tuxedo took it from his arm. Marcus flashed a smile at Jacob and joined Megan and Ostride who were admiring the carving on the fireplace mantel.

"Incredible," Jacob said under his breath.

"Right this way," Albert said, extending his arm down the hallway behind the podium. Marcus took Megan's arm and followed Albert to a closed curtain. When he opened it, Megan gasped. In front of them was a large window, the length of the room, looking out over the edge of the mountain. The stars above filled the night sky and showered down on the valley below. Megan walked to the window and softly stroked the edge of its pane. She turned back to Marcus and Albert who were smiling at her.

"It's like a thousand glittering diamonds," she said, turning back to the window. Albert dimmed the lights so that they could get a better view.

"Oh Jacob, it is absolutely stunning," Ostride said. Jacob seized an opportunity to put his arm around Ostride, something he had been aching to do since he had met her.

"Thank you, Albert," Marcus said, standing beside him.

"It is my pleasure," Albert said and bowed. "I will return with champagne." The heavy velvet curtain swung closed and Marcus walked up behind Megan.

"We're on the edge of Mount Petra. Below is Lake Nami and around it are the villages of Canton," Marcus said.

"I don't think you're going to be able to pry me away from this window," Megan told him, still watching the lights of the city below.

"You will come eagerly," Jacob told her. He and Ostride were already sitting at the dining table next to one another. "The only thing better than the view at Albert's is the food!"

CHAPTER 6

"That was a culinary delight!" Megan said to Albert. The portly restauranteur had returned with two servers who removed the dinner china and had poured coffee for the guests. Albert nodded in appreciation and they left silently, leaving a silver tray of decorated sugar cubes and heavy cream on the table.

"I love the popovers," Ostride said, picking apart another that was left in a basket in the middle of the table. "It's a good thing I don't know how to cook or I would be feasting on popovers day and night."

"The trick is that you have to boil the butter in the popover pan before you put in the batter," Megan said.

"Why is that?" Ostride asked.

"I don't know but it works," Megan said.

"You enjoy cooking?" Jacob asked Megan.

"My mother and father told me it was chemistry. I bought into that argument until I realized I was the only one doing all the experimenting in the house. Then I realized my experiments tasted better than theirs so I kept doing it. Now I'm living on cereal, more cereal, cookies, and an occasional sandwich."

"And pretzels," Ostride reminded her.

"Ah yes, and bags of pretzels. Our lunch," Megan said. "I can't understand why they don't have a cafeteria in our building."

Marcus watched Megan closely, how she flipped the corner of her napkin with her thumbnail and pressed it out again with her hand while she spoke, how she slowly stroked the stem of her water glass, and how she kept her eyes fixed on whomever was speaking, listening intently. Her eyes, he thought, are a still burning fire like the reflection of a sunset in the depths of the Caribbean Sea. Marcus eased back in his chair, holding his coffee cup in his hand and thankful he had relented to Jacob's nagging and accepted his invitation. He's usually right, Marcus thought, glancing at him. His childhood friend had always seemed to be a part of his life, waiting, watching, and patiently guiding.

They had poured themselves into their studies at medical school but Jacob could see in the last few months that Marcus' demons were beginning to return, the discontent that seemed to simmer and then boil over in his soul.

"There is no satisfaction," Marcus had said a few days before as he slammed his book shut, staring vacantly out the window of his study.

"I never thought I would be saying this, but you need to get out," Jacob had said, standing in the doorway. "You've been locked away working or studying for months."

"I thought my responsible new life was considered to be a marked improvement," Marcus returned sarcastically. Jacob wagged a pencil between his fingers as he leaned against the door frame. "Extremes, Marcus. Always extremes," Jacob had said, stepping into the study. "I've made arrangements with Ostride. We're going out."

"Ostride," Marcus said, "you finally asked her."

"Yes, and I asked her to bring a friend," Jacob said.

"I can get a date," Marcus said petulantly as he opened the book again with the point of his pen.

"No," Jacob insisted, "someone new."

"You don't approve of my female companions either?" Marcus asked.

"Think of it as an adventure," Jacob had said. "Be ready tomorrow at six. We have to pick them up at seven."

Tonight, thanks to his persistent friend, he was laughing again and strangely confortable in the company of a woman he didn't know. There is something about her, Marcus thought, as his eyes rested on her dark spiraling curls and then her green-blue eyes. What is it about her that is so compelling, he asked himself.

"Will there be anything else?" the waiter asked, popping into the room from the closed curtain.

"Yes, another bottle of champagne," Marcus said. "I feel like celebrating." The waiter bowed and pushed the red velvet curtain aside.

"I have a question," Megan said. "Why does the waiter bow every

PLANS · VICTORIA J.M. HOFFBECK

time he leaves the room? I've been to plenty of restaurants since I've been here and no one has ever done that before."

"I guess I hadn't noticed," Marcus said. Jacob rolled his eyes and finished his coffee. "Jacob and I have been to your state, Minnesota," he continued.

"For business or pleasure?" Megan asked and stirred some more cream into her coffee.

"A little of both," Jacob replied. "We went to observe at the Mayo Clinic and then we took a trip to that large park in the north."

"The Boundary Waters?" Megan asked. The waiter returned with the champagne and filled the tall fluted glasses. Megan watched and waited for the man to exit, wondering if he would repeat this peculiar custom.

"Yes, that is it," Marcus said, putting his hand on the back of her chair and touching her shoulder. Megan looked away from the waiter to Marcus.

"You haven't said why you are visiting Dreiholm. It is a long way from Minnesota and the United States of America," Marcus said. The waiter slipped out of the room and Marcus rested back into his chair.

"I'm working on a research project I started some time ago. I hope to finish it here," Megan said, lazily playing with the corner of her folded napkin that was resting on the table. "I suppose I shouldn't say that I will finish my research. Professor Clayton would say that I would only answer a question that will lead to the next question and a next research project."

"You have a class with the legendary Professor Clayton?" Marcus asked.

"No, I haven't had the pleasure. He's my advisor," Megan said. Marcus looked surprised as he took a drink of the bubbling wine.

"You're leaving out one small detail," Ostride chided her, leaning into the table. "Megan is the Scoly." Marcus choked on his wine and grabbed for his napkin.

"You won the Scolengard?" Jacob asked.

"Yes," Megan said. She had been resting her elbows on the table and now put her hand under her chin and fixed her eyes on Marcus, who had quickly regained his composure. "Surprised?" she asked.

Marcus noticed that her eyes had turned a jade green and even though her voice was sweet he knew his next words had better be keenly phrased.

"We had heard that it was an American but, I guess we didn't expect..." Jacob started.

"Didn't expect what?" Ostride asked. "That it would be a woman?" Jacob turned to Ostride who had recoiled to the back of her chair. Megan picked up her coffee cup and took a sip and waited. Marcus and Jacob looked at each other and then at the women and back at each other again.

"Well, are you disappointed? Or offended?" Megan asked.

"Neither," Marcus said, and took hold of her hand. "I think the words I am looking for are pleased and impressed." For the first time Megan looked deeply into Marcus' dark blue eyes. His solid frame and defined face reminded her of the pictures she had seen as a child of the Viking explorers idealized at home, except that his features were more refined and unblemished.

"And you?" Ostride asked, looking at Jacob.

"I am surprised," Jacob said. "I'm surprised that two of the most talented and beautiful women on earth are having dinner with me."

Ostride rolled her eyes. "Good save, Romeo."

"How about a movie, Juliet?" Jacob asked and nuzzled up to Ostride.

"The last show was at ten, and it's now midnight," Ostride said.

"And we have to get up early tomorrow," Megan chimed in.

"Tomorrow is Sunday," Marcus said. "It is the day of rest."

"Megan and I go to the early church service and we trade off making breakfast, the only meal I know how to make, and then we hit the books again," Ostride said.

"It's my turn this week," Megan said.

"I suppose we should get our coats then," Jacob said, pulling Ostride up and out of her chair.

"I guess we will," she said, as she was being pulled out the door. Megan stood up and went to look out the window one last time.

"We can stay longer if you would like," Marcus said, walking up close behind her. "I can get a cab for Jacob and Ostride." The heat of his body radiated through her clothing and penetrated her skin.

"All good things must come to an end," Megan said, gazing at a very bright star.

"There is nothing I could say to change your mind?" Marcus asked. Megan turned to him and for a moment their eyes met.

"Change your mind about what?" Jacob asked.

"I'm trying to convince Megan that the evening is still young."

"Canton seems to have fallen asleep," Megan said, looking down at the few remaining lights shining in the darkness, "and I think Albert would probably like to go home too."

"We can take you to some places that are very much awake," Jacob offered.

"I can tell you're in your last year of residency," Ostride said, holding on to the back of a chair.

"You're right," Jacob said, putting his arm around her. "And I'm loving it."

"Was everything to your satisfaction?" Albert asked, coming into the room.

"Everything," Marcus said, watching Megan.

CHAPTER 7

A sharp winter wind whisked through the alley awakening wisps of latent snow, twirling and whirling in loose, white funnels across the dark pathway. A light from the top of the restaurant pierced the night and exposed the spinning cyclones as they unwound themselves at Megan's feet. Ostride and Jacob had already run to the car and were huddled up together in the back seat. Megan flipped the collar of her coat up around her neck, buried her face into the soft trim and hurried into the car. She had noticed another car in the alley when they stepped outside the door but didn't see anyone inside it until now. Two men with short hair and dark coats were parked behind them. Megan rubbed her hands together watching them. The driver had a scar on the side of his face and the other was young, with shaggy brown hair. Both seemed to look back at her with grim, menacing faces until Marcus sat down next to her. "It will only take a minute for the seats to warm up," he said, and quickly pulled out onto the road.

"I should be used to cold weather by now," Megan said, still looking at the car behind them through the rear-view mirror. It sat idling as they pulled out from the alley but then popped up behind them again when they reached the main road.

"What is it?" Marcus asked. "What are you looking at?"

"I know this is going to sound ridiculous but I think we are being followed," Megan said. Ostride and Jacob turned around to look at the car. Marcus glanced at the rearview mirror and paid little attention to the pair of lights shining behind them.

"Do either of you have any enemies?" Megan joked. Marcus and Jacob sat silently as Marcus glanced again into the mirror. He shifted into gear and sped through a series of traffic lights.

"I'm sure it's nothing. See, they've turned off at the last block," Marcus said. Megan and Ostride turned around and watched the car travel down the side street.

"I guess I wouldn't make much of a detective," Megan said, still watching the rear-view mirror.

"Jacob told me that you work on the weekends," Marcus said.

"At Brier Pharmaceuticals, Wednesday evenings and Saturdays."

"A very good company," Marcus noted.

"We know Mr. Payton," Jacob said.

"You do? I'll have to ask him about the both of you," Megan said.

"I don't think he would recall two medical students," Marcus grumbled, glaring into the rear-view mirror at Jacob but it was too late. He had already turned his attention to Ostride and was whispering something in her ear.

"I wouldn't be surprised if he did remember you. He seems to remember everything," Megan said over the sound of cooing and kissing noises coming from the back seat. She rested her elbow against the door and put her hand over her face as she tried to peer out the window.

"What's that?" she asked Marcus, pointing to a large gray building with a red arch intersecting the massive columns of the Greek-looking structure.

"The Museum of Fine Art."

"And that?"

Jacob moaned passionately and Ostride laughed in a hushed voice. She tried to quiet him with whispers and more kisses.

"The electric company," Marcus said flatly, looking back at Jacob with an irritated frown.

"Oh," Megan said. The streetlights were swiftly passing by as Marcus drove faster and faster down the deserted highway while the constant cooing continued. He turned off onto a street Megan had never been on before, and then slowed down to turn another corner where Megan could see her apartment on the next block. Thank goodness, Megan thought, at the sound of another mournful moan.

"I'm going to walk Ostride to her apartment. Pick me up after you have dropped Megan off, will you?" Jacob asked, and opened the door before the car came to complete stop.

"After that big meal we could use the exercise," Ostride said.

"Go," Megan and Marcus said in unison. Megan laughed and before she could unbuckle her seat belt, Ostride and Jacob had both jumped out of the car and were walking down the sidewalk, hand in hand.

"What do you think? In love?" Megan asked.

"Madly," Marcus said, and got out of the car. Megan climbed out before he could reach her door. Megan looked down the sidewalk. "Well, I don't think they will need us for their next date," she said, watching the couple fade into the darkness. "But thank you for this date and for going along. I had a wonderful time and I'm sure I never would have found Albert's without you."

"You're welcome," Marcus said. The wind had subsided and small white snowflakes had begun to drift lazily down from the velvet sky. Megan took a deep breath of the cold air and looked up into the heavens. "I love nights like this."

"It's very cold," Marcus said, and put his gloved hands into his pockets.

"No, no, listen," Megan whispered. Marcus stood still waiting to hear some sound.

"I don't hear anything."

"Exactly," Megan said, still looking up at the sky. "No cars, no train or planes, no books reverberating their words in my head, no labs, no experiments, just peace and quiet." A snowflake found a home on one of Megan's long, dark eyelashes and others laced her hair. Suddenly, she felt Marcus' hand reach around her waist and pull her close to his chest. Captivated by the dizzying, swimming warmth of his kiss she could feel her heart beat and then race as it sent an unstoppable current through her body. She stepped back and stumbled over her own feet. Marcus grabbed onto her small waist and steadied her until she regained her balance.

"Either I'm out of practice or you're good," Megan said, fanning her face and walking toward the apartment steps.

"I would like to see you again," Marcus said, taking her keys from her hand as they walked up the stairway.

"I think that can be arranged," Megan said, laughing at her own eagerness. Marcus opened the door and stepped back to let her go inside. He stood in the doorway flipping her keys in his hand.

"What?" Megan asked. "You look like you want to say something."

"I..."

"I...," Megan started for him again.

"I am in my last year of my residency," Marcus said, straightening his shoulders.

"I know that," Megan said.

"I can't have a meaningful relationship now," Marcus said coolly.

"Oh, I see," she said and stepped back, gently taking her keys from his hand and putting them into her pocket. "Your work is important to you, time consuming, isn't it?" she said sweetly.

Marcus nodded his head.

"And you certainly can't have any personal distractions in your last year," she went on. "I know, a demanding relationship would be unmanageable and who knows when an opportunity might come your way? You certainly couldn't impede your career with a relationship," Megan said, twisting the gold doorknob.

"It would be difficult for both of us," Marcus said, stepping closer to her. Megan gritted her teeth and felt her skin begin to burn as anger surged through her.

"So what you're suggesting is that you want an understanding," Megan said. "A relationship, where we could go out occasionally, catch a movie, have dinner, a little kiss, a little cuddle,..." she said wrinkling her nose.

"Exactly," Marcus said, stepping even closer to her with his deep blue eyes searing into hers with the intensity of a hungry wolf. "And more," he whispered, his voice so low it was almost a growl. "You understand," he said, as his lips brushed up against hers. Megan put her hand up to his chest.

"Perfectly," she said, in a whisper that pulsed against his lips, and then she shoved him, hard, out the door and slammed it shut. Marcus grabbed onto the wrought iron railing to stop himself from falling down the stairs and watched the windows on either side of the door rattle.

"Jerk!" Megan hollered through the panes of glass and stomped up the stairs to her apartment.

CHAPTER 8

"Can you believe that? Neither one of them knew who you are?" Jacob said, as he bounced into the car with an exuberance that reeked of romantic bliss. He pulled off his gloves and put his hands up next to the heat vents. Marcus looked straight ahead, his glazed eyes set on the road and his jaw clenched.

"What happened?" Jacob asked.

"Women," Marcus muttered.

"I thought you and Megan were getting along. She's certainly attractive enough and there is no doubt she's intelligent. I couldn't believe she's the Scoly. With all the notoriety, she'll be sought after by every pharmaceutical firm in the world and the best universities, not to mention half of the men on campus," Jacob said.

Marcus groaned.

"What's wrong with you?" Jacob asked impatiently.

"Why do women take everything you say the wrong way?"

"What exactly did you say?" Jacob asked.

"I asked her if she would like to go out again."

"And,..."

"She seemed willing."

"And,..."

"I told her that we had to start out slow."

"That's reasonable. What else?"

"That it wouldn't be right to have a steady relationship," Marcus said quickly. "That it would be better for both of us."

Jacob put his hand up to cover his eyes.

"Did she ask for one?" Jacob asked, looking through his fingers.

"No."

"You just volunteered the information?" Jacob asked amazed. "I guess you can kiss that one goodbye, if you even got that far."

"I was doing it for her own good. I didn't want to give her any false expectations."

"False expectations, what are you talking about?"

"She's an American," Marcus said defiantly.

"So what?" Jacob snapped. "You went out with that Countess, what's her name? The Russian, and that obvious money-hunting dimwit, and so-called actress from France. What's wrong with an American?" Jacob asked. Marcus leaned his arm against the car door and rubbed his forehead.

"Nothing," Marcus said. "I don't know what I was thinking."

Jacob shook his head as he watched his friend in the passing strobe of city streetlights. "You saw something in her, didn't you?" Jacob asked, half wondering why he even felt a shred of sympathy for Marcus when it came to women. Marcus kept his eyes on the road, and then looked back to see the familiar headlights in his rear-view mirror.

"I want to go out with her again."

"Then I suggest you apologize," Jacob said. "And be honest with her. Tell her who you are and why security cars follow you. She'll find out one way or another."

"No. I don't want her to know." Marcus came to a stop inside the gates of the townhouse. Jacob opened the car door. "Jacob, try to understand."

"You can't change who you are, Marcus."

"Look at the women in my life," Marcus said. "They're caught up in some fantasy. They think I live in a fairytale, or worse, they think I can provide them with one. You know I'm telling the truth. For once, I would like to know if a woman could love me for what I am and not who I am."

"Did you ever think it might be the women you choose?" Jacob asked as he got out of the car. Marcus looked across the roof of the car at Jacob, streams of frozen air spewing from his nostrils and then he looked up into the starry heavens. Marcus closed his car door and dismissed the security guards with a wave of his hand.

"I don't know," Marcus admitted.

Jacob sighed. "Marcus, in the grand scheme of things we really are insignificant. We just happen to be fortunate. Honestly, I don't think that Ostride or Megan are looking for fairytale lives. If they were, they wouldn't be sitting in a sterile laboratory fifty hours a week trying to find the cure to the world's diseases. They'd be at some party somewhere or at some beach resort doing what those women do. They don't need us. They're not going to come running after us. They don't have to. They have to want us."

"Why didn't you tell Ostride who I was when you arranged this date?" Marcus asked.

"I don't know. I guess because I didn't want to. And you're twisting the argument, that isn't the point."

"Admit it. You didn't want all the noise, the hype, the gushing, am I right?" Marcus asked, looking at his friend. "Well, neither do I."

Jacob shifted his weight as he stood holding on to the car door. He raised an eyebrow as he wondered why he wasn't forthcoming with Ostride or Megan. "I really did think that they would recognize you when you took off your glasses."

"But they didn't," Marcus said.

"Marcus, think. What would you do if Megan did fall in love with you?" Jacob's question was met with silence. "She's not a toy, Marcus."

"Of course she's not."

"Then why, Marcus?" Jacob asked. Marcus silently stared at Jacob. Jacob could see beyond the stubbornness and at the deep sadness that dwelt in his soul. "Marcus, you are the Prince of Dreiholm and one day you will be king. That is who you are. You cannot wish it away even if you wanted too," Jacob said.

Marcus leaned against the car with his hands folded over its roof, listening but staring into the blackness of the night. "I just want to know," he said.

Jacob raised his arms and let them fall to his sides. "You are my best friend and if you ask me to hold my tongue I will, but I can only imagine that this path you are taking will only lead to heartache."

"It is a risk worth taking," Marcus said.

"I wonder."

CHAPTER 9

"Good morning!" Ostride said with a big smile. Megan stood by the window with a steaming mug of coffee in her hand while watching the butter yellow sun melt away the few gray clouds left in the sky.

"Cold?" Megan asked.

"Freezing," Ostride said, as she tossed her hat and coat onto the small wooden chair next to Megan's apartment door.

"Coffee?"

"Yep." Ostride scurried to the kitchen table and slid into the chair, rubbing her red cheeks and nose. "Okay, enough idle chatter, what did you think of him?"

"Jacob?" Megan asked. "He seems nice and you're right, wow! He's a heart-stopper, very handsome." Ostride grinned from ear to ear as Megan handed her an oversized blue mug filled with rich, black coffee. Ostride wrapped her hands around the cup, absorbing the warmth into her cold fingers.

"He's like a dream come true. He's good-looking, smart, decent and he can actually speak in complete sentences. I keep wondering what's wrong with him."

"Why does there have to be anything wrong with him?" Megan asked.

"I can usually find a guy who is good looking and a talker or decent and smart but I've never been able to find one that has it all wrapped up in one package, and single!"

"Slim pickin's out there?" Megan asked.

"You haven't noticed? I've had to travel half way around the world to find a guy like this."

"That's not saying much for the guys back home," Megan said, refilling her own mug.

"No, it's not," Ostride said. "Hey, I started this conversation wondering what you thought of Marcus."

Megan plunked a lump of sugar into her cup and looked at Ostride's chipper face from the kitchen island. "It was nice to get out," Megan conceded, trying not to spoil her friend's good mood.

"After Marc took off his hat and sunglasses, I was stunned."

"Like you said, there's more to a man than his looks," Megan grumbled.

"I could have sworn you were having a good time last night," Ostride said.

"I did," Megan said, looking up from her coffee. Ostride twitched her nose and set her cup down. "Did something happen after Jacob and I left?" she asked.

Megan didn't answer and Ostride assumed that her intuition was correct. "He didn't try to hurt you, did he?"

"No, no nothing like that," Megan said. She braced herself on the kitchen counter top, seething as she thought of Marcus kissing her. "He's such a jerk," she said, turning to get a loaf of bread. "I don't want to talk about it. But it just makes me angry." Megan spun around with the bag of bread in hand. "Toast?" Megan asked. Her voice was edgy.

"Sure."

"He kisses me good night, not just any kiss, mind you. You know the kind, I practically fell over! Then as he's wooing me, he proceeds to tell me that I shouldn't hope for any kind of meaningful relationship," Megan said, dragging out the words.

"You're kidding!" Ostride exclaimed, stiffening in her chair.

"Really," Megan said, getting a plate. "Doctors! Ha!" The toast popped up from the toaster and without missing a beat, Megan grabbed the slices of bread and buttered both sides. "'It would be difficult for both of us,'" she said, imitating his whine. "Can you believe that? What he wanted was a roll in the hay," she said, setting the toast down in front of Ostride and thumping the jelly jar on the table. "Men! I know exactly what he wants," Megan said, her eyes flashing. "He wants somebody he can prance around with, and I don't care what he looks like, those big blue eyes, it's not going to be me!"

"So, he thought you were out for a MRS. Degree? Or just fun and games?" Ostride said. "Jerk."

"That would be the day," Megan said drumming her nails on the counter. "I don't know why I'm letting myself get all worked up over him. It was one date and I'll never see him again. That was my first and last date with Dr. Love."

The door buzzer rang and Megan looked at Ostride who ran to the window. "It's a delivery truck," Ostride said.

Megan pushed the intercom button. "Hello, can I help you?" she asked into the speaker.

"We have a delivery for a Miss Megan Buchanan."

Megan unlocked the door and heard a number of footsteps coming up the stairwell. Ostride peered out into the hall and watched men dressed in blue uniforms march up the stairs and into the apartment. "What is this?" Megan asked. "I didn't order anything."

"A gift," a young deliveryman said as he set the small tower of boxes on the table and handed her an envelope. Another man brought in two baskets of flowers, and another handed Ostride a large, warm box and a card.

The men left and Megan opened the note and read it aloud. "I'm sorry. Please forgive me. Marcus."

She looked up at Ostride who was opening hers.

"Good morning! Hours go much too slowly until I will see you again. Jacob," she read with a dreamy, lyrical voice. "Popovers!"

"It's from Albert's," Megan said dryly, as she broke the seals on the pale blue boxes. "They sent breakfast." The fragrance of the glistening caramel rolls and hot tins of bacon, cheese, mushrooms, and hot scrambled eggs filled the room. The church bells began to ring and Megan looked at Ostride.

"Well, it looks like you're going to see him again," Ostride said biting into a steaming popover.

"We're late for church."

"Meg, all this food!" Ostride cried as she watched Megan stuff everything into the refrigerator.

"Come on, my rock of Gibraltar." Megan took Ostride by the hand and pulled her toward the door. Ostride reached for the box of popovers and snatched another hot puff.

"For the road?" she said, tearing it in half and giving the other half to Megan.

Megan popped the pastry in her mouth. "Yeah, yeah, come on."

CHAPTER 10

Megan dropped off her weekly report and picked up her mail at the University's post office. She skipped through the bills and advertisements and opened a letter from her uncle and read it on her walk home.

...and all's well. The fundraiser went as planned and they met their goal. It looks like the school will get the new equipment your aunt was shooting for. Your aunt had an exceptional time. She won one of the door prizes. What she plans on doing with one of those crazy kid game machines, I have no idea. She tells me she's going to donate it to the children's cancer center here at the University. Maybe they'll know what to do with it. As far as I can tell, all it does is make noise.

Mr. Payton tells me that he's extremely pleased with your work and that his grandchildren are especially happy to see you on the weekends. Time is flying by. It's not too early to start making plans for Christmas break. I'll shop around for a good price on an airline ticket. Aunt Julie has already dressed up a room for you for when you come home and has set her sights on a short trip to the ranch. Don't worry, we'll make sure you have plenty of time to see your friends. We miss you...

Megan stopped when she heard a sound nearby, like the rub of canvas. She looked up and saw Marcus at the top of her apartment steps brushing off snow from his ski jacket and jeans. Megan shoved her mail into her pockets and began searching for her keys. She could feel her face begin to burn the longer she dug into her purse. Without any success, she ceased her quest and faced her visitor.

"You haven't returned my calls," Marcus said, looking down at her.

"I've been out of town for a few days. I would have sent a note but I didn't know where to send it. Thank you for the breakfast," Megan said, with a mere hint of gratitude. Dry leaves tumbled across the sidewalk, chasing a dusting of snow that was curling along the street.

"But, you haven't forgiven me."

"Look," Megan said, with her arms stiff and fists balled up. "You made it clear what you want and I've got news for you, you're barking up the wrong tree." A couple of teenagers, holding hands, ran across the street toward Megan. Marcus casually turned into the door, eased up the collar of the jacket and then slid his hands into his coat pockets. The young man glanced up at him but then quickly ran past Megan, pulling the girl with dark braids behind him. The girl smiled at Megan and then giggled as she huddled into the young man's arms. Megan smiled at the couple and then looked up at Marcus. Her eyes narrowed and she took off her gloves and began patting down her coat pockets for her keys.

"I didn't mean what I meant," Marcus said in a low voice.

"What?" Megan asked.

"I mean, when we went out, I didn't mean how it sounded," Marcus said hesitantly.

She stopped, opened her coat and pulled out her keys from an inside pocket. She walked up the stairs past Marcus and opened the apartment door. He quickly slipped in behind her.

"Hey!" Megan protested.

"I'm trying to say I'm sorry. I wasn't thinking," he said firmly. His thick sun-streaked hair was windblown and damp from the snow, and his face was getting red from the cold and now the warm heat of the apartment house.

"Now what are you thinking?" Megan asked.

"I'm thinking that it was one date and that one date leads to a second date," Marcus said sheepishly.

"Maybe." Megan's green-blue eyes beamed through the slits of her thick dark lashes and she began walking up the stairs. Marcus followed and then in a leap stepped up next to her.

"Can we try again?" Marcus asked.

"I have a better idea," Megan said, pausing on the landing. "Where I come from, contrary to popular belief, we become friends before we start to date. How about we try that?"

"No kissing, no..."

"No," Megan said sharply. "Friends."

"Yes, friends," he agreed, grudgingly.

"How long have you been outside?"

"Not long, about an hour."

"An hour?" Megan exclaimed.

"I had a book," Marcus said, and pulled a paperback from the inside of his coat. "A study on spinal cord injuries."

"Would you like some coffee? You must be frozen."

"Yes," Marcus answered, feeling relieved she was now more relaxed. When Megan opened her apartment door, the fragrant aroma of cinnamon and cloves filled the air. It was warm and the setting sun had painted the quiet room a golden yellow. "Apple pie?" Marcus asked.

"Yeah, I think I'm a little homesick. I ran to the store yesterday and picked one up." Megan hung her coat up on a hook and went to the kitchen. "Have you eaten yet?"

"No," Marcus said. "We could order something."

"Do you like fettuccine?"

"Yes, I do."

"Good," Megan said, getting out a pot. "Take off your coat. It will only take a few minutes." Instead of cooking, Marcus wanted to coax her to sit with him by the fireplace. Patience, he thought, as he watched her begin to put the meal together.

"Do you have any wood?" Marcus asked.

"In the utility closet." Megan pointed to a corner of the room as she filled the pot with water. Marcus opened the door and found a basket of dry, split logs and kindling. He located a book of matches on top of the mantle. Soon a log popped as the flames took hold.

"Can I help?" Marcus asked, turning to Megan.

"Nope," Megan said, "I'm almost done."

Marcus let out a sigh of relief and put another log on the fire. He hadn't been in a kitchen since he was a boy and even during his camping and military excursions, food had been prepared for him by servants or delivered to him in dehydrated foil packages. Megan called him over to the simple table and sat down opposite him and bowed her head in prayer.

"Lord, for this meal and for Your many blessing we give thanks."

"Amen." Marcus couldn't remember the last time he had prayed, he thought, as he took the roll and some butter Megan had offered him. As a boy, his mother had taught him the Lord's Prayer. Now, he only joined his parents at Christmas and Easter church services and even then his mind wandered. Jacob prayed often, he thought. It's different for them, he said in the private recesses of his mind. Nothing stirs my soul, no great revelations or divine calls, just silence, deafening silence, from a silent God who has forgotten this world and me. Megan twisted the long flat noodles around her fork and glanced over at Marcus. He could feel her eyes on him, awakening him to the outside world.

"Megan, what do you do for Payton?" Marcus asked.

"I was doing some sales work at first, now I'll be continuing some of my research at Payton's labs. They all seem to be in a hurry. I'm ahead of schedule but the dean and Mr. Payton feel that I can make better progress with Brier's equipment."

"What are you working on?"

"I can't say. I'm under contract with the university and now Brier Pharmaceuticals and they don't allow me to talk about my work. No one can. Ostride can't tell me about her project and I can't tell her about mine," Megan said. "I miss my sales job. It was nice to hear some familiar voices, but Mr. Payton lets me call home whenever I want to."

"Do you miss the States?"

"Sure," Megan said softly. "I think everyone misses home." Megan thought about her aunt and uncle and what was happening back home in the river valley. She sighed, and then smiled. "Dreiholm is missing two important things," she said.

"What?" Marcus asked.

"Baseball and family," she said with a smile, but with sad eyes. Marcus hadn't thought about what it must be like for Megan, being alone in an unfamiliar land. He suffered from just the opposite problem, rarely ever being alone at all. "And you don't have potato chips, root beer or any shopping malls."

"We don't have baseball, but we do have hockey," Marcus said with a hint of pride. "Potato chips have too much fat and I don't know what root beer is but it sounds as if it were better left in the States." His unintended quip made Megan laugh.

"I guess you have to try it," she said, separating a roll and tearing off a bit.

"We don't have shopping malls, but we do have some of the finest gift shops, clothing stores and restaurants in the world. And as for family, we can't replace family, but give us time, it won't be long before we all become familiar to you," he said sympathetically. Megan smiled and listened intently as Marcus told her about the orchestras, folk music and festivals of Dreiholm and told her stories about mountains, lakes and the people who lived in the foothills below. The images took Megan on a whimsical tour of the wildflower meadows in early spring to the colorful celebrations of fall with ribbon streamers and music and harvest dances for young and old. Marcus' enthusiasm and passion bubbled over into laughter and into a tune that he hummed as he kept time with his fork.

"You're a good salesman. I think I'll stay," Megan said, laughing with Marcus. "On a more serious note, no pun intended, maestro, the other night you never did tell me about the government here." Marcus held his breath. "Would you like more?" Megan asked, pointing to the pasta.

"No, no thank you. I'm quite full," Marcus said. "It was very good." Megan put the plates aside and took her cup and sat down by the fire.

"Our government is a monarchy," Marcus said, following her and sitting down on the floor next to her.

"That much I know," Megan said, grabbing a pillow and putting it behind their backs as they leaned against the couch. "Is it like England?"

"Not exactly," Marcus said carefully.

"It seems so foreign to me," Megan said. "I've always lived in a republic. It seems almost unfathomable to think that there are still monarchies that exist today."

"We have a senate, similar to yours. They have the ability to create and establish laws and, like your president, the king has the power to veto any law or changes the senate might make. The difference is that once the king decides to veto an act, it is final and cannot be overturned by the senate."

"Do the people have rights, like what we have in our Bill of Rights? The right to free speech, to assemble and so on?" Megan asked.

"There have been kings and queens in the past that have quashed the rights of the people, and paid dearly for it, but the current king knows that he is only in power because the people will it so. If he were to trample what has been so amply stated as inalienable rights, the people would eventually crush his throne and he would be remembered as nothing more than a dictator."

"I saw a picture of the royal family in a hotel when I arrived," Megan said. She took a sip of her coffee and Marcus sat still. "Do they have only one young son?" Megan asked.

Marcus let out a breath when he realized Megan must have seen a dated portrait of his family.

"Yes," he replied.

"Cute little boy," Megan said, recalling the photograph. "He has a mischievous glint in his eye. I bet his parents have their hands full with that one."

"Yes," Marcus said, looking into the fire and considering his past years. His sweater brushed up against Megan's shoulder but she made no effort to move.

"Really, I can't complain about anything here," Megan said, wrapping her hands around her cup. "Everyone has been kind and honest with me. I love my little apartment and the work has been abundant but not discouraging." Marcus felt a twinge of guilt and he gripped the foot of the table next to him and played with the edge with his thumb. "I just miss home, I guess." The sun had set behind the mountains and the only traces of light were the pale yellow and blue shadows from the crackling fire.

"Give Dreiholm time, Megan," Marcus said.

"Oh, I'm locked in now," Megan said looking into the fire. "I can't renege on the scholarship. I have to finish what I started."

"It won't be long before the fall festival and Christmas. That's something to look forward to," Marcus said. "Exams will be over and we will be able to enjoy ourselves for a week in the fall and a month at Christmas."

"I have to decide what I'm going to do," Megan said.

"What do you mean?"

"My uncle and aunt are expecting me home at Christmas but I know I should work. It just depends on how the next few weeks go."

"You mean you would go home for the whole month?"

"If I can manage it," she said. Marcus rubbed his hands together, thinking about the possibility that Megan might be leaving.

"Your hands are like ice," Megan said. She set down her mug and cupped her warm hands around his. Marcus sat mesmerized as he watched Megan in the firelight, her eyes, the spiraling curls that framed her face, and the curve of her body. He took hold of her hand and looked deeply into her eyes. Megan blushed and stood up.

"You need to warm up. Why don't you get on the couch," she said, and turned on a light. "That's better." She opened the old trunk at the end of her bed and pulled out a quilt. Marcus grimaced as he sat up on the couch, realizing he felt stiff and tired. The overstuffed couch was soft and the pillows molded into his back. Megan spread the patchwork quilt on top of him and gave him another pillow with a cool, white cotton pillowcase for his head.

"I'm glad you brought a book," Megan said, handing it to him. "I have to catch up on some of my reading." She nodded to the piles of paper against the wall. After turning on a small light behind him, she picked up a file and two books and put them on the end table next to the chair and ottoman. Marcus watched her go to the kitchen. She poured two glasses of water, picked up a pen and highlighter, and put the bow of her reading glasses into her mouth. She set a glass of water beside him, turned on another light and nestled into the big chair, opening her book.

Marcus released a deep sigh and turned to the page where he had left off. His eyes ached and stung as he strained to read the fine print. He closed his eyes for a moment to moisten them and was startled by the sound of a loud thump. Megan looked at Marcus from above the frame of her glasses. His book had fallen from his chest to the floor.

CHAPTER 11

"What time is it?" Marcus asked, reaching down to pick up his book.

"About eight o'clock. You fell asleep for about an hour and a half."

"I'm so sorry," Marcus said.

"Don't be. My mother told me that you wouldn't fall asleep unless you needed to sleep." Megan had turned off the light by the couch while he slept and Marcus stretched to turn it back on. Marcus opened his book again. He looked at Megan who was searching through a file and then he looked around the room. He tried to center his attention on his studies but found himself looking at Megan and the objects she had in her apartment, a collection of blue glass bottles, a few woolly sheep ornaments, bookends, and a laptop computer.

"Why don't you have any pictures?" Marcus asked. "I thought you would have a picture of your parents or friends in your apartment."

Megan took off her glasses and came over to sit on the end of the couch. She picked up her Bible from the table behind it and showed him a photograph that was tucked inside the pages. "We're not big picture takers. I only brought this one, and the few others I have are at home. These are my parents," Megan said, handing him the picture. "It was taken at my last graduation."

Marcus could see the resemblance Megan had to her mother, a beautiful woman, with the same jewel-like eyes and warm, inviting smile. Her father, Marcus thought, looked as rugged as the mountains. In the picture, his chin rested on Megan's head and his arms wrapped around both Megan and her mother. His skin was as tan as leather and his eyes were a piercing steel blue.

"Your father looks like an American," Marcus said.

"And what do Americans look like?" Megan asked, laughing.

"A cowboy. He looks like a cowboy."

"He would have enjoyed that analogy."

"Would have?" Marcus asked.

"My parents have both passed away."

"I'm sorry," Marcus said, wondering if his words had troubled her.

"So am I."

"They would have been very proud of you winning the Scolengard," Marcus said. Megan smiled and put the picture back in between the pages of her Bible.

"My father was a biochemist and my mother a pediatrician and research scientist. When I had any trouble in school my mother and father were right there to help. I wasn't stretching myself choosing this field."

"They gave you a gift," Marcus said.

Megan looked down at her Bible and played with the corner of its pages, stopping at the family photograph. "They were a gift," Megan said, tears pricking her eyes. She quickly changed the subject. "After I'm done here," she said, taking a deep breath, "I want to go back home and go to medical school. I know my uncle will hate the idea but it's my dream and I want to do it."

"We have a good medical school right here," Marcus said proudly.

"You certainly do. And we have a few back in the States," Megan said with a wink and a smile. "Would you like some tea?"

"Yes, thank you," Marcus said.

Megan left her Bible on the couch and she went to the kitchen. Marcus picked it up and started scanning the pages. He stopped at one of the scraps of paper marking a passage.

"You have to explain this," Marcus said when Megan returned and set down the cups. She took the scrap of paper Marcus handed to her. On it was written, "Don't spread manure on an evil seed."

"My great aunt," Megan said with a laugh, "with good ol' Texas common sense."

Marcus looked at her, more bewildered than before, as she sat down on the end of couch. "You found that in First Kings, right?" Megan asked. Marcus looked down at the Bible and read the chapter.

"Yes."

"The passages about King Solomon," Megan said spooning sugar into her tea. "Well, we know that Solomon was blessed. He was a wise man, the wisest man to have ever lived, an intelligent man and certainly a wealthy man, but he couldn't seem to help throwing a little manure around already fertile fields."

"What do you mean?"

"He liked women," Megan said flatly. "All sorts of women. Women he had no business being with. Women he was told to stay away from. Instead of doing what he knew was right, he turned his head from the truth, and his thoughts became an act, and the act became an obsession, and the obsession became his downfall. So as my aunt puts it, don't spread manure on an evil seed, because something's bound to grow!"

Marcus thumbed the worn cover of the Bible and kept his eyes on the fragmented gold letters.

"Megan, do you believe in the Bible?" he asked.

"Yes, I do," Megan answered. She looked over at her books and thought about the work she had to do the next day and then she looked at Marcus. He kept thumbing the pages of her Bible and then closed it with the heavy palm of his hand. She blew over the top of her steaming drink and leaned back on the couch.

"How do you know that Jesus is the Son of God or that there even is a God at all?" Marcus asked, sitting up. "How do you know?"

Megan took her time and thought for a moment, drank from her cup and then set it down again. "How do I know?" Megan repeated thoughtfully. "I guess I never really considered it because as far back as I can remember I have always known God."

"Blind faith," Marcus said dryly.

"Yes, by faith, but that doesn't mean I haven't questioned or tested or even been tested by God."

"How? How do you know He's there or that prayers are not just wishful thinking or that happiness is not just a stroke of good luck?" Marcus asked.

Megan put her arm on top of the couch and leaned her head into her hand. "I work in the world of the itsy-bitsy, as Ostride and I like to call it." Megan smiled and said, "We don't get to see a whole person, like you. We don't have the opportunity to know their personality. We can't hear their laughs, their growls and grumbles, their wit or introspection. We can't see their hearts." She paused and focused on her books and papers on the floor and ran her fingers through her tumbling hair. "But what we do see at work is the mechanical, the factual workings of their smallest parts known to us at this time. And in it, and the translucent specks of tissue and minute beads of blood," Megan said, "I can see God's hand, His design. There is order in every detail, in the smallest fragments of life. I can see the evidence of God's hand in those places, His mastery and genius, His love and His mercy. To me, there's no question that our bodies are well-thought-out designs. The human body itself is proof of God."

Megan went on, "I know it sounds trite but I see God's work everywhere, in every star in the sky to every living creature in the depths of the ocean. The more I learn the more I am convinced. We have evidence we can see and touch, there is the historical and physical evidence of the accuracy of the Bible, and there are the prophets and the recorded fulfillment of their prophecies. We have witnesses in the Bible and witnesses today who testify for Christ."

Megan looked into Marcus eyes. "In our work we believe much with so much less and here," she said looking at the Bible, "the evidence is conclusive. We just have to want to look at it."

"What about this?" Marcus asked. He reached for the book he had been reading and pulled out an envelope he had been using for a bookmark. He handed it to her and Megan opened the folded letter inside. It was the laboratory results of a patient he was treating. Megan could tell from the results that the four-year-old boy was gravely ill.

"A child suffering," Marcus said. "We've tried everything. I keep going over and over his records hoping that I can find something, anything. We're losing the battle." He rubbed his forehead and wiped his eyes with both of his hands trying to erase the picture of the boy's small hand wrapped around his fingers and looking up at him with trusting eyes from his hospital bed.

"If there is a God, why an innocent child, Megan? What could this child have done to deserve this?" Megan reread the letter and looked over the test results and set them on her lap. She said a silent prayer and looked up at Marcus who was waiting for an answer.

"Not long ago, I was told my father was dying," Megan said. "I asked 'why' until my eyes were swollen with tears and my heart was numb.

You see, I was preparing for my mother's death. She had been fighting cancer for two years, but like you say, she was losing the battle. When she decided to come home from the hospital, I dropped out of school to take care of her. We spent as much time together as we could. We prayed together and shared our thoughts. Whatever came to pass, we were ready." Megan took a deep breath. "I was so sure that God was going to take care of it all.

"Then one day my father walked through the door. I knew he had gone for a checkup. I didn't even think about it. He'd never been sick a day in his life. He sat down at the kitchen table, folded his hands and didn't say a word. I remember I didn't want to hear it. I didn't want to hear what I already knew somehow," Megan whispered. "It seemed like the day after he was diagnosed with leukemia he passed away. We didn't have that special time, there was no time to prepare, just this horrible emptiness. I didn't understand. My mother was too ill to make arrangements or to go to the funeral. When I came home she tried to comfort me and reminded me that Dad was at home, safe and more alive than we are right now. I didn't want to hear it. I wanted them both with me. I didn't want to be alone. But I didn't have time to be angry or arrogant with God. When I looked at my mother I could see the same shadow of death coming to collect her soul. I begged God for a miracle, and she prayed for God to give me the faith and strength to carry on. She passed away exactly two months after my father. It was almost like a dream, or rather, a nightmare," Megan said.

"I arranged my mother's funeral, sorted through years of belongings, sold our house and paid, signed, sealed and stamped a mountain of bills, legal documents, and thank-you notes. When I realized everything was finished, I sat alone in my apartment one evening and I remember listening to the refrigerator hum. It was a miserable sound. I remember thinking this is it, I'm alone in this world without my parents and without a home, and when I needed God the most in my life, He deserted me, and left me behind to fend for myself in this fallen paradise. I wanted to collapse and let someone else pick up the pieces. I couldn't believe that I had managed everything to that point. And then I realized something: I hadn't. God did. When I couldn't carry on He did. The many times I wanted to crumble, Jesus gave me strength. When I was certain that my heart would break in two,

He sustained me. And He sent friends and family. My uncle and aunt left Texas to be with me. My uncle was offered my father's position at the university and my aunt teaches school to disabled children in the town where I grew up. Why were the two people I cherished more than my own life taken from me? I don't know. God knows, and I have faith that He will see me through," Megan said with conviction. Then she added, "God knows this boy, Marcus. He is not alone."

"Does God really care?" Marcus asked.

"So much that He was willing to die for this little boy and for you and me. Look at the evidence, have faith and pray. God will see you through."

"I've forgotten how to pray," Marcus said harshly, his thoughts on the suffering child.

"Then just talk to Him. The Lord is sympathetic to those of us who are more analytical than eloquent." Marcus gripped the Bible and kept his eyes on the faded gold letters. "Pray," Megan urged. "There isn't a question He can't answer. There isn't a hurt He can't heal."

She picked up her book and went over to her chair.

CHAPTER 12

The next time Megan looked up from her book Marcus had slumped down into the pillow and had fallen asleep again. His thick, feathered hair had fallen lazily down on his brow and his dark brown eyelashes were fanned against his wind-burned face. Megan shook as she felt a chill run down her back. Ostride is right, Megan thought, he is so good looking. Megan slowly crawled out from underneath her afghan and tried to revive the fire from the few glowing embers that remained. It's still early, she thought, as she watched Marcus asleep on the couch. A few hours of rest might be just what we both need. She turned off the lights and took the book from his chest and gently laid her afghan on top of the quilt that covered his legs. The low burning fire cast a warm glow over the entire room. As she looked down at him, she could almost feel the slow, steady rhythm of his deep long breaths lulling her to sleep. The fire snapped and a log hissed. She turned and wrinkled her nose, picked up her books, and quietly stepped away toward the kitchen.

* * *

Only black ashes and a few remaining scattered embers were left in the fireplace when Marcus' arm stretched above the couch. As he flexed his chest, Megan could hear his shoulder and arm crack and a deep sigh that was muffled by a pillow. He sat up and ran his fingers through his hair. He found Megan sitting at the kitchen table that was covered with papers, books and an empty coffee mug.

"What time is it?" Marcus asked. Megan pulled her glasses down to the end of her nose and looked at the clock on the kitchen wall.

"It's almost midnight," she said.

"If I am going to sleep, I'd better do it at home," Marcus said and dragged his hand through his hair again. "I don't know why I am so tired." He folded up the quilt and afghan, picked up his book and made his way to the door to put on his jacket.

"Marc, I want you to have this," Megan said. "I dug it out. It's not as old as it looks. It's just well used." The black leather Bible was tattered and the binding shifted in Marcus' hands. He opened it and read the inscription on the inside cover.

"This was your father's!"

Megan pulled her turtleneck sweater closer to her chin and nodded. "In the margin of each chapter he would write down short notes. They helped me answer some of my questions, so maybe Dad can help you answer some of yours," Megan said, holding her glasses with both hands.

Marcus closed the Bible. "Megan, I can't take this."

"Take it," Megan said and smiled. "Read it."

His eyes rested on hers. "I'm glad I came," he said.

Megan put her reading glasses on top of her head. "Me too."

"Can I call on you again?"

"Friends are always welcome," she said.

"Tomorrow at six? I will bring dinner," Marcus said, and reached for her hand.

"You don't like my cooking?" Megan teased.

"No, no it was very good."

"Good night, Marcus."

"Good night, Megan." His words were slow and deep and Megan felt the same chill travel up and down her back, causing her to tremble. She let go of his hand and began to rub her arms through her sweater.

CHAPTER 13

"It's time for a break," Megan said, snapping off her gloves and throwing them into the garbage. Ostride peered through the maze of glass beakers, rubber and plastic tubes and caught a glimpse of her friend. Megan had been quiet all morning and Ostride knew that she was feeling the pressure to spend longer hours in the lab to reach her goals.

"What's the trouble?" Ostride asked.

"I don't know. This should work, it did at Brier's, but it isn't here. I can't figure it out." Megan stared at the glass slide and then walked away. "Maybe I just need to leave it alone for a while. Can I buy you a soda?" Megan asked, as she washed her hands.

"Sure, I think you can pull me away for a minute or two," Ostride said. "Hey, did you hear they're going to be adding a cafeteria to this building?"

"No, when?"

"It was in the school newspaper. An anonymous donor gave funding for the construction project to start in the spring. In the meantime they're going to set up a temporary deli cart downstairs."

"That will help. I'm getting tired of pretzels from the vending machine," Megan said as they walked down the hallway. The lounge was empty. Ostride emptied her pockets onto a table, picking up the coins among the rubber bands and tissues that filled her pockets. "It's my turn," Megan said. "Soda and pretzels or soda and cheese snaps?"

"Let shake it up and try cheese snaps," Ostride said, as she stretched out onto one of the stiff aqua blue vinyl chairs. Megan joined her and they both kicked their feet up onto the plastic cube that separated them.

"All I have to do is finish one last group of slides and I'm done for the day, thank goodness! Then I can go out for something real to eat,"

Ostride said, tipping her head back, looking at the speckled ceiling as she popped a cheese snap into her mouth.

"One of these days you're going to have to learn how to cook," Megan said. Ostride waved her hand in the air to dismiss the idea.

"Never!" Ostride said, as if she were sounding out a charge. "Besides, eating is a minor detail. I'm going out with Jacob tonight."

"Where are you going?" Megan asked.

"I don't care as long as there are no books, papers, computers, cell phones or pagers in sight." Ostride took a swallow of her soda. "Maybe we'll go to a movie. I haven't been to a movie in eons. Would you like to come along?"

"No, no thank you." Megan laughed. "I think you'll have more fun on your own."

"That's not true," Ostride chided. Megan squinted, cocked her head and waited. "Okay, we're going through a stage," Ostride admitted.

"A stage for two, not three. But thanks for asking," Megan said, and broke a pretzel into bite-size pieces. "Besides, Marcus is supposed to stop by tonight."

"Marcus Holcombe?" Ostride said. "You've been holding out on me."

"He apologized, we're friends and that's about it," Megan said, avoiding making eye contact with Ostride. When she finally did, she saw that Ostride had an impish grin on her face. "Stop that," Megan said. "I know what you're thinking and you're wrong. Marc has been coming over to study." Megan stood up and reached down deep into her lab coat pocket and pulled out a few coins to feed into the vending machine.

"Marcus is coming over to study," Ostride said. "Right."

"Yes, study."

"Uh huh...."

"There you are Megan!" Jacob said, coming through the swinging doors, "I've been looking all over for you."

"Already he has eyes for another woman," Ostride said from the corner of the room.

"Ostride," Jacob said happily, as he went to her side and bent down to kiss her.

"He can't help it," Megan said, parading over to the trash can. "It's the designer lab coat, matching bonnet and safety glasses that get 'em every time." She threw her pop can into the recycling basket. "What can I do for you, Jacob?" she asked.

"Marcus wanted me to tell you that he won't be able to make it tonight. He's not feeling well. I feel a little guilty leaving him alone this evening."

"Where's Phillip?" Ostride asked.

"I don't know. He left a note and said he would be gone. Who knows what that means. He's like a stray cat, he might be gone the evening or he might come back next week."

"Who's Phillip?" Megan asked.

"Phillip is Marcus' cousin. We all share Marcus' townhouse," Jacob said. "Maybe I should cancel tonight, Ostride. Marcus is quite ill."

"It's up to you," Ostride said with the expression of a disappointed child. "We could go out Sunday after church?" Ostride asked.

"No, that won't work for me," he said, putting his arm around her. "Tuesday?"

"I have an exam Wednesday. How about next Friday?" she asked, clutching his hand.

"Good grief!" Megan exploded with a laugh, as she watched the two sulking in the corner. "I can go over and make sure Marc gets through the night."

"That would be great," Jacob said as he scribbled the address on his business card. "We're right in Hebl across from the Government Square. Thank you, Megan"

"My contribution to save true love," Megan said as she watched the two huddle together.

"We do our best," Ostride whispered to Jacob.

"What?" Megan asked, as she turned around from the snack counter. Ostride had reached up and pulled Jacob to her lips and was kissing him passionately.

"I see my mission is complete. True love prevails," Megan said. She opened her second bag of pretzels and walked out the door.

* * *

Propped up in bed by three large pillows, Marcus surveyed the files and books sprawled out on his bed, nightstand and floor. His cell phone buzzed as another hourly report from the hospital entered his email. He looked at the screen, read it and closed his eyes. Letting the phone drop to the blanket, he rested his head onto the pillows and stretched his arms out and to his side. His hand rested on a sheet of paper. He lifted it and looked at the picture of the small boy he was trying to save, lying helplessly in a hospital bed. He couldn't help him by lying in bed, he thought. Pushing the papers aside, he swung his legs out of bed and sat up in one slow motion. His head throbbed and his arms and legs felt like weights attached to his weakened and hot flesh.

Megan's greeting faded when she walked into the room. "Marc, what in the world!" she exclaimed. His white tee shirt was soaked with perspiration and his face was as pale as the cotton sheets on his bed.

"Megan," he said slowly. "What are you doing here? Didn't Jacob find you?" He swayed slightly and then seemed to find his balance again as he sat on the edge of his bed.

"Yes he did," Megan said, pushing up her sleeves and putting the palm of her hand on his forehead. "That's why I'm here. He thought someone should be home with you if you weren't feeling well, but you're downright sick. You have a fever and from the looks of it, influenza. Take off your shirt," she said, picking up the papers around his bed and on the floor. "Where's the bathroom?"

Marcus turned his head to the left side of the room. Megan went in and found a washcloth and soaked it in cool water and turned on the water in the tub.

"Come on," she said brushing back his hair and wiping his brow, "you have to get out of those wet clothes, get cleaned up and cooled down." She helped him up from the bed and walked with him to the bathroom. Marcus leaned over the sink. His teeth ached as his head pounded from the short walk. "Where are your tee shirts?"

"In the closet, top drawer," Marcus said and closed his eyes.

"I'm going to get that man, the butler who let me in, to help you out in here," Megan said.

"I'll manage."

"It's either him or me." Megan found a set of thick, white towels in a closet and set them on the counter. "I'll have him check on you in a few minutes. I don't want you to be in the warm water very long."

PLANS · VICTORIA J.M. HOFFBECK

"Yes, Dr. Buchanan," Marcus whispered. He put his hand on top of hers but kept staring down into the sink.

"Don't worry, I'll have you fixed up in no time at all," she said and rubbed his back.

Marcus closed his eyes and hung onto the marble counter. "I'll be all right," he protested.

"Sure," Megan said. "Take your time." She turned off the water in the tub and closed the door behind her as she left. She quickly started to pick up the room, setting empty glasses and crumpled up pieces of paper and tissues on a tray and called down the stairs for the butler.

"Yes, Miss?" The Englishman suddenly appeared behind her. Megan jumped and the tray leapt in her hands. The glasses rattled together and a balled up piece of paper dropped to the floor.

"I am terribly sorry, Miss, I didn't mean to frighten you."

"I didn't see you coming," Megan said, with a little chuckle.

"I came from the servants' door, Miss." He opened up the hidden door from the hall. "This way we can move about the house rather quickly." Megan looked blankly at the door that fit perfectly into the paneled wall. "Can I take that from you?" he asked.

"Yes, please," Megan said. "I never would have noticed that door. That's remarkable."

"If you need additional assistance you can press any of the ivory buttons you see on the walls. The electronic system will pick up your voice and we will get whatever you need."

"Thank you," Megan said, looking at a set of buttons next to the door, and trying not to seem surprised.

"Will there be anything else?" he asked

"Yes," Megan said. "Could you check on Marc in a minute or two. He's taking a bath. And I was wondering if you could point me in the direction of the kitchen. I would like to make some tea with lemon and honey if you have it."

"I'll have Cook make the tea and I'll bring it up in a moment."

"Cook?"

"Yes, Miss."

"Oh," Megan said, surprised. "Then maybe you can tell me where the linens are kept. Marc's bed is drenched and it needs to be changed."

"I'll have one of the house maids come up straight away."

"House maids?"

"Yes, Miss."

"I guess I'm not in Minnesota anymore," Megan said.

"No, Miss," the butler said. "Will there be anything else?"

"No, I don't think so," Megan said. Before she could collect all of the papers and books on the floor and nightstand, a maid had appeared in the bedroom with a stack of pressed bed linens. Megan began to help her strip the bed. The maid's eyes widened and she gasped, "Oh, no need, Miss."

"It's no problem," Megan said, piling the damp sheets on the floor. Megan took one of the pillowcases and waved it in front of a down pillow and stuffed it inside.

"I don't know if you should be doing this, Miss. It's just not proper."

"Excuse me?" Megan said, stuffing another pillow and then helping the girl tuck in the sheets. "I've been doing my own bed for as long as I can remember." The butler knocked on the door, holding the tray with the tea on it with one hand. He snickered as he watched Megan put the finishing touches on the bed and the maid nervously scurrying out the door with the bundle of used linens in her arms.

"Tea, Miss?" he asked, setting it on top of a large dresser. Megan had put her hair up in a knot and secured it with a pencil she'd found on the floor. She looked around at the tidy room with her hands resting on her hips.

"Thank you," she said, turning to the butler. "I'm sorry, I don't know your name."

"Broderick, Miss," the butler said. He had a friendly face and a winsome smile. He had jet-black hair and an impeccably groomed salt and pepper mustache and beard that Megan favored.

"Nice to meet you, Broderick," Megan said. "I suppose Jacob already told you who I am."

"Yes, Miss," he said, pouring her a cup of tea. "I've checked on Marcus and he will be out momentarily. Will there be anything else, Miss Buchanan?"

"Megan, please."

"I am afraid I cannot," he said, looking toward the bathroom door.

"Why not?" Megan asked. Marcus opened the bathroom door looking refreshed but still pale and tired.

"Can I help you, Sir?" Broderick asked.

"No, thank you," Marcus said, shuffling to the bed. He took off his robe and slipped between the soft, clean sheets.

"Broderick, do you have any chicken broth?" Megan asked, looking at Marcus, "Maybe a few noodles in it, and some toast?"

"Yes, Miss."

"That will be all, Broderick," Marcus said. The servant nodded toward Marc and left the room without hesitation.

Megan walked to the dresser and poured a cup of tea for Marcus. "Well, this isn't the way my mother would make it but it will do you some good anyway."

"How would your mother make it?" Marcus asked, taking the cup from Megan.

"Besides the lemon and honey she would have added a shot of brandy."

"You don't seem the type."

"Medicinal purposes only," Megan laughed. "My mother believed that her tea and a little tender lovin' care could kill just about any virus known to man."

"It would certainly make the tea taste better," Marcus said sarcastically.

"I love tea," Megan objected.

"I quite agree, Miss," Broderick said, holding the tray of broth and toast.

"That was fast," Megan said.

"Cook had a hunch that chicken soup should be on tonight's menu."

"Broderick came to Dreiholm fifteen years ago from England. He is responsible for introducing tea to this household," Marcus said. Broderick flipped the feet down on either side of the tray and set it in front of Marcus.

"I'm not hungry," Marcus growled. Broderick immediately took the tray.

"Try a little," Megan coaxed. "If it doesn't taste good to you, then don't eat it."

Megan went into the bathroom and found the medicine chest. "Here, you can take two of these with your tea," she said, setting the pain relievers on the tray that was back on his lap. Megan picked up her tea cup and stood watching him.

"Will there be anything else, Sir?" Broderick asked.

"I think we'd better ask the lady," Marcus said.

Megan looked at Marcus and wrinkled her nose. "Not right now, but thank you, Broderick." She pulled the chair from the desk over to Marcus' bedside and put her feet up on the bed. Marcus took a bite of the toast and noticed that Megan had taken all of his files and set them on top of his blanket chest. Megan followed his eyes to a blue file on top of the pile.

"It's the boy I was telling you about," Marcus said. He put the toast down on the plate. "I keep going over it and over it again, but nothing."

"Can I?" Megan asked, picking up the blue file. Marcus nodded his head and took some broth from the cup.

She opened the file and found the child's medical history. He had never been ill before and his parents and grandparents were, in all respects, in excellent physical condition.

"When his mother brought him into the clinic he had a headache, a fever, and was weak – all the signs of a viral infection. We have had similar cases. It's common this time of year but the next time she brought him into the clinic he was much worse. No treatment has helped. He has chills and is confused and lethargic and now his left kidney is failing. He's slowly deteriorating and there is nothing I can do about it," Marcus said, angrily pushing aside the cup and brushing his hair back with his fingers. "It's driving me mad."

"At least we got some food in you," Megan observed, as she took the tray away and set it by the door. She dug through her bag and pulled out her reading glasses. She sat back down in the small chair and started to reread the child's history.

"He has a rash?" Megan asked. "Rash. Hum. Fever, chills, rash..." Megan repeated the words, tapping her thumb against the papers.

"A faint rash. Patches on his body," Marcus sighed, with his head tipped back on the pillows. "We think it is from the fever. It's not very pronounced."

Megan wrapped her hand around the teacup and laced her fingers through the ear of the cup. Her eyebrows were knitted together as she turned a page of the boy's file and then flipped the page back again.

"What?" Marcus asked.

"If we were in the States, I'd have a guess," she said, "but you don't have ticks in Dreiholm."

"Ticks?" Marcus asked.

"An insect. A tick," Megan said. "A tick bite can spread disease, Lyme's disease or a better guess is Rocky Mountain Spotted Fever. Not common but not uncommon in the States, it would be checked for anyway. Your little boy has all the right symptoms. The trouble with my theory is that he would have had to have been somewhere where these ticks are, exposed to a park or some kind of wooded area, and he would have to have been bitten by an infectious tick. Highly improbable," Megan said, eyeing the chart. She heard Marcus' cup fall to the floor and watched him as he frantically sat up in bed, grappled for his cell phone and tapped out a series of numbers.

"Dr. Wolf, immediately," Marcus ordered.

"Marc, I know there aren't any ticks here, I had to take classes and go through immunization before I came to Dreiholm," Megan whispered. Marcus held up his hand to quiet her and then reached out to her hand and pulled her to his side. Megan could feel the heat of his fever radiate from his touch.

"Ren, where are you? Is the boy's mother there? Put her on ... Ah, Mrs. Becker. When did you say you went to the United States? Oh, and where did you stay? And then you went camping? Thank you, Mrs. Becker, very much. Could you put Dr. Wolf back on the telephone.... Ren, we need another blood test right away for Rocky Mountain Spotted Fever. Yes, Rocky Mountain Spotted Fever, it's a tick-borne disease. Let me know as soon as you find out the results."

Marcus hung up the phone. "He's going to call me back," he said to Megan, his voice not as strong anymore.

"They were in the U.S.?" Megan asked.

"Vacation," Marcus said, still holding on to her hand. "One night I couldn't sleep and I went to the hospital and Mrs. Becker, the boy's mother, was there by his bed. We started to talk and she told me that she and her family had visited her brother in New York. After their visit they decided to tour the south and west of the United States."

"Did she mention that her son had been bit?"

"No, but it is worth a try," Marcus said. "I've exhausted every other possibility. We all have." Together they watched the silent telephone and then after a moment, Megan picked up the fallen cup and went to the bathroom to find a towel to soak up the few drops of tea on the floor.

"Megan, you don't have to do that," Marcus said as she came back into the room.

"A watched pot never boils," Megan said wiping up the spill. "If I just sit there watching that phone, I'll jump right out of my skin." She flung the moist towel over her shoulder and eased Marcus back down into the bed. She pulled the sheet and blanket taut to his chest and put the telephone by his side. "There is nothing you can do now but wait. Try to rest."

His eyes closed and Marcus drifted off to a restless sleep, stirring every few minutes. When Megan had looked up from her book an hour had passed.

The cell phone rang.

"Yes," Marcus answered. "Yes!" His smile brightened up his face. "How did I know?" Marcus said as he looked at Megan twisting the edge of the towel still draped over her shoulder. "It was an answer to a prayer, Doctor, an answer to a prayer."

CHAPTER 14

After the jubilation and a celebratory cup of tea, Marcus finally began to lose focus as sleep began to claim him. Megan felt his forehead again. The fever had subsided somewhat, but was still present. "Now physician, it's time to heal thyself," Megan said. "I think you had better get some rest."

"Don't leave," Marcus said, holding on to her hand. "I just need a short nap."

"I think you're going to be able sleep through the night," Megan said, as she stood to leave.

"No, no," Marcus said wearily. "Just a half an hour. Wait for me." The evening light was fading in the sky and Megan looked for a small lamp she could work by.

"I saw a room down the hall, I'll study down there."

"Anywhere you like," Marcus said, half asleep. He could feel Megan tucking the blankets tightly in between the mattresses. With his one arm outside the blankets, he caught Megan's hand again and without opening his eyes he brought her hand up to his lips and gently kissed her fingers.

"I'll leave the door open," Megan said. She turned out the lights and looked down on him lying in his bed. The same chill of electricity she had felt before now surged through her body and tingled in her hands. Stop that, she thought. He's delirious, he has a fever. We're just going to be friends. That's it. Trying not to rattle the teacups, she picked up the tray and walked out of the room and down the staircase. At the bottom, she found Broderick readjusting the logs in the foyer fireplace. "Broderick, where is the kitchen?" Megan asked. He saw the tray in her hands and quickly came to her side.

"No need for you to do that, Miss. I'll take care of this," Broderick said, taking the tray. "I realized coming down, I neglected to ask you if you would like anything from the kitchen?"

"I'm starving," Megan admitted.

"I'll see what Cook can come up with," he said, smiling warmly. Megan liked the way his mustache wiggled when he smiled and how his eyes shone above his round cheeks.

"Broderick, may I look around the house. It's so beautiful and filled with so many things, I would love to explore."

"I'll take you for a tour if you would like, Miss."

"I would like that very much," Megan said, looking twice at a small painting to her side. "Is that really what I think it is?" she asked.

"It is a Picasso," Broderick said. Megan looked at the disjointed and bloated figure and cringed. It looked out of place, Megan thought as she surveyed the other beautiful portraits on the wall.

"Humph," Megan said.

"I agree," Broderick whispered. "It was a gift and I suppose it would be in poor taste not to display it. Let me bring this to the kitchen and while Cook is making you supper, we'll take our tour."

"Can I see the kitchen?" Megan asked. "I have never been in a kitchen where there has been a hired cook."

"It's not terribly interesting. I'm sure you will enjoy other parts of the house much more."

"Oh, I'd still love to see it," Megan said.

"Then follow me, and I'll bring you to the kitchen." They went down a narrow stairway with worn stone steps to the basement level. At the bottom was a wide hallway with rows of doors on each side. One door was open to the back driveway. A man in overalls was carrying boxes through the door and down the hall, as another man dressed like Broderick waited by the door counting boxes and watching the deliverymen make their trips back and forth. "We receive all our deliveries through this door," Broderick said, proceeding further down the hall.

"Late delivery," Megan mentioned.

"Much of the goods are air freighted to the house. As soon as they arrive we accept delivery, unless it is too late, of course." At the end of the hall was a wooden door with the upper half made of frosted glass. Inside, Megan could hear voices, one she recognized as the young maid who had helped her strip Marcus' bed.

"You mean she has no idea," Megan heard someone say.

"None at all," said the young housemaid.

"How can that be?" another voice said. "Is she completely daft?"

Broderick kicked open the door and entered before Megan, giving each of the servants a stern glare. "This is the kitchen, Miss Buchanan. As you can see it is not very interesting at all," Broderick said, handing off the tray to a young woman who glanced at Megan and then hurried to put the dirty dishes into one of three dishwashers. Megan noticed the small group seemed to stand at attention when Broderick entered the room, everyone except the elderly woman wearing a white chef's hat and jacket.

"Hello," Megan said, looking at all the unfamiliar faces. The elderly woman didn't speak but watched Megan carefully as she walked into the room. "What a wonderful kitchen," Megan said, looking at the large worktable of stainless steel that almost went the entire length of the room and a smaller butcher-block table by the stove, surrounded by sturdy wooden chairs. Pots and pans hung above the workstation and every culinary tool imaginable was placed in orderly open cubes attached to the wall or below the countertops.

"Something smells delicious," Megan said.

"That, Miss?" Broderick said, twitching his nose. "I was almost embarrassed to bring you down for fear of the vulgar smell." Cook raised an eyebrow and gave him a searing glance.

"Oh, no, it smells wonderful to me. It smells like sauerkraut and stuffed cabbage." Cook's eyes lit up. "One thing my mother did cook well was sauerkraut and stuffed cabbage and the few other recipes her parents had brought with them from the old country."

"Would you like some?" Cook asked.

"Yes, please," Megan said. Broderick shook his head as he retrieved a clean tray. Megan sat at the butcher-block table as Cook ladled two rolls of cabbage and a heaping serving of sauerkraut onto a plate.

"I will gladly bring it up to the dining room for you, Miss."

"That's all right Broderick, if you don't mind. It's nice and warm in here," Megan said. Cook gave Broderick a sharp look and set the plate in front of Megan and waited for her to take a bite. The entire staff, curious about the unexpected visitor, quietly crept into the kitchen and peered at her from behind carts, cupboards and half-closed doorways. Megan took one bite and then another and took hold of Cook's hand. "This is fabulous!" she said, cutting another piece with her fork. Cook's shoulders set back as she grinned and turned up her nose to Broderick.

"Nothing could taste this good," Megan said. The young woman who had taken the tray from Broderick inched up beside her.

"Get Miss Buchanan a drink," Cook ordered. The young woman hurriedly filled a glass with ice and poured red punch into it from a silver pitcher.

"Is this all right, Miss?" she asked.

"Wonderful," Megan said. "Thank you."

"Miss, is it true that all Americans live in mansions?" she asked in a low voice.

"No," Megan said. "Why do you ask?" The girl shifted from side to side and kept looking down at the table. "You can ask me whatever you like, I won't be offended. I have a pretty tough skin," Megan said, taking another bite.

The young woman waited and looked at Broderick and then hesitantly sat down. Cook took a chair as well and sat beside Megan.

"I get a magazine from the United States and all the houses look so grand. I read once about a housekeeper who had saved enough money to build a home of her own and on her own land!" The other servants in the back of the kitchen laughed out loud and the young woman's face turned a bright red. "She even had her own garden and an automobile." The laughter rang louder than before and Megan could see the young woman's lip begin to quiver. Cook sat quietly and when the laughter continued, Broderick snapped his fingers and the staff quieted to a hush.

"What you read is most likely true," Megan said.

"How could it be?" a young man snapped. He stood beside the workstation in a starched white shirt and a button down vest that clung to his thin frame. His arms were folded across his chest and his dark blue eyes laughed at her in disbelief.

"America is a land of opportunity and possibilities," Megan said, taking another bite before setting down her fork and dabbing her face with a napkin. "When people are allowed to be creative and are ambitious they can do amazing things."

"Not everyone has a house and an automobile in the United States. Certainly not a housekeeper," the young man grumbled.

"Mind yourself," Broderick said. "Miss Buchanan is a guest."

"That's all right," Megan said. "You're right, not everyone can afford a house or a car or even food. There is suffering everywhere in the world, even at home, but our country has been greatly blessed by God and by the people who came with little more than their faith, determination and imagination, for which I am eternally thankful."

"Where are your people from?" Cook asked.

"Well, let's see, my mother's family came from Lithuania," Megan said, trying to swallow as she spoke. Cook smiled broadly and pulled her chair closer to her. "My great-great grandparents left Lithuania when they heard about the free land being offered in the West.

"Free land!" Cook exclaimed.

"Yes," Megan answered. "The government was trying to entice people to populate the West, and to do that they offered free land to settlers who would stay and farm the territory. My family stayed for some time but then hard times came and they moved on to Texas."

"Cowboys!" the young woman said with great enthusiasm.

"Definitely, cowboys," Megan said. "They became ranchers. It's a hard life but they prospered enough to send their children to school. My grandfather became a doctor and moved to a state called Minnesota and his daughter, my mother, became a doctor too."

"It takes generations then?" the young man beside the workstation said.

"Sometimes," Megan said. "Other people with good ideas and the drive to enter the marketplace, they can be very successful in a short period of time. And I have to say, it isn't uncommon for a housekeeper in America or any other working person to save and own a car and a home of some kind." The young man huffed and Broderick glared at him. He knew from his superior's face it was his last warning.

"You have to remember," Megan continued. "America is not like Dreiholm. In America, there is a great deal of land. That makes the price of building and owning a home less expensive. And because so many of us live so far from where we work, cars become essential."

"It's hopeless," the young man said. "We're destined to live as we always have with our parents and grandparents. There are not enough homes being built to buy, even if we did have the money to purchase them." Megan could see that the young man was struggling and that his dissension was turning to anger.

"The government owns all the land," Broderick explained. "They lease the property to the citizens for one hundred years. When the lease expires, the recipient's children have an option to renew the lease. Most do. If they choose not to renew, a house becomes available for another family. The problem is aggravated by the shortage of land and the few new building permits issued each year by the government. It is only in the mountains, where very few people build at all, that the restrictions are less stringent," Broderick said. Megan thought for a moment as she ate her meal. She stared at a bowl of tomatoes sitting in the middle of the table.

"Cook, everyone calls you Cook. What is your name?" Megan asked.

"Elizabeth," the cook said clearly.

"Elizabeth, what are you going to do with the overripe tomatoes?"

"I am going to make some sauce out of them."

"What else can be done with them?" she asked the girl beside her.

"I don't know, Miss. I suppose we can make some soup out of them."

"What else?" Megan asked.

"My mother use to make a dye out of them," a woman said.

"An artist in the group," Megan teased. The woman smiled shyly. "What else?"

"Compost," came another voice.

"How about you?" Megan asked the young man by the workstation, tossing him a small and still firm tomato. He held it in his hand, looking at its smooth red skin and bright green top.

"Fuel," he said.

"Ah! The future," Megan said. "All good answers. Now let's answer another question," Megan said, scraping her dish to get the last of the sauerkraut. "How can I buy a home? But first we have to define the issue."

"What do you mean, define the issue?" the young woman asked.

"First, we have to consider the known facts. We know money is a problem and we also know that even if money were not a problem, there still wouldn't be a house to buy. So we really have a number of questions to answer, that could be summed up in part by asking, how can we create affordable housing in Dreiholm that would be acceptable to the government and people?"

"We could build in the mountains," a woman in the back of the room said. "There are beautiful slopes that are fine for building."

"How would we get to work?" another asked.

"The tram!"

"The tram doesn't go up there."

"How would we get the money?" the young man snorted. "Almost all of my wages go to my family or taxes and other necessaries."

"You could take a second job like my Mike does," the woman in the back said.

"Or become entrepreneurs," Megan suggested.

"What is an entrepreneur?" Elizabeth asked.

"A businessman or woman," Megan said, "selling goods or services for profit. You could become an entrepreneur by selling your cabbage rolls, for example," Megan said.

"Would you like some more?" Elizabeth asked.

"I'm full," Megan said, patting her midsection. "But I loved every bite."

"I'll put some away for you to take home," Elizabeth said, getting up from her seat.

"It would take a lifetime to make enough money to buy the materials to even build one house," the young man grumbled again.

"I don't believe that," Megan said. "There are many questions to be answered but the task is not insurmountable. It can be done."

"How?" the young man asked.

"By working together," Megan said. "Start by answering the questions and remember that there are many ways to reach your goal. If you hit a roadblock, step back and figure out the right way to get around it."

"It's impossible," the young man repeated. Megan sighed.

"My father always told me 'Nothing is impossible for God.' I believe that. You have to believe it too," Megan said, looking directly at the young man. "You can do this. The first step is prayer and the second step is to try."

"Can you help us?" asked the young woman sitting beside her.

Megan looked down at her empty plate.

"I have a few of my own questions to answer in a laboratory," Megan said.

The room became silent except for the sound of Elizabeth closing the lid on the container she was preparing for Megan to take home. Then Megan's face lit up. "Do you have a pen and paper?" she asked. The girl went to a drawer and handed them to her.

"I do know someone who may be able to get you started in the right direction. Just tell Rose, his secretary, that you want to talk with him and tell her that I sent you. He'll listen to you and he may be able to help you get started." The young man came to the table and stood beside her. Megan stood up, folded the paper in two and handed it to him. She turned to the cook. "Thank you, Elizabeth."

"The rest will be waiting for you when you are ready to leave, child." Elizabeth said. Broderick puffed at Cook's rare expression of affection.

"I'll appreciate it even more tomorrow."

"Are you ready for the rest of the tour of the townhome, Miss?" Broderick asked, holding the door open for her.

"Absolutely. Thank you again and it was good to meet all of you," Megan said. She waved goodbye and Broderick led her up the stairway. Back in the kitchen the servants hovered around the young man as he opened up the note. "Mr. Charles Payton," he read.

"Charles Payton - he's the American billionaire that owns Brier Pharmaceuticals," the woman from the back said. They looked at each other, puzzled.

Cook didn't join the small crowd. She carefully stirred the remaining cabbage rolls, watching the juices bubble. "Maybe," she said thoughtfully, "maybe."

CHAPTER 15

Megan was awed by everything she saw in Marcus' townhouse. She was fascinated by the finely carved doors that told a story about a young boy exploring the mountains, playing with woodland friends, and another of a boy opening gifts beneath a Christmas tree.

"This door is beautiful," Megan said. The carving was of a group of young men in uniform sitting around a campfire by a stream. As she looked more closely she saw two faces in the thick woods. One menacing face was watching the men around the campfire and the other was approaching the menacing one from behind. "What is this one about, Broderick?"

"This evil fellow," Broderick said, pointing to the menacing face, "was about to attack these men at the campfire but this young man came from behind and saved his friends." Megan bent over to look more closely at the faces.

"Do you know what I find most fascinating about these doors?" Broderick asked, as he swung the door open before Megan could take a closer look. "Each door fits into the wall," he said, locking the door into place. Megan saw that the vine carvings on the backside of every door completed the wall panels to the door's side.

"Incredible," she said, touching the door at the flawless seam. "You can't even tell it is a door when it's closed. Amazing." Megan looked around the room and smiled. "I don't know what I was expecting, but I wouldn't have imagined Marc living in this type of house," Megan said as they strolled down the hall.

"This is the Capital Apartment. One of the family estates," Broderick said. "Marcus, his cousin Phillip, and Jacob only live here when the university is in session."

"Oh. Oh my!" Megan said. "Where does he live the rest of the time?"

"For the past few years he has been traveling abroad; otherwise, he will visit his home in the mountains."

"The mountains?" Megan thought out loud as she put her one finger to her lips. "I don't know if that fits him either," she chuckled. "Well, Broderick, he's a mystery to me. Thank you for the tour. This has been a wonderful distraction, but I am afraid my fun is over," she said, looking at her watch. "I have to get back to my studies."

"Can I get you anything, Miss Buchanan?"

"No, no. I'll be fine. Thank Elizabeth again, will you? I had such fun meeting everyone. Don't tell Marcus, please, but I've had almost as much fun tonight as we had on our first date," Megan whispered. Broderick grinned and his mustache wiggled from side to side. Megan tiptoed up the stairway and slipped into Marcus' bedroom. From the dim light of the hallway she found her book bag. She could hear Marcus breathing quietly, deeply. She slipped out of the room undetected and found the study down the hall. Megan turned on the light and partially closed the door. She spread her books out on the desk, opened her laptop and began.

The next time Megan looked at her watch two hours had passed and Broderick was at the door holding a silver tray. "We thought you might like some tea and cake," he said, setting it on a small table by the window. Megan pulled her glasses down to the end of her nose.

"Can I bring you home with me?" Megan pleaded. Broderick laughed.

"If you need anything, Miss Buchanan, just ring."

"Thank you, Broderick," Megan said and turned out the light to rest her eyes. The light from outside the window was enough to find her way around the study. She poured a cup of tea and reclined in the window seat. The grand white, grey and blue government buildings towered like the mountains in the distance and the black lantern street lamps outside her window glowed with a halo of yellow light as snow steadily fell down from the dark sky. She cuddled back into the corner and wrapped her hands around her cup. She noticed a small spot in the corner of the window, tiny spires of frost laced together in the shape of a star.

"Difficult to study in the dark, isn't it?" Marcus said. He stood in the doorway in his bathrobe and slippers and Megan felt the familiar tingle in her fingertips.

"My eyes were burning," Megan said. "Broderick brought up this tea and it seemed like the perfect time for a break. How are you feeling?" she asked. Marcus sat opposite her on the window seat, with his hands in his pockets and one foot on the floor.

"Much better," he said and leaned back against the wall and looked out the window.

"You look much better," Megan said and put her hand on his forehead. "Your fever broke. You're on the mend." She took a sip of her tea.

"I called Dr. Wolf. Now that we know what we are dealing with we'll be able to prevent further damage and the boy will be fine."

"Good," Megan said.

"I started reading your father's Bible last night," Marcus said. "He had many notes."

"He could expound," Megan agreed.

"He asked the same questions that I ask myself."

"Any answers?" Megan asked.

"Yes, some. 'The answer is in the word and the word is God,'" Marc quoted from Megan's father's notes.

"Dad would ask God anything and everything," Megan said. Marcus remembered the witty bits written in the margins of the worn Bible and grinned.

"I like him," Marcus said.

"Me too," Megan said softly. When Marcus looked up he saw Megan staring out the window. Her eyes glistened. He was about to reach for her hand when he heard the front door open and close with a thud and the muffled voices of Ostride and Jacob traveled up the stairs.

"Broderick, how is Marcus doing? Is he still in bed?" Jacob asked.

"I believe so. Miss Buchanan is in the upstairs study."

"I'll be just a minute," Jacob said to Ostride. "I want to check on him."

Marcus held his fingers up to his lips. "Maybe he won't notice us and will go away," he whispered.

Jacob leapt up the stairs, passing the dark sitting room and knocked on Marcus' door. Not hearing a sound he went to the study.

"Megan? Marcus? What are you doing sitting in the dark?" He

turned on the lights and Megan shielded her eyes from the bright glare.

"We were enjoying the view," Marcus said.

"The falling snow in the city lights is mesmerizing," Megan said, finishing her tea.

"I hadn't noticed," Jacob said and poked his head between them to take a look. "Yes, it is worth a look, isn't it?"

"We don't want to keep you from Ostride," Marcus hinted.

"Marcus, you look much better," Ostride said, entering the room. Marcus rose to his feet with a sigh.

"His fever has broken. I think he is on the road to recovery, " Megan said. "My first successful patient." Jacob took off his suit coat, and with one hand folded it and draped it over a chair.

"You still need time to recuperate," Jacob said.

"You're right," Megan said. "And now that Jacob is here I'd better be going."

Marcus reached for her hand and held it tightly in his. "Jacob, why don't you and Ostride go downstairs and get something to eat," he suggested.

Just then the front door slammed shut and Marcus cringed as he heard Phillip running up the stairway.

"You can thank me later!" Phillip shouted, throwing a rubber costume mask with long fur ears and mane onto the desk where Megan had been working, scattering her papers to the floor. He shook his head and pulled out a thick strand of costume fur out of his blond hair and threw it onto the rug. "I finally got that bore, Count Vangardner, to let us use his villa for the fall break. It took some doing but I did it. And that isn't the best part," he said, crossing one hoofed leg over the other and leaning against the desk. "Nicole and Babette and her sister Simone will be joining us."

The room was silent and Marcus felt sick again.

"What's the matter with you two?" Phillip asked, his dark blue eyes darting between Marcus and Jacob. "You've been telling me to do this for months and now that I get the job done, you don't have a word to say? And Nicole and Babette besides!" he wiggled his eyebrows.

"Phillip!" Marcus roared. "This is Megan Buchanan." Megan twisted her hand free as Phillip glanced at the woman next to him.

"The American," Phillip said and sneered.

"Hi," Megan said briefly, then went to the desk and began to pick up her papers that had fallen.

"I've been to your country, once," Phillip said as he walked over to the tea tray and looked at the cake. "I can see why you decided to leave."

"Phillip!" Marcus shouted. Megan stuffed her books and laptop into her bag, brushed past Jacob and walked out the door.

"Megan, wait!" Marcus called, following her down the stairway. Broderick was standing at the bottom waiting for her.

"I called a cab for you, Miss," Broderick said, as he retrieved her coat.

"Thank you, Broderick," Megan said.

"Megan, wait!" Marcus pleaded. He stood beside her and was about to take her arm when she turned around to look at him. Her mouth opened, closed and then she snorted and stomped out the open door. A few steps down the walk Megan turned around and looked at his pale face through the wet clumps of falling snow.

"You have enough friends in your life, Marcus Holcombe. Goodbye and good luck."

"Megan, please!" Marcus called as he stepped out onto the walkway, watching her run to the cab. "Megan!" he yelled and started to cough. His robe had opened to the cold air and the long tails of his sash hung in the gray slush. He watched aimlessly as the cab drove away. He picked up his sash and tied it into a knot, wet drops streaming down the robe as he went into the house.

"So, we were the floor show until the real talent arrived?" Ostride asked Jacob. Phillip flopped down onto a stuffed chair and hung his furry legs over the arm, enjoying the animated rift.

"Ostride, I didn't know anything about this," Jacob answered.

"Yes, you did," Phillip chimed in. "We just talked about it last week."

Jacob held onto Ostride's coat. "Don't listen to him."

"Which one was yours?" Ostride asked, jerking her coat from his hands.

"Babette," Phillip said, "definitely Babette."

"Phillip!" Jacob screamed. Ostride ran down the stairway and Broderick held the door open.

"A cab is waiting, Miss," Broderick said. Ostride ran out the door and Marcus stood in the dark watching her follow in Megan's footprints in the snow. He took the door from Broderick's grip and slammed it shut. Then he marched up the stairway with Jacob right behind him. Phillip sat eating the piece of cake Megan had left untouched on the tea tray. Marcus and Jacob stood glaring at him from the doorway.

"What did I do?" Phillip asked. "You both told me to ask the Count for his villa and I did. I arranged it, like you asked and now you're standing there ready to bite my head off?"

"How could you have been so rude and thoughtless?" Marcus thundered.

"What? That American?" Phillip said, looking out the window. "You told me that you two were just friends. A friend would be happy that you're going to have a good time. And as for my comment about America, I don't like it," Phillip snapped. "Should I lie?"

Jacob collapsed on the couch holding his head in his hands. "All right," said Phillip, "I'm sorry. But I took great pains to arrange this trip, sitting through a dinner with the Count and his wheezing wife, so that I could get you both what you said you wanted. Am I right?"

"I'm going to bed." Marcus said, coughing again, "to sleep and pray this was all a bad dream."

"You pray?" Phillip scoffed, taking the last bite of the cake. Marcus' hand slammed down on the desktop.

"Phillip," Marcus began, "you will apologize to Miss Buchanan and you will do it as soon as possible. I would make you go now except for the way you look, you're an embarrassment to Dreiholm."

"It was a costume party. I went as Bottom from *A Midsummer Night's Dream.*"

"Perfect," Marcus said, "an ass."

"And Simone was Titania, Queen of the Fairies," Phillip said with a wicked smile. Marcus looked down at Phillip dressed in the donkey costume and then left the room.

"What's the matter with him?" Phillip asked. Jacob got up and slammed the door behind him as he left.

CHAPTER 16

With his coffee still steaming on his desk, Mr. Charles Payton strolled about his office opening the morning mail. He recognized a letter from his broker in New York and pulled it out from the pile. It was a cloudy day in Dreiholm and even with the desk and floor lamps turned on he still was having trouble reading the handwritten letter. He walked closer to the picture window, unfolded the creases in the page and caught a loose slip of green paper before it fell to the ground.

Chuck:

Here's an unexpected dividend from your investment in BCT. Now you can go and buy that boat we were looking at on our last fishing trip.

Give me a call when you get a chance. Betty and I would love to have you and Annie meet us in Marco in February.

Jake

Inside the letter was a check for two hundred and fifty thousand dollars. A plane flying across the sky drew his eyes to the window. He looked out onto the horizon and then to the many buildings he owned, filled with busy people going in and out of the many glass doors.

"Lord, my cup overflows. My wife and children and grandchildren are taken care of. We have more than we need. And I certainly don't need another boat. I like the boat we saw, but I don't need another boat," he prayed out loud. "Lord, this one's yours. What would you like me to do with this gift?"

His intercom buzzed and Rose's melodic voice pierced the morning quiet. "Chuck, there are two people downstairs to see you."

"I don't have any appointments this morning, do I?"

"No. They came without an appointment. It's two servants of Prince Marcus."

"Servants of Prince Marcus?"

"Yes, they said that they got your name from Megan."

"Megan?"

"What would you like me to do?" Rose asked.

"Send them up. And find out if Megan is in today."

"Right away," Rose said. Mr. Payton sat down and set the letter and check on the corner of his desk. He scanned the rest of his mail and sorted it into three piles for Rose to dispose of, respond to, or transfer to the appropriate employee. As he finished, Rose knocked on the door and opened it, ushering in the two visitors. One was a young girl who couldn't have been more than eighteen, Payton guessed, and the other was a young man probably in his twenties. Both were dressed in what Payton called Sunday best and were trying to appear confident even though he noticed the girl's hands were trembling.

"Mr. Payton, this is Sarah Quinn and Peter Bach," Rose said.

"Thank you for seeing us," the young man said.

"Sit down, sit down. Would you like a cup of coffee or tea?"

"No thank you, sir," Peter said and Sarah shook her head.

"If there isn't anything else,..." Rose said.

"Here's the morning mail," Payton said, crisscrossing and stacking the piles and then handing them to her. "The usual."

"Good enough."

"Thanks, Rose," Payton said. Sarah watched the conversation closely and was astonished at the friendliness between the man and his secretary.

"Now, what brings the two of you here?" Payton asked.

"Well sir," Peter started, "we have a problem and Miss Buchanan thought that you may be able to help in some way."

"I will if I can," Payton said. Sarah smiled nervously and Peter took a deep breath.

"You see sir, as you probably know, the government owns or controls most of the land in our small country and very little of it is made available each year for new homes. We are a growing population and many of us are tired of living in homes acquired by grandparents and great-grandparents. Since the only land available to us that is not restricted in its entirety by the government is the mountain territory, we would like to build there," Peter said. Payton's thoughts traveled as Peter spoke to a thousand places, to lawyer's offices, government councils and committees, lobbyists, builders and to roads, equipment and construction, transportation and weather conditions in the mountains.

"The trouble is that we have little experience in this area and very little money. Miss Buchanan thought maybe you could point us in the right direction."

Payton was silent, still contemplating the possibilities and risks of such a venture. This could cause quite a stir, he thought, still wondering how Megan fit into all of this. Peter and Sarah glanced at each other and then back at Mr. Payton who was rocking back in his chair. The furnace started and the gust of warm air caused the papers on Payton's desk to heave. The letter and check from his broker inched across his desk and Payton set them back on the corner from which they had come and put his mug on top.

"What you need is a group, an organization," Payton said, sitting up to his desk and folding his hands. "You have to legitimize yourselves."

Sarah and Peter looked at each other and then back at Mr. Payton.

"There is a group of us," Sarah said, "about a dozen or so."

"Good," Payton said. "And you'll all have to pull some weight, work hard to get it going."

Peter sat at the edge of his chair. "What do we have do first, sir?"

"First, we have to establish an organization," Payton said again, and pulled out a pad of paper from his desk drawer. "We'll need a chair for your organization, at least a temporary one, until a permanent one can be elected and a co-chair and secretary and treasurer. Peter you'll be the chair, Sarah you'll be the co-chair and I'll be the secretary and treasurer, temporarily." Sarah was now sitting on the edge of her seat with her hand on Mr. Payton's desk. "We're going to need some expert advice on government and construction, and for that we are going to need some money." Peter's smile turned to a frown and Sarah's lips tightened.

"I have a little saved," Sarah said. "About a thousand U.S. dollars." Peter looked at her in surprise. "That should help, shouldn't it?" she asked. Payton looked at the letter from his broker. The corners of the letter were wafting up and down from the warm air billowing below.

Is this where you want this to go, Lord? Payton silently prayed. He reached for the letter and turned the check over and signed the back. "That won't be necessary," he said. He hit his intercom. "Would you come in here for a minute, Rose?"

Rose's electric wheelchair hummed into the room. "Could you take a letter to Shannyn Olin?" Rose held the memo pad firmly, waiting for his next word.

"Dear Ms. Olin, please set up an organization in accordance to current laws and regulations of Dreiholm. The organization is to be established for the purpose of providing additional housing for Dreiholmian citizens. The chair of the this organization will be Peter Bach, co-chair Sarah Quinn, and myself as secretary and treasurer until the first formal meeting held on the first Thursday of this month, et cetera, et cetera, " Payton said. "At said meeting, permanent officials will be elected. Please furnish the chair and co-chair with guidelines for proper organizational meetings and responsibilities and please plan to attend the meeting at my office, either yourself or one of your associates. I will provide a check to the chair and co-chair and they will open a bank account in the organization's legal name,..." Payton looked at both Peter and Sarah.

"Westwind Housing Group, that should be its name," Sarah blurted out, and Rose wrote it down.

"And they will provide you with account information. Best regards."

"I'll have it ready for you in a few minutes," Rose said.

"Thanks, Rose." She wheeled off to her office and Payton pulled an envelope out of his desk drawer. He picked up the check, endorsed it to the Westwind Housing Group, put it in the envelope and handed it to Peter. "Bring this to Dreiholmian National Bank, ask for Mrs. Steinhauser. If she has any questions, tell her to call me," Payton said. "We'll see where it takes us."

Peter and Sarah stood to thank Mr. Payton. "This was more than we expected," Sarah said. "We are so grateful."

"Thank you, sir," Peter said. "Thank you. We'll look forward to our next meeting." They shook Payton's hand again and walked to the door. Peter peeked inside the envelope. He stopped and showed the check to Sarah. Payton watched the two as they turned back to face him.

"This is a fortune. You trust us with this much money?" Peter asked. "You don't even know us."

Payton stood beside his desk and put his hand in one pocket. "God didn't make me a fool, son. I know where you live five days out of the week, I know Prince Marcus, and I know his father, the King, very well. All in all, I think I have my bases covered," Payton said with a grin. "But more important, experience has taught me a thing or two. I believe you both can be trusted. Now, pick up a copy of that letter from Rose and I'll see you here next Thursday."

Rose buzzed Mr. Payton's office after Peter and Sarah had left her office.

"Yes, Rose."

"You inquired about Megan. She isn't in today but she has scheduled a lab for Saturday morning. Today she is at the university until five."

"Thank you," Mr. Payton said. "Rose, I'm going to go to the hospital and find Prince Marcus. If you need me just give me a call."

"Will do."

CHAPTER 17

Charles Payton stomped off the wet snow from his shoes, walked into the hospital and marched directly to the doctors' lounge. He scanned the room and saw only two disheveled interns dozing in the corner among a stack of coffee cups and candy wrappers. He picked up the telephone hanging on the wall and was about to call the front desk when he saw Marcus and Jacob come through the doorway.

"Marcus," Payton said, in more of a call than a greeting.

"Chuck, what are you doing here?" Marcus asked, shaking his hand.

"Good morning, Jacob," Payton said with a nod. "Nice to see you."

"Good morning, Mr. Payton."

"I have some business to discuss with Marcus. Could you excuse us for a few minutes?" Payton asked as he took off his coat and draped it over his arm.

"Certainly. Either of you want anything from the snack counter?" Jacob asked. Neither said a word. Jacob could see gray clouds of a storm thickening in Payton's icy stare. "No. Okay. I'll be going," Jacob said and quickly exited.

"Medical or father?" Marcus asked as Jacob left.

"Megan," Payton answered. Marcus opened one of the adjoining conference room doors and Payton dropped his coat on an empty chair.

"How did you find out?" Marcus asked.

"You do know her then," Payton said. Marcus sat down in an empty chair, realizing he had foolishly confirmed Payton's suspicions.

"We've been dating," Marcus said.

"Dating?" Payton exclaimed. "Where would she meet you? She doesn't hang out at bars or discos." Marcus' eyes narrowed and he was about to speak when he remembered Payton's close friendship to his father.

"Jacob arranged the meeting," Marcus answered. Payton looked out the conference room window and saw Jacob sitting at a table reading a magazine and having a soda.

"Remind me to thank him," Payton said, with his hands in his pockets.

"What does this have to do with you?" Marcus asked. Payton sat down opposite him and looked at him squarely in the eyes.

"Megan Buchanan has been put in my charge and I'll have none of your shenanigans interfering with her work, life, or you breaking her heart. Do I make myself clear?"

"The last time I looked she was over the age of 21 and, Chuck, I find it offensive that you find me so unsuitable," Marcus said in a heated but diplomatic tone. Payton calmly picked up an empty foam cup left on the table and tossed it into the trash can.

"You know, I'm surprised Megan hasn't told me or Annie or any of the kids about meeting you, you being the Prince and all," Payton said. "And not one picture in the papers. You'd think they would want to make a story out of a young American girl going out with a prince."

Marcus looked away. "She doesn't know," he admitted.

"She doesn't know what?"

"Who I am," Marcus said. Payton looked at him suspiciously. "And I'm doing my best to keep it that way."

"Why?"

"It is best that way," Marcus said.

"For whom?" Payton asked, pressing him. Marcus stared off toward the corner of the room.

"For me," he confessed. Marcus closed his eyes and suddenly he felt tired. He knew that he had been taking on more at the hospital since Megan walked out of his home but he knew it was more than that. "I want to know if she loves me as me," he said calmly.

Payton slowly leaned back into his chair. His eyebrows were twisted into two white bristled burrs as he cocked himself in his chair and began tapping his hand on the table.

"Could it be that you have finally fallen in love?" Payton asked.

"The truth is I'm not certain about anything anymore," Marcus said miserably, "It may not matter anyway. Things aren't going well at the moment."

"Why?" Payton asked.

"We had a misunderstanding."

"What kind of misunderstanding."

"At first it was my fault, I take full responsibility. I insinuated something," Marcus said, looking at the wall and then at Payton. "It's embarrassing to repeat it."

"Try me," Payton said.

"I mentioned that I couldn't consider a permanent relationship but that I would like to keep dating her."

"Date, date, you meant you wanted to have an affair with Megan?" Payton said with a deep frown.

"Yes," Marcus admitted.

"So, she didn't take too kindly to that?"

"No, she didn't," Marcus said. "She slammed the door in my face."

"That's my girl," Payton said, slapping the table top.

"After I finally got her to believe that I was truly sorry and to give me another chance, Phillip managed to undo the whole thing in minutes."

"How's that?" Payton asked.

"Megan, Jacob, and Ostride, Megan's friend, were at my home the other night. Phillip came home, barged into my study and announced to the world that he has reserved Count Vangardner's villa for the holiday break." Payton shrugged his shoulders. "And that he had arranged for three female companions to join us."

"Hum," Payton grunted.

"It wasn't my idea," Marcus said. "The villa yes, but the women, no." He stood up and settled into a corner of the room, bracing himself between the two walls. "These years I've been in medical school I've been trying to change. I guess Phillip hasn't noticed. It looks like no one has," Marcus said, looking at Payton directly. "I wondered why. I thought perhaps I hadn't tried hard enough. Then recently, I realized that trying isn't enough. I can't try hard enough or be good enough or give enough to make up for my past or even change who I am," Marcus said and bowed his head. "There are days I would give anything to take it all back, but I can't."

He looked up at Payton. "Did you know that when I first started practicing here, a patient refused to see me? I thought it might be because I'm the prince, so I had the nurse reassure him that I was to be treated like any other doctor on staff and that he had no reason to worry. But the man still refused. I was curious so I went in to see him and inquired why. He handed me a newspaper he had found in the lobby. In it was an article about me, a history of my sordid past, including some choice pictures." Marcus wiped his face with his hands. "One certainty about being in the spotlight is there is never a shortage of critics to summarize your life."

He closed his eyes and sighed. "I've embarrassed myself, the king and queen, and my people. I have broken their trust. They deserve better and so does Megan," Marcus said, "and the worst part is that I have wasted so much time."

Payton noticed the signet ring on Marcus' finger. It was the same ring Payton noticed so often on the king's hand, the family ring of sapphire blue and gold. It had looked so clumsy and awkward on Marcus in his youth and now it fit perfectly.

"I'm not one to defend your virtue but you do have something you can keep in your pocket," Payton said. Marcus looked up. "You have an education and you have served in the military, they must have taught you something. You're a doctor, and according to Dr. Weisman, despite yourself, a rather fine one at that. You're right, you haven't had your proudest moments in the past but today you've convinced me that you have learned something, something more important than the how-to's of life," Payton said. "Something you're going to need on that road ahead of you."

"Humility," Marcus said, almost as a question. Payton flipped his palm up and nodded his head.

"Humility is an important lesson but it's not the only one you've learned. Keep working on it." Payton tapped his finger on the black surface of the table. "Right now it sounds like you have other troubles."

"Megan," Marcus said, sitting back down at the table. "She looks at me from the inside out. I'm beginning to think that she wouldn't care who I was, what I looked like or how much money I had. She's more concerned about what I think and what I believe in and what I want to be. I don't know how to attract a woman like that when what she wants is inside of me. If she doesn't like what she sees then there is no hope."

"Has she gone out with you more than once?" Payton asked.

"Several times, yes."

"She picks up the phone on the first couple rings?"

"Yes."

"Chemistry?"

"She doesn't pull away when I take her hand, if that's what you're asking," Marcus said, "except for this last time."

"Hum," Payton said, picking up his coat. "I guess I wouldn't give up yet. But, I warn you, I'll be watching. No shenanigans. And tell her the truth. The truth always comes to the surface and it will be less of a shock from you than from someone else."

"I plan to after I get back from break."

"Why wait?"

"She has exams, and Jacob and I will be pulling a few extra shifts until we leave."

"You mean you're still going to the villa with those women?" Payton asked.

"I told Phillip to undo his deed but that we could still go to the mountains. I need some rest and time to think."

"You're going to your family's place?"

"Yes," Marcus said, as Payton put on his coat.

"Before I leave, I want you to do something, a favor."

"What?" asked Marcus.

"I want you to go home, visit your parents, and tell them what you told me. They'll want to hear it. And something else – I do have some business with you. Could you to come to my office next Thursday about seven? I want you to meet some people," Payton said. Marcus nodded in agreement. "Thursday then, don't forget."

"Seven," Marcus said.

CHAPTER 18

Megan awoke early and was at Brier Pharmaceuticals before the evening security guards had left their shift. She trudged down the hall, taking off her scarf as she went. She could see Mr. Payton in the next lab through the glass doors, reading a report and talking to Dr. Juhl. He waved at her as she passed by and she managed to smile. Alone in her lab she put her coat on a hook and traded it for a fresh white lab coat in the closet.

"Good morning, Megan! How are you today?" Mr. Payton asked as he walked in with a cheerful smile.

Megan looked at the flannel shirt he was wearing. It was red plaid with thin green, black and gold lines crisscrossing his chest.

"My dad had a shirt like that," Megan said, getting a set of gloves out of a drawer. "It looks nice and comfortable."

"It is," Payton said, patting his hands on his chest. He noticed Megan was moving slower than normal and that her voice had trailed off to barely an audible whisper. She had completely avoided his question. "I've been checking the progress on this project and Dr. Juhl thinks it is two months ahead of schedule. He is very impressed with your work." Megan was listening but kept gathering the materials she needed to begin her work for the day. Her eyes were red, even blood shot, he thought, and the lab coat looked rather large on her small frame.

"Didn't we order you a small lab coat?" Payton asked.

"This is a small," Megan said, as she looked down at the coat, "I think I've lost a little weight. Actually, I'm glad you stopped by; I wanted to talk to you."

"It couldn't wait until Sunday dinner?"

"It's about my work here. I was thinking that during the fall break and Christmas holiday I could work full time, if you wouldn't mind.

The faster this project gets done the faster I will be able to get home and get on with my life, medical school I mean. Besides, I could use the extra money."

"So, you're not going home for break?" Payton said, stroking his chin.

"It just didn't make sense to spend all that money and time going home for a week at break and a month at Christmas when I could get so much more done here. It always takes me so long to get back into the swing of things when I've been gone for awhile. Uncle Joe wasn't happy about my decision but I think that if I work hard enough I'll be able to cut this program in half or at least by eight or ten months," Megan said, and filled up a beaker with water.

"You need some time off," Payton said sternly. She shrugged her shoulders and clicked on the computer at her desk.

"Ostride isn't going home either. We thought we might catch a couple of movies and spend Christmas together."

"I don't know, Megan," Payton said. "I don't know if I want you hanging around here through break."

Megan stopped what she was doing and looked at him in surprise.

"If you wear yourself out you'll be no good to me or yourself. I'll tell you what, I have a cabin in the mountains. Why don't you and Ostride go up there for semester break? You can ski, skate and even swim. It has an indoor pool and if you come back refreshed and a few pounds heavier, I'll think about letting you work here full time over Christmas holiday."

"But,..."

"No buts," Payton said, "just go and have a good time. You need a break Megan. You can't be working yourself like this and expect it to last. Now, you're coming to dinner tomorrow night, right? Annie's cooking up a pot roast and a ham. Those grandkids of ours are starting to eat like horses."

"I'll be there."

"I'll have the keys for you then. We'll see you tomorrow."

* * *

Megan hurried around the corner to her apartment on her walk home from work, hoping she would find Marcus sitting at her doorstep. The street was deserted and the only thing at her door was a small brown paper package. She heard the sound of voices behind her and turned around to find two young boys playing hockey in the street. They ran from side to side passing a puck. One of the boys ran down the sidewalk and slid on a patch of ice while the other ran his hockey stick along the iron fence. The boys laughed and checked each other, bumping and sliding down the road. She stuck her hands deep into her coat pockets as the two boys ran by, clutching her keys and laughing with them as they slid by. She picked up the box at the foot of the door and saw that it was addressed to her. She peeled off the envelope that was attached to it and opened the letter as she walked up the stairs to her apartment.

Megan,
Thank you for nurturing me back to health – and much more.
Marcus

Megan stuffed the note into her pocket and unlocked her door. She set the package on the kitchen counter, took off her gloves and drummed her fingernails on the counter, staring at the package. The telephone rang and she picked it up while ripping the brown paper from the box.

"Hello," Megan said, pinching the receiver between her chin and her shoulder.

"Hi Meg," Ostride said.

"Who died?" Megan asked, throwing the box of chocolates on the counter, "you sound awful."

"I got flowers from Jacob and a note."

"I got the candy," Megan said. "And a note. Well, I guess that's that." Megan could hear Ostride whimpering on the other end of the line. "Hey, we have to pick an attitude," Megan said.

"I don't think I can," Ostride said sobbing.

"I have some good news that might help."

"What could help?"

"We're going on vacation," Megan said. "Mr. Payton came in today and offered to let us use his cabin during break."

"When do we leave?" Ostride asked, tearfully.

"Right after our last exam," Megan said. "Why don't you come over and we'll make a list of things we'll need before we go."

"I'll be over in a minute," Ostride said and blew her nose.

"Good. See you in a few minutes." Megan hung up the phone and picked up the box of candy. The hand-dipped chocolates were wrapped in bright pink foil and each truffle sat in a tiny decorative chocolate cup. She picked out a raspberry cream and dropped the box on the counter again. The chocolate melted in her mouth. She leaned over the counter and gazed into the box.

"Just friends," she said and chose another, a white chocolate oyster with a dark chocolate truffle held between its jaws. Who am I trying to kid, she thought, nibbling at the chocolate. "I'm not going to get fat mooning over you, Mr. Holcombe," she said to herself and threw the chocolate back down into the box. Megan took off her coat, hesitated, then picked up the discarded chocolate, popped it in her mouth and walked away.

CHAPTER 19

Rose was waiting for Mr. Payton to complete his thought, her pencil and steno pad in hand, when the telephone rang. "Mr. Payton's office," Rose said as she picked it up. "Just a minute, Frank, I'll ask." Payton looked at Rose from over the top of his reading glasses.

"Who is it?"

"Peter and Sarah and the others are waiting downstairs for you," Rose said. Payton looked at his watch.

"It's only six-thirty. Didn't I say seven?" Payton asked. Rose had a broad smile.

"Yes, you did. I hope you know what you're getting yourself into."

"Eager bunch. You can't fault them for that."

"What would you like me to do?"

"Send 'em up. It might be good to talk to them before the prince arrives. Is the conference room ready?"

"All I have to do is call food service and have them bring up the trays and refreshments I ordered this morning."

"Good," Payton said.

Rose pushed a red button on the telephone and connected to Frank. "Frank, I'll be down in a minute to get them," Rose said and hung up the phone. "Do you want me to fill in the blanks on this letter?"

"Yes, that would be good," Payton said, opening up his desk drawer and pulling out a file and some papers. Rose already started for the door.

"Hey, aren't you working a little late tonight?" Payton asked.

Rose spun around to face him. "And miss a chance to meet the 'Partying Prince'? Not on your life. You couldn't kick me out tonight."

* * *

A few minutes later, Rose had just closed the conference room door when Payton came around the corner to meet her. "There's a few more than we expected," she said. "I'm going to see if I can get a couple more trays, another pot of coffee, and some chairs."

"How many more?" Payton asked.

"I'd say there's at least twenty-five or thirty in there," Rose said. She put her wheelchair in high speed and zipped back to her desk. Payton looked at his reflection in a glass panel and straightened his tie and put his glasses in his breast pocket. He coughed once to clear his throat and then opened the door. Peter was standing near the entrance to greet him.

"Peter," Payton said warmly.

"Mr. Payton," Peter said. "Good evening. We wanted to thank you again for helping us and letting us meet at your facility tonight."

"I'm honored," Payton said and looked around the room. The large conference table was filled, each guest was standing beside his or her chair and the others were standing in the back of the room. Payton noticed that the visitors had left the head of the table empty, awaiting his arrival.

"You know Sarah, and the others will introduce themselves. We are all servants of Prince Marcus or at the palace," Peter said.

"Good evening, Sarah. How are you tonight?"

"Very good, sir," Sarah said, briefly meeting her eyes to his.

"Sebastian Broderick, sir," Broderick said, extending his hand. "Housemaster, butler and personal servant to the prince."

"Good to meet you, Sebastian," Payton said.

"Elizabeth de Benedictus," the sturdy, expressionless woman said. "I am the head chef to Prince Marcus." Payton took her outstretched hand and held it in both of his.

"Ms. de Benedictus, may I call you Elizabeth?" Elizabeth's cheeks flushed an apple blossom pink.

"You're most welcome to, sir." Without letting go of Elizabeth's hand Payton addressed the group.

"Then please, all of you, please call me by my given name," Payton said. "My mother calls me Charles and my friends call me Chuck." The maintenance men arrived with the extra chairs while Payton met each man and woman in the room. When the extra coffee arrived Payton went to the head of the table and started the meeting.

"I want to say a few words before we get started this evening. First, I agreed to help in this effort for a number of reasons. One being that I know many of the people who work here, in my company, have the same complaints you people do. They can't find a house to buy at a fair price and they're getting frustrated. Another reason is that I believe that you might be the group that could make a difference and change things around here. You're in a unique position. You know the royal family, and more importantly, they know you," Payton said. He shifted his weight and with his hand in one pocket he scratched the back of his neck with the other.

"I've invited someone else to the meeting here tonight, besides Ms. Olin, who is the attorney that will help us with the legal decisions that go along with this project. In fact, before this project ends we are going to need a great deal of advice from many professions: builders, real estate specialists, financiers and so on, but tonight I invited someone who might be able to help us speed things along politically, our biggest hurdle. I invited Prince Marcus to attend the meeting tonight." A few panicked gasps echoed throughout the room and a man in the back stood up and addressed Payton.

"But sir, we could lose our jobs."

"Now, settle down, settle down," Payton said, raising his arms and pressing them down before the group. "There is no reason to worry. He doesn't know that any of you are here. I asked the Prince to come to my office to meet some people. And if need be, Ms. Olin, her associate, and I will carry on without a word about anyone else. There is a door in the back of this room and if you decide to, you can leave. What I am suggesting is that you vote on whether you want to go forward with this cause or not. What you want to do has been asked and answered before. It has always been voted down by the lords and never brought before the king, even though I know he is eager to implement a project like this. Someone must intervene and pass it through the Senate. I believe Prince Marcus could help us, but you're right, there is a risk. I don't know how he will react. I don't know what he will say. I only know that to succeed you must take risks. Now, you all have to decide if this is a risk worth taking."

Payton saw the blue light flashing on the conference room

telephone, Rose's signal to him that the prince had arrived and was waiting. "I'm going to hand this meeting over to your Chair, Peter Bach. I will be in my office meeting with the Prince. When you decide what you want to do, send someone out to tell Rose and she will discreetly get the message to me. There are other ways to do this but if the Prince cooperates, I think this will be the best way," Payton said. He then left the conference room in the midst of low grumbling voices.

When the door closed Peter stood up and took his place at the head of the table.

"That man is going to get us all sacked," a man in the back said.

"I don't believe that," Sarah said, "at least not intentionally."

"Intentional or not, I can't support my family without a paycheck," another said.

"This is your fault," an elderly woman said to Sarah. "If you would have just left well enough alone and not talked to that American girl. You had no business talking to her. Filling your head with dizzy ideas."

"Wait a minute," Peter said. "It's not Sarah's fault. It's not my fault. It's everyone's fault, everyone in this room and outside of it. We don't have places to live, our houses are busting out at the seams and we aren't doing one thing about it." He looked out at the troubled and some angry faces. "Joseph, you were just telling me that you were thinking about moving out of the country because you want to get married and you can't imagine living with your parents, and your fiancée's parents already have two daughters with their husbands living in their home. And Sigrid, you were telling Sarah that you felt that you couldn't have another baby because your first little one had colic and kept your grandparents up all night. That's not right."

"Nearly all my friends have gone off to Australia, England or to America," Sarah said.

"Mine too," a young housemaid said.

"I have been a bachelor all my life, saving as much as I can and still I can't afford to retire here," Broderick said. "I'll have to return to England, to my family."

"If we don't do something now, we will all end up leaving. We will either do what we must or we must go where we can, leaving what we love behind us. We have no other choice. The choices have been made for us and the king," Peter said. "We must try."

"Pray and try," Sarah said softly.

"Yes, pray and try," Peter echoed.

"But Peter, Prince Marcus?" a man said to his side. "Can he be trusted? We've all noticed some change in him of late but can he be trusted? Will he cooperate and help us?"

"I don't know," Peter said, "but can the risk be any worse than the reality? Will our children be better off if we don't try? A door has been opened. We have an opportunity, a chance. Who will take it with me? Raise your hands," he said.

There was a quick count.

"I'll tell Miss Rose," Broderick said.

CHAPTER 20

"It looks like the people I wanted you to meet are ready," Payton said. "Thank you for being so patient."

"Not a problem," Marcus said, following Payton to the door. "I didn't have any plans tonight and I haven't been inside your building since you remodeled. It is very impressive."

"Thank you," Payton said as they stood outside the conference room door. He hesitated, wondering if he should warn Marcus before they entered. "Like I mentioned to you in my office, these people need help with a project and I think you might be just the man to help them."

"Do I know any of these people?" Marcus asked.

"A few I'm sure," Payton said, smiling. He opened the door and all of the guests bowed low or curtsied before the prince. Payton noticed that a few of the guests were missing and those remaining looked anxious and alert.

"Broderick," Marcus called. "What is going on here?"

Broderick was about to answer when Peter came forward.

"Begging your pardon, Sir. We are a committee, an organization to create affordable housing in Dreiholm."

"Who are you?" Marcus demanded.

"I am Peter Bach, a butler in your house, Sir," Peter said. Marcus shifted his eyes away from Payton, embarrassed by his own ignorance.

"Peter Bach, do you speak for all these people?" Marcus asked.

"I am the chair of this organization, temporary chair, until we can elect a permanent chair. Mr. Payton has been kind enough to help us get established."

"Marcus, why don't you have a seat and listen to what these people have to say," Payton said softly. Peter offered his seat at the head of the table and took a vacant chair for himself. Marcus reluctantly sat down.

"I don't like surprises," Marcus said in a low voice, directing his comment to Payton.

"This is a meeting, not a surprise," Payton said quietly.

"A meeting I am not prepared for. Therefore I reserve the right to end this meeting when I choose," Marcus said.

"Fair enough," Payton said.

"Now, what is this about?" Marcus asked, looking around the table.

"I'll let Peter take over," Payton said. He could see the young man stiffen at the mention of his name. "Go on, Peter." Peter looked at Sarah, who urged him on with a smile as he stood and faced the prince.

"Many of us in Dreiholm lack the means to purchase a house. There are so few homes available that the price of an existing dwelling costs a small fortune. We have resorted to living with parents and grandparents with little or no hope of ever obtaining a home of our own. As a result, and as you know, many of us, young and old are being forced to leave Dreiholm. We don't want to leave. We love our country, the king, our neighbors and friends, and our families, but we have few choices. A solution would be if we were allowed to build in the mountains. We realize the land is limited, yet with the right plan we think we could create affordable homes and communities we could be proud of, like they did years ago."

Marcus knew the situation was serious. Anonymous newspaper editorials and keenly phrased news reports voiced the people's discontent, and applications for exit visas testified to the truth.

"Those of us in the business community are concerned," Payton added. "Technology is your strength in Dreiholm. Because of it and your dedication to education and business, and Dreiholm's natural beauty and low crime rate, we are able to attract the talent we need, but they won't stay. They want homes of their own, not government properties. It has come to the point that even I have had to consider relocating," Payton said.

"Have you approached the king about this?" Marcus asked.

"Yes. We have had many discussions. The problem is that his efforts are being blocked by a few, and without their support, the king's hands are tied," Payton said.

Marcus knew Payton was referring to Lord Greven and his

followers. They were adamantly opposed to any new building, redistricting or even restoration of failing communities. If it hadn't been for his father's insistence, Dreiholm would not have the few new villages that now existed or the improvements that had been made, Marcus thought. Even with the people's support and gratitude for the small improvements, Greven's followers had grown in strength, often challenging the king's authority.

"We don't mean to complain, Sir," Sarah said in a meek, tender voice. "It's just that it is becoming unbearable and when we were talking to Miss Buchanan, she thought that if we worked together we could come up with a solution, just like they do in America."

Broderick's eyes rolled when he heard Sarah mention Megan's name.

"Miss Buchanan?" Marcus asked, blinking.

"Yes, Sir," Sarah said. "Oh, she doesn't know that you're the prince, we made sure of it. We even hid the royal stationary and used the plain silverware so she wouldn't inquire. I can't imagine how she doesn't know, but she is a wonderful woman and she got us in touch with Mr. Payton."

"She did, did she?" Marcus said, looking at Payton. Payton smiled. "Megan," Marcus whispered. Even when they were apart her presence was before him, he thought.

The room was silent as Marcus contemplated the situation. "I am not certain what I can do. This is my father's kingdom and I am a doctor," he said and then looked at Sarah who was close to tears. "But, I am also a prince," Marcus conceded, "and now we will find out what that really means."

"Does that mean you will help us, Sir?" Peter asked. Marcus looked down and folded his hands.

"I will help, but I will not be a part of this committee. You must act independently. When a plan is completed and we have discussed it, I will present it to the king, and then to the senate," Marcus said. "I will do what I can." Payton smiled. "But first, I want to visit your homes. Three homes should be enough, I want to see how you live."

"Right now, Sir?" Broderick asked, incredulously.

"Yes," Marcus said.

"But Sir, we haven't any notice. We haven't cleaned or prepared a meal," Elizabeth said.

"Exactly," Marcus said, rising. "I don't want to intrude but I want to see real life, not a life prepared for a prince. Who will volunteer?"

After a few moments, Joseph raised his hand and then Elizabeth.

"One more," Marcus said.

"I would offer, Sir, but I live in your home," Sebastian Broderick said.

"Have you been to Sebastian's quarters?" Payton asked drily.

"No, I don't believe I have."

"Well, then you've got three," Payton said, patting his hand on the tabletop. "We just have a few details to clean up before we adjourn and we'll be on our way."

CHAPTER 21

Marcus had his driver stop at the first house on his tour, the home of Joseph Ortman, the assistant buyer of general merchandise for the palace. Payton had accepted a ride with Marcus and together they walked down a narrow sidewalk to the front door. Marcus noticed that the townhouse had a small front yard; no more than ten feet square, and that it was open to the street. The customary flower boxes had been emptied for the season and were now filled with fragrant pine boughs and bright orange bittersweet. As soon as Marcus stepped onto the front stoop, Joseph opened the door, and what looked like a dozen curious little faces with large blue eyes peered at him through decorative twisted spindles of the staircase.

"Prince Marcus," Joseph said and bowed. "Welcome to our home." A little girl with a wreath of blonde braids and dressed in a pleated gray jumper had wrapped her arms around Joseph's leg and held on tight, looking first at Marcus and then at Mr. Payton. "This is Isabella, my niece," Joseph said.

Payton crouched down to greet the tot face to face. "How do you do, Isabella?" Payton said in a very grown-up voice. The little girl buried her face in Joseph's pant leg and then giggled and reached her arms up to the gray-haired man with a big smile on his face. Payton picked her up and held her to his shoulder. "Are those pink flowers on your dress?" he asked.

"Pink," she said and giggled.

"Please come in," Joseph said. Marcus and Payton huddled together in the narrow foyer as the other children dodged up the stairway.

"I think they're a little frightened," Joseph said apologetically. He invited Marcus and Payton into what Marcus assumed was a small sitting room. Two chairs, a small table and a desk filled the tiny room. Marcus could see the kitchen and two adults standing in the doorway.

"These are my parents, Reinhold and Gretchen Ortman," Joseph said. They bowed and curtsied before the prince as the woman nervously pulled at her apron.

"Thank you for allowing me to visit your home," Marcus said.

"It is our pleasure, Your Highness," Mr. Ortman said.

"We only wish Joseph would have given us more warning and I would have prepared something special for you. All I have freshly baked is plain sourdough bread," Mrs. Ortman said apologetically.

"I didn't want anyone to go to any trouble. That is why I asked to come with such short notice. Forgive me for interrupting your family's activities."

"We are very honored to have you visit us," Mr. Ortman said.

"Joseph would not have heard the end of it if he had not volunteered. We are very pleased, very pleased indeed," Mrs. Ortman said. "Please come in." She led Marcus and Payton through a white tiled kitchen, no bigger than Marcus' bathroom, and into a living area at the rear of the home. Every inch of the home was immaculate and painted in pale yellow, bright blue and white. In the far corner of the living room sat an old man in a reclining chair. A blanket covered his legs and he smiled broadly when Marcus entered. The blanket shifted and exposed the plastic flesh underneath. He quickly readjusted the afghan as he begged the guests to come in.

"Please, please," the old man said, "come in, sit down."

"My grandfather, Reinhold Ortman," Joseph said. Payton sat in a rocker as Isabella touched the shiny metal on his gold watch.

"It is my pleasure to meet you, Mr. Ortman," Marcus said as he sat next to the old man who was sitting silently on the edge of the couch with his hands folded together. He seemed to be examining every inch of Marcus' face.

"I remember your grandfather," he said.

"The war," Marcus commented.

"Yes, yes. The Nazis made life bitter for all of us," the old man said, "but now, Joseph tells me that you are going to have a battle of your own."

"It is not even comparable to your sacrifice," Marcus said. The old man raised his hand in protest.

"We all have our battles to fight. Don't underestimate yours. What is more dangerous, a silent killer or a noisy one?"

"Poppa," Joseph's father admonished.

"I am an old man, I have nothing left. I have served the king, and I have raised my children, grandchildren and great-grandchildren. Now, in my old age, I will speak my piece."

"Have you raised all your children in this house?" Payton asked. Isabella had put her head against his shoulder and was now running her tiny fingers up and down the satin lining of his coat. Her eyes were beginning to close and her little heart-shaped lips yawned as Payton slowly rocked her.

"Yes. Some have gone now, but my son and one daughter and their families have stayed. The rest are in Canada. They ask me to come and be with them in Canada but I can't leave. This is where I was born and this is where I will die." Marcus got up abruptly and bowed deeply before the old man.

"Thank you, Mr. Ortman. Thank you for allowing me in your home."

"God bless you, son," the old man said.

Marcus went directly to the front door and left without saying good-bye to the others. Joseph gently took a sleeping Isabella from Payton.

"I'll see myself out," Payton said. "Thank you and I will be seeing you, Joseph, Monday at the meeting."

"Yes, sir."

The driver was waiting for Payton, dutifully holding the door to the black limousine. Marcus was staring out the window when Payton got in. "Did you see the picture on the wall?" Payton asked. "Reinhold was a member of the Lion's Head during the war. I've read about them. They were a courageous bunch of kids. Who knows how many lives they saved blowing up Hitler's storehouses."

"That's how he lost his legs," Marcus said, still looking out the window. "I saw the medal." Marcus took a deep breath and exhaled slowly. "Along with the many other medals from the Royal Guard."

The limousine turned, wound down a gravel road and then came to a slow stop outside the village at a quiet cottage.

"Tired?" Payton asked.

"No, I'm fine," Marcus said, stepping out of the car and looking at the stone cottage with the arched doorway and slate roof. "So this is Cook's house," Marcus said. A wrought iron streetlamp lit the path to the door, and Payton gingerly bounced up the step and tapped the door with the brass doorknocker.

"It's sure a cute cottage, isn't it?" Payton said, looking at the bay window with its diamond shaped grids. Marcus stood on the step taking in the whole view with its picture-perfect yard, complete with a stone path and cone-shaped shrubs. A man in a gray cardigan sweater and gold wire rimmed glasses opened the door.

"Professor de Benedictus!" Marcus exclaimed.

"Prince Marcus," the middle-aged man said, bowing in respect. "Mr. Payton. Come in. Come in. The air is cold."

"What are you doing here?" Marcus asked in surprise.

"I live here, of course, Elizabeth is my wife."

"Cook?" Marcus asked.

"I think she prefers Chef," Professor de Benedictus said, taking their coats. The fragrant smell of sweet chocolate filled the house and Marcus was beginning to feel hungry. "Elizabeth has studied all over the world, in France, Morocco, America, and in the Netherlands. Cooking is my hobby, but for Elizabeth it is her passion."

"I never knew," Marcus said, as he and Payton followed the professor into the living room.

"There are many things I wish you knew as well as your organic chemistry, young Marcus."

The living room was warm and exactly as Marcus would have guessed his professor would have it. The bay window would have let in much light in the day, but at night the reading lamp by the two chairs and foot stools tendered a soft glow for reading the volumes of books stacked on the many shelves on either wall. Professor de Benedictus led them to two beige couches that faced one another in front of the fireplace. "Please sit down. I'll find out where Elizabeth is hiding."

Payton stepped over a golden retriever who was sprawled out on the floor by the corner of one of the couches. "Don't mind Maggie. She is completely harmless and this is her only sanctuary. Elizabeth will not allow her in any other part of the house." The dog barely lifted her head as the two men passed over the top of her and she didn't twitch an ear when a log popped from the heat of the fire. As they sat down, Elizabeth came into the room with lemon cake and tea.

"Why, Elizabeth," Payton said. "You have an absolutely charming home." Elizabeth acknowledged the prince with a slight curtsy as she balanced a silver tray.

"Thank you, Mr. Payton, it was my first husband's family home," Elizabeth said as she set down the tray on a side table. "Tea and some cake?" she asked Marcus and Payton.

"Yes, please," Marcus said.

"Elizabeth bakes the best lemon cake in Dreiholm," the professor said.

"Hans."

"It is true. It has won the blue ribbon at the fall festival three years in a row."

Marcus bent over and scratched Maggie's ear.

"I appreciate Mrs. de Benedictus' cooking very much," Marcus said.

"This was your husband's home?" Payton asked.

"Yes," she said, setting a piece of cake and a cup of tea before the prince. "When my husband died I was afraid I was going to have to give it up."

"Why would you have to give it up?" Payton asked.

"We didn't have any children, and since I was not a blood relative of the family, I would have to leave and defer the home to my husband's brother," she explained. Payton looked at Marcus.

"It is because of the lease rights," Marcus said, uneasily. Elizabeth handed Payton a cup of tea and piece of cake.

"What happened that you were able to live here?" Payton asked.

"I applied for a five-year extension," Elizabeth said, holding her cup.

"Then I came into the picture," the professor said, holding on to the fireplace mantel and putting one foot up on a small needlepoint stool. "Three years after Otto had passed away I met Elizabeth and we began courting. We married, and since professors have special privileges to lease property close to the university, I made a deal with Elizabeth's brother-in-law and we have a house. Otherwise, Elizabeth and I would have had to find another place to live, or leave."

Marcus was less hungry now and slowly sipped the tea. Maggie put her head on his knee and he stroked the dog's soft amber coat.

"You have a friend, Prince Marcus," Professor de Benedictus said.

"Is that chocolate I smell?" Payton asked.

"Yes, I am experimenting with chocolate candies," Elizabeth said.

"May I see them?"

"Certainly," she said, and the men followed her into the large white kitchen.

"We once had another room in this house but we decided that we were always cooking so we might as well make it comfortable," the professor said. On either side of the fireplace in the kitchen were more books and a small dining table with a bright red candle in a white porcelain candlestick. The rest of the room was a menagerie of stoves and copper and silver pots and pans. The well-used butcher-block island was over ten feet long and was covered with wire racks filled with chocolates. A painter's palette of colored frostings sat on the counter and drizzles of lace-like chocolate dotted the waxed-paper table covering.

"What is that?" Payton asked, looking into a pot of a ruby red mixture.

"A raspberry glaze that I use to coat a truffle. Would you like to try one?" she asked, handing Payton and Marcus a tray of dark chocolate truffles with tiny pink frosted flowers on the top of each one.

"This is exceptional," Marcus said. "Really."

Elizabeth's cheeks became a rosy red. "Thank you."

"There will be no living with her now," the professor said, kissing his wife on the cheek. He showed the prince and Payton the rest of the cottage including his greenhouse where he grew fresh herbs and vegetables, and then led them back to the front door.

"Thank you again for letting us into your home," Marcus said.

"You are entirely welcome," the professor said. Elizabeth hurried down the hall with two white boxes tied with raffia ribbon.

"Take these home with you. They will be good with coffee," she said, and handed one to the prince and another to Payton. "There is a sample of each of my chocolates inside."

"Thank you, Elizabeth," Payton said. "I am sure my Annie will be very thankful too," he said, walking out the door.

"Prince Marcus," Elizabeth began, "thank you for helping us."

"Good night, Chef," Marcus said and then looked down at the box of chocolates in his hand. "Thank you."

When they were seated in the limousine, Payton opened his box of chocolates. "Tempting, aren't they," he said, peering into the little box. "I've never had anything like these."

As the driver pulled into the gated estate, Payton said, "I'll let you know how we are progressing after our next meeting. He doesn't know it yet, but Peter Bach is going to be a good leader. He's got spunk." The driver opened the door and Payton hesitated before he got out of the car. "You're doing the right thing, Marcus. Thank you."

"Good night, Chuck," Marcus said.

"Good night, Your Highness."

When Marcus arrived home he stopped at the entrance and looked up at the stars. It was a clear night and the stars were bright in the deep blue sky. He slowly opened the door and Broderick was there to greet him. Broderick took his coat and in the late evening silence, Marcus sighed.

"It has been a long night, Sir. We can do this another time."

"No. I want to do it now," Marcus said.

"Very well, Sir," Broderick said. Marcus followed Broderick down the hall and up four flights of stairs to another narrow, low hallway. Broderick stopped at the first door at the top of the stairway and opened it. A few curious onlookers peeked through cracked doorways down the hall, and others whispered among themselves behind closed doors. Marcus had to duck to get into the attic bedroom. It was a plain and colorless room, Marcus thought. The small gray bed took up the majority of space and the few other pieces of drab furniture with the backdrop of beige walls made the room look like a muddy clay cave. Marcus looked at the only other door in the room.

"The bathroom?" Marcus asked.

"Down the hall, sir."

Marcus sat down on the bed and wiped his face. When he looked up he noticed a picture on the top of the dresser. It was of a young woman in a long white dress standing on a beach, holding the straw hat on her head from blowing away in the wind. Her bright, sunny smile made Marcus smile back at her.

"Esther, Sir."

"Who is she?" Marcus asked.

"My godchild, Sir." Marcus looked around the room once more.

PLANS · VICTORIA J.M. HOFFBECK

He hung his head and then pulled himself up with the help of the bedpost. "Thank you, Broderick, for letting me into your room. I'll take care of myself tonight. Good night." Broderick watched Marcus walk down the staircase.

"Sir, I could make you something to drink if you would like?"

"No, I'm fine," Marcus said, "good night."

"Good night, Sir."

While Marcus walked down the stairs he could hear the doors behind him creak shut as he left the floor. The house was dark and quiet. Shadows of blue moonlight illuminated the hall. Marcus opened the courtyard doors and went outside into the night. He took a deep breath of the cold air and looked up again at the stars and then collapsed on a stone bench.

"O God, O God," Marcus said, holding his head in his hands and watching his tears fall to the ground. "Forgive me," he cried out. "I have not honored you with my whole heart. I have not loved my neighbors as myself. I have let heroes – men of honor – live in poverty and widows are without homes. And even in my own house, my own house, I have neglected faithful and loyal servants. O God, O God, forgive me."

There was a sound of quiet footsteps on the walk. In a long coat and hat, the mammoth figure of a man came towards him.

"Son," the king called softly.

"Father?" Marcus said, jumping to his feet. His father stepped out of the shadows of the garden path.

"Father, I'm so sorry for what I have done. I'm sorry," Marcus said. The king embraced him.

"This is the day I have prayed for. I am blessed beyond measure. Praise God! Praise God!" he said.

"What am I to do now?" Marcus asked.

"Come," the king said, putting his arm around his son's shoulder. "It is time to begin."

CHAPTER 22

"Have you ever seen so much snow in your entire life?" Megan asked. She ran to the top of the white pile beside the road and then flopped down on her back, laughing as she kicked her feet.

"I can see you've never been to Banff," Ostride said, opening up the back of their rented Jeep. She took a look around the vast mountain terrain and then grabbed a bottle of water. "Hey, there's a truck coming," she said. "Let's find out if they know where Mr. Payton's cabin is." Ostride's braids flipped up and down as she bounced and waved for the truck to stop.

"It can't be too far," Megan said, dusting off the snow from her pants. "There's a lodge over there, we could just go there and ask." The red truck filled with bales of hay pulled up next to Ostride.

"Are you girls lost?" asked the woman from the passenger window.

"Maybe," Ostride said. "We're trying to find Mr. Payton's cabin."

The elderly couple began to laugh, "There's no address markers out here," Megan said, "or they're buried in the snow, but we can't seem to find 100 Pine Peak."

"You couldn't get much closer," the woman said. "That's Mr. Payton's right over there."

"The lodge?" Megan asked.

The driver rolled his window down. "That isn't a lodge," he chuckled. "That's his cabin."

Megan and Ostride looked at each other and then at the cabin. "Wow!" Ostride exclaimed.

"We take care of the cabin when he's away," the woman said. "You two must be the girls from the university."

"Yes," Megan said.

"Well, everything is ready for you and I stocked the refrigerator as Mr. Payton asked. Do you want us to let you in?"

"I have a set of keys," Megan said, still looking at the cabin.

"Have fun. And if you need anything we left our telephone number on the kitchen table," the woman said. The elderly couple went off and Megan and Ostride grabbed each other's coats and jumped up and down in the snow. "That's our cabin!" they screamed to each other.

"Let's go!" Ostride said as they hopped back in the Jeep. Megan peeled off the embankment and ventured up the steep driveway and parked in front of the door. "Wow," Megan breathed, looking at the cabin before turning off the engine.

"Let's go see what our vacation home looks like," Ostride said giddily. Megan found the ring of keys Mr. Payton had given her and tried every one before being able to unlock the door. "It's the gold one," Megan said.

"I swear, Megan, you and keys." Side-by-side Ostride and Megan walked in slowly and then stopped in the foyer to take it all in.

"Look at that!" Ostride said, "I've never seen such a big fireplace. You could put a whole tree in there." She took off her boots and ran up the open staircase, opening and closing doors. "Where would you like to sleep?" Ostride asked from the balcony. "Bedroom one, two, three, or four, and if those won't do, we have the sunset view with bedrooms five, six, seven and eight."

"This is incredible. Hey, there's a bedroom down here too," Megan yelled, opening a door next to the fireplace. Ostride ran down the stairway and looked inside the room.

"Wow!"

Megan continued to the living area and sat on one of the buffalo plaid chairs. Ostride sprawled out on the leather couch facing the fireplace.

"This is the kind of place you dream about as a kid," Ostride said. "A place where you can do cartwheels in the living room."

"Mr. Payton said there was a swimming pool," Megan said. They both jumped up and went to the back of the cabin through the kitchen and there, off to the side, was a large indoor and outdoor swimming pool. Steam rose from the outdoor half of the pool that was surrounded by towering spruce trees covered in snow. Ostride squealed in delight.

"Let's go swimming!"

"Swimming or skiing?" Megan asked.

"Skiing, swimming, skiing, swimming. I died and went to heaven," Ostride said.

"We still have some daylight. Let's ski and then we'll come back and swim and soak in the hot tub," Megan said.

"I'm halfway to the slopes," Ostride said, picking up her suitcase. They both headed for the bedroom next to the fireplace. "It has two beds," Ostride said. "Why not? We'll be up talking all night anyway."

* * *

Ostride walked out of the bathroom looking like she always did, Megan thought, like she'd walked off the cover of a fashion magazine. Her long blonde hair shimmered down her back like a ray of sunlight against her jet-black jacket and pants.

"Woo, woo!" Ostride said, admiring Megan's ski suit.

"I know, I panicked and bought new gear," Megan winced and then looked into the mirror to pin up her hair. The tight white suit hugged her curved shape and the metallic blue and silver stripe that began at her shoulder and ended at her right ankle wound around her like a loose ribbon.

"Looks good," Ostride said, digging in her satchel for her goggles.

"Okay, I have money and keys," Megan said, feeling the pockets in the arm of her jacket. "You have our goggles and gloves."

"Check," Ostride said and handed Megan her gloves.

"The skis are in the car. I guess we're set."

"We're off!" Ostride shouted, linking Megan's arm to hers, and together they ran out the door.

CHAPTER 23

Two hours later, Ostride took off her goggles and poked her head into a well-lit lounge at the ski lodge. "Meg, over here," she said, waving her hand. Megan wiped the mist of snow from her face and made a slight detour to pick up a brochure from the reservation desk on her way to catch up with Ostride.

"What'd you find?"

"Food. Come on, it looks like we could get something to eat in here." Megan followed Ostride into the multi-tiered dining room that funneled down to a stage. The maître d' was dressed in a black jacket and tie for the dinner hour and the busy restaurant was dotted with glittering patrons ready for an evening night out.

"I don't know, Ostride. We're not really dressed for the occasion."

"It's quite all right, Miss. We are used to casual attire at the lodge," said the host.

"Do you have a booth on top over there," Ostride asked, pointing to an inconspicuous corner.

"I am afraid those tables are reserved, but I do have a table in front of the stage. We have entertainment tonight, a band from America. They will start in an hour."

"What do you think?" Megan asked Ostride.

"Why not? I'm starving."

"Right this way." The maître d' said, and led them through a labyrinth of tables to the front of the nightclub.

"I feel exhilarated now, but I have a feeling I'll be paying for that last run in the morning," Ostride said, taking off her jacket. She dragged an empty chair from their table to prop up her feet and began rubbing her knee. A waitress soon stopped at their table and both girls ordered hamburgers and sodas.

"I think I got sunburned," Megan said, taking a tissue out of her pocket.

"We certainly slathered on enough sun block," Ostride said, while she read the small card listing the appetizers. "Um, egg and anchovy mousse, caviar and salmon squares. Whatever happened to stuffed potato skins and chicken wings?"

"They have hamburgers. I'm happy," Megan said.

"There are burgers, all right, but what kind?"

"What do you mean?" Megan asked. "Forget it. Don't tell me, I don't want to know."

Megan sat back in her chair and suddenly felt tired. She opened the brochure she had picked up at the reservation desk and began reading some of the highlights to Ostride.

"Hey, we can get a massage here," Megan said, "and they have mineral springs in the spa."

"We have our own hot tub," Ostride said. "And believe me, I plan on using it tonight."

Their meals came quickly and even among the increasing noise and chaos of the nightclub they ate slowly, enjoying their time. A man came out from behind the stage curtain and began testing equipment, making pinging, whooshing and screeching noises on the amplified system. When he had finished, recorded music from the stacks of massive speakers began to play. Ostride was about to put another french fry in her mouth when she abruptly put it back on her plate.

"What's the matter?" Megan asked.

"I hate to coin an old phrase, but of all the gin joints, he had to walk into mine."

Megan turned around and saw a line of people at the door of the restaurant waiting to get in, and spotted Jacob huddled inside the door, arm-in-arm with a short, redheaded woman wearing a tight ski sweater and dangling gold earrings. "It must be Babs," Ostride said.

"What do you want to do? Do you want to leave?" Megan asked.

"Don't look now, but here comes the rest of the troupe," Ostride said. Megan turned again, and saw Phillip and Marcus surrounded by women. Through the maze of people their eyes connected and Marcus, with his entourage in tow, scuttled out of the room.

"There's no reason why we should leave," Ostride said defiantly. "I wonder who's playing tonight," she said, flipping over Megan's brochure. Even through her cool exterior, Megan could see Ostride was fighting back tears. The lights dimmed in the lounge and Ostride wiped her eyes quickly, flashing a painful smile at Megan.

"A group called Major League is playing tonight," Megan said. "Ostride, we don't have to stay. We can go back to the cabin and try out that hot tub." Waiters were hurriedly setting up more tables in the back, when red, green and blue lights flashed on the stage to the rhythm of the recorded music.

"Following us?" Jacob asked, as he sat down in a chair next to Ostride. Marcus stood next to Megan. At the sound of their voices, Megan became rigid.

"Don't flatter yourself," Ostride said, and then looked around the room. "Where is the rest of your crew?"

"Ostride, they're just friends, people that happened to be here. Phillip is getting them a table."

"Just friends," Megan said, looking at Marcus. "They're very friendly," she said to Jacob. Marcus pulled a chair up next to Megan and sat down. He was going to take her hand but she reached for her glass.

"Megan, I...."

"Feeling better?" Megan interrupted.

"Much better," Marcus said.

"That's good. I hadn't heard from you and I was wondering."

Jacob tried to put his arm around Ostride by putting his arm on the back of her chair but she leaned forward to the edge of the table. Jacob picked up a clean fork and teetered it between his fingers as he sat back in his chair. He glanced at her out of the corner of his eye and she glared ahead at the black stage. Megan shook the ice in her glass and took the last of her water.

Just friends, Megan found herself repeating over and over in her mind, we're just friends. They're just friends. Friends. Megan sensed every movement of Marcus body, his hand close to hers, their shoulders touching, their knees accidentally bumping together. Maybe it's not as it seems, she thought. They could be just friends.

Megan's chair jolted forward. A woman in a low-cut black sweater slid between two tables and stepped behind Marcus, wrapping her arms around him and pressing her hands down onto his chest. "Marcus, we have been getting lonely for you," the sultry brunette said.

Or maybe I'm just gullible, Megan thought, taking a chunk of ice from her glass and rolling it around her mouth with her tongue. She could see Jacob mumble something and shield his eyes as a giggling Babette scurried to his side. The redhead squeezed in between Ostride and Jacob and ended up tumbling onto Jacob's lap. Jacob yanked a vacant chair from an adjoining table and sat Babette down on it. She cuddled up to him, laughing in a skittish, high-pitched giggle.

"Friends of yours?" Ostride asked Jacob sarcastically. Marcus unlatched the grip of the woman clinging to his neck and she sat down on a chair beside him.

"Marcus, you are being very rude not to introduce us," she said, directly to Megan. "I am Countess Nicole de Sonnete.'" Her dark brown eyes darted to Megan but then lingered on Marcus.

"Megan, you must let me explain," Marcus pleaded uneasily.

"Explain what, darling?" said Nicole, as she picked a celery stick off of Ostride's plate. She brushed it against her glossy red lips, and then snipped off a bit.

"Please, go ahead. A french fry?" Ostride said, pushing the plate to her. Nicole ignored her, and Ostride looked at Megan unbelievingly.

"Our little holiday has been exhausting," Nicole said, curling a smile. "I just hope we have the energy to enjoy the other recreational activities before we have to leave." The music boomed and Marcus turned to Nicole, frantically speaking to her in his native tongue. Megan closed her eyes and smiled as she touched her forehead, wondering why she was still sitting in her seat and not walking out the door. Not only am I gullible, I'm a glutton for punishment, she thought.

"We're just friends," Megan said aloud to no one. Marcus stopped and stared at her. Megan could see Ostride and Jacob were embroiled in a heated conversation when the band leapt out from behind the curtain and a roar of applause and screams erupted from the audience. People were standing around the tables, jumping up and down and clapping their hands.

"Check, please," Megan yelled to the waitress as she passed by. The waitress nodded to her as she was swallowed up and drifted off with the crowd of people going to the dance floor.

"Megan, this is not what you think," Marcus said, holding onto her arm.

"I've got the picture," she said yelling above the noise of the crowd.

"No, you don't"

"Did we move the party front and center?" Phillip bellowed, holding onto a blonde in a rhinestone mini skirt and a fuzzy pink sweater.

"Sit down, Phillip," Jacob said. "Join the party. It can't get any worse."

"Oh, it's the American," Phillip said sarcastically, surveying the guests and then taking his date to the dance floor. Megan threw some money on the table and she and Ostride got up to leave. The song ended, the lights went out and a spotlight beamed on stage.

"Ladies and Gentlemen, Major League!" a voice said over the speakers. Another roar erupted from the audience as Megan grabbed her coat. The guitarist stepped into the light. "We'd like to introduce a new member of our group tonight, David Erickson."

Megan held on to her coat and watched as the figure in the shadows appeared on stage.

"David?" she said, turning slowly.

CHAPTER 24

The thunder of applause came in a wave of screams, whistles and catcalls from the women in the audience. The tan, sandy-haired musician came into the light singing in a low raspy voice that made the women scream even louder.

"Meg, what's the matter?" Ostride asked, in the wake of the romantic ballad.

"It's David," Megan said slowly, looking up at the stage, over the heads of dancers.

"That's David?" Ostride asked, sitting back down.

Phillip returned to the table and stood in the way of Marcus' view.

"Phillip, sit down," Marcus ordered. A man in a black coat appeared and provided a chair. Phillip sat down next to Babette and soon his blonde date shared his lap. With Phillip out of the way, Marcus could now see the man singing on stage. In an open baseball shirt and jeans, the musician looked more like a California surfer than a baseball player, Marcus thought. Like the audience, Megan was captivated by the singer's voice. After he had finished, the band hurried to their next song in the midst of more catcalls from the women. The waitress stopped at their table and her eyes widened when she saw Marcus. He casually put his finger to his lips and shook his head, begging her to keep his secret. She took their orders with an impish grin and a wink to Marcus. She left, looking back at him as she darted through the crowd.

The music stopped and David wiped away the perspiration from his brow. "Thank you! Thank you! Is everyone having a good time?" Cries and whistles came back from the audience. "All right then. Let's rock!" An electric guitar howled, reverberated and squealed in a seductive, racing energy and the drummer, dripping in sweat, hammered out a strong steady beat that sank and thumped into the crowd and came out again in an electrifying motion on the dance floor. David jumped off the stage, bounding onto tabletops and chairs, singing to women as he made his way around the audience. A waiter holding a tray above his head walked by and David grabbed a glass of water from it, taking a gulp and setting it back down before the waiter disappeared. When he looked down, he saw Megan below and then looked again. Megan waved shyly and he jumped off the table in front of her.

"Megan!" David said, lifting her from the dance floor into his arms. "It's really you!" He kissed her and lowered her back down, clutching the back of her sweater.

"You're great!" Megan said, laughing. "You're really great!"

The band continued to play with the guitar players looking in the sea of dancers for David. Marcus was at Megan's side with Nicole clutching him.

"What are you doing here?" David asked. "Wait, don't move," he said and bounded for the stage. The band stopped playing when he reached them and the crowd looked up at the stage curiously. "We'll be taking a short break. Back in fifteen," David said to the swarm of people. The crowd booed and groaned when his announcement came over the microphone.

"I'll be back in five if I can get her to say yes," he said. The crowd laughed. "We'll make it up to you, I promise."

The band cranked up the recorded music and one of the guitarists, seeing an opportunity, helped an eager young woman to the stage and began to dance with her. David jumped down to Megan and gave her another hug.

"What are you doing here?" he asked.

"I was about to ask you the same question," Megan said.

"You know me. Some friends were in a bind and were short a lead so I volunteered. It's only for a few weeks," David said, looking into her eyes. "It's great to see you again. Now, why are you stuck here in this Icelandic cold front?"

"I'm going to school."

"School? What for? And why here? Come home and I'll teach you everything you need to know."

"She is the recipient of the Scolengard," Marcus said quietly.

"You're kidding! Meg, is it true?" She nodded. "That's fantastic!" David said, picking her up again and twirling her around the floor.

"Marry me! I need someone to support my lifestyle," he said, slowly setting her down. "Don't make me beg like the way you made me last time."

"You're crazy."

"Of course I am. Just don't tell anybody."

"Don't worry, your secret's safe with me," Megan said.

"Megan, perhaps you would like to introduce us to your...friend," Marcus said. He had sat back down and was no longer shunning Nicole's advances.

"David, this is Marcus Holcombe, Nicole, Ostride, a good friend of mine from school, Jacob, Babette, Phillip and,...."

"Simone," the young blonde girl said, anxious to meet the American singer. David gave a half-hearted salute to all, returning his attention toward Megan.

"You're a musician?" Marcus asked.

"I guess I am, part-time," David laughed. "Not even part-time. I'm a temporary worker. Hey Meg, is this yours?" David asked, pointing to a glass filled with ice. She nodded and he grabbed it and her, pulling her in front of him so that they both faced Marcus. He wrapped his arm around her waist and kissed her on the neck. He shook the ice in the glass and emptied it into his mouth. "I fill in here and there. Wherever I'm needed."

"Jacob and I are at Dreiholm Medical," Marcus puffed.

"Good school," David said, swallowing the melted ice. "I taught there about a year ago," he said, inching his hand across Megan's stomach, bracing her to him. Marcus watched David's hand venture across her waist. "Meg, I only have a few more minutes. Where can I meet you after this gig?" he asked. Marcus drew closer to the table.

"What did you teach?" Marcus asked, with an unbelieving smirk on his face.

"I didn't know you were here before, in Dreiholm," Megan interrupted, looking up into his wanting hazel eyes.

"The heart stent Jack and I developed was finally approved," David said. "We've been showing our esteemed colleagues how to use it."

"You did it!" Megan screamed as she hugged him again. "Oh, good for you David. That's fantastic!"

"Thank you very much," he said, in a silly German accent. "That's what happens when a guy gets his heart broken: work, work, work."

"You're Doctor Erickson, Doctor David Erickson, the heart surgeon and inventor?" Jacob asked in disbelief.

"In the flesh," David said, looking down at Megan. The drummer called out to David. "I'll be right back," he said and slipped away to the stage.

"Is that your neighbor, David, the one with the brother and the car?" Ostride asked.

"Uh hum," Megan said. She quickly looked at Marcus who was sitting back in his chair. Nicole was playing with his hair and stroking his neck.

A little later David bounced back to the group. "Meg," he said, "I have to get back. How about we meet for dinner after."

"Sure."

"Ostride," he said, "I don't know if you have plans but, Bill, the drummer, would like you to come along. We could all go together."

"I don't have any plans. I'd love to go out," Ostride said, getting up from the table. Jacob reached out his hand to stop her but she slipped by. "Jacob, it was nice to see you again. I hate to go, but I have a date."

"Come over and meet Bill. He's a great guy." David said, taking both Megan and Ostride by the hand. Nicole watched Marcus' eyes follow the two women to the stage.

"I don't think they will be lonely tonight," Nicole said, whimsically, tracing the design of Marcus' sweater on his arm with her long fingernails.

"No, I don't think they will either," Marcus said as he rose to his feet. "Good night, Countess."

"Marcus!" Nicole called out petulantly. A whirl of carnival-colored lights raced around the room and a cheer exploded as the band began to play and Marcus disappeared into the crowd.

* * *

Marcus found refuge from the noise and the stinging appearance of David in an empty banquet room looking out over the dark mountain slopes. In the dim light of the room he could see clearly the men and women passing by on the balcony outside, holding hands and kissing in the moonlight. He leaned over the brass railing, folded his hands and looked out the gigantic window to the jagged edges of the mountain peaks hidden in the black of night. He listened to the ticking from the heat vent overhead.

The door opened and Jacob poked his head inside. "There you are," he said as he slowly sauntered over to join him. He picked up a pretzel from a half-filled bowl that was left on a reception table and slumped over, resting his elbows on the railing. He broke the pretzel into pieces and scissored the bits with his front teeth. He tossed the remaining piece into the bowl and looked out the window.

"I love her, you know," Jacob said.

"I know," Marcus said, looking ahead.

"And I think you feel the same way about Megan," Jacob said, turning to his friend. Marcus paced up and down the ramp, putting his hands into his pockets.

"I don't know what I think or feel," Marcus said. He stopped and watched the midnight skiers weave down the mountain slopes holding pink flares in their hands, crisscrossing as they went down the peak. "I know I'm attracted to her," Marcus said, leaning over the railing again, twisting his family ring on his finger. "I notice how other men look at her, how David looked at her, and I know what they're thinking," Marcus said. "But what if what I'm feeling is just a natural reaction or instinct? I want her, but is that the same thing as being in love with her? I've confused desire and possession with love for so long that I'm not sure I can distinguish between the two anymore."

"Look at the facts," Jacob said. "You've told me how you feel about her. How she excites you and how she makes you happy. You've told me how she encourages you and is interested in your life and in your work. She's beautiful, hardworking, resourceful, and we know she's intelligent. She's a good conversationalist, motivated and interesting, and has a good sense of humor. But more importantly, from what I can see, she has a kind and faithful heart. Any three of those are good enough reasons to fall in love with her."

"We aren't dealing with facts or characteristics or whatever they are, we're dealing with love! Love is a feeling and I can't trust mine," Marcus said.

"Love is more than a feeling," Jacob said. "Feelings come and go. They change with the music or a bad meal," he continued. "Love is more than that. Love is enduring. It lasts and it's a choice."

The skiers were at the bottom of the slope standing together in the shape of a large firecracker. A whistle shrieked as a rocket darted into the sky and exploded into a glittering display of gold dust fireworks. The short display called an end to the evening's festivities and the onlookers on the balcony began to retreat to the warmth of their cabins and the lodge. Marcus watched a middle-aged couple in front of the window. The man put his arm around the woman and tucked her into his side and she pulled the scarf he was wearing up to his hat to cover his neck.

"Love is patient and kind, never jealous or envious, never boastful or proud, never haughty or selfish or rude. Love does not demand its own way. It is not irritable or touchy. It does not hold grudges and hardly even notices when others do it wrong. It is never glad about injustice, but rejoices whenever truth wins out. If you love someone you will be loyal to him no matter what the cost. You will always believe in him, always expect the best of him, and always stand your ground in defending him. All the gifts and powers from God will someday come to an end, but love goes on forever. First Corinthians, thirteen, verses four through eight," Marcus said.

"I see you have been putting that memory of yours to work again," Jacob said with a smile.

"Will she love me like that?" Marcus asked, still looking at the couple outside.

"Will you love her like that?" Jacob asked. Marcus looked down at the floor. The red and gold pattern of the carpet was a web of vines and gold leaves, muted colors blurred by the dark of night.

"I love Ostride," Jacob said. "She's everything I need or could ever want. It's more than passion. Love's an act, a commitment. A commitment I am going to make to her, if she'll have me."

"Congratulations," Marcus said, looking across at him and still leaning against the brass railing.

"Keep it," Jacob said. "Tonight she is going out with a drummer."

Marcus dragged his hands through his hair, groaning. "David," he moaned.

"Megan has as much feeling for David Erickson as I have for Babette," Jacob said.

"How do you know that? She seemed happy enough to see him," Marcus said. "And she wasn't exactly shrinking back from him."

"And you weren't exactly running from Nicole," Jacob said. "Let's face it, it didn't look good. None of it looked good."

"I know, I know," Marcus admitted, "and then I had to open my mouth about being a medical student." He closed his eyes and shook his head.

"I couldn't believe it was him," Jacob said. "Erickson's a genius, when it comes to cardio work anyway. What is he doing singing in a band? It's such a waste of his time."

Marcus looked out the window, remembering his conversation with Payton.

"They're trying to get even with us," Jacob went on, "and who can blame them. I even have a hard time believing that Nicole and Babette just happened to be here."

"They didn't," Marcus said. "I invited Nicole."

"What! Why?" Jacob asked. Marcus looked out the window and saw the couple he had noticed before kissing each other warmly under the stars.

"I'll tell you on the way," Marcus said. "Come on, let's go."

CHAPTER 25

Ostride and Bill were playing a game of chess by the fire while David and Megan were reminiscing over a cup of hot chocolate in the kitchen.

"I'm sorry we went so late but I felt like I owed the crowd something for taking a longer break," David said.

"If you didn't mind a cold sandwich for supper, I'm okay with it," Megan said, putting their few dishes into the dishwasher.

"It was great," David said. He looked out at the pool and at the trees surrounding it glowing with white lights. "This cabin is incredible. I have to get to know this Payton guy."

"I'm sure he'd like to meet you," Megan said, sitting down at the table. "By the way, I sent you a letter before I left, telling you I was moving, and it was sent back to me. Where are you living now?"

"I bought a house."

"You did? Where?"

"On the west side of town overlooking the lake," David said.

"My, my, my, the hoity-toity side of town," Megan teased.

"Marry me and I'll share."

Megan shook her head. She looked at his braided leather bracelet, torn jeans and high top tennis shoes. "David you're a thirty-something working on eighteen."

"Ouch!" David said with a laugh.

"It works for you," Megan said, "and it looks good on you and I am proud of you, really."

"Thanks," David said, kicking back in his chair. "Hey, who's the guy?"

"What guy?"

"The guy. The one glaring at me every time I touched you."

"That's why you were holding on to me, kissing me and all that baloney? You were just trying to get his goat."

"What are you talking about, I'm madly in love with you," David said, kissing Megan on the neck as he reached for more cocoa.

"Yeah, yeah, yeah," Megan said, shooing him away.

"Let's just say I was conducting a little experiment with one of the many non-invasive methods of rapidly elevating one's blood pressure. I think I was successful," David said, filling up his cup. "So, who is he?"

"Just a friend," Megan said.

"Who was the viper wrapped around his arm?" David asked, leaning back in his chair.

"Countess Nicole de Sonnete," Megan said, sharply.

"Ah, so he is more than a friend?"

"What are you talking about?"

"Admit it! Come on, admit it!"

"I'll admit nothing. We went on a few dates, we're just friends, apparently," Megan said.

"Nicole is an enticing creature," David said, looking down at the table. He could feel Megan glaring at him and he began to laugh. "Average. She's average," he said insincerely as Megan wrinkled her nose. "Down right plain," he conceded in a gruff, exaggerated tone.

"Who are you trying to kid? She's drop-dead gorgeous," Megan said. "I know it."

"I won't go there again, but I can tell you this, he wasn't looking at her tonight."

"We're friends," Megan said, looking into her cup.

"Yeah, right," David replied.

"David, don't you ever get scared?"

"Of what?"

"That we missed something? All the school and work and more school and more work."

"You mean because we're not following the norm? We didn't get married after college and have kids right away and open up a retirement account? No, not really," he said. Megan rested her elbows on the table and blew over the top of her mug that she held in both of her hands. "Meg, life runs us, we don't run it."

"Really?" Megan said with a touch of cynicism.

"What I'm trying to say is that we can't control everything in our lives," David said. "One thing leads to another, circumstances bring us to places. Look at you, school led to research and your research led you here. The same for me, research led me to medicine, medicine to cardio work, cardio work to stents and transplants. It's been a fast-paced ride and almost everything else in life took a backseat while we've been on it, particularly the norm."

"You seem to have found time for other things," Megan said. Her ruffled eyelashes knitted together to a point where David could barely see her eyes.

"What I can control, I make the most of," David said.

"Maybe you're right," Megan said and set her cup down on the table.

"Sure I am. All those unanswered questions of yours will run their course," David said, reaching for her hand. "It just takes time, some patience and a little persistence."

"And what if it's not the answer you wanted?" she asked, staring at the dangling fringe on his bracelet.

"You get up and go on," David said and laced his fingers in hers.

CHAPTER 26

"How long do you think they'll stay in there?" Jacob asked, his eyes set on the dimly lit cabin as his frozen breath spewed out of his nostrils like a fire-breathing dragon. Marcus parked at the bottom of the hill watching every movement in the cabin between the drifts of snow that hid his car. In the burning glow of firelight inside the cabin he could see two people but that was all.

"I can't believe they brought them to their cabin," Marcus said. "They could be staying the night."

"That's not going to happen," Jacob said. "I know the restaurants were closed by the time the band finished, but if they aren't out of there in fifteen minutes I'm going in."

"A light just went out," Marcus said, reaching for the door when the light came on again. "They're coming out," he said, watching the four standing outside on the porch. "Why are we doing this? I've never lurked around corners in my life. If we want to see them we should go to the door, and if not, we should leave."

"Right," Jacob said as he stretched his neck to watch Ostride wave goodbye to Bill in her stocking feet. The drummer ran to his car, yelling something to Ostride as she laughed and ducked inside the cabin. Marcus leaned over to see Megan alone with David outside the cabin door. David pulled her into his arms and when he went to kiss her she began to laugh and pecked him on the cheek. She hugged him once more and he ran to his car waving goodbye.

"We have to trust them or we have to confront them, we can't be groping around at night," Marcus said, and turned on the engine when he saw David get into the car with Bill. "I think we should trust them."

"I agree," Jacob said, looking back at the cabin one last time to watch David and Bill drive away in the opposite direction as they traveled down the road. "Let's get back to your place."

* * *

Ostride are you asleep?" Megan asked.

"No."

"I can't sleep," Megan said.

"Neither can I," Ostride said, tossing one of the pillows that was under her head to the chair in the corner of the room. "Bill said that he and David were going to another resort tomorrow."

"Yep."

"David seems nice."

"Yep," Megan said. "Ostride, do you think I'm being too hard on Marc?"

"Are you crazy?" Ostride said, punching her pillow. "They didn't have to rub salt into the wound by stopping at our table. They both could have just minded their own business and left us alone."

"But we're just friends and we've never promised each other anything."

"Ahh!" Ostride gasped in frustration as she pulled her blankets over her head. "Megan, if you and Marc are just friends then I'm a monkey's uncle."

"We're not exactly a couple," Megan said.

"Well, you were," Ostride said. "Everyone could see it. I could, Jacob could, Nicole certainly did and so does David." Megan lay staring up at the ceiling. Ostride wrestled with her blankets as she twisted and turned in bed and then settled down with her arms to her sides, staring up at the beams above her.

"That obnoxious, baby doll giggle," she said. Megan knew she was referring to Babette, and she covered her eyes, thinking of her bouncing into Jacob's lap, laughing hysterically with her shrill, reverberating hee hee hee.

"I don't know why anyone would intentionally act that way. If I were a guy I wouldn't have the time of day for a ditzy, sugar-coated... oh well," Megan said rubbing her face trying to wash away the image of the redhead. "Why do I even try understanding, I'm not a guy. I was actually embarrassed for her," Megan said, as she turned to her side and pushed down the plump pillow. Ostride didn't answer. In the blue moonlight Megan could see Ostride with her hands folded on her chest, tapping her thumbs together.

"The trouble is that I thought I found the right one," Ostride whispered in a strained voice. "But, he's just like the rest of them." A glistening tear fell down the side of her face onto her pillow.

"Oh, Ostride, I'm sorry."

"If I just stay busy, I'll be fine," she said in a shaking voice. The cabin creaked and moaned in the cold night as if it were sympathizing with their pain. The thought of Nicole with her arms wrapped around Marcus entered Megan's mind and stung at her eyes. She looked at Ostride crying silently.

"Then, for the rest of the trip we'll be busy," Megan said firmly. "Tomorrow we'll pack the day so full we won't have time to think. And we'll start by going to no man's land, to the village shopping!" Megan said. Ostride cracked a smile, slowing down the steady stream of tears falling from her blue eyes.

"It won't help, but it can't hurt," Ostride said, with a little laugh.

"I have to pick up a few Christmas presents and I have to get a turkey."

"A turkey?" Ostride said, wiping her face dry.

"Thursday's Thanksgiving in the U.S. and I plan on celebrating."

"Can't we settle for a frozen turkey dinner?" Ostride pleaded.

"No way. It's tradition!"

"All right, all right," Ostride said, pulling the covers over her head. "I'll make a pie," she said in a muffled voice.

"Good night, Ostride."

" 'Night, Meg."

CHAPTER 27

Phillip awoke early and found Marcus and Jacob having breakfast in the dining room of Marcus' family villa. The sun was bright, and through the picture windows overlooking the mountain he could see brightly colored skiers in the distance, dotting the slopes for a morning run.

"I hope you're both satisfied, Phillip said. Nikki and the others are leaving this morning."

"Have a seat, Phillip, I want to talk to you," Marcus said. Phillip straddled a chair and sat squarely in front of him.

"Phillip, I want to thank you for taking care of the details and arranging this holiday for us." Phillip's one eyebrow peaked when he heard his cousin's unexpected words. He glanced at Jacob, buttering his toast, and then looked back at Marcus from the corner of his eye. "When you first arranged our holiday at the Count's, we knew you had our best intentions in mind and not so long ago I wouldn't have given the arrangement another thought," Marcus said, putting down his knife. "But things have changed. I've changed."

"It's the American and the Canadian, isn't it?" Phillip asked.

"No, it's not just Megan or Ostride. I've turned a corner in my life and I'm not going back," Marcus said sternly. "And I'll thank you to refer to Megan and Ostride by their given names." Phillip sneered and took a piece of toast from the plate in the middle of the table. "Nevertheless, we can salvage this vacation if we want to. The snow is good so we can ski or maybe even play a little hockey if you like. It may be just what the doctor ordered." Marcus paused and wrinkled his brow. "Where have I heard that before?" he muttered. Jacob shrugged his shoulders as he drank the last of his juice.

"There's an open hockey game every day at the lodge," Phillip said enthusiastically. "I could sign us up for this afternoon's game."

"I'm willing," Jacob said.
"Sign us up!" Marcus added as they high-fived.

* * *

The mountain village was a maze of tiny shops and boutiques bustling with tourists and early Christmas shoppers. The restored log cabins with their brightly painted gingerbread cutout shutters were tightly packed together and lined the narrow streets. Savvy proprietors, whose log cabin shops did not conjoin with the others, instead built enclosed heated walkways from split logs, where they served hot chocolate and strudel to weary customers. Horse-drawn sleighs with jingling bells zipped by on the snow-packed streets, and cross-country skiers raced on the trails beside them.

"I think we did it!" Megan said, readjusting the bags in her arms. Ostride was gazing into a storefront window. Megan watched her taking deep breaths of the mountain air and letting out somber sighs as she burrowed down into her scarf, hiding. Ostride had laughed at her jokes and had painted a smile on her face most of the day but Megan could feel the agony of her broken heart. On the drive back to the cabin Megan loosened the laces of her boots and wiggled her toes.

"Well, they're still there," she said reaching down into her boots, rubbing her toes through her wool socks. "After we drop off the bird and the bags, do you want to get something to eat at the lodge?"

"Sure," Ostride said. The Jeep sputtered to a stop in front of their cabin. "If nothing else, I feel like we accomplished something today. I got most of my Christmas shopping done," she said, grabbing two of her bags from the back seat.

"I know my uncle and aunt are going to love the music box I found for them," Megan said. "It will make a nice addition to their collection." She hoisted a large package wrapped in brown paper into her arms. Ostride hurried to the front door to let her in before she dropped the bird.

"When the butcher asked us to come back in an hour I had no idea that he was going to actually go out back and, you know, get a bird," Megan said with a sour face.

"You asked for a fresh turkey and that's about as fresh as you can get."

"You know," Megan said, shoving the turkey into the refrigerator, "ever since I came here I feel like I have stepped back into some kind of time warp. The villages are a step back one-hundred years. Then, in other ways, the cities in this country are more modern than anywhere else I have been. It's the strangest thing," she said, closing the refrigerator door and blowing a stray curl out of her eyes. "Okay, do you want to walk down to the lodge?"

"Can your feet make it?" Ostride asked.

"Sure, I just need to freshen up a bit and I'll be ready for a hike."

New snow had fallen and being out in it revitalized their energy. Ostride snapped pictures as they charged through powder snowbanks. They made snow angels in the untouched canvasses of white and then hiked up steep snowy hills to stand next to the towering pines just to slide back down again.

"Look at that!" Megan breathed. Ostride saw a fox running across the ice on the lake below and snapped a picture.

"No, no, not that! That!" Megan said, pointing. Ostride looked a few feet down the road where a large ram was standing, licking the salt left behind by the snowplows.

"Oh, he'll move once we get close enough," Ostride said. The solid beast, with bulging round muscles kept licking the pavement as they crept closer, all the while keeping his eye on them.

"He doesn't seem to be moving," Megan whispered, as they walked closer. Ostride pulled her red scarf out of her coat and waved it back and forth, yelling at the ram.

"Go on now. Get going!" The ram raised his head and looked directly at Ostride. He stomped his right foot and snorted.

"Okay. We lose. Let's try this other path," Megan said, and pulled Ostride off the road.

"If we go that way we'll have to walk all the way around the lake," Ostride protested, looking at the park map carved into a marker by the side of the road.

"Yeah?" Megan asked. The ram grunted again and stared unflinchingly at Ostride.

"The scenic route it is," Ostride said, linking her arm into Megan's. They climbed up the cleared path that twisted and turned as it went deep into the woods. The setting sun touched the tops of the gigantic pine trees above them and dipped its fingers to the ground below, illuminating twigs and boughs heavy with snow. Small birds with puffed breasts fluttered in the branches of the trees, readying themselves for a night's rest. In the distance, Megan and Ostride heard a loud cheer and then the blast of an air horn that made them both jump.

"It must be the hockey games," Ostride said. At the top of the hill they were able to see down to the ice rinks below. One rink was jammed with spectators waving flags and blowing horns and whistles while the other two rinks were empty.

"I wonder why there is such a big crowd tonight?" Megan asked, as they approached the rink, dragging Ostride behind her.

"I'm sure it's just another game, Meg, slow down," Ostride said. "These people love hockey more than most Canadians I know."

A woman in an overstuffed down parka with a fur-trimmed hood cinched tightly around her face was walking with her husband at the bottom of the trail. They'd overheard the conversation and began to laugh. "I think you're right," the man called, as Ostride shuffled to a stop from their slide down the hill.

"We're from Ontario and we love the game but these people are nuts about hockey. Our travel guide said that he heard that the Prince of Dreiholm was down here playing with some of the people. We wanted to see if we could get a picture of him," the woman said.

"He's a cute boy," Megan said. The woman looked at Megan strangely as Ostride jumped up onto the corner of the crowded bleacher. Megan stood below, standing on her toes. All she could see were the tops of hats in the vast crowd.

"Can you see anything?" Megan yelled up to Ostride.

"The score is three to two and it's the third period," Ostride said. A loud cheer roared through the excited crowd.

"What happened?" Megan asked.

"I don't know. I can't see," Ostride said. A large man with a banner jumped up in front of Ostride and he began singing a cheer. A woman standing next to her in the bleachers called out "The Prince made a goal! The Prince made the goal!" The banner slipped from the large man's hands and slid down between the bleachers.

"Megan, you'll never believe this!" Ostride said looking out at the ice.

"What?" Megan asked impatiently. Ostride jumped down from the bleachers and landed next to Megan.

"Jacob, Marcus, and Phillip are on the ice," Ostride said incredulously, "Can you believe that? They're probably trying to meet the royal family."

"How much time is left in the game?" Megan asked.

"It's in overtime now. Let's get out of here," Ostride said. Megan tried to get a glimpse of the game and then saw Ostride's tear-filled eyes.

"Where would you like to eat?" Megan asked.

"Let's try The Pub at the lodge. It's small and quiet," Ostride said. "They all go to the big clubhouse restaurant after the game."

"Okay," Megan said. By the time they reached the lodge their fingers and feet were cold and their faces a bright red. Megan stopped at the front desk and picked up a newspaper and Ostride went into The Pub.

"They don't have anything in the main dining room but they have a small meeting room they're willing to open up for us, off to the side there," Ostride said, pointing to the back side of the room.

"Great. I picked up a Chicago paper. It's the closest thing they have to home," Megan said, following Ostride into the room. "Hey, this is perfect."

A crackling fire was glowing in the fireplace of the cozy room and the three dark brown tables shone in its light. Cushy wingback chairs with matching stools to rest their weary feet were positioned at each table along with small pillows to place behind their backs. Ostride hung up her jacket on a hook and pulled down her sweater. "Where do you want to sit?"

"The corner is fine," Megan said. The table was near the only natural light in the room by a large brown, red and gold stained-glass window. A waiter took their order and left the room with Ostride following him, closing the door behind him to shut out the noise of the outside world.

"Do you mind if I look at the arts and entertainment section? I want to see what movies we'll be missing," Ostride asked.

"Be my guest," Megan said, handing her the section of the paper.

"Hey, Minnesota had its first winter welcome," she sighed, looking at the headlines. "Twenty-four inches. It's a record. I wish I could have been home for that."

Ostride bent the corner of her paper to look at Megan. "Take a look out the window. It's the same stuff."

Megan laughed as she picked up another section of the paper. "Ostride, have you ever seen a picture of Dreiholm's royal family?"

"Yeah, I think so but I think it was pretty old," Ostride said, as she skimmed an article. "It must be getting cloudy. I can't see a thing over here." She slid her chair next to Megan's and tipped her paper to the window.

"I still don't know very much about this country," Megan said.

"Umm," Ostride said, still reading, "neither do I."

"While we're on holiday break we should go to a few museums. It would probably be good to find out a little more about this place. That woman we met going down to the ice rink gave me the strangest look when we were talking about the prince."

"I wouldn't take it to heart. She probably just didn't hear you," Ostride said. "Well, we aren't missing anything at the movies."

A rush of pounding feet and the sound of the lodge doors opening and closing resounded even in the small room. "The game must be over," Megan said, holding her part of the paper up to read a medical article.

"Yep," Ostride said and flipped the page of the newspaper.

CHAPTER 28

Marcus, Jacob and Phillip came into the lodge on the tops of shoulders of their triumphant teammates. Phillip jumped up on a chair in the midst of ringing cowbells, whistles and the blast of horns, and screamed a cheer of victory. The excited crowd answered back in a shout of celebration. Marcus took pictures with his teammates and shook hands with as many Dreiholmians as he could before his security guards became impatient. Well-wishers and curiosity seekers surrounded Marcus and Phillip, pressing in on them on every side. Jacob cornered the concierge and asked for a private room for the prince at the closest restaurant.

"I'm sorry, but we do not have private rooms in our restaurants," he explained. "All we have are small conference rooms adjacent to our restaurants and the closest one is in The Pub."

"That will do," Jacob said. He motioned to Marcus and Phillip and the security guards opened up a path for the prince and his cousin to follow Jacob into the restaurant, closing off the entrance to the other patrons.

"If you will wait for one moment, I must vacate the room," the maître d' said. "There are two young ladies dining in this room at the moment. I will ask them to leave."

"Two we can handle," Phillip said, anxious to eat.

"That won't be necessary, thank you," Marcus said. "Could you have a waiter bring us a bucket of ice and orange juice?" he asked, holding the doorknob to the small room.

"Soda," Phillip demanded.

"Right away, sir. You must be thirsty after your victory."

"It was a spirited game," Marcus said, and opened the door. Megan peeked over the top of her paper, expecting to see the server with their meal. Instead, she saw Marcus, Phillip and Jacob hurrying into the room. Megan kicked Ostride's foot, and Ostride looked at her from behind her newspaper. Megan jerked her head toward the door and Ostride peered between the pages. Marcus threw his jacket on the bench and reclined in a chair next to their table. "I haven't felt this good and so tired in a long time," Marcus said.

"That Czech, what a player! Ten more minutes and I wouldn't have been able to keep up with him," Jacob said, unlacing a boot.

"You old men," Phillip laughed, "I'm ready for another round."

"He's only fifteen years old," Marcus said. "Hans told me that he's already been recruited by a professional American team."

"I can see why," Jacob said, slowly straightening his back.

Megan and Ostride folded their papers and put them beside their plates. When they were noticed, the group sat speechless looking at each other, except for Phillip who let out a miserable groan.

"Good game?" Megan asked.

"Yes," Marcus and Jacob said simultaneously.

"Eat with us," Jacob said, unable to take his eyes off Ostride. He got up from his chair in his opened jacket and unlaced shoes and came to her side.

"No, thank you, we've already ordered," Ostride said firmly.

"Please, Ostride," Jacob asked in a whisper, bending over her chair. His dark hair was wet and tousled and his face was rough with the shadow of a beard and ruddy from the wind and sun.

Ostride looked away and without further comment, Jacob pulled the women's table to theirs. Neither Megan nor Ostride moved from their seats. Jacob waited behind Ostride and Marcus behind Megan.

"How was your evening last night with your friends?" Megan asked too sweetly, looking up at Marcus.

"Less eventful than our evenings out," Marcus said, picking up the chair with her in it and dropping it by the table. "And yours?" he asked, sitting down beside her. Phillip snickered, openly relishing the squabble.

"Watch it, Holcombe," Megan warned. The waiter came into the room and Marcus shouted an order in his native tongue. The waiter stopped, looked at the guests, served the drinks and left without a word.

"What's that all about?" Megan asked.

"I ordered dinner."

"Dinner?" Megan said. "That didn't sound like dinner."

"Before I join the festivities, where are the other guests?" Ostride asked Jacob.

"They left, thanks to you two," Phillip complained.

"Phillip!" Marcus snapped.

"I'm surprised. Nik and Babs didn't seem like the type to give up so easily," Ostride said.

Jacob pulled Ostride up from her chair. He looked deeply into her eyes. "Ostride, I'm in love with you. I have been since the first moment I saw you," he said. Ostride stepped back from him. "I don't care about Babette or any other woman, except you."

"But,..." Ostride began.

"Ostride, listen to me," Jacob said, coming closer to her. "I love you. Marry me."

Ostride put her hands to her mouth.

"Please, Ostride," Jacob pleaded. Ostride's hands began to shake and Megan could see her friend's eyes begin to fill with tears.

"Say yes," Megan sounded out in a tiny whisper as she watched her friend.

"Yes," Ostride said and Megan clapped her hands. Jacob picked her up off the floor and kissed her until they couldn't breathe.

"Please, this is making me sick," Phillip said, as he watched the two embrace and kiss.

"I love you too," Ostride said laughing, holding Jacob's face in her hands. Megan smiled, watching the scene through blurred eyes. Marcus sat tapping the tabletop with his cold fingers and looking at Megan.

"Ostride, I am so happy for you," Megan said, giving her friend a hug and wiping away her own tears.

"Yes, congratulations," Marcus said, "to you both. We will now celebrate."

"It's not official until you have a ring is it?" Phillip asked. Marcus glared at him.

"Well, is it?"

"It's official," Marcus pronounced.

"Wait a minute, I'll be right back," Jacob said.

"Jacob, where are you going?" Ostride asked.

"I'll be right back," Jacob insisted and then ran out of the room as the waiter came in with their meals.

"Ostride, what would you like to celebrate with?" Marcus asked.

"I don't know," Ostride said, looking around flustered. Then she looked at Megan. "I know, chocolate caramel mocha layer cake. That is something I don't let myself have every day."

"Done," Marcus said and looked at the waiter.

"Right away, Sir," the waiter said, departing quickly. Jacob came back running into the room holding a small black velvet box.

"Here," he said holding it out to Ostride. "When I saw it, I knew this is what I wanted to get you." She opened it up and looked at the small circle of gold and brilliant, square, sparkling diamonds. "It's an eternity ring – the time I am going to spend with you," he said, placing it on her finger while she started to cry again.

"It's beautiful."

"Our meals are getting cold," Phillip announced in a very bored tone of voice. Ostride wiped away her tears and sat down and showed Megan her ring. Phillip sat in his chair eating his meal, becoming more annoyed with each utterance. He avoided looking up from his plate and when he did, Megan noticed that he would not look at her at all. He looks so much like Marcus, Megan thought, same thick blond hair, piercing bright blue eyes and imposing athletic physique, but there was something different about Phillip, too. She looked at Marcus and then to Phillip. Marcus was tempered, disciplined and meticulous in look and tone but Phillip had a ruggedness, a steely eagerness that kept the unsuspecting on edge. Her observation lasted too long and Phillip glared at her from across the table.

"So, you won the hockey game," Megan said, diverting the conversation away from wedding plans. "Do you play hockey at the University, Phillip?"

"No," Phillip answered shortly.

"Any sports?"

"No," Phillip said and then glanced at Marcus who was obviously unhappy with his curt answers, "not in competition anyway."

"You're probably as busy as Ostride and I are in school," Megan said. Phillip intentionally put a hot roll in his mouth to avoid speaking to Megan. O Lord, help! Megan prayed.

"Phillip is majoring in journalism," Marcus said, lowering his glass to the table while he glared at Phillip. Phillip could see his anger and it perturbed him that Marcus would rebuke him in public even if it was done in silence.

"Photojournalism," Phillip corrected him.

Thank you Lord! This might be the answer, Megan prayed again.

"Phillip is very good with a camera. He was asked to go to the United States for a competition but we had a few difficulties when we got there," Marcus said.

"Difficulties!" Phillip snorted. "Everything I brought was stolen from me - my equipment, my pictures, my passport. The authorities were of no use and the people, the people were inhospitable and offensive, not to mention boorish. By the time I had straightened the whole mess out, Chet had already left that miserable country."

"Chet," Megan whispered, "the war correspondent?" she asked.

"Chet Garrett, not that you'd know him," Phillip said.

"Oh, I know him," Megan said. "He's my godfather."

"You're lying!" Phillip exclaimed. Megan could sense Marcus' anger and she intentionally tipped her glass, spilling a drop of water onto the table and splashing Marcus' hand.

"I'm sorry," Megan said, dabbing his hand with her napkin. "No, Chet's my godfather."

"How?" Phillip asked.

"I didn't have much to do with it," Megan said, "I was a baby when it all happened. But if you're asking how my parents knew him, he's from Texas, a state in that miserable country I call home, that you had to visit," Megan said, putting her napkin aside. "You might say we were all neighbors in Texas, and when Chet moved to Minnesota, my uncle, who knew him well, told him to look up my parents. They invited him to go to church with them and they became friends and bingo, I got a godfather. In fact, he sent me one of his cameras before I came here and I can't make heads or tails of it."

"You have one of his cameras?" Phillip asked. "Can I see it?"

"I don't have it with me but you can stop over at the cabin and take a look at it if you'd like," Megan offered.

"It's a small world isn't it?" Ostride asked rhetorically. "So I guess you were bound to meet one of these days," she said to Megan and Marcus. The waiter returned to the room, cleared the dishes and set a dark chocolate cake in the center of the table. Caramel oozed out from between the layers and the smooth chocolate icing covering the top of the cake cascaded down the sides.

"Ostride, you might as well practice for the big day. Why don't you cut the cake," Megan said. Ostride took the knife and made the first slice and her eyes welled up with happy tears again.

"Please, not again," Phillip begged.

"You're right, you're right," Ostride said. "But, I'm getting married to the man I love!" She shouted and kissed Jacob again and then again. Megan laughed and Phillip groaned.

"Okay, okay, I'm in control of myself," she said wiping her face. She served another piece of cake and kissed Jacob one more time. "On to other subjects. Here's something: we heard the prince was here today and was playing hockey. Did you get a chance to meet him?"

"He's just a boy," Megan insisted to Ostride. "He couldn't have been playing hockey with the men, could he?" Megan asked turning to Marcus.

"There was that Czech,"Ostride said, "He was only fifteen, right?"

"The prince looked younger than fifteen," Megan said. Phillip thought Marcus looked pale.

"The pictures you saw of the royal family when you first came to Dreiholm were probably dated," Marcus said carefully.

"Did he play? Did you get a chance to meet him?" Ostride asked.

"What was he like?" Megan asked. Jacob and Phillip waited for Marcus to say something but when he didn't, Phillip took advantage of the rare opportunity.

"He's a bore," Phillip said, stabbing his piece of cake with his fork. "But Marcus knows him better than I do. They're very close."

"You are?" Megan asked. "What does he look like?" Marcus shrugged his shoulders.

"Like everyone else, I guess," Phillip said, and Megan let out a sigh of disappointment.

"Why? What were you expecting?"

"I don't know," Megan said, resting her arm on the table and playing with the caramel drizzle on her plate. "I suppose every woman expects a prince to be tall, dark and handsome."

"And with a sword by his side and a hundred medals on his chest," Ostride added, laughing at the fairytale image.

"That about sums it up," Megan said.

"You'd both be disappointed," Phillip said. "He's not much to look at. Marcus was being generous. In fact, I think he's rather plain-looking."

"Oh well, what he looks like really doesn't matter anyway," Megan said. "Is he a good man, this prince of yours?"

"He's trying," Marcus said, wiping away a crumb from the linen tablecloth.

"Is he a just man, someone who should lead the country?" Ostride asked.

"He's a changed man," Jacob said, "and by God's grace he will be the man he is destined to be, honorable, wise and faithful."

"And what do you think of the prince, Phillip?" Megan asked. Phillip casually wiped his mouth with his napkin.

"Oh, he's like family to me."

CHAPTER 29

"It's a good thing you're taking us to the cabin or we never would have made it back walking," Megan said. The wind and snow were blowing against the SUV, making it wobble as Marcus fought to keep it on the mountain road.

"This isn't good," Phillip said, looking out the window.

"It was fine just a minute ago," Ostride said. "We could see the stars at the lodge and now it's just all white."

Marcus sped up the driveway hoping to plow through a snowdrift that was cutting across the faint path. The car stopped in the middle of the drift, unable to move forward or backward. The lights going up the driveway and at the front door were barely visible in the blowing snow.

"I think we can make it from here," Megan said. "Come on, human chain, we're going in."

"As soon as we get you inside we'll start digging out," Marcus said.

"You're not going out in this again. That's crazy. I don't know what you call it here, but at home we call this a blizzard. You have to wait until it passes," Megan said, putting on her gloves.

"I'm with her," Phillip said and pushed the car door open, shoving it into a drift. A gust of glacial wind and icy snow burst in and hit their faces like dry sand. Jacob found a thin rope underneath the back seat and tied it to his belt and then tied it to Ostride. "Here," Jacob said, passing the bulk of it on to Phillip. Phillip threaded it through a toggle on his jacket and the three got out. Phillip kicked the snow away from Megan's door and opened it. An icy gust blasted into the vehicle and pushed her against Marcus. Their eyes met and she turned away, wrapping the rope around her waist. Megan took Phillip's hand and he pulled her out into the storm. She threw the rope to Marcus and in a moment Marcus was beside her.

"Let's go!" Phillip yelled through the howling wind. They waded up the driveway, pushing through dunes of waist-deep snow drifts, gasping for air, while following the blurred lights that edged the path. Ostride was the first to reach the front door. She opened it and they all fell in, slipping and sliding down on the wood floor. Megan fell on Phillip's back and Marcus landed on top of her and Jacob. Megan started to laugh and tried to blow her snow-matted hair away from her eyes. Marcus brushed the hair away from her face and began to laugh.

"We made it!" Jacob said, struggling to sit upright, kissing Ostride as he did.

"Get off of me," Phillip grunted. Marcus stumbled to his feet and forced the front door shut. A mighty gust blasted the heavy door, making it rattle. Marcus locked it and then held out his hand to Megan, who was still sitting on the floor.

"I'm sorry, Phillip, are you okay?" Megan asked, getting up.

"Fine," Phillip gasped.

"I've got to clean this up before it ruins the floor," Megan said.

"Where's your maid?" Phillip asked.

"You're looking at her," Megan said. "Where's the maid?" Megan muttered under her breath, taking off her coat. Then she said to Phillip, "I've got a surprise for you. While you're here you are the new assistant to the maid, as well as the cook and bottle washer."

Jacob rolled on the floor laughing.

"And what are you laughing about?" Ostride asked.

"You don't have to worry about me. I've been in his majesty's service. I was the bottle washer," Jacob said. Ostride kissed his cheek and she crawled to her feet.

"Come on, Junior, you can help me find some rags," Ostride said to Phillip. Phillip got up from the floor and followed Ostride in his wet boots. "Phillip! Your boots!"

* * *

Marcus turned off his phone as he walked through the kitchen door. "Where is everybody?" he called out. Megan came out of the pantry carrying a plastic tub of flour.

"Phillip found the pool and Jacob and Ostride decided to join him," Megan said, measuring out some flour and putting it into a mixing bowl. Marcus walked around the granite island and peered through the window. Phillip was running off the diving board wearing hot pink shorts.

"What is he wearing?" Marcus asked, stunned.

"My running shorts," Megan said. Marcus just shook his head, grinning. "It was better than the alternative," Megan said. "Did you get through to whoever you had to let know that you were stuck here?"

"Yes," Marcus said, watching Megan. She had rubbed her cheek with the back of her hand and had unknowingly smeared her face with flour.

"Good," she said, measuring a few other ingredients carefully.

"It wasn't Nikki," Marcus said.

"I didn't ask," Megan said, popping the top back on the flour tub.

"Yes, you were," Marcus said. "You can put your mind at ease."

"My mind at ease?" Megan said, dumping water into the mixing bowl. "You mean like the way you waited outside our door while David and Bill were here?"

"How did you know?" Marcus asked.

"I didn't, thank you very much," Megan said, putting the flour away, "but I do now. What did you think you were going to do, charge in here and drag them out if they didn't leave?"

"They shouldn't have been here in the first place," Marcus said.

"Oh, really!" Megan said sarcastically, cracking an egg on the edge of the bowl. "I'll be wearing white at my wedding, Holcombe, how about you?" Marcus sheepishly looked away and watched Jacob and Ostride by the pool. Jacob was wrapping a towel around Ostride's damp shoulders and gently patting her dry.

"There are many things I regret," Marcus said, "Nikki is just one of them. But it's not like that anymore, Megan. If I never see another Nicole or Babette or nightclub or casino again, I wouldn't miss it. They tempt me no more."

Megan picked up a towel and wiped her hands and stood over by Marcus, watching Ostride, Jacob and Phillip through the window.

"I'm sorry about my past. Now I have to face the future and fill up the voids with a life more worthy."

Megan squinted her eyes and tugged at the towel hanging over her shoulder. "That sounds like something my father would say," Megan said.

He leaned back against the island. "It's strange, two people an ocean apart struggling with the same questions, having the same thoughts, caring for the same people." Megan wanted to touch him, his blond hair streaked with gold and brown, but didn't dare. She followed his gaze out to the pool.

"Ostride is so happy. She loves him so much," Megan said.

"Megan, we're not just friends, are we?"

"Probably not," Megan said, keeping her eyes on Ostride and Jacob. "I think we're somewhere in between here and there," she said. Marcus stepped in front of her and brushed the flour from her face. He kissed her deeply, erasing any separation between them until they both fell captive to the passion ignited in their hearts.

"Megan, I think I...."

"I think I need some help in here," Megan interrupted and twirled around to reach for the salt. Marcus grabbed the container and turned her around to face him.

"Megan, I want to...."

"Don't," Megan said, putting her fingers up to his lips. "Let's just enjoy the moment."

Marcus tossed the salt from one hand to his other. He opened Megan's hand and placed the container into it and then looked into her eyes. He looked away from her and then at the smattering of ingredients on the table.

"What are you making?" he asked.

"Dinner rolls for tonight."

"What can I do to help?"

"You're a surgeon, you can clean the turkey. I was planning to have it Thanksgiving but since we have guests...."

"Where is it?" Marcus asked.

"In the refrigerator," Megan said. "There's a knife in the first drawer to your right. Go for it."

Marcus took the bird out of the refrigerator and placed it on the stainless steel cutting board near the sink. Megan watched out of the corner of her eye as Marcus meticulously took off the wrappings and then thoroughly washed his hands, all the time looking at the bird as if it were going to fly away.

"Marc, where did you meet Jacob?" Megan asked, kneading the

bread dough.

"When I turned twelve I was sent to a private school. Jacob was the first person to say hello to me and we've been best friends ever since."

"Where did you go to school before that?"

"I was tutored at home."

"You don't have any brothers or sisters, do you?"

"No."

"Then that must have been pretty lonely."

"Not really. Well, at times," Marcus added. "I traveled with my parents and made a few friends along the way, and when I wanted to play sports my parents put me into a conventional academic setting. And you, you're an only child. Were you lonely?" Marcus asked.

"Sometimes," Megan answered.

"Do you want children of your own?" Marcus asked.

"Funny, we were just talking about that," Megan said, thinking of David. "I guess I do, but I don't see it happening in the near future."

"Why not?"

"Well, I always thought I would like to do things the old-fashioned way, a husband, a home and then maybe children," she said.

"But you're open to it?" Marcus asked.

"Yes, I'm open to it," Megan said, holding on to the pan and turning to Marcus. "What did you do to that poor turkey?" Megan gasped.

"I cleaned it and cut it up," he said. Jacob came into the kitchen and looked at the carefully dissected turkey laid out on the counter.

"Good job," Jacob said. "I couldn't have done that better myself." Ostride followed him, pinning her wet hair to the top of her head.

"What happened to the turkey?" she asked.

Marcus and Jacob looked at her puzzled. "I haven't finished filleting it yet," Marcus said.

"I'll help," Jacob offered.

"You don't fillet a turkey, you roast a turkey," Ostride said, exasperated. "You've never cooked before, have you?"

"No," Marcus and Jacob said in unison.

"I take that back," Jacob said. "We cooked when we went camping."

"Yeah," Marcus said proudly.

Megan looked at the cut up pieces and sighed. "Ah well, Happy Thanksgiving," she said.

CHAPTER 30

"Delicious," Jacob said, stretching lazily at the dining room table. The wind was pounding against the walls of the cabin as white sheets of snow passed by the windows.

"I never knew cooking could be so much fun," Marcus said, eating the last black olive on his plate.

"Grilled turkey, that was a change," Megan admitted.

"I like cooking on that grill contraption," Phillip said, and took another scoop of mashed potatoes.

"I think we had a little southwestern thing going here," Ostride said, looking at the leftover plate of seasoned turkey.

"Meg, since you and Marcus and even Phillip helped to cook, we'll clean up," Jacob said.

"It's about time," Phillip said, buttering a roll. "You two might as well be married already, the way you prattle and coo over each other." Ostride stood up and took Phillip's plate.

"I'm not finished yet!" he yelled.

"You are now," Ostride said. "You just elected yourself to serve my pie. Come on, get up." Phillip was about to protest when she picked up another plate. "One word and you're drying the dishes too." Phillip scowled and followed Ostride into the kitchen, grabbing a turkey leg on his way.

"If the snow doesn't let up and Phillip has to stay with Ostride much longer, she'll have him ready to take over Broderick's job when we get back," Jacob said, taking Megan's and Marcus' plates.

"Optimist," Marcus chuckled. Megan took her cup and went over and sat on the couch by the fire. Marcus sat down next to her and Megan shot up and headed toward her bedroom. "I forgot something, I'll be right back," she said. When she returned she was carrying a blanket and a small black leather bag. She set the bag on the floor and wrapped the blanket around her feet as she sat down on the couch. Marcus pulled her to his side and she rested her head against his chest. "What's that?" Marcus asked, looking at the bag.

"Chet's camera."

"That's it?" Phillip asked, hurriedly setting down two pieces of pie on the coffee table. "Can I look at it?"

"Go ahead," Megan said. Phillip sat down on the floor. He carefully opened the leather case and slowly lifted the heavy metal camera, cradling it in his hands with the same tenderness as one would hold a newborn baby.

"His name is engraved on it, and a date," Phillip said. "Megan, this is the camera he used in Rwanda."

"One of them, I think," Megan said. Phillip stopped and put his finger over a smooth dent in the camera's metal body. "A bullet," Megan said somberly. Phillip kept rubbing the wounded camera.

"Would you mind if I take a few with it?" Phillip asked.

"Be my guest. I thought I might have time to figure out how to use it while I was up here but so far I haven't had time to even open it up," she said. Phillip spun the dials and popped the lens cap off and began shooting pictures. Marcus turned Megan's face to his and kissed her. Megan could hear the series of clicks of the camera.

"Hey, hey!" Megan said. "I'm not sure I want you taking pictures of me and your cousin kissing."

"He's used to it,"' Phillip said, snapping some more. "Don't worry I can always edit him out."

"And then what would be in my place?" Marcus asked.

"I can think of a few subjects. I'm available," he said, winking at Megan. She shook her head and put her hand on Marcus' chest.

"Phillip, why don't you keep that camera?" Megan said. Phillip stopped taking pictures and looked at Megan, holding the camera close to him.

"Megan, do you know how valuable this camera is?" Phillip asked.

"To you or to me?" Megan asked, resting on Marcus' shoulder. "You should have it. Go capture the world's faces with it."

"I can't," Phillip said.

"Sure you can," Megan said.

"I've never had such a gift," he said. He gripped the steel casing with both hands. "Thank you," he said softly.

"You're welcome," Megan said. "When I call I'll let him know his gift is in good hands."

"Megan, can I be there when you call," Phillip said, pushing her coffee mug aside, and sitting on the table facing her.

"Sure," Megan said.

"Hey, how do you like my pie?" Ostride shouted from the kitchen.

Megan sat up. "Eat," she commanded to Marcus and Phillip. "She worked so hard on this," she said in low voice, taking a bite of the pumpkin pie. Megan closed her eyes and began to cough, gagging and her eyes watering as the pie slid down her throat. Phillip clicked the camera.

"What's the matter?" Marcus asked.

"Don't eat the pie!" Ostride screamed, running out of the kitchen. "I must have mixed up the allspice with the ginger and the teaspoon with a tablespoon!" Megan coughed again and took a drink of her coffee. Jacob came out of the kitchen with a glass of water and a beet red face.

"I'm so sorry," Ostride said, "they're both brown and I must have mixed them up." Jacob coughed and then sneezed and Phillip snapped another picture.

* * *

Megan awoke at dawn, smiling and burying her face into her pillow. She rolled over and saw Ostride sleeping in the next bed. The snow had stopped falling and the furious winds that rattled the windows had calmed to a wisp and were swirling icy crystals on top of the frosted drifts. Megan tiptoed out of the shower and went out into the living room with a book in hand.

"Good morning," Marcus said, standing by the window.

"What are you doing up this early?" Megan asked.

"I like the morning," Marcus said. "I now know how to make coffee. Would you like some?"

"Sure," Megan said and looked out the window. "Wow, they already cleared the road and our driveway too? I wonder how they did that so quickly." Marcus put his arm around Megan and led her into the kitchen.

"As soon as Jacob and Phillip get up, we'll be going."

"Why? What's the hurry?" Megan asked.

"I have some things I have to do and I can't do them from here," Marcus said. "Why don't we meet for dinner?"

"Dinner," Megan said, as she backed him up against the kitchen door and kissed him.

"What's this?" Marcus asked catching his breath.

"I'm taking a chance," Megan said, "any complaints?" Her sweatshirt rose up on her waist as she put her arms around his neck. He felt the soft skin of her back and pulled her to him.

"No complaints," Marcus said, kissing her again.

"Ouch!" Phillip yelped as he ran into the blocked kitchen door. Marcus begrudgingly stepped aside and let his cousin in. "What were you doing standing in front of the door?" he asked and looked at Megan and Marcus who were awkwardly silent. "Don't answer that. I don't want to know."

"Nothing I would be ashamed to tell my grandmother," Megan said. "Coffee? Marcus made it."

"I don't know your grandmother and I'll take my chances on the coffee," Phillip said and sat on a bar stool, ruffling his hair. "I see the storm passed."

"We'll be leaving as soon as Jacob and Ostride get up," Marcus said.

"Why? I like it here."

"So do I, but people will get the wrong idea," Marcus said as Megan poured Phillip some coffee. While Megan had her back to him, Marcus flashed his telephone at Phillip. A picture of Nicole popped up on the screen and faded away. "We'll all have dinner tonight," Marcus said and casually slipped the phone back into his pocket before Megan turned around.

"I'll go rattle Jacob's cage," Phillip said as he grabbed his mug and a piece of streusel. "Or maybe I should start with Ostride."

CHAPTER 31

"Marcus was on his cell phone a lot. Who was he calling?" Ostride asked.

"I have no idea," Megan replied.

"It looks like it's warming up between the two of you?" Ostride sat down on her bed while Megan got ready to go to dinner.

"Um hum."

"That's all you're going to give me?"

Megan found a tube of lotion and sat on the floor across from Ostride.

"I'm just not sure what to think," Megan said, rubbing the lotion into her hands.

"Why are you so scared?" Ostride asked.

Megan thought for a long moment. "I don't know," Megan said, "there's something about him and I can't put my finger on it. I want to give him the benefit of the doubt, and obviously I'm incredibly attracted to him, but something keeps getting in my way."

"Have you asked Payton about Marcus and Jacob?"

"Yes," Megan said rolling her eyes. "'Upstanding citizens of Dreiholm,' is all he said."

"There you go," Ostride said, waving her hand.

"Yeah, you're right, I shouldn't be so suspicious," Megan said, throwing the capped tube back into her bag. The brass luggage tags hung down over the edge of her bed. One tag still had her mother's name on it. "But something's up. I want someone I can trust, someone who will love me forever, like my parents did," Megan said. "Maybe I am scared, but my instincts tell me I'm missing something."

"Like what?"

"I don't know, something."

"I know Marcus cares for you," Ostride said.

"Okay, spill," Megan said.

"That's all I can say," Ostride said with a mischievous grin. "Just take my word for it. But they are different."

"What do you mean they're different?" Megan asked.

"Not one of them knows how to do a blasted thing!" Ostride said, dropping to the floor to sit with Megan. "It's like they have never seen the inside of a kitchen before. Didn't you notice that they didn't even know how to turn on the stove? The three of them were trying to figure out how to use the washer and they got it running but ended up washing their clothes with fabric softener instead of detergent. I was going to stop them but they had already dumped it in, and Jacob stood there so proud of himself, I just couldn't burst his bubble or what should have been a bubble."

"At least they smelled baby fresh," Megan said, reaching for Ostride's arm so they could help each other get up off the floor. "It doesn't surprise me. Marcus has a servant for everything."

"I had a nanny and we had a maid who came in once a week when I was growing up but I still knew how to boil an egg and I knew how to do my own laundry," Ostride said.

"Now who's dreaming up conspiracy theories?" Megan asked.

"No theories, it's just that Jacob is going to be zero help around the house."

"He's a fast learner. You can sign him up for a home economics course and while he's there you can take Baking 101," Megan said.

"Very funny!"

* * *

"They're going to be late," Ostride said, tucking her cell phone into her purse. "Jacob said they'd be a half an hour or so."

"Why?" Megan asked, opening the lodge door.

"A land deal of some kind. I guess Marcus is involved with a housing group, and Jacob and Phillip are helping out. That must be why Marcus was on the telephone so much," Ostride said as she and Megan walked down the indoor shopping mall of the lodge. "I've been dying to try one of those ever since we got here," Ostride said, pointing to the window. Megan knew exactly what she was talking about. They had walked past the bakery every day they had been at the lodge and they both were tempted by the raspberry tart piled high with fruit and

PLANS · VICTORIA J.M. HOFFBECK

swirls of pure white whipped cream.

"We're on vacation," Megan rationalized, "let's do it." The small bakery was warm and filled with the sweet, rich aroma of caramel and chocolate.

"A piece of heaven," Ostride said, smacking her lips as she took a mouthful of tart. A dollop of whipped cream was on the edge of her upper lip when a man with a camera in his hands and his back loaded with equipment pulled out a chair at the table beside them. He began shedding his bags while a woman, wearing a fitted business suit and carrying two cups of coffee, joined him. She set the cups down and dropped her large leather handbag next to Ostride's feet.

"Can you believe that Babette?" the woman asked the man with the camera. Ostride licked her lips and looked up at the woman. The trim woman sat down, crossed her legs and leaned back in her chair. The man laughed as he put a new lens on his camera.

"She gave me a camera full. That picture will make the front page," he said, unzipping one of his bags. Megan rattled her cup to startle Ostride who was obviously staring at the woman. Ostride looked at Megan and took a fork full of tart.

"I hope she and her friends froze out there," said the woman."

"That's not a worry. Babette has enough padding to keep her warm," he said.

"Padding? Mostly silicone," she said, as she checked her telephone.

"Babette is nothing compared to that cat, Countess de Sonnete. I swear that woman would do anything to get her claws into the prince."

"Oh, I don't know. I was talking to Trevor at *People Watch,* the rag, and he seems to think she has her sights set on that industrialist's son, the one in Parliament, you know, what's his name? What is his name?" the woman said, taking a drink of her coffee as the man checked his camera. "You know who I'm talking about...oh whatever, it will come to me. Anyway, I hear he really loves her."

"Then love is blind," the man said. "She's only toying with him until she can get her hooks into the big fish."

"You're right," the woman said, "I know you're right."

"Excuse me," Megan said, looking across the narrow aisle. "You're reporters?"

"That's generous," the photographer said.

"I was wondering if you might have a picture of the prince?"

The two looked at Megan and then at each other and then back at Megan and Ostride. Ostride had managed to swallow but was still unable get a word out of her mouth. "We're visitors here and the only picture we have seen of him is one with the king and queen, and he must have been only about twelve years old."

"He's about 20 years older, and do we ever have pictures!" the woman said. "He's been on the cover of every paper here for years and on the European circuit for as long as I can remember. When did you get here?"

"This summer."

"And you've never seen his picture?" the woman asked, startled.

"No."

"He's here at the lodge, you know," the man said.

"We heard," Megan said.

"I have one on my other camera, him and Nicole, ah yes, here it is," he said digging into his bag. The woman's cell phone rang. "I have to go through a few of these. Yes, here it is," he said looking at the small screen.

"We've got to go," the woman said to the man, picking up her bag. "It seems Nicole is putting on a show in the lobby. The prince is there and that industrialist's kid is there too, looking for trouble."

"This will be a good one," the man said, jumping to his feet.

"Sorry," the woman said calling back to Megan and Ostride and running down the hall. "Look for him on the cover of *Deep Dish*."

"So they didn't leave," Ostride said, her face as red as her raspberry tart.

"No, they didn't," Megan said, watching Ostride stomp out of the bakery. "Where are you going?"

Ostride stood inside the bakery door as people began to gather and hurry toward the lobby.

"I'm going to have a talk with my fiancé," Ostride said. "Are you just going to sit there?"

"And where are you going to look?" Megan asked.

"Where there is Nicole, there is Babette and if my guess is right that's where we'll find Jacob."

"And Marcus," Megan said.

"They're like glue. If you find one, you'll find the other," Ostride said. The lobby was filled with people and cameras flashing at every man coming in or out of a set of doors beyond the hallway. Megan couldn't pass through and was shoved into the woman who had sat next to her at the bakery.

"I'm sorry," Megan said.

"Don't worry honey, you get used to it in this business," the reporter said. "Here she comes!"

The woman yelled up to the cameraman perched on the arm of a metal statue of a mountain climber. Flashes of light from the multitude of cameras dotted the room as Nicole came out of the hallway with a man beside her, partially hidden behind a marble column.

"It's the industrialist's son," the woman said. Megan and Ostride stood on a step and saw Marcus hand-in-hand with Nicole. Jacob and Phillip were behind them, beside Babette and Simone. The crowd roared and whistled at Nicole as she bared one shoulder for the cameras and snuggled up to Marcus.

"No, it's the prince!" the woman cried out. "Now you can say you have seen him," the woman said, turning around to tell Megan, but Megan was gone. She found herself face to face with a disgruntled maid carrying an arm full of towels. "Oops," she said to the maid and turned back to see Nicole kissing the prince.

"Get a picture!" she yelled to the cameraman scaling the statue. "Get a picture!"

CHAPTER 32

"What did you think you were doing?" Marcus demanded, closing the door to the mob of cameramen and reporters. Nicole slowly sat down on the settee.

"She knew exactly what she was doing," Phillip said. "You never intended to donate your property to the housing project, did you? You just wanted to get the press together so you could get one step closer to the altar."

Nicole slipped her red silk scarf through her fingers and curled a smile.

"If that was your plan, you're going to be sorely disappointed. The land will be released to Westwind or I will call my own press conference," Marcus said and walked toward the door.

"We're late," Jacob said, shedding Babette from his arm.

"Very," Phillip said, watching Nicole.

"Marcus, I didn't say you could leave," Nicole said, pouring herself a drink from a golden flask. Phillip froze in place as he watched Marcus stop at the doorway. Nicole turned to him, twirling the liquid in the crystal snifter she held in her hand, her long painted nails ticking against it as Marcus walked back to her. She cocked her head and with a delicious sensation of victory she wet her lips as her dark eyes gazed into his. Marcus put his hand over the top of her glass.

"No one," Marcus whispered evenly, "no one in this kingdom dictates to me when to stay or go." He wrenched the snifter from her hand and threw it into the fireplace, shattering it into pieces. "Vacate this property. I will not ask again."

"Don't say anything you might regret," Nicole said.

"Regret? Marcus said, "I am ashamed I was deceived so easily by what I thought was a gesture of nobility." Nicole's eyes narrowed. Babette winced at Marcus's words.

"You came willingly and you'll come again," Nicole said, and turned her back to him to pour herself another drink.

Marcus put his lips to her ear. "Why, Countess, would I come for something I can take, or for that which is so eagerly given?"

Nicole turned around, her eyes dark and filled with hate.

"I will never come to you again," Marcus said and left the room. Jacob followed him but Phillip lagged behind. Simone was cowering in the corner and Babette had run to Nicole's side pursing her plump, red lips. Nicole picked up a glass. "He will come back to me. He will beg to come back to me," Nicole said.

"Be careful, Nicole," Phillip warned. "Whatever you have conjured up in that little mind of yours will not succeed. Your traps are obvious and your beauty has faded with your true intention." Nicole threw her glass at Phillip, but missed him and hit the door.

"You missed your mark again," Phillip said, and kicked the broken bottom of the glass into the fireplace. "Good evening, Countess."

* * *

"This is getting out of hand," Jacob said. "Marcus, you have to tell Megan who you are. With this housing project and Nicole and the press, she's bound to find out, and then what?"

"I know, I know," Marcus said, pacing the small conference room of The Pub. "Why aren't they here?"

"Considering we are a half an hour late from the last time we called, it doesn't surprise me. They probably went home," Phillip said.

"I told Ostride we might be later. She wouldn't leave without telling me," Jacob said.

"It's hot in here, Phillip, open that window," Marcus said. Phillip cranked out the stained glass window and heard voices below.

"Can you believe those two girls? They didn't even know who the prince was."

Phillip grabbed Marcus by the arm and pulled him over to the window, putting a finger to his lips. Jacob stood by the edge of the window trying to listen above the noise of the fan above him. He found the thermostat and flipped the switch to shut off the heat.

"They're travelers, college students, my bet, probably skipping from country to country. They both had an American accent."

"Still, you would think they would have known. Do we really have to do a night shoot on a night like this? I'm freezing."

"The office said they wanted night shots," the photographer said. Marcus, Phillip and Jacob heard a series of clicks and could see the flashes from the camera below. "I wish I had those girls here now. They would add to the picture."

"The blonde?" the woman asked.

"She is stunning, very chic, and the other one, I've never seen eyes like that before. Move the light over to the right."

"Here?"

"That's fine."

"Well, we gave them an education anyway. They know who the prince is now," the woman said. Marcus slid to the floor underneath the window and pulled back his hair.

"Why is that?" the cameraman asked.

"They followed us to the lobby," the woman said. "Is this far enough to the right?"

"Good, good," the man said. "So, they saw the prince."

"Sure, we all did."

"One more, tip the light down a bit."

"I guess I can't say for sure that they saw him," the woman said. Marcus put his ear to the window. "When Nicole came out, I thought she was dragging that industrialist's kid behind her, but when I saw Gustavson and Phillip with Babette and that other girl, I knew it had to be the prince. When I turned around, those girls had already gone."

Jacob pounded the pub's wall shaking the window.

"They're probably on their way to Zurich by now and not giving it another thought. I know I wouldn't," the photographer said, bending to one knee to take a shot.

"Office or not, my feet are getting cold. We're done," the woman said.

"Hold it!" the man said, clicking the camera one last time. "That will do."

When Phillip heard them walk through the door below he closed the window.

"I knew this would happen," Jacob said, "I knew it!"

"They aren't late. They obviously left," Phillip said. Marcus and Jacob both headed for the door. "Where do you two think you're going? Thanks to Nikki, we have a hundred reporters outside that door. Do you want to drag them over to see Megan and Ostride?"

"He's right," Marcus said, halting.

"I'm not going to just sit here while Ostride thinks...I don't even want to know what she's thinking right now," Jacob said, frantically dialing Ostride's cell phone. Marcus called Payton's cabin but no one answered.

"They're not answering," Jacob said.

"Or they're not there," Phillip said.

"Ostride, call me. It's urgent," Jacob said and hung up. "Just her voice mail," he said. Marcus called the cabin again and let the phone ring.

"Megan, pick up the telephone."

CHAPTER 33

Megan gently closed her Bible and sat at her kitchen table pushing the scrambled eggs on her plate from one side to the other. The sun was rising over the mountaintops. The warm rays of light pierced through the picture window illuminating the tiny particles of dust as they danced a slumbered waltz in the air. She thought of her uncle's office back home and a faint smile passed her lips. With a quick glance at the clock, she raced to put her dishes in the sink, picked up her bag and coat and dashed out the door. The snow was heavier in the city, she thought. It clung to her boots as she hurried down the sidewalk to the bus stop. She could see the red bus turning the corner and began to run. Before she could stop Megan stepped on a sheet of ice. Reaching in all directions, Megan caught a branch of a small tree that broke off in her hand and she landed in a snow bank. She waved her mitten hand at the bus driver and he stopped where she sat in the pile of snow.

"You almost had an accident, Miss Buchanan," the driver said. "You have to be careful. The stone sidewalks are slippery this time of year." Megan brushed the snow from her coat and, without looking at the other passengers, she stepped onto the bus. "Thank you for stopping, Henry. I was late this morning," Megan said, handing him a token.

"I look for you in the morning," he said.

"Thank you, Henry," Megan said. She sat by a window, brushing the snow from her hat. As the bus rumbled on, she stared out the window, watching the buildings pass by and thinking up sad stories about every elderly woman she saw walking to the market and every stray dog sitting beside the road.

I'm not going to do this to myself, Megan thought. I'm not going to help myself to feel miserable. If Marc and I were not meant to be then there will be someone else, somewhere else. It's like David said, life will go on and so will I. Lord, you know the story of my life and I'm confident that you'll help me lead a purposeful and fulfilling life no matter what, she prayed. Who knows, maybe there is someone right around the corner, she thought, sitting straight in her seat.

The bus stopped in front of Brier Pharmaceuticals and Megan hopped off, quickly walking around the corner to the front door. The street and courtyard were empty and gray. Megan slid her security badge into the lock and the gate and glass door opened. A security guard looked up from his desk and nodded. She heard the sound of the fountain in the courtyard and the birds fluttering from tree to tree but she didn't look up. Instead she kept her head down, following the blue carpet to the laboratories.

"Good Morning, Megan," Mr. Payton said in a cheerful voice from the hallway. "Did you have a good time at the cabin?"

"Your cabin is indescribable. Ostride and I couldn't believe it," Megan said and dug to the bottom of her purse for his keys and a thank you note she had written for him. "I was going to stop by your office this afternoon."

"Have fun skiing?" he asked, walking with her to her lab. "You look better. There's more color in your face."

"Ostride and I were out skiing the first day and we used the hot tub the second," Megan laughed.

"Meet anybody interesting?" Mr. Payton inquired, trying to act inconspicuous by looking through the notes on top of Megan's desk.

"Yes," Megan said with enthusiasm, as she hung up her coat. Mr. Payton looked up excitedly. "I met up with a friend from home. Can you believe it? Here in the mountains of Dreiholm." Mr. Payton's anticipation waned.

"Who was that?"

"Dr. David Erickson."

"The stent man?" Payton asked, referring to an article he had read about the boy wonder.

"That's him."

"I'd like to meet him someday," Payton said, still thumbing through her notes. "Do you have your last report?"

Megan opened the safe behind her desk to retrieve a flash drive. "There you go," she said and handed it to him.

"I'll be out of your way in a minute," Payton said. "You know, I actually came down here to make a special delivery." Megan was wondering why he was holding a package of envelopes in his hand. "This one is for you," he said. He handed her a large creamy white envelope with a hand-painted spray of pine covering the front and a small golden pine cone printed on the back.

"I don't know how it happened," Payton said, disgusted with the situation. "Every year Annie and I hold a benefit for the hospital and every year it goes like clockwork. But yesterday I found out that some of the invitations weren't sent, to my own employees no less. So, today I'm personally inviting them. I hope you're able to come. This is what happens when Rose isn't in charge of things." Megan opened up the envelope and read the card.

"The eighth of December," she read aloud.

"I know it doesn't give you much time. For the life of me, I can't understand how this happened."

"It's at the royal palace," Megan said.

"Yes. The king is gracious enough to let us use one of the ballrooms and North Star hall for our benefits. Don't lose the invitation, you'll need it to get in. They're very particular about security at the palace." Megan set the invitation on her desk and put on her lab coat and safety glasses. "Should I tell Annie that you'll be coming?"

Megan wrinkled her nose and shook her head. "Probably not, she answered."

"Why?" he asked.

"I haven't a thing to wear," she said and laughed, but in reality she knew it was true.

"There are plenty of dress shops in town. I know that for a fact. My daughters have found every one of them," Payton mumbled.

"I don't have a date, and you can't pick up one of those at a convenience store," Megan replied, setting out her trays and pulling up a program on her computer.

"Oh, there must be some nice young man out there. Or, if you'd like, I could arrange a date for you," Payton said.

"No, no, no. No more blind dates for me," Megan said.

Mr. Payton wondered what else he could say to convince her to come.

"Chuck, you and Annie have been more than wonderful. You've

given me a job, you've invited me into your home and your family, you even let me and Ostride use your cabin. I can't thank you enough for everything," Megan said. "It's just that right now it's better if I focus on my work and not worry about parties, dresses, dreams, or men."

"Nonsense!" Payton said standing up. "The benefit is Saturday evening. You'll be on break from school, I'm sure you will be able to find a dress, and as for an escort," Payton waved his hand in the air. "Aren't you supposed to be a woman of the twenty-first century? I thought they didn't need a date!"

Megan smiled and opened a file. "I'll think about it," she said.

"You will, won't you?"

"Yes, I will."

* * *

Megan trudged up the stairway to her apartment and hesitated at the landing when she saw a pair of boots between the spindles of the staircase.

"I was wondering if you were ever coming home," Ostride called, hanging over the railing. Magazines blanketed the floor of the hallway and a stack of sticky fluorescent green bookmarks that she and Ostride used in their studies sat beside the door outside Megan's apartment.

"Hi. What are you doing here? And how did you get in?"

"Mr. Grutner," Ostride said. "Meg, guess what? I'm getting married again!" she said with that famous smile.

"You are?"

"Jacob came over and I decided I better let him in because the landlord was getting ticked that he was making so much noise outside. He explained that the whole thing was all part of that land deal and he brought the paperwork to prove it," Ostride said.

"Is that why Marc was hand-in-hand with Nicole?" Megan asked, opening the door.

"You were right about Nicole, she does have a thing for Marc but Jacob told me that it's all one-sided," Ostride said, following Megan into the apartment.

"Lucky him," Megan said and took off her coat. Ostride stood with a stack of bridal magazines in her arms and a fading smile. "I am glad for you and Jacob," Megan said. "I really didn't think he had any part of this in the first place. So, what's with all the magazines?"

"I want you to help me pick out a wedding dress and your bridesmaid dress," Ostride said.

Megan headed straight for the refrigerator. She opened the freezer and looked at the half eaten quart of ice cream. She glanced at Ostride spreading out the magazines on the small table and then opened the refrigerator. "What would you like? Leftover spaghetti or leftover chicken?" Megan asked, holding out two plastic containers.

"Spaghetti," Ostride said. Megan put the sauce in the microwave and put a pot on the stove to boil the noodles. "Meg, is this okay? I mean to talk about the wedding and all."

"Absolutely," Megan said. "This is supposed to be one of the happiest days of your life and I'm happy for you. Honestly. Have you told your parents yet?"

"Last night."

"Were they excited?"

"Excited? My mother wanted grandchildren three years ago. I don't think she would be this happy if I won the Nobel Peace Prize," Ostride said. "Go figure. I'll have two doctorates when I'm done here and she thinks getting married is my biggest accomplishment."

"But she's happy? And you're happy?"

"Very," Ostride said. "Meg, what do you think of this dress? I was thinking of a garden wedding." Megan looked at the picture of a strapless, full white gown with a train that looked like it went on for miles.

"Perfect!"

"I think so too," Ostride said, wearing a delightful grin as she loosely bit her bottom lip.

The magazines were full of elaborate gowns, hats, shoes, jewelry and anything else that Megan could possibly imagine for a memorable wedding, and somewhere in the middle of dinner she caught the spark of Ostride's excitement.

"How long does it take to get a dress?" Megan asked.

"It depends, but not long," Ostride said, "anything we pick out will be here by August, that's for sure. Why?"

Megan began to clear the table, taking Ostride's plate and putting it in the sink. "I was invited to a benefit but I don't know if I want to go. It's this week."

"The hospital benefit at the palace?" Ostride asked.

"Yes. How did you know?"

"I'm going, too!" Ostride said. "Jacob was invited and now I am too."

"Do you have a dress?"

"I bought a dress last year that is going to knock Jacob's socks off," Ostride laughed, pulling apart a crust of bread. "For a while there, I didn't think I was ever going to get a chance to wear it."

"I've wondered what the palace looks like inside. It looks so massive sitting up on that hill," Megan said.

"There's only one way to find out. Besides, if you don't go, who will Jacob and I have to talk to? I don't want to be stuck talking to another old Professor Grogens, like we did at that last University tea. I like my work as much as the next person but the last thing I want to do is spend the night exchanging theories. That's one of the many things I like about you," Ostride said, helping Megan with the dishes. "You know how to work and when you're done for the day you're done."

"With my luck, if I go to the benefit, Marc will be there with Nicole and there I'll be with no one."

"So don't go alone. Go with a friend. Take Phillip."

"Are you out of your mind? I'm avoiding that whole family, thank you very much."

"Oh pooh!" Ostride said. "If you don't go you'll regret it for the rest of your life. How many times are we going to get invited to a palace?" she said, dialing the telephone. "Jacob and I will be there so you'll have nothing to worry about."

"Who are you calling?" Megan asked, her hands deep in the soapy dishwater.

"Hi, Phillip," Ostride said.

"Did she get the invitation?" Phillip asked.

"Yes," Ostride said turning away from Megan who was waving her hands and silently screaming at her.

"Payton really did forget to invite some guests and Megan was one of them. It looks like we managed to get through phase one of this scheme," Phillip said on the other end of the line.

"Phillip," Ostride began, "Megan received an invitation to the Hospital Benefit Ball and I thought it would be a good idea if you would take her." Megan rolled her eyes back in disbelief.

"She won't go without a date?" Phillip laughed, "I hadn't thought about that."

"Good," Ostride said smiling and turning back to Megan who had buried her face in her hands. "You've got a date then for the ball."

"Now I just have to figure out what I'm going to do with the date I already have," Phillip said.

"I'm sure that won't be a problem. Goodbye, Phillip," she said and hung up the phone.

"Ostride!" Megan pleaded.

"You're all set," Ostride said, sitting back at the table. "Now, the fun part – looking for a dress for you."

CHAPTER 34

Marcus sat down in the doctors' lounge, rubbing his face and setting his stethoscope on the coffee table in front of him. The door of the lounge cracked open and the bright lights of the hallway streamed into the dimly lit room, making it difficult to see who was joining him.

"Good evening, Marcus," the familiar voice said from the doorway.

"Chuck, thank you for coming. I would have stopped by your office but a surprising number of our doctors are suddenly on maternity leave and we have found ourselves shorthanded."

"It's not an inconvenience. Besides, you sparked my curiosity on the telephone this morning," Payton said. "I talked to Phillip and he filled me in on your visit to the mountains."

"I have sent flowers and candy and notes and still Megan will not take my calls," Marcus sighed. Payton sat listening, flinging a speck of lint from his trousers. "At least we have the land for the first phase of Westwind."

"Was it worth the price?" Payton asked.

"What else could I do? We needed that land to get a road built to the proposed site and that site has the best chance of being approved by the Senate."

"Maybe," Payton acknowledged.

"Surprisingly, Nicole relented. But what other choice do we have?" Marcus asked.

Dr. Weisman then strolled into the lounge and poured himself a cup of coffee. He sat down next to Payton.

"There are some things we just don't seem to learn without God's help," Payton said. "Wouldn't you agree, Abe?"

"Most definitely," Dr. Weisman said.

"You have it in your head that if you don't do it, if you don't make it happen, it won't get done," Payton said.

"Is that how you started Brier, by some miracle it just came to be without your developing it or driving it forward?" Marcus asked.

"I'm not saying God doesn't expect us to work. What I am saying is that we cannot compromise ourselves, go against our Christian faith for a business deal, a political victory, or even goodwill."

"But I didn't," Marcus protested. "Nicole sent the deed to me with a note that she wanted Westwind to have the property as a donation to the cause."

"You pushed the envelope," Payton said. "And I don't know what it is but my guess is that pretty little thing has something up her sleeve."

"God is in control," Dr. Weisman said. "He has a plan for the world, for your housing development, and for you and me. With or without schemes, it's going to work out as God planned. Next time, ask God first."

"Ask Him the tough questions. There isn't one He hasn't heard from either one of us," Payton said, and Dr. Weisman laughed. "Now, what is it that you wanted to ask me?"

Marcus looked at Dr. Weisman and then at Payton.

"Is it about Megan?" Payton inquired.

"Who is Megan?" Dr. Weisman inquired.

"Megan Buchanan," Marcus said.

"The Scolengard recipient?" he asked.

"That's the one," Payton said.

"I was wondering if at the benefit you would be willing to announce my father and mother, and me, during the introductory ceremonies, and then wait until after the dinner for any further recognition. Phillip will be bringing her to the ball."

"Phillip is in love with this girl?" Dr. Weisman asked, puzzled.

"No, no," Marcus said, sheepishly.

"You haven't told her yet?" Payton asked.

"She won't return my calls."

"You are interested in this girl?" Dr. Weisman asked, surprised.

"Yes." Marcus wrung his hands.

"Then why is Phillip taking her to the ball?"

"Because she won't go with me."

"She loves Phillip?" Dr. Weisman asked.

"You have to get up to speed on this, Abe," Payton said. "Megan

PLANS · VICTORIA J.M. HOFFBECK

is from the United States. She came here and met Marcus on a date. She didn't, and still doesn't know that he's the Prince of Dreiholm, and Marcus hasn't volunteered the information as of yet, even after getting good advice to do so. The problem is, he has gotten himself into a few messes by not telling her the truth and now if he wants to salvage any kind of relationship with her, he has to tell her before it is too late."

"Is this true?" Dr. Weisman asked. Marcus nodded his head. "And you thought my classes were difficult. Ha! When she finds out that you have been lying to her all this time you will be fortunate if the only thing you lose is your pride."

"I'll make the arrangements, but I don't want this to go on much longer. I've been talking to Joseph and he wants to know if Megan has been getting out and meeting anybody. He's worried about her and I won't lie to him."

"Megan hasn't mentioned me to her family?" Marcus asked, shocked.

"Yes, she said she has been seeing a Dreiholmian doctor off and on, but not a prince."

"She'll know on Saturday night," Marcus said, looking down at the carpet.

The two men said their goodbyes to Marcus and walked out talking to each other about the next symphony performance. Alone in the lounge, Marcus stared at the coffee table where a soft beam of light shone on the metal pieces of his stethoscope, making it look like polished silver.

"This is a lie, isn't it Lord?" He reached for his telephone and dialed Megan's telephone number again.

* * *

"I can't understand why Megan wouldn't answer my telephone calls. I know she was there. She just wouldn't answer. I hate bow ties," Marcus said petulantly, pulling at the white satin ribbon.

"Don't worry, she'll be there. She has been angry but I think she is warming up to you again. Ostride told me she hasn't called you a derogatory name for days now. That's progress."

"Progress," Marcus grumbled. "Why do I keep trying? There are other women out there."

Jacob shook his head and rolled his eyes at Broderick.

"Do you need help, Sir?" Broderick asked.

"No!" Marcus snapped. "No, thank you, Broderick. I'll get it, it just isn't cooperating," Marcus said, untying and starting over again.

"Part of the reason you haven't been able to get Megan is because she and Ostride have been inseparable after work making wedding arrangements. Can you believe that Ostride wanted me to wear a pink cummerbund! By the way, thank you, Broderick for talking them out of that."

"You talked to Megan?" Marcus asked Broderick, letting his tie unfurl as he stood in front of the mirror.

"Cook asked me to send over a box of her confections to Miss Buchanan's home and I agreed to stop by on my day off. When I was there, the two young ladies were trying to match the groomsmen's ensemble to the bridesmaid's gown."

"How come everyone else is able to talk to Megan and I'm not?"

"We all had tea, Sir, it was quite pleasant. I enjoyed the company of Miss Megan and Miss Ostride very much."

"I can hardly wait until this whole charade is over," Jacob said, putting on his jacket. "Then I can tell Ostride that we will be married in the palace gardens and in our country's colors and I will never in my life wear pink."

"Just remember, I have to be the one to tell Megan," Marcus said.

"Phillip and I will do the best we can, but try to tell her as soon as possible. I don't know how long we will be able to divert the obstacles at the ball."

"All I need is fifteen minutes alone with her," Marcus said, as Broderick helped him on with his jacket.

"You may only have five," Jacob said. "Phillip, are you ready!"

"Yes, yes, I'm ready," Phillip said walking down the hall to Marcus' study.

"Why aren't you already gone?" Jacob asked.

"Because I have to be late, remember?" Phillip said. "We have to arrive after all the guests have been announced."

"You're right, you're right, my mistake," Jacob said nervously, as they all went down the stairway.

"I must say, gentlemen, you all look smashing tonight," Broderick said, holding their topcoats over his arm. "I wish you all good luck."

"Say a prayer!" Marcus said. "We'll need it." I'll need it, he thought.

"I will," Broderick said. "Sir, I took the liberty of calling for three limousines from the motor pool." He opened the door and the shining black stretch vehicles were waiting in the driveway. Marcus hesitated at the door.

"All will be well, Marcus. Relax," Phillip said, and put his hand on his cousin's shoulder.

"I just wanted to thank you," Marcus said.

"We know," Jacob said.

CHAPTER 35

Megan put the finishing touches to her hair and gazed at the woman in the mirror. "You're going to have a wonderful time," she told herself aloud and then turned away. She looked at the dress hanging in the doorway. Who knows, maybe Annie is right, she thought. Maybe all I need is a change of scenery. A party at a palace is certainly a change for me. But no matter what, Lord, I pray that I won't become angry or jealous or act like an idiot if I see him there with her. I just want to have a good time. Megan gently stepped into the dress and twisted her arms to fasten it in the back. "Shoes, purse, wrap, and all I need now is Phillip."

She checked the clock on the wall and then on her nightstand and caught sight of her nails. "My nails! How could I have forgotten to finish my nails?" She hurried to her dresser and quickly painted them and walked around the apartment waving her hands as they dried. The buzzer sounded and she sped to the door, pushing the lock and opening the door with her elbow. She heard Phillip running up the stairway and opening the jarred door as she put away the bottle of nail polish.

Without noticing Megan, Phillip brushed off the snow from his coat. "Megan, I'm sorry I'm late,..." he began, but when he finally looked at her, his voice dropped, trailing off to a hush. "The traffic was bad and it is starting to snow again. Megan, you look beautiful."

Megan smiled and turned around, unfurling the many layers of her dress. Her dark eyelashes fanned against her fair skin and her bare shoulders hinted of stardust.

"You look very handsome yourself," she said, coming closer to him. She evened his silk scarf that was hanging underneath the lapel of his topcoat. "Very romantic," she said rolling her r's with a Latin flair. Phillip felt his face getting warm.

"We'd better get going, we're already late," he said.

"I just have to get my bag," Megan said. Phillip watched her as she appeared to glide to the table. She turned, feeling his eyes on her. "Phillip, what's the matter? Is something wrong?" Megan asked, twisting around trying to see every angle of her dress. "Be honest with me. I don't want to make a fool of myself." The deep blue dress wrapped so tightly to her small waist that Phillip was certain he could encircle it with one hand. From her waist the dress was a profusion of rippling, flowing and beguiling darkness, illuminated by a petticoat dotted with glittering rhinestones that flashed when she moved. Megan held out her glittering handbag.

"Phillip, is this appropriate? I've never been to a ball before," she asked.

"Meg, truly you have captured the winter sky on the canvas of your gown. You are very appropriate," he said, taking her wrap and putting it around her shoulders. Breathtaking, he thought as he carefully fastened the cape at her neck and looked into her eyes. "Megan, I was wrong about you. I acted poorly. These past few days we have been together I've wanted to tell you. I don't know why I haven't. Can you forgive me?"

"If you'll forgive me," she said.

"For what?" Phillip asked. "You haven't been anything but kind to me, even when I was unkind to you."

"I may have been cordial to you but my thoughts weren't exactly warm and fuzzy," Megan said, tapping his chest. "You can sure test a soul but I know a good heart when I see one."

"Forgiven then?" he asked.

"Of course."

"And no matter what, we'll be friends for life?"

"What could happen?" Megan asked.

"Friends?" Phillip insisted.

"Always."

"Come on then," he said, taking her hand. His mischievous grin returned as he opened the door. "We'll have a ball tonight."

* * *

"Phillip, look at that!" Megan exclaimed. Her eyes were like a child's, wide and full of wonder and excitement, Phillip thought, as she pointed to the ice sculptures on the palace grounds. A life size crystal carriage and frozen snow white horses waited at the bottom of the steps of the palace as imaginary guests, elegantly dressed as eighteenth century ladies and gentlemen. Some ice figures exited from a frozen cabbie while others appeared to be walking up the palace stairway in their carved ice hats and capes. When they reached the top of the stairs she looked back to the gardens around them. Every tree glittered with white lights and the black streetlamp poles were wrapped with pine garlands and red bows. Small feather-like snowflakes drifted in the dark blue night and rested delicately on her evening wrap while others caressed her dark eyelashes.

"Close your eyes," Phillip said and he touched the lace of snow. "We'd better get in or you're going to catch a cold."

She looked up and saw the huge columns at the palace entrance, an iron fixture burning bright, and massive arched windows.

"It's so big. I have only seen it from a distance. It's absolutely breathtaking."

Phillip doubted if Marcus knew how much he was missing out on, not having shown Megan his home for the first time. Megan opened her handbag and handed Phillip her invitation to the ball.

"Here," she said handing it to him. "I think you'll need this at the door." Phillip smiled and took the card from her.

"There is much more to see," he said, taking her arm. He paused when he saw the guards posted at the door. Even though Marcus had warned the staff and guards of their ruse to hide their identity, he still wasn't certain that they would disregard what had become habitual protocol.

"Megan, do you see that statue over there?" Phillip asked, pointing to the courtyard. Megan looked to the lit park, as Phillip guided her to the door. The guard took the invitation and nodded a bow as he opened the door for the guests. "It was a gift from the French, like many of the paintings you'll see in the main corridor. The collection of art in the palace has been recognized as one of the best private collections in the world," Phillip said, taking Megan's wrap and his coat and handing them to the servant waiting for him inside the door.

Megan followed the few others to the foyer, looking at the enormous portraits on the wall. Phillip caught up with her and quickly directed her to the ballroom, being sure to avoid familiar faces.

"You have been here before?" Megan asked, puzzled at his familiarity.

"Look, there's Jacob and Ostride!" Phillip said, looking across the room. Megan was relieved to see her friends and took Phillip's arm as they made their way to them, navigating through the people congregating on the outer edges of the room. The orchestra began playing a waltz, and pairs of dazzlingly dressed couples responded to the invitation to dance. The vibrant colors of the ladies' dresses reflected off the gold walls making the room a holiday bouquet of beauty.

"I feel completely out of place, but I'm glad I came," she whispered to Phillip, as she gazed around the room.

"No, Megan, you fit perfectly," Phillip said.

"You made it," Jacob said, with a smile.

"Better late than never," Phillip quipped, winking at Megan at his attempt at an American cliché.

"Isn't this fantastic!" Megan exclaimed, watching the dancers on the ballroom floor.

"It's incredible. I only wish we could have made it here on time," Ostride said. "The driver got lost. Can you believe that? On the way to the palace, he got lost." Jacob looked at Phillip from the corner of his eye. "We missed the first few minutes of the program, but we made it just in time to hear the children's choir. They were adorable. I told Jacob I wanted a dozen just like them," Ostride teased.

"We've been compromising ever since," Jacob said.

"I don't know, Jacob, Ostride has a way of getting what she wants," Megan quipped.

"She forgets that I have been in the delivery room. She might have second thoughts after the first one."

"We'll see," Ostride said. "Phillip, why are you wearing that sash? What does it mean?"

Phillip looked down at the royal blue and gold sash across his chest. "Boy Scouts." He looked around the room. "Marcus, where are you?" he muttered under his breath.

"I'll tell you later darling," Jacob whispered in Ostride's ear as he kissed her. Megan was watching a woman dressed in a bright pink satin gown waltz in the arms of a tall and very attractive man. The woman glittered with diamonds and sparkling pink tourmaline. Large pear-shaped drops hung from her necklace and from the small tiara that she had tucked into her mound of black hair.

"Isn't she beautiful?" she said to Phillip. Phillip gave the woman a glance.

"With the English Ambassador? Married," Phillip said, fussing with his jacket.

"You'd better hurry up Phillip, all the good ones will be gone," Ostride said.

"I'm not worried," Phillip said, "and I'm in no hurry. Aren't I talking to the most beautiful women in the room?"

"Charm, charm, charm, charm, charm," Megan said lyrically, watching the dancers glide across the ballroom floor. "You'll go far with your flattery with the willing ones."

"And there are so many willing ones," Phillip said, slipping his arm under hers as she watched the dancers.

"Megan," a voice from behind her called. Without turning to see who it was she knew it was Marcus. She could feel him behind her and she could feel her heart pounding and a welling inside her throat promising to cut off her voice if she didn't speak. In a tone she hoped sounded confident and indifferent she turned around to greet him.

"Marcus, I wasn't sure if you were going to be here tonight," she said with dry politeness. He was more handsome than she had imagined he would be, flawlessly dressed with a blue and gold sash like Phillip's across his chest, and his rich, warm sun-touched skin and golden hair. She forced herself to look to the other guests. She saw Chuck and Annie across the room and smiled at them. Chuck lifted his glass and Annie waved at her, smiling back and watching with a curious glint of anticipation.

"A dance?" Marcus asked, extending his hand.

"Why is it that whenever you ask a question it always sounds like an order?" Megan snipped.

"Please, my lady, may I have this dance?" Marcus said, sarcastically. Megan's eyes squinted to a narrow line of black.

"I am sure I owe the first dance to Phillip," Megan said sweetly.

"He won't mind," Marcus said.

Megan looked to Phillip for support.

"He's bigger than I am, Meg," Phillip said, picking up a drink from a tray offered to him by a wandering waiter.

"I wouldn't want to keep you from your date, she said to Marcus."

"I came alone," Marcus said and pulled her by the waist to the dance floor. Megan looked back at her friends who were all raising their glasses in a toast, with smirks on their faces.

"What is going on here? Is this some kind of conspiracy?" Megan asked. Marcus swept her across the room to a quiet corner away from the other dancers and guests.

"It was the only way I could talk to you. I've tried calling you every hour of the day. I have sent notes, flowers, chocolates. I would have sat outside your door if I wasn't certain you would let me freeze."

"And what do you expect?" she said in a hushed scream.

"To freeze," Marcus said, exasperated. The fire in her eyes had subsided and Marcus detected a hint of a smile. "Megan, it is not what it seems. Nicole was a business deal, an arrangement to purchase some land."

"So I've been told," Megan said. "I knew it had to be something other than what it appeared to be, or otherwise you would have to be the most ignorant man I ever met. Who would ask a woman to dinner and then have another tryst going on in the same hotel, and bring the press to cover it?"

"Then why haven't you answered my calls?"

"Because I wasn't sure if you weren't the most ignorant man I've ever met."

"Megan, it was a business arrangement, I swear to you."

"I don't know if I like your business," Megan said, flashing a smile at a passing dancer when she realized they had stopped dancing and were standing on the edge of the ballroom floor. She looked into Marcus' agonized face and rumpled brow.

"I'm learning, Megan," he said, holding her hand close to his chest. "Be patient and forgive me again," he whispered.

"It's simple," Megan said. "Tell me the truth, good or bad. I can cope with the truth, but not lies. All the guessing and wondering about your intentions and these business dealings of yours will drive us apart, permanently," Megan said flatly. She felt uneasy as she noticed that the other guests were whispering and watching them as they talked in the corner of the room. "Why is everyone staring at us?"

"There is something I have to tell you," Marcus said, desperately looking around the room for an escape.

"What is it?" Megan asked. "Just tell me."

"I want to be alone with you when I tell you," Marcus said. A palace servant approached Marcus from behind and tapped him on the shoulder.

"Excuse me, Sir," the servant interrupted, "but the ambassador from England wishes to be introduced to yourself and the lady."

"He will have to wait," Marcus snapped. The servant bowed, turned dutifully and walked away.

"Marc?" Megan asked in surprise.

"I just need two minutes alone with you but I see now it will have to wait," Marcus said angrily.

Even though he was standing beside her, Megan could feel every muscle in his body tighten and his posture elevate until he seemed to grow inches in every direction. Chuck and Annie were approaching them along with the tall, attractive man whose tuxedo jacket was decorated with medals and ribbons. Chuck tried to distract the Ambassador by introducing him to other guests but he was not dissuaded and proceeded directly to his destination. Chuck shrugged his shoulders as he looked at Marcus from behind the Ambassador, acknowledging his failed attempt to head him off before he reached the couple.

CHAPTER 36

"Megan, you look lovely," Annie said, reaching the couple first. "I'm so glad you decided to come."

"It would have been a great loss for us all if you hadn't," the Ambassador said, kissing her hand and bowing deeply to Marcus.

"Megan, this is Sir Westin Langley," Payton said, and took a drink from his glass.

"How do you do, Miss Buchanan?"

"I hope you are finding our small country interesting and hospitable," Marcus said, positioning himself slightly in front of Megan.

"Yes, I've already found it to be very interesting," Westin said, keeping his eyes on Megan. "I understand you're an American, Miss Buchanan."

"Yes, I am," Megan replied.

"I am infatuated with the United States, the western folklore, Chicago pizza, and Dixieland jazz."

"And baseball," Megan added, "you can't forget baseball."

"No, by all means, I cannot forget baseball," the Ambassador said, tracing each smooth curve of her body with his eyes. "I would..." the Ambassador began reaching for Megan.

"I'm sure you would," Marcus said, taking Megan by the waist again. "If you will excuse us..." he said and whisked Megan to the dance floor.

"What's wrong with you?" Megan asked as they danced in the middle of the crowded room. "The Ambassador was just trying to make conversation."

He looked around the room again for an escape and found one at an unguarded passageway.

"We have to talk," Marcus insisted, leading her across the floor to the hidden door.

"What is it that you have to tell me?" she started to ask when Marcus felt a tap on his shoulder.

"Excuse me, may I cut in?" The English accent put a frown on Marcus' face. For a long moment Marcus ignored his question.

"If you are willing to risk scuffing your shoes, Mr. Langley, yes," Megan answered, trying to mask Marcus' foul mood.

"A small sacrifice to dance with a beautiful woman," the Ambassador said. He cut in front of Marcus and took Megan's hand. Before Marcus could protest, Jacob grabbed his arm.

"Let's get a glass of punch," Jacob said. Ostride led the way off the dance floor to where the Paytons were talking to Phillip.

"Where have you been, Phillip?" Ostride asked. A waiter offered her a glass of golden punch that matched the color of her gown and the ribbon that laced her hair. Phillip sipped from a long fluted glass filled with bubbling champagne, keeping his eyes on the dance floor.

"Since my date has been preoccupied,..." he began, turning his attention to his cousin. Marcus held his glass up to Phillip in thanks. "I have been pursuing other possibilities."

"Anyone interesting?" Ostride asked.

"I don't know if you would call them interesting," Phillip said, as he and Marcus both watched Megan and the Ambassador twirling on the dance floor. "Nicole and Michele Ferrer are here."

Jacob could see Marcus' jaw grind at the mention of their names.

"What are they doing here?" Marcus asked.

"I don't know," Payton said. "Annie, do you remember either of these women on the guest list?"

"I recall a Pierre C. Ferrer on the guest list. He gave so generously to the hospital after his heart surgery last year, remember?" she replied.

"That explains that. Pierre is Michele's father," Jacob said. "Who cares, let her come. The worst is over."

Marcus adjusted the cuff of his shirt, letting just the edge of his sleeve protrude from his jacket, avoiding looking directly at anyone. "No, it's not, I haven't told her yet," he said quietly.

"What do you mean?" Ostride said. "You were in the corner of the room and then on the dance floor."

"We were interrupted."

PLANS · VICTORIA J.M. HOFFBECK

"I'm sure she knows how you feel," Ostride said sympathetically as she set down her glass.

"If it were only that simple," Phillip moaned.

"What are you talking about?" Ostride asked impatiently. Jacob looked at Marcus, waiting to be released from his promise of silence.

"You have been more than patient," Marcus nodded to his friend.

"Ostride, I would like to introduce to you to the Prince of Dreiholm," Jacob said, gesturing to Marcus with a flip of his hand and slight bow. Ostride looked at Marcus, then at Phillip and finally the Paytons.

"And who are you?" Ostride asked Jacob, putting her hands on her hips. "A duke from Buldavia?"

"I'm afraid Jacob is telling the truth," Payton said to Ostride. "Marcus William John Holcombe is the Prince of Dreiholm, and Count Phillip Andrew Scott Holcombe is his cousin."

"Then who are you?" Ostride asked Jacob again.

"I am who I always claimed to be," Jacob said, taking hold of her hand, "a doctor whose father happens to be in the diplomatic service to the king. And I'm a good friend of Prince Marcus."

"For Pete's sake, Marcus, why didn't you tell us right from the start?" Ostride asked, in anger.

"To be honest, it's all becoming a blur exactly why, but right now I need your help. I need to get five minutes alone with Megan before anything else happens," Marcus pleaded.

"I'm afraid you're too late," Phillip said, looking over the crowd, "something else is just about to happen."

Marcus looked beyond one of the towering Christmas trees and saw Michele approaching him in a red velvet dress that was being held together by diamond chains at her waist and her breast.

"She looks hungry tonight," Phillip said into his drink.

"Good evening, Michele," Marcus said in a trained, even tone. "May I introduce Mr. and Mrs. Charles..."

"Dance with me," she rudely interrupted him with a husky voice. "I think one dance is not much to ask for after Poppa decided to make such a large donation again this year."

Marcus gritted his teeth and saw that Megan was still dancing with the Ambassador. Michele took her little finger and locked it onto his and brought him to the ballroom floor.

"That boy has a lot to learn," Payton said, as he watched Marcus being lured to the floor.

"What kind of people did you hang around with anyway? And I emphasize did," Ostride asked, turning to look at Jacob squarely in his dark eyes.

"The wrong kind," Jacob said uneasily.

"And here comes another example," Phillip said. "Nikki! I thought after our last encounter you would make it a point to miss this little get together tonight." She took the drink out of Phillip's hand and set it on a ledge.

"Why is that?" she asked, playfully stroking his face, "when there is so much work to be done, for the good of the people of course," she finished flippantly. "I think we have a dance."

"I am busy, Nicole," Phillip said reaching for his glass. She came closer to him and dragged her fingernail across his chin as she whispered in his ear. "You wouldn't want to cause a scene in front of all of these people, would you?" she asked, stepping back but still coiled around his arm.

"Oh look, Phillip, isn't that Lord Brighten, Camille's father? She was telling me about your trip to Morocco." Nicole winked at the white bearded Lord and blew him a kiss enticing him to come across the room. Phillip walked out on the dance floor and waited for Nicole to join him. Nicole started toward him and stumbled into Phillip's arms.

"Oh, excuse me," Ostride called to Nicole. "My heel, it must have caught on the hem of your dress." Nicole turned her head back at Ostride, flashing a searing glance.

"Are you okay, darling?" Jacob said casually, steadying Ostride.

"I'm fine, just fine," Ostride said. Chuck nonchalantly turned to the wall and Annie gulped down her punch, hoping she wouldn't laugh out loud.

"You were a bad boy bringing me all the way up to the mountains without providing me a prince like you had promised," Nicole said with indisputable venom. Phillip firmly gripped her hand as they waltzed around the room.

"The Prince summoned you to finalize a purchase and I promised you nothing. Any other aspiration of yours was your own," Phillip retorted. "I am sure it was your delicate manner and quiet modesty he found easy to resist," he said, looking down at her revealing attire. "Coming as Lady Godiva this evening?"

Nicole pulled her hand back but couldn't escape Phillip's grasp. "Uh, uh, uh Countess, remember your station. People are watching." As soon as Phillip felt the tension in her body subside, he released her hand. "The contest is over Nikki. It's time to retract your claws and look for new game."

"What are you talking about? Michele is no threat to me," she hissed.

"I didn't mention Michele, did I?" Phillip said. Nicole watched Marcus and Michele dancing. Michele was clinging to his chest but his eyes were elsewhere, to a woman dancing and laughing with the Ambassador from England.

"That common American," Nicole laughed. Phillip's eyes dimmed as he danced with the wily creature. "No matter. Tonight is his one last chance."

* * *

"Marcus, why haven't you called?" Michele asked, forcing weepy eyes and pouting red lips. "I have left messages and still nothing."

"I have been extremely busy with my work," Marcus said, trying to watch Megan while they danced.

"Your work! Why do you insist on playing doctor at that hospital when there are so many more interesting things for you to do with your time?" Michele pouted, pressing herself closer to him. "Soon you will rule Dreiholm. Why should you waste your time as a doctor."

"My father is a fit man. He has many years of service before he entrusts his responsibilities to me. Until then, being a doctor will be my contribution to my country."

"Leave the tedious monotony of daily tasks to those who have to pursue them," Michele said in a sly voice. She traced the back of his neck with her fingertips. "As for you and I, Marcus, let us enjoy life. Come back with me to France."

Her words, once sweet temptation, were now the foolish seductions of an idle woman, a woman who repulsed him. Marcus led her off the dance floor and bowed graciously. "There are other guests to attend to, Michele. I pray that you will have a safe trip back to France. Have a good evening."

CHAPTER 37

Marcus found Payton and Annie mingling with guests where he had left them. "Where is Megan?" he whispered in Annie's ear.

"She is still on the dance floor with Langley," Annie said as her husband finished a conversation with a colonel and his wife.

"I've been noticing that she has been trying to catch a glimpse of you on the dance floor. You better clear this up as soon as you can," Payton advised. The music stopped and Megan and her partner were the last to retreat from the floor. Marcus met Megan halfway.

"Westin, thank you for the dance, you're absolutely fascinating," Megan said. "Marc, did you know that Westin has raised a Siberian Tiger?" Marcus didn't answer as he walked Megan to Payton and Annie.

"Two actually," Westin said, walking behind them, "ferocious appetites."

"Megan, you're flushed," Marcus said, putting his hand against her cheek.

"I haven't danced in a long time," Megan said. Annie handed her a glass of punch. "You should be a bit tired yourself," Megan said to Marcus, glancing at Michele as she drank.

"Dinner should be in a minute or two," Chuck interrupted, "we all can take a break from the dance floor."

"I must be inspired by my dance partner. I am ready for another round," Westin said, cracking a faint smile.

"I love to dance and Chuck never does. If you don't mind I would love to have your next dance," Annie said to the Ambassador. Marcus smiled, knowing the Ambassador wouldn't refuse the hostess of the party.

"Certainly, Mrs. Payton," Westin said, taking a glass of champagne.

"Where did Ostride and Jacob run off to?" Megan asked and set her glass down.

"They're taking a walk around the palace. He's showing her the sights, paintings and all. Might not be a bad idea for the two of you," Payton suggested.

"Yes, we should," Marcus said. He looked about the crowd and saw Michele at the far corner at the entrance of the hall and Nicole at the other.

"I would like to see the paintings of the royal family. I feel rather guilty not knowing who or what the royal family looks like," Megan said. Westin looked up from his glass at Megan and then at Marcus, lifting one corner of his mouth, smiling secretly as he sipped his wine. The orchestra began to play a slow, sweet melody.

"Marcus, you promised me a dance and I have come to collect on your debt," Nicole said as she wrapped her arm around Marcus' waist.

"Please do, Marcus," Westin said informally and held out his hand to Megan. "I would be happy to keep you company, Miss Buchanan. I will be back momentarily, Mrs. Payton, for our dance."

"Isn't this my dance?" Phillip said, cutting in front of the Ambassador and pulling out an imaginary dance card reading it aloud. "Young, handsome, witty and charming. Yes, by all accounts that's me," Phillip said and lifted Megan to the dance floor laughing. Payton put his arm around his wife. "Annie, he said, "I have never been so happy to be happily married."

Phillip twirled Megan around to make her dress billow out in a full circle and then pulled her in to his side. "I'm surprised you're not looking over my shoulder to watch Marcus and Nikki," he said. Megan shrugged her shoulders and then looked at the couple behind Phillip. Marcus was stiff and silent.

"I know he would rather be with me," Megan said.

"You're so sure of that?" Phillip asked.

"I think so," Megan said. A wonderful childlike vulnerability and innocence radiated from her face, making her more beautiful and desirable than before.

"I think so, too," Phillip sighed, and held on to her a little more closely. The music stopped and Payton and Annie stood by the exit, encouraging guests to be seated for dinner.

"I'm going to visit the ladies room. I'll meet you by the door."

"I'll find Ostride and Jacob and meet you there," Phillip said.

"I'll only be a minute." Megan said as she followed the others out the door. Phillip checked the ballroom floor looking for Marcus and found him in the corner of the room with Nicole, partially hidden behind a curtain. He could see Marcus talking to her and then Nicole stomping off and disappearing out the doorway. Phillip smiled. "Good for you Marcus. Good for you."

Down a wide, red-carpeted corridor, Megan was distracted by the sculptures and paintings that hung on the walls. Portraits of men in military uniforms and women in ornate gowns with shimmering jewels posed with their children who were sitting on ponies and thrones of gold.

"Can I help you, Miss?" a guard asked in English.

"I was looking for the restrooms."

"You just passed them, around the corner and to your right."

"Thank you."

"My pleasure," the splendidly dressed guard said and returned to his post.

Megan found the rooms and pushed open the first door and stopped when she saw two women quarreling in the parlor. Michele and Nicole ended their bickering when they saw her and followed her as she sat in front of one of the gold-framed mirrors. She tried to ignore their whispered words and their taunting giggles and glares and busied herself by looking for her lipstick in her bag. When she looked up into the mirror, she saw Michele and Nicole staring back at her. "You are the one from the ski lodge, no?" Nicole asked.

"It's good of you to remember me, Nicole," Megan said, "and I believe Phillip mentioned to me that you are Michele Ferrer," she said, nodding to the other woman.

"She is nothing more than a peasant," Michele said. "He is having his fun with her, that is all. Look, she doesn't even have a pin to wear." Michele fanned one of her cascading diamond earrings that touched the bottom of her neck as she sat down next to Megan on a velvet cushion. "A gift from Marcus," she said playfully.

Nicole stood behind Megan twisting a lariat of diamonds around her finger. A large ruby teardrop necklace hung provocatively between her voluminous cleavage.

"A token of his gratitude," Nicole said.

"How generous of Marc," Megan said. She stood up to leave.

"The prince is always generous,..." Michele said, putting one of her long red fingernails to her mouth. "...How should I say, to those that please him." Nicole looked at the small ring Megan wore that her parents had given her.

"Obviously you do not," she said and then laughed out loud.

"The prince?" Megan repeated.

"Marcus, of course," Michele said dreamily. Megan felt the weight of deception fall to her feet and anchor her to the floor.

"You did not know!" Nicole said, and began laughing hysterically. Michele snorted and joined her, rattling on in French.

CHAPTER 38

The mysterious cars, servants, half spoken phrases, private rooms, and the sashes of blue and gold whirled through Megan's mind like pieces of a puzzle in a wild tornado that fell together in a clear, picture-perfect thud.

"Liar," Megan muttered, "how stupid could I have been?" She pushed past Nicole and the restroom doors. Mixed up and turned around, she began hurrying in the wrong direction down the hallway. She slowed when she felt her face getting hot and her heart racing wildly in her chest. Tears began to blur her vision. Oh no. I'm not going to cry over this, she thought, wiping away the wet streams. Oh Lord, help, she prayed and took a deep breath, inhaling and exhaling until the shock passed and the trembling subsided. She looked in both directions of the corridor and went in the opposite direction of the ballroom. There's got to be another way out of here, she thought, coming to another passageway.

Phillip was in on this, Megan thought, as the reel of events became pieced together. "And Jacob and Ostride," she said aloud, as she scurried down the passageway looking for an unobstructed exit. No, not Ostride, she wouldn't, Megan decided, shaking the handle of a locked door. We were just fools, duped for their fun and games. And Chuck and Annie, Megan paused thinking of them. What a fool I have been! I can't believe it. I'm supposed to be this intelligent mastermind, a whiz kid. I'm an idiot! Megan let out a squeal through clenched teeth as she rattled another locked door. The only way out was through the ballroom. She backtracked, hurrying through the decorated hall, smiling pleasantly at the few lingering guests waiting to be seated, while she focused on getting to the door leading out of the palace.

"Megan!" Marcus called out to her. Megan picked up the length of her dress and ran out of the ballroom.

"Could you please hurry?" she asked the young man at the coat check.

"Yes, Miss," the young man said, sprinting to the door with her wrap in hand.

"Thank you," she said as she grabbed it from him and ran down the stairway, missing steps as she fled.

Marcus caught her by her arm as she was stepping out of the palace. "Where are you going?"

"Home," Megan said, dragging Marcus outside and down the palace stairway. She stopped and Marcus slipped on an icy step, wobbling as he regained his balance. "Or didn't I say that correctly," Megan said, stomping her foot on the step and just missing Marcus' toe. "Let me try again. I am going home now, Your Highness!" she said sarcastically and wrenched her arm free from his grasp.

"Megan, wait! I've been trying to tell you all evening," Marcus called out as she ran down the steps.

"Save it for your collection of lies," Megan yelled back. The guards at the door came to Marcus' side and he waved them off as he ran to catch her.

"I was going to tell you but we haven't had a chance to be alone," Marcus said. The snow was falling in thick wet clumps, leaving pools of gray slush on the sidewalks.

"You've had a chance to tell me every day for months!" Megan said evenly, wiping the melted snow from her face. "Ever since we met, you...have...been...lying...to...me. Why should I believe anything you have to say?" she asked.

Marcus snapped his fingers and his limousine appeared. "I'm taking you home," he said.

"Ha!" Megan huffed and marched down the sidewalk to the gate, throwing her wrap over her head and neck. The muddied snow crept into her high-heeled shoes and soaked her feet with icy water. Marcus didn't wait for the driver to stop at the curb as he opened the limousine's door. He motioned to the driver to follow him and ran ahead to catch up to Megan.

"Megan, get in. I'm taking you home," Marcus said. When she didn't stop, he stepped ahead of her and picked her up off the sidewalk.

"Put me down!" she yelled, as she hung over his back, kicking her feet. Marcus stuffed her in to the car, pushing her dress aside and waving the driver on as he shut the door. A glittering hair comb that had held Megan's hair up was hanging from a twisted knot at her shoulder. She pulled at the silver car door handle and thrust herself against it only to find that the car doors had been locked.

"In my country we have a law against kidnapping!"

Marcus looked out the window. They had passed the palace gates and turned onto the thoroughfare outside the palace grounds. "And in this country, I am the law," Marcus said coldly.

"Our destination, Your Highness?" the driver asked.

Marcus pushed down on the intercom. "To the townhouse."

Megan flung herself across him and pressed down the button. "To 145 Seventh Street. Pronto!" Megan shouted. The driver continued toward the townhouse.

"To Seventh Street," Marcus said, pushing down on the button again. The driver turned the car around and Marcus plucked the comb from Megan's hair. She felt the warmth of his hand on her bare shoulder and she retracted back to her seat. "There is no reason to be frightened, I wouldn't...."

"Frightened! You big baboon!" she said, hitting him on the shoulder with her handbag. "Don't you even imply that I should be frightened! Don't you even think of it!"

"Megan...."

"Don't start! I don't want to hear any more," she said, taking her hair comb from Marcus' hand and twisting her hair up into a knot on top of her head. She drummed her fingernails on the leather armrest and stared out the window, watching the streetlights race by.

"You're acting like a child," Marcus said.

"Oh, really! Let's talk about who's acting. What role are you playing tonight? Marcus Holcombe the wealthy medical student, the rich industrialist's son, or Prince Charming?" Megan raged. Marcus turned away from her. "Tell me something, were you just bored or did you want to see what it was like on the other side of the tracks?"

Marcus turned to her with eyes as dark as ink. "Enough, Megan," he said, as the limousine came to a stop.

"You're right. I have had enough," Megan said, with tears in her eyes. As soon as she heard the doors unlock, she bolted out of the car and up to the apartment building door. She fumbled with her keys until they fell to the ground at her feet. Marcus had followed. He scooped up the keys and opened the door. She wiped away a tear and reached for her keys in his hand. He held onto them and to her.

"How could you do this to me?" she asked. "How could you lie to me?"

Marcus started to speak and then his voice failed. Megan took her keys and ran up the stairs to her apartment.

"We must talk," he said as he closed the front door and sprinted up the stairs after her.

"Is that a request or another order?" Megan asked, looking down at him from the landing.

"Why are you being so difficult?"

"Me?" Megan barked, "when did this become about me! You're the one who lied! And those, those cats!"

An elderly neighbor that Megan had met only once before opened her door and looked at the arguing couple. Seeing the prince, the old woman gasped and closed the door.

"I'm not going to have this conversation with you in the hallway," Marcus said. Megan marched up the last flight of stairs, opened the door, kicked off her wet shoes and threw her wrap over a kitchen chair. The streetlight outside her window lit the room with long, drawn shadows rippling across the floor. Megan waited in front of the bright window with her arms crossed.

"You have five minutes."

"Now that you know who I am, I would think you would give me a bit more deference."

"I am. I'm giving you five minutes, that's more than I would give any other person."

"Humor," Marcus said, "I didn't think you would be in the mood."

"I'm not. You think respect comes with a title or what family you happen to be born into?"

"In some times and in some places, yes."

"Fear is not respect," Megan said, "and you're wasting your time. What did you want to say? Do you have a final play in your little game?"

"This was not a game!" Marcus shouted. He turned away from her and held on to the back of a chair. He looked down at the small kitchen table and remembered the nights they ate together, laughing and working beside each other.

"The first night, I admit, when I realized that neither you nor Ostride knew who I was, selfish as it may have been, I took advantage of an opportunity. I wanted to find out if someone could love me for who I am and not what I am," Marcus said, turning to her and pounding the sash across his chest. "Is that so wrong?"

"I'm sure you were disappointed," Megan said. She turned to look out the window and thought of their first date.

"Ah!" he growled, clenching his fists. "You're infuriating! You don't understand what it is like."

"Oh really, I don't? You mean to have somebody want you because they want something from you and not because they love you?" Megan asked. She could see him clearly in the darkness looking back at her. "I have a pretty good idea," she said. "You're not the first man who has tried to seduce me, nor the last." A still silence rang out in the room. Megan rubbed her bare shoulder. She could hear the crinoline of her skirt rustle and saw the flash of light from the shimmering rhinestones below. When she looked up, Marcus was in front of her, searching her eyes.

"I'm so sorry," Marcus said, holding on to her waist. "I'm sorry," he said again. "I was trapped in my own lie, wondering how I was going to tell you the truth without losing you." He inched closer to her and as he did Megan could feel herself becoming a captive to the relentless passion they shared. He kissed her and her body heightened to his every touch and ached to surrender to the ecstasy within her grasp. When he released her, she looked down, feeling her heart beating within. He stepped back and pulled a long thin velvet box from his breast pocket.

"After I told you the truth tonight, I was going to give you this," he said and placed the gift into her hand. She opened it and inside she found a gold bracelet embellished with diamonds. The images of Michele's glittering earrings and Nicole's necklace mingled with the beautiful diamond bracelet, and tears flooded her eyes. She opened up Marcus' hand and placed the closed box into it.

"Please leave, Your Highness," Megan said. She turned to face the window and watched the snowfall from the light of the street lamp and then looked at the limousine still parked in front of her door. "He's waiting," she said stiffly.

"Megan, what's wrong? Say something. I'm sorry. I'm sorry I lied to you."

Megan walked past him and stood by the kitchen counter. "Do you know how I found out tonight?" she asked quietly.

"Michele or Nicole," Marcus guessed.

"The conversation was enlightening," Megan said. "Michele showed me her earrings and Nicole her necklace. They told me they were gifts for pleasing you," Megan said bitterly. "What have I done to please you, Marcus? Or is that supposed to come after the gift?" Marcus threw the velvet box from his hand across the floor. Megan stiffened as she watched it ricochet off the baseboard, breaking the box open and sending the string of diamonds spinning into a small crumpled pile in the corner of the wood floor.

"I'm just like the others to you, and I won't stand for it," Megan said, taking off her long evening gloves and making them snap against her dress. "Nicole got the necklace, Michele the earrings, and I get the bracelet. What I want to know is who gets the ring?"

Marcus stood silently in the shadows.

"All right, I've got my answer and you've got yours: I fell in love with you. Now leave," she commanded, ready to burst into tears. "Your five minutes is up and your little experiment is over."

CHAPTER 39

Megan rinsed her face and let the cold water linger on her tear-swollen eyes. Her face stung. She reached for her lotion and knocked over the bottle of shampoo. Before she could catch it the contents had left a slippery puddle on her bathroom floor. She wiped it up and wrapped herself into a thick fleece robe and curled up on the couch. It was painfully quiet. She looked at her dress and wondered if Phillip knew she had gone, and if he, Jacob and Ostride had waited long for her at the dining room door. She shook her head as she thought of Annie and Chuck and questioned their reason for keeping Marcus' secret.

What do I do now Lord? Megan prayed. I can't trust him. She closed her eyes and listened to the music that ran through her mind, a gentle, soothing dream like a lullaby that drifted over her and beckoned her to sleep. "Lord, you first," Megan whispered. "You decide what happens next. The trouble is, somewhere along the way I fell in love with him," she said before she fell asleep.

The door buzzer rang and Megan jumped, jolting her raw nerves. She looked at the clock and ran to the window and looked outside. The street was empty. "Hello?" Megan asked as she pressed the intercom button.

"Miss Buchanan. Megan. It's Westin Langley."

"Westin?"

"I saw you leaving in a hurry and I wanted to make sure that you were all right. I saw Prince Marcus run after you and...."

Megan tripped the security door and waited for Westin at the top of the stairway. In footsteps that were barely audible, Westin leapt up the stairs, barely stopping at the landing. He looked up at Megan in her thick white robe and bare feet. She had a pink ribbon holding back her dark hair and he knew he had been right, she was the most beautiful woman he had met at the ball.

"Westin, what are you doing here? You should be at the benefit. And how did you know where I live?" Megan said.

"My conscience wouldn't let me have a moment's peace after I saw you run away," he said. "Are you well?"

Megan wondered if her eyes were still swollen and went back into the apartment. "I'm fine," she answered.

"As for knowing where you live, you're listed online," he said, following Megan into her apartment. Megan went to the kitchen and opened the refrigerator. Westin scanned the room and noticed her dress in a heap on the bed, her wet shoes strewn across the floor, a broken box and a small strand of diamonds lying in the corner of the otherwise meticulous apartment.

"Megan, are you all right?" Westin asked.

"I'm fine," she said, following his line of sight to the bracelet on the floor. She went to it, picked it up and put it into its box.

"It's exquisite," Westin said, looking at it as she put it away.

"Yes, well it's going back," she said, dropping it on the table by the front door before she returned to the kitchen.

"You look like you're ready for bed. I'll leave," he said.

"You're welcome to stay if you like." Megan got out a small pan. "I need hot chocolate. Would you like some?"

"No, thank you," Westin said, putting his coat aside and closing the apartment door.

"Have a seat," Megan said, "how about some tea, then?"

"Yes, it is cold out," Westin said rubbing his hands together and sitting down in the rocking chair by the fireplace. He watched her pour the milk into a pan and then pour water into the teapot. "I have a confession to make," he began.

"This would be the night for it," Megan said dryly, getting out two cups.

"When I saw you and the prince leave, I followed you."

"Why?"

"When I saw him pick you up and throw you in the car, I thought it might be a good idea,"

"Baboon," Megan muttered, stirring the tea. "Sugar?"

"No, thank you," Westin said.

"Have you been waiting outside all this time?" Megan asked, handing him the cup and setting hers down on the table.

"After I saw that you let him in, I thought it would be best to wait a minute or two."

"It's been over an hour and a half since he left."

"I didn't know if I should intrude or not," Westin said. "And, here I am." He watched as Megan opened a large trunk and pulled out a pair of fluffy red socks. "It seems as if the benefit ball exceeded its expectations."

"It did? I suppose it helped to have the prince there," Megan said. She huddled back on the couch with her knees to her chest, putting on her socks. "I'm sorry it's so cold in here. The heat kicks down after ten o'clock."

"I'm perfectly fine," Westin said, rocking back on the chair. "I have a feeling that the cat got out of the bag tonight."

"Was I the only person in the room who didn't know that Marcus was the prince?" Megan asked, covering her face.

"It's my business to know. I am sure there were one or two others who didn't have any idea. If it isn't prying, how did you find out?"

"Two of his friends informed me," Megan said, staring at her feet, holding her cup of hot chocolate.

"Oh," Westin nodded wisely. "Nicole de Sonnete and Michele Ferrer."

"You know them too?" Megan asked in surprise.

"You might say they have a reputation in certain circles."

"They're the jet-set type, aren't they?" Megan asked, looking down into her mug.

"More or less."

Megan sipped her chocolate. Westin watched her, noticing the small freckles on her nose and her pink lips that matched the ribbon in her hair.

"What are you thinking, Megan?"

"I was just wondering if Michele or Nicole have a pair of red slipper socks and if they sleep in flannel night gowns."

Westin laughed. "I can almost guarantee that they don't," he said.

Megan thought of Michele's vampish beauty and Nicole's translucent veils, and her own red socks.

"Megan, I wouldn't be envious of Michele or Nicole. Besides, it seems to me that you have managed to captivate the attention of the prize they most want to win," he said. "And you did it with red slipper socks."

Megan smiled and set her cup down and hugged her legs. "Maybe that's their problem. They think of Marcus as a prize."

"Perhaps," Westin agreed. Megan yawned. He rose from the chair. "It is getting late. I had better leave. Thank you for the tea."

"You don't have to leave."

"No, it is late," he said.

"It's nice to know someone is watching out after me," Megan said, walking him to the door. "Thank you." The tall ambassador smiled as he put on his coat.

She sighed, "I've wondered at times, coming to this country, being here all alone, if this was the smart thing to do."

"There is no escaping our destiny," Westin said, "and you're safe," he added with a wink. "Don't worry." The ambassador looked around the apartment one last time and then settled on her sad eyes. "Megan, I was wondering...."

"What?" she asked.

He tugged on his white scarf but did not turn away from looking steadily into her eyes. "I was wondering if you were going to see him again?"

"I don't know. I suppose so," Megan said, tightening the knot on her robe. "Mutual friends of ours are getting married. I'll probably see him there."

Westin's eyes brightened and a faint smile washed across his face as Megan yawned. "As long as I know all is well I feel much better," Westin said. He started putting on his gloves. "Rest. It will all look better in the morning."

"Thank you, Westin," Megan said. "Not many people would have cared enough to come. Good night."

"Good night, Megan."

* * *

In the back of the limousine, Marcus gazed out at the passing street lights decorated with red ribbon. I think I lost her, he thought. I was going to tell her the truth, but.... His words played back in his mind like an endless recording. "I was going to tell her the truth but I didn't," he said aloud. Cars passed by in the opposite direction with bright white lights. Marcus closed his eyes. The limousine rolled across the uneven cobblestone road, spraying melted snow onto the sidewalk in constant drumming beats. Marcus lowered his head. I didn't listen. I ignored your warnings. I've been selfish and it is an empty, desolate place, Marcus prayed silently. The driver parked in front of the townhouse that tonight looked tired and dark and was covered with a shroud of snow. He looked down at the limousine's silver buttons by his hand and then again at his house. Marcus pressed the intercom, "Take me to the hospital," he said wearily.

CHAPTER 40

The hospital was as quiet and seemed as drearily asleep as his home, Marcus thought. The offices and halls were vacant and the lights in the halls and stations were muted for the late evening hours of rest. He pulled a blue surgical shirt over his head as he came out of the locker room and headed for the nurses' station. Marcus could see Nurse Houser sitting behind her desk with the blue glow of her computer illuminating her face. He turned on one of the under-counter lights at the circular station and picked up the computerized chart lying on the desk. "Is there anything I can do for you, Doctor Holcombe?" Nurse Houser asked.

"I was just going to look in on a few patients," Marcus said, activating the chart. He touched the chart's monitor and located a patient he had assisted Dr. Weisman with in surgery earlier in the week. The patient's vital statistics were clearly improving and he could see from the screen that the patient was resting without any discomfort.

"Everyone is resting well tonight," Nurse Houser said, scribbling on a note pad. "The only patient awake is Ida. She refuses to take anything to help her sleep."

Marcus looked to her room. The door was closed but a bright light was shining from the bottom of her doorway, spreading out like a yellow fan across the hall. He enjoyed talking to Ida. Now in her sunset years, Ida would eagerly reminisce with Marcus about the days of old when she was the governess to his father. Simpler times, she would recall fondly. Marcus opened her door quietly in case she had drifted off to sleep.

"Ida, what are you doing up at this time of night?" Marcus asked, scolding her in a voice just above a whisper. Ida set down her magazine and smiled at the large figure of a man standing in her doorway.

"Prince Marcus," Ida said, bowing her head and then reaching out her hand. "What are you doing here at this time of night?" she asked inquisitively as Marcus closed the door.

"I believe I asked you first," he laughed, taking her hand. He sat next to her on the bed and quickly looked up her chart.

"And what does that thing say?" Ida asked. "I will tell you what it should say, that I am an old lady." Marcus laughed again and put the chart down on the bed. "I can't sleep thinking of all the things I must do. I should be home baking Christmas cookies for my great-grandchildren instead of lying here taking up space." Marcus noticed that her magazine was open to a picture of a plate full of decorated cut-out cookies and rocking-horse ornaments. "They are keeping me here against my better judgment, but what is the sense of arguing. My doctor insists I stay one more night and one more night I will stay. Now, what is your excuse for being here at such a late hour?"

"I couldn't sleep either," he said, and noticed Ida looking at his feet.

"Fancy shoes for a doctor at a hospital," Ida said suspiciously.

"Father didn't get away with much while you were his governess, did he?"

"Not often," Ida said sternly.

Marcus put his hand on top of hers. "I was at the hospital benefit this evening," Marcus said. Ida sat up in her bed anxious to hear all the details.

"All the nurses were aflutter about the dance tonight. Will we have a new wing on the hospital next year?"

"Yes, yes," Marcus said, fidgeting. Ida waited for more but Marcus had turned his attention to the colorful picture in the magazine.

"What is troubling you, child?" Ida asked. Marcus kept his eyes on the magazine and focused on the white rocking horse with gray spots on its back and its gold-braided bridle.

"Rocking horses, fairytales and castles on a hill," Marcus said. Ida's joy turned to somber concern. Marcus wished he could take back his words knowing he had upset his favorite patient.

"I just need a little sleep," he said, patting her hand and getting up to leave. Ida held on to him and he sat back down. She reached over to her nightstand and pulled out a tabloid from the drawer. Ida handed it to him. On the cover was a picture of him with a headline that read

"Dreiholm's Playboy Prince Partied Out?"

"My niece brought this magazine to me today. She thought it might be entertaining for me to read." The tabloids' exaggerations and lies about his personal relationships, successes and failures always angered him. He'd had to learn at an early age to ignore the puffed up papers entirely, yet he was compelled to read the headlines when he saw his picture on their covers. He recognized the picture as one taken after his first year exams in medical school. His wrinkled shirt hung outside his jeans as he grimly looked into the camera with a pale, unshaven face.

"What did our nosey newshounds find this week?" Marcus asked, turning the page.

"When I looked at the picture, I realized it had been taken some time ago, so I knew it must all be lies."

"Ida, are you saying that I have lost my youthful good looks?" Marcus said, as he passed by the advertisements for miracle face creams and diet pills.

"No, Marcus. Your handsome face you have retained, but there is something different about you."

"The quiet life suits me, Ida," Marcus said, putting down the tabloid. "I am content in my work."

"Then why do I see sadness in your eyes?" Ida asked.

He folded the tabloid in half. "Because in finding contentment and peace, I also found some*one* and tonight I am not sure if..." Marcus took in a labored breath of air, "well, if it will all work out." He quickly forced himself to appear confident and unconcerned.

"Do you love her?" Ida asked. Marcus began to pace the floor. He ran his hand through his hair as he looked at the tiny woman in the hospital bed.

"She is stubborn and disagreeable and jealous," Marcus complained, "and even ungrateful."

"She must be a horrid, ugly woman."

"No, Ida, she's beautiful and intelligent and loving and kind and not like anyone I have ever met before," he said. "And Ida, she makes me laugh and she's not afraid of anything."

"Then I was wrong," Ida said with a tender, knowing glint in her eyes. Marcus reached up and rested his hand against the window frame.

"I've done some idiotic things," he said, gazing out the hospital window. His mind drifted along the cityscape and in the distance he could see the red lights at the top of the skyscrapers and the buildings shimmering below. A nearby billboard that looked like a rolled-up newspaper tied with a red bow unfurled in red and green lights reading, "Everyone at the Dreiholmian Press wishes you a Merry Christmas." And then it rolled back up again.

"Ida, do you trust God?"

"Of course!" she said, her eyes wide with surprise.

"How are you so sure?" he asked.

"Marcus, during my long life, the Lord Jesus has let me be witness to many answered prayers. We are an impatient lot," she went on, "like children. We want immediate answers to our questions, just like that device," she said, pointing to Marcus' computer chart. "We want to push a button to God and have Him give us an instant reply."

"But that is what I want Ida, I want answers."

"God answers in His own time and in His own ways," she said slowly. "When you get to be my age you'll realize his timing was perfect and because of it our faith has been strengthened."

"But, Ida...."

"Patience, child," she said softly, "God wants the best for us. Let Him give you the best he can give."

"But what if I lose her."

"Trust God. His thoughts are not our thoughts, His ways are not our ways, and His abundance is beyond our imagination."

CHAPTER 41

Jacob found Marcus asleep in the doctors' lounge, lying on the couch with a bunched up sweatshirt for a pillow and a hospital copy of the Bible draped over his chest.

"Marcus," Jacob said as he jostled his shoulder. Marcus groaned and rolled over to his side. Jacob caught the Bible from falling to the floor when Marcus' bloodshot eyes fluttered to life.

"Phillip and I were wondering where you were when you didn't show up last night", Jacob said as he sat down on the coffee table. Marcus groaned again and wiped his face. "All I can say is that I was thankful that the king and queen left the benefit early last night."

Marcus stretched his arm until the tingling pain from sleeping on the narrow, makeshift bed dissipated. "I came to the hospital after I dropped off Megan," Marcus said.

"I heard about your riff."

"Discussion," Marcus said, sitting up. Jacob's eyebrow peaked. "Heated discussion," Marcus said, rubbing his neck. "Have you talked to her?"

"No, Ostride did."

"How is she?" Marcus asked.

"Fine. Upset but fine," Jacob said, getting himself a cup of coffee.

"You and Ostride?"

"Heated discussion," Jacob said, looking at Marcus. "Coffee?" He asked holding a cup.

"Yes, please," Marcus said. Jacob opened up the cabinet on the wall and found a jar of powdered cream and some sugar.

"But making up was worth the fight. Nevertheless, I'm not going to make a practice of keeping secrets or testing her patience after we get married," Jacob said, exaggerating a shiver. Marcus smiled and tried to smooth out his bent hair.

"What time is it?"

"Almost six-thirty. It will be at full boil around here in a few minutes," Jacob warned. Doctors and nurses passed by the doorway holding coffee mugs in one hand and papers in the other, rushing to get to staff meetings on time. "What did you do here last night? When I left, it was as quiet as a church."

"I couldn't go home. I came here and ended up talking to Ida," Marcus said, "and I read and prayed." He looked at the Bible. He drank some of the coffee and then looked down at the tar-colored syrup in the foam cup. He smacked his lips and stuck out his tongue, still tasting the pungent bitterness in his mouth. He tossed the cup and its contents into the trash can, flopped back down on the couch and began plumping up his sweatshirt.

"I hate to add salt to the wounds but you weren't the only visitor Megan had last night," Jacob said, stirring his coffee. Marcus' eyes opened wide.

"What are you talking about? I left her apartment late last night. No one would have stopped by."

"Langley did," Jacob said.

"What was he doing there?" Marcus asked, sitting up.

"He contended that he wanted to make certain she was all right. Thought she might have been abducted," Jacob said.

"Abducted!" Marcus roared. "Abducted, right," Marcus said as he shot up from the couch and headed for the door.

"Where are you going?" Jacob asked.

"Out," Marcus said.

"Here, have another cup of motor oil," Jacob said, handing him his own coffee. "You're on duty in fifteen minutes."

"Cover for me," Marcus pleaded.

"I switched with Gertz. I'm working with you today," Jacob answered.

"Great!" Marcus said, throwing the cup in the trash. "My luck."

"It might be good luck," Jacob said.

"I don't trust him," Marcus said, thinking of the Ambassador's advances toward Megan the night before.

"Relax, if anything sordid went on, Ostride would be the first to know. And if anything did happen she would have been the first to take him to task," Jacob insisted. "Don't worry. You and Megan both need some time. I hear it didn't end well last night."

Marcus brushed back his hair with his fingers. "No."

"Then better to let some time pass," Jacob advised.

"I don't have much choice in the matter, do I," Marcus said, looking at the clock on the wall.

"Not today. Dr. Weisman is coming in," Jacob said, walking out the door. "And do yourself and everybody else a favor: hit the shower before staff update."

* * *

When Megan reached her laboratory at Brier she found a note from Rose attached to the door. All the laboratories had been shut down for a maintenance check and if she wanted to stay, she would be reassigned to a sales desk for the day. Megan took the elevator to the fifth floor and found she had a choice of any office. The sales staff took their vacations during December and she was told it would be especially quiet the day before and after the night of the hospital benefit ball. Megan chose a deserted office in the back of the room that looked over the tropical park below. She opened the sealed manila envelope Rose had left for her. After reading the typed list of details, she noticed a hand-written reminder, written in bold red letters, on the bottom of the last page. *Call home.* Rose had intentionally made her list of calls short, and by early afternoon Megan called her uncle and aunt.

"...I just finished."

"Why couldn't you work in the lab?" her uncle asked.

"Maintenance," Megan said, jostling her pen between her fingers. Just then she spotted a bright red bird with yellow feathers, perched outside her window. It paid little attention to her as it nibbled on the ledge and then shuffled down a flag pole.

"Megan, what's the matter?" her uncle asked. "Something must be wrong."

"I'm tired," Megan said.

"Meg, why don't you come home for Christmas?" her uncle asked, "even if it will be a short stay."

"I've survived so far," Megan said. "I'll make it until the end but thanks for asking. I miss you both so much."

"Come home, Meg darling. We'll go skiing and have a party with your friends here and maybe we could squeeze in a quick trip to the ranch." Megan thought of the familiar places, her aunt and uncle's cozy home tucked in the woods. Then she thought of David, and riding in the warm sunshine of the ranch.

"It's tempting," Megan said, "but I have to try and stick it out. Besides, I want you to save your money for your visit here this spring."

"Are you sure, Meg?" her uncle asked.

"I'll be fine." Megan said. "Really I will. I love you."

"We'll call you on Christmas Eve then," her uncle said. "We love you, too."

"Bye, honey. You give us a call anytime if you change your mind," her aunt cut in. "You know that we are aching to see you."

"I will," Megan said and hung up the phone. Megan began to bundle up the files Rose had given to her, and wondered if she had made the right decision. She went to the file cabinet and thought about her aunt and uncle's Christmas tree, her aunt's famous turkey and stuffing and her parents' cabin. She went back to the desk and picked up the telephone.

"Megan!" She could barely hear Mr. Payton calling her. She put the phone back in its cradle and looked outside her office door. He was standing in the doorway of the sales department office.

"I'm back here," she called with a wave. "I'm in Callaway's office." She returned to her desk and sorted through her last file and wrapped a rubber band around it. She could hear Payton talking to someone as he walked down the hallway and assumed that Rose had come to collect her papers.

"Good afternoon, Megan," Payton said. She looked up from her desk, surprised by his uncustomary formality. Westin Langley was standing behind him. "Mr. Langley stopped by to bring over a check for the hospital and he asked to see you."

Westin stepped into the office from behind Payton. Dressed in a black leather jacket, dark sunglasses and blue jeans, he projected an air of mystery Megan had not detected in him before. He smiled and hooked his glasses onto the neck of his sweater.

"Hello."

"Hello," Megan said, slowly.

"Have I interrupted you?" Westin asked, looking at her desk.

"No, I just finished making my calls."

"Did you get a chance to call Joe?" Payton asked, shifting between Megan and Westin.

"Yes, I called home," Megan said and put the completed files into an envelope. "All is well. Joe wants you to give him a call about a project he's working on."

"I'll give him a call tonight," he said, watching Megan and then glancing at Westin who was staring at her.

"Does that mean you're finished for the day?" Westin asked eagerly, stepping around Megan's desk.

"Yes, unless there is something else I can do?" Megan asked Payton, handing him her files. He looked at the computer print-out clipped to the manila envelope.

"You went through all the reps?" he asked.

"All that I could get hold of today. I only had to leave messages for two," she said, closing her notebook and putting her extra pencils away.

"Did you tell them about the changes we will be making come January?"

"Absolutely."

"And Fed regs?"

"They'll all be getting copies after the holidays."

"Good," he said, looking at Westin out of the corner of his eye. "How about the lab?"

"Shut down," Megan said, "I thought you knew."

"Oh, yes," Payton said. "It slipped my mind. Well, then, I guess you're done for the day."

"Excellent!" Westin exclaimed. "Miss Buchanan, how would you like to join me for dinner?"

"Thank you for asking, Westin, but I'll have to decline," Megan said. Payton walked to the filing cabinets and smiled. "I wouldn't be good company anyway," she said apologetically. "I'm beat. I thought I would pick up a few groceries and a small Christmas tree for my apartment on my way home and then call it a night."

"Perfect," Westin said. "I'm tired of restaurant dining. We'll stop for a few groceries and I'll help you with your tree and I can make you dinner." Payton shuffled through the file cabinet waiting for Megan's response.

"It sounds like fun but I shouldn't."

"Sunday then?" Westin asked.

"No!" Chuck said hurriedly, turning to Westin. "Megan is having Sunday dinner with my family, Annie's expecting you," he said to Megan.

"That's right," Megan said, "I guess tonight will have to do."

"Good, my car is out front," Westin said, helping Megan with her jacket. Payton followed them out of the office and turned out the light.

"I tried, Marcus," he said to himself, watching Westin and Megan leave the building. "I tried."

CHAPTER 42

Westin put the bag of groceries in the back seat of his car and searched for Megan in the square. He found her standing in front of the city bulletin board outside the small grocery store. "What did you find?" Westin asked.

A faint spicy scent of cloves wafted in the still winter night air, which Megan quickly recognized as Westin's cologne. She felt him come up behind her from the shadows and step into the light, resting his hand on her hip.

"The crown jewels of Dreiholm are going to be on exhibit," Megan said, stepping closer to the photograph of the jewels and away from Westin's hand.

"They're on exhibit every year at this time," Westin said. Megan thought of the bracelet Marcus had given her that were now lying in a crumpled pile in the corner of her apartment. "It's one of the few complete collections left in the world. The royal blue diamond set in the queen's crown is rare indeed."

"All those carats would make a happy rabbit," Megan said with a quiet smile as she looked at the square diamond in the photograph.

"And his friends as well," Westin said. "You see that necklace?" He pointed to the poster. The multi-strand necklace was a chain of diamonds woven together with gold and semiprecious stones. "It has been said that it belonged to the czarina of Russia and that she gave it to the then king of Dreiholm as payment for refuge for the czar's youngest child during the revolution. I have a hard time believing it but tales are spun around such things."

"Why don't you believe it?" Megan asked.

"The design. The stones," Westin said, putting his arm around Megan. "Let's just say it would have hardly been the czarina's choice. Most likely Spanish."

"How do you know so much about jewelry and history and royalty?" Megan asked. Westin was looking down at the sidewalk, teetering on the back of his feet, and gave Megan a provocative glance with a hint of a smile.

"Don't tell me. You're expected to know such things," Megan said, rubbing her hands together.

"We had better get back to your apartment," he said, and opened the car door. "The wind is picking up and you're getting cold."

* * *

With groceries in one arm, Megan dug through the closet and found the tree stand in the utility room right where Mr. Grutner said it would be. Westin carried the tree up the three flights of stairs, bending and swerving on the way up so that not one needle touched the banister or one spindle. Megan hurriedly opened her door and raced to the far end of the apartment to set the tree stand by the fireplace. "Right here," she said, setting the groceries aside and feverishly untwisting the screws that would secure the tree in the stand.

"Take your time, it's not heavy," Westin said, watching her kneeling on the floor. Westin waited until Megan had dropped back and pushed away on the smooth floor before he dropped the tree in the stand. Megan threw her coat on her bed and slid underneath the tree, crawling on her stomach.

"I really appreciate your help," Megan said from under the branches, twisting the screws tight to the tree.

"Not at all," Westin said, holding the tree as he talked to the pair of legs on the floor in front of him.

"It should be safe now," Megan said. "It's not as small as I wanted but the price was right." Westin let go of his grip on the tree, then took off his coat and threw it on the bed next to hers. Megan shimmied out from underneath the tree and picked off a few dry needles from her sweater. Westin crouched down beside her and put his hand up to her face. Megan paused and looked at Westin who was staring into her eyes. He plucked a pine needle from her hair, spun it between his fingers and then made it disappear.

"So, you're a man of many talents," Megan said, sliding over to pick up the bag of groceries from the floor. Westin reached over the top of her and grabbed the bag's paper handle. Their eyes met again, his lips parted and then in one sudden motion he jumped to his feet and pulled Megan up from the floor at the same time.

"I'm making dinner, remember?" he said, going to the kitchen and opening the refrigerator. "You're well stocked," he commented, making room for the few things they had bought. Megan went to her closet and pulled out a bag.

"A friend of mine keeps me supplied with her culinary creations."

"Well, let's see how you like mine," he said, and opened a bottle of wine that he had bought at the store. "What have you got there?"

"Christmas lights and a star for the top of my tree. I found it when Ostride and I went on a trip to the mountains," Megan said. She carefully pulled the glass star from its box. The cut crystal shone in the afternoon light, reflecting rainbows onto the white walls and ceiling. She struggled to get it to the top of the tree, stretching over the extended branches and bending the highest bough towards her. "Other than a few strings of lights, I'm afraid this poor tree is going to be pretty bare," she said in disjointed syllables as she fought to get the star on top of the tree.

"Megan!" Westin yelled, leaping over the couch and pushing her quickly aside. He caught the glass star in his hand before the tree fell on top of him.

"Westin!" Megan gasped. All she could see was a hand holding the star, rising above the tree's branches. She picked up the tree and pushed it aside. "Are you all right?"

Westin spit out a pine needle that was in his mouth. He handed Megan the star.

"Thank you," Megan said timidly and sat next to him. "Are you all right?"

"Fine," he said, and brushed the needles off of his sweater. A drop of pinesap smeared across the cashmere knit. Megan covered her face.

"I'll make dinner," Megan said.

"I'll make dinner. You hold the tree and I'll tighten it up," Westin said, as he put the tree back into the stand and shoved the star on the top bough. Megan looked at the crooked star and began to laugh. He adjusted it and looked at Megan and then at the tree and his stained sweater and smiled. "Prop it up, no tree will get the best of me!"

CHAPTER 43

"Good evening, Sirs," Broderick said, greeting Marcus and Jacob as they came through the door.

"Good evening, Broderick," Marcus said, shedding his rumpled sweatshirt.

"Good evening, Broderick," Jacob said and sat down in the closest chair to the door. "I'm exhausted. It's a good thing Ostride is going to be out tonight. I don't think I'll be able to stay awake past eight."

"That's five minutes from now, Sir," Broderick mentioned.

"Exactly," Jacob yawned.

"Is Ostride going out with Megan tonight?" Marcus asked Jacob anxiously. Phillip came running down the stairway and hung onto the banister as he leaned over to see Marcus and Jacob sitting in the foyer.

"Not too late tonight," Phillip commented, "it must have been a slow day at the morgue."

Jacob groaned and closed his eyes as he leaned back into the soft chair. Broderick took Jacob's coat and Marcus' wrinkled and dirty sweatshirt.

"I will have this cleaned right away, Sir. Would either of you like something to eat?"

"We ate at the hospital," Marcus said, looking across the room. "Jacob, you didn't answer my question."

Jacob bobbed his head and rubbed his temples. "What question was that?"

"Is Ostride going out with Megan tonight?" Phillip glanced at Broderick.

"No, Ostride was going to the beauty salon and to some store for something," Jacob said, tipping back his head on the pad of the chair.

"Sir, a package came for you today," Broderick said. Phillip handed Marcus the small velvet box sitting on the step.

"She sent it back this morning," Phillip said. "I tried to reach her all day but she must have been at work."

"Was there a note?" Marcus asked.

"No, just the bracelet."

Marcus slapped the thin box in his hand and put his shoes on.

"Off to see her?" Jacob asked, looking up. Marcus grabbed the soiled sweatshirt from Broderick's hands and pulled it over his tangled and bent hair.

"Not a good idea."

"Why?" Marcus asked his friend, not caring if he got an answer.

"Because you're tired and you're angry and you don't even know why. You're running on pure adrenaline. Not a good combination for decision making," Jacob said. His bloodshot eyes closed and he tipped his head back into the chair again. Marcus looked at the velvet box in his hand. Megan had carefully put the broken pieces of the box back together and taped the hinges. He opened it up with his thumb and saw the diamond bracelet coiled up at one end.

"If you're going to go, it wouldn't hurt if you took a shower first, and definitely don't wear that sweatshirt," Phillip said. Marcus snapped the box shut and handed it to Phillip as he walked up the stairs.

"I'm not going," Marcus said, "and I did take a shower!"

"I don't want it! I learned my lesson," Phillip said. He tossed the box to Broderick who caught it on the top of Jacob's coat.

* * *

"That was good." Megan said, chewing on the last bit of a crepe as she arranged the lights on the Christmas tree. Westin had taken off his sweater and rolled up the sleeves of his white monogrammed shirt. He was swirling the last bit of wine he had in his glass.

"Why white lights?" he asked. "A variety of colors are more festive."

"Flip the switch," Megan said, pointing to the panel by the door. Westin pressed it down and all the lights went out except for the tiny white lights on the Christmas tree.

"Now, can't you imagine that you're looking at the stars in the sky through the branches of the tree?" Megan asked. "Minus the cold night air." She looked at him across the room and then turned back to her tree. "Isn't that beautiful?" she asked.

"Yes, it is," Westin said, looking at Megan and setting down his empty glass. "Some music?" he asked, turning on the radio as Megan dug in a box for a spare bulb.

"Sure," Megan said, as she exchanged a bulb into a tiny light socket. An orchestra played a medley of Christmas carols and Westin searched for wood near the fireplace. "I haven't restocked the firewood. Mr. Grutner keeps it locked up behind the building and I haven't made it back there in the morning when he's home to get any."

"We'll have to improvise," Westin said, lighting a candle that was on the coffee table.

"There," Megan said, sitting on the floor looking up at the tree.

Westin sat on the edge of the couch watching Megan. "I take it you're not going home for Christmas."

"No, I'm going to stick it out here. How about you? Are you going home for Christmas?" Megan asked.

"No," Westin said, folding his hands together and looking down at the floor. "No, I have to work."

"I'm sure your family will miss you."

"My family is gone now and there doesn't seem to be any reason to go back."

"I have never been to England."

"England?" Westin asked, puzzled.

"Your home?" Megan asked.

"I'm actually from Scotland," Westin said hurriedly.

"Really?" Megan asked, curiously.

"Why are you staying on?" Westin asked.

"Obligations," Megan said, "and it's a learning experience. This is my first extended stay outside the United States."

"And what have you learned so far?" Westin asked.

Megan stretched out her legs on the floor and leaned against the side of the chair as she thought about her adventure.

"I've learned that the unfamiliar becomes familiar in not too much time," she said.

"What else?"

"Well, I've learned not to even try to do your wash on Saturday at the laundromat; if you want to send a package home do it on Thursdays because that's the only day Wilma is on duty and she's the only one who knows how to process the package; and never tell a Dreiholmian that you prefer German sausage over their own," Megan said with a smile. "One morning while my friend Ostride and I were having breakfast we received a lecture on the merits of the hand-processed, premium select Dreiholmian pork patties that we will never forget," Megan jested.

"And what about the people?" Westin asked.

"Oh," Megan said, getting up from the floor and settling into a chair next to the tree. "I can't complain. When I left home I thought for sure I would wither away in this isolated mountain village, but somehow God always seems to bring the right people together. I don't know what I would do without Ostride."

"Your friend from Canada, who I met at the hospital benefit?"

"Yes, and Chuck and Annie Payton. If I really need a shot of home I spend time with their grandchildren. They keep me up on the latest and greatest. The Paytons have everything and anything the children want shipped into Dreiholm. If I can't find it in the stores Annie has it in her kitchen," Megan laughed.

"And Prince Marcus?"

"Prince Marcus," Megan repeated to herself. "I thought he...." Her words trailed off as she felt an ache inside of her grow and prick her eyes. "We live in two different worlds. And besides, my life is... complicated."

"Are you certain of that?"

"That we are worlds apart or that my life is complicated?" Megan asked.

"That you are worlds apart."

"Absolutely," Megan said, watching the bright flame of the flickering candle.

"But you love him?" Westin asked. Megan turned her attention to the lit tree and began to rub her arms.

"I don't know."

"Fair enough," Westin said, coming close to her. "Megan, there is something I have to tell you."

CHAPTER 44

When Marcus came down the stairs, he saw Broderick and Sarah setting out the china and crystal goblets for the Westwind Housing Project meeting the next day.

"Prince Marcus," Broderick said, setting down the plates. "Can I get you anything? Perhaps some soup, or Cook has made stroganoff."

"No, thank you, I'm not hungry," Marcus answered. "Where is everyone?"

"Phillip has gone out to a hockey game and Jacob has retired for the evening," Broderick said. Marcus had picked up the velvet box and bracelet in the hallway and was tapping it in his hand. He sat down at the dining room table playing with the box, then opening it up and looking at the sparkling gems. Sarah tried to busy herself with the silverware but couldn't help looking at the embellished bracelet.

"Is something troubling you, Sir?" Broderick asked.

"I don't understand," Marcus said, "I don't understand why Megan did not like this gift. I thought it was very becoming and yet she would just as soon pitch it at me."

"No wonder," Sarah muttered under her breath and then stiffened, knowing she had spoken aloud. She shuffled through the assorted spoons, clanging forks and knives in the drawer, hoping his Highness missed her indiscretion. Broderick's mustache twitched.

"What was that, Sarah?" Marcus asked. Sarah timidly looked up at Prince Marcus and then at Broderick and back to the prince again, barely lifting her eyes to his.

"I'm terribly sorry, Your Highness. I didn't mean to say anything."

"What did you say?" Marcus asked.

"No wonder," she said cringing as she said it.

"Why?" he asked. Sarah set a handful of spoons on the table and glanced at Broderick with sad, childlike eyes. Broderick whisked his mustache with a brisk swipe of his finger and then braced himself for what was next.

"Perhaps, Sir, you inadvertently did something to aggravate Miss Buchanan."

"Like what?" Marcus asked. "I profusely apologized for keeping my identity from her and I bought her this diamond bracelet. What is there to be angry about? Frankly, I think she is being entirely ungrateful. I know a thousand women who would love to have it. So tell me what could be so aggravating that she despises my gift?"

Sarah looked at Broderick and they both took a deep breath. Sarah realized the Prince was waiting for her to answer.

"Perhaps by giving the lady an expensive gift, Your Highness, a woman might feel as if she were obligated to make you happy. You said it yourself, 'I know women who would do anything for it'."

"That isn't exactly what I said."

"Same thing," Sarah said spitefully and then put her hand to her mouth.

"Speak freely. I'm not about to send you into exile because you happen to disagree with me, even though I am right," Marcus grumbled. "Go on."

Sarah looked at Broderick again.

"Sir, perhaps it is better if we finish our work here another time. We are disturbing you," Broderick said.

"No!" Marcus protested. "One thing doesn't have to do with another. That is what Megan cannot seem to get through her head. Sarah continue," Marcus commanded. She took a deep breath again and exhaled.

"It is like this," Sarah said, holding a bouquet of forks. "Peter and I, we wish to marry but we cannot because we cannot afford to right now, and because my parents want us to wait until I turn twenty-one. Until then, Peter bought me a dining room table and chairs, and I, well, I will have saved up enough by this Christmas to buy him an automobile," she said proudly.

"My goodness!" Broderick exclaimed.

"Nothing fancy but something we'll need if we are going to be able to have a house in the mountains someday soon," Sarah said. "You see, it's not the size of the gift, it is under what circumstances it is given.

If Peter would have given me my dining room table and chairs without the promise of being wed, I would have felt obligated to reciprocate in some way."

"And a diamond bracelet?" Marcus asked.

"I could never," Sarah said. "Peter and I are building a life together, but without that commitment, the gift would be a purchase for my affection. I don't think anyone likes to be bought," she said earnestly.

"Some do," Marcus said.

"Some," Broderick agreed, "but perhaps those that do are in love with the manna more than the man."

"Why, Broderick, I've never heard you once speak to me in such a way," Marcus jested.

"Sir, may I continue?"

"By all means," Marcus said. Broderick looked at Sarah. "Don't worry about Sarah," Marcus said, "there isn't much you could say to me that the tabloids haven't said more than once."

"A lady should never be treated as common and those that are common should be treated like a lady. Miss Buchanan is most certainly a lady."

"You are fond of her?"

"Very much, Sir. In my opinion, we have never had anyone of finer quality as a guest in this house."

Marcus flipped the velvet box shut and wiggled it on the smooth surface of the table and then slid it to Broderick.

"Return it and deposit the funds in the Westwind account," Marcus said and then left the room.

* * *

"This will be our final meeting before we go before the senate. Be ready," Marcus said, standing before the housing committee. "We have little room for error. As your prince I have only one opportunity to advance such a civic operation and I have only one vote among the senate members."

"We are prepared for any circumstance, Your Highness," Peter said. "The land has been inspected and surveyed…"

"And nearly killed us doing it," the surveying engineer said.

"What's that?" Marcus asked.

"Someone took a shot at my men while they were up in the mountains," the engineer said.

"We had the police look into it," Peter said. "They told us that it was most likely a stray bullet from a hunter, Sir."

"One stray I can see, but three,..." the engineer said angrily, "someone didn't want us up there."

"Why wasn't I notified of this?" Marcus asked. "Payton didn't mention it."

"He didn't know, Sir. Mr. Payton is out of town and will not be back until this evening."

"Why didn't you tell me?" Marcus asked Peter. "Are you or are you not the chair of this committee?"

"The police reassured us that it was unintentional and they asked us not to mention it further until the final report was issued. I received it late last night," Peter said, handing the report to Marcus.

"When did the shooting take place?" Marcus asked, flipping through the pages of the report.

"Four days ago," Peter said. Marcus motioned for Broderick, who was standing nearby, and then whispered instructions in his ear. Broderick quickly left the meeting room.

"Are all the preparations in order?"

"Yes, Sir," Peter said. "I have compiled the committee's findings, the history of the land, the surveys, land usage records, designs, costs and impact studies."

"Is everything in this package?" Marcus asked, holding up the thick brown-covered report.

"Yes, Sir."

"Everything?"

"Yes, Sir."

"Good. Then I will expect to see you all tomorrow," Marcus said. The committee members filed out of the room and Peter lagged behind the rest. He hesitated at the door and then glanced back at Marcus who was reading through the report again. Peter hesitated and then walked out the door.

"Sir, the chief of police," Broderick said as he handed the telephone to the Marcus.

CHAPTER 45

Megan wrapped protective bubble sheets around the music box she had found in an antique shop in the mountain village. Carefully bundling it up, she made sure not to crush the bow on the top of the Christmas package. She inched it down into the cardboard box and stuffed crumpled newspapers around every side until it was snug in the package. "That should get you safely to America," she said, as she sealed the box with a roll of wide tape. She dug through her kitchen drawer until she found a red marker, and wrote the address on the top of the package, wishing she were home to watch her uncle and aunt open the gift.

"You'll have to go to the post office today if you're going to make it to your new home by Christmas," she said, talking to the music box. Megan jumped at the sound of her door buzzer.

Why in the world can't they use door bells in this place, she asked herself as she ran to the door.

"Who is it?" Megan asked.

"Ostride." Megan pressed the release button to unlock the outside door, and then heard a number of footsteps coming up the stairs. She opened her apartment door to find Phillip bounding up the stairwell with Jacob and Ostride close behind.

"Hi, Meg!" Phillip said, holding onto his hat and walking into her apartment.

"What's going on?" Megan asked.

"We're going to see the crown jewels," Ostride said. "Do you want to come along?"

"I have to show Ostride what she will be missing," Jacob said.

"I haven't felt neglected," Ostride said, looking at her engagement ring. "Yet," she teased, and then kissed him on the cheek.

"So, what do you say, Meg?" Phillip asked, picking through the assortment of hard candy in a bowl on the kitchen counter.

"I'm going to see them tomorrow," Megan said, setting the music box by the door. "Westin asked if I would go with him, but thanks for asking."

"Westin! You've seen enough of him," Phillip chided. Megan wrinkled her nose at him.

"I know, I go out so often. No time at all to eat or sleep, and I've completely given up working," Megan replied sarcastically, putting away the red marker.

"You've gone out with him every night this week."

"And what would you know about this?" Megan asked as she closed the drawer.

"Just checking, Meg."

"It's not true," she said, going to the closet. "Well, not entirely." She stepped inside the closet to put the packaging supplies away. When she came out, Marcus was standing in the doorway of her apartment.

"The door was open downstairs," Marcus said, looking at Megan.

"I thought you were on duty tonight," Jacob said.

"Smith called and asked to switch," Marcus said, his clenched fists causing his black leather gloves to tighten on his hands. "Broderick told me your plans."

"Come on, Meg," Phillip prodded, "you'll have much more fun with us." Marcus took her coat off the rack and held it out for her.

"I have to go to the post office," she said.

"I'll take you," Marcus said, and turned to Ostride and Jacob. "We'll see you at the museum's south entrance."

"We're going to have to hurry," Ostride said, looking at Megan and Marcus and then at her watch. "We'll be cutting it close the way it is."

"We don't have to worry. We can get in anytime," Phillip said.

"Come on, boy wonder," Ostride said, taking him by the arm and directing him out of the apartment door. "It's time for us to go," she said, shifting her eyes back to Marcus and Megan.

"Oh, oh yeah!" Phillip said. "Frankly, he would be better off if I stuck around," he said in a low voice.

"Yeah, well, we need you to get into the museum," Ostride said and pushed him out the door.

"We'll see you there," Jacob said carefully as he closed the door.

Marcus put Megan's coat back on the hook and looked at her across the room. She hadn't moved and he couldn't tell from the expression on her face if she was glad to see him. He cautiously walked forward, taking off his gloves as he went.

"Megan, I shouldn't have lied to you. For that I am truly sorry. And as for the gift, I didn't mean it to offend you or hurt you in any way. I wanted to give you something. I didn't expect anything or want anything in return. It was just a gift. I understand now what you were thinking, and it was not like that at all."

Megan slowly closed the closet door. She leaned against it with her hands behind her back and looked at him. "I believe you," she said slowly. "I'm just not sure where that leaves us."

Marcus walked toward her and with every step she could feel her heart beat faster. As he stood in front of her she could see the pain in his eyes and feel the pulsing tension without a single touch.

"It leaves you with me." He kissed her and was overwhelmed by the warmth of her body, her lips, the soft brush of her eyelashes, and the sweet fragrance of her soft skin. He traced the silhouette of her body until the longing he had tried to control had now risen above the height of passion, leaving him aching, hungry and wanting. He could feel the muscles in his arms quiver as he looked down into her tear-filled eyes. "Megan," he said, and kissed her again.

"I missed you too," she said, brushing aside a lock of his hair. "They'll be wondering where we are," Megan said softly, putting her hands under the warmth of his jacket.

"Let them wonder," Marcus said, kissing her again. The door buzzer echoed in the room and Megan inched away.

"Don't answer it." Marcus pleaded, pulling her to him.

"I have to. If it's work I have to," Megan said. Marcus followed her, kissing her neck and hands. "Yes," she said into the intercom.

"Delivery for Ms. Boocannon," a voice said. Megan unlocked the door.

"Did you send me something?" she asked Marcus.

"No, I haven't had very good luck with gifts of late," he said, taking off his coat and putting his arms around her waist. The delivery man was having trouble lifting the box up the stairs and finally made it to the third floor. He set the package down in front of the Christmas tree.

A card was attached to the box and the delivery man tore it off and handed it to Megan.

"Could you sign here, please?" the man said. Then looking at Marcus, "You know, you look like...." he started to say as he waved his finger at Marcus.

"He gets that all the time," Megan said, showing the man the door. "Thank you. Thank you very much." Megan closed the door. Marcus picked her up off the ground and began kissing her again as she opened the card.

"Who is it from?" Marcus asked.

"My aunt and uncle. It's my Christmas present," she said. "Dear Meg, we wanted to get you something extra special this year. We hope you like it. Love you, Uncle Joe and Aunt Julie," she read aloud.

Marcus sat down on the couch and put Megan on his lap. "Are you going to open it?"

"No, I'll wait for Christmas," she said, "and that's their gift over there." Megan nodded toward the door.

"We better get it to the post office before it closes," Marcus said.

"Yes, we better," she said softly. He touched her lips, tracing the delicate pink flesh with his finger while he looked deeply into her eyes. The desire within him surged through his veins, stretching to his fingertips and reverberating throughout his body. He picked her up and then delicately stood her back down on the floor.

"We must go now," he said, kissing her again, "or I will never leave."

CHAPTER 46

"Prince Marcus." The royal guard saluted as he stood at attention.

"The exhibit is closing?" asked Marcus.

"Yes, Your Highness, the last tour is on its way out," the guard said. He unlocked the sealed outer steel door and then a set of glass doors inside. Megan held on to Marcus as they passed through the gates and noticed the guards at the desk watching her with exceptional interest.

"Your cousin, the Count of Weinbourgh has also just arrived. He and his guests are entering the exhibit now," the guard said, pointing to the live camera monitoring the exhibit. Megan could see Ostride and Jacob following Phillip into the dimly lit room. "I will lock the door behind you and notify the guards that you are the last persons to enter this evening."

"Thank you," Marcus said. Megan could hear the doors bolt shut behind them. Small lights on the floor and those beaming up from the exhibits were the only illumination lighting the path in the black hallway. Megan looked at the many displays as she and Marcus slowly walked on. Life-sized mannequins of Nordic warriors with grim faces and fur pelt clothing stood on either side of them, prepared to lunge their thick wooden spears and sharp metal daggers at unwanted intruders.

"Relatives?" Megan inquired.

Marcus chuckled. "Not that I know of but I can't be sure." He opened the exhibit's black door and Megan's eyes lit up at the rainbow of color before her. Sealed glass cases lined in black velvet stood against the walls and were filled with blinding jewels.

"You made it!" Jacob said, surprised.

"You're buying supper," Phillip said to Jacob, as he was pointing out a necklace to Ostride. "That piece is supposedly Russian."

Megan looked at the necklace and recognized it to be the same piece Westin had told her about. "Spanish," Megan interjected.

"Yes," Marcus said, "you have an eye for art?"

"Not really," Megan said, moving on to the next display case. In it were the royal scepter, swords, and the king's crown. Marcus stood with his feet apart and his hands behind his back, looking on them with a calm acceptance. "It looks heavy," she said. "The crown, I mean."

"Yes, very," Marcus answered. Megan stepped back and leaned against Marcus' chest. "Luckily, Father doesn't have to wear it often."

"That's good," Megan said.

"There is no place to put in hair pins," Ostride said, inspecting the crown. "How do you keep it on?"

"With God's grace and a bit of balance," Marcus answered.

Ostride drifted over to the queen's display, "Megan, come here. Look at that diamond!"

"It's one of the largest diamonds in the world," Phillip said. Megan turned around and looked at all the jeweled dresses, robes, necklaces, broaches, earring, bracelets and rings.

"It's astounding," Megan murmured.

"My grandmother ruled Dreiholm for a short period of time after my grandfather died. She was very fond of excess and nearly bankrupted Dreiholm," Phillip said.

"And put the people in great danger," Marcus said bitterly.

"Have you recovered?" Ostride asked.

"After her untimely death, the king and his brother, Phillip's father, rallied the remaining assets of our land and restored our security and wealth," Marcus said. "I am indebted to their efforts."

"Members of the royal family are natural entrepreneurs," Jacob said, taking Ostride's hand. "If not for their position, I think they would be giving Payton a run for his money."

"Mother gave up her emerald ring this year," Phillip said, peering down into a glass case filled with a kaleidoscope of gems.

"It's like shopping at Tiffany's," Ostride laughed. "Oooo, I like that one," she said, pointing to a blue topaz ring surrounded by perfectly white diamonds. "It looks like melting ice against a pond of blue water."

"Don't get too attached," Jacob warned, "it was a gift from his majesty to her majesty."

"And what's your choice, Meg?" Phillip asked.

"I got the bracelet, remember," Megan said. Marcus was behind her and gently put his arm around her waist and rested his head on top of hers as she looked down at the jewels.

"Come on, Meg," Phillip nudged, "just pick one."

"Phillip, I work in a laboratory. I could never wear rings like these," she said, walking on to the next case. Curiously, she looked inside. It was a small display with one small ring resting on a pillow of blue velvet. "Now here's a ring a woman can wear, simple and elegant but definitely eye-catching."

"Of all the rings in this room, this is the one you would choose?" Phillip asked. Megan looked around the room again and then back at the small ring.

"Uh hum," Megan said. "It's perfect." She looked down at it again.

"But that one?" Phillip asked. Jacob stood behind Ostride, holding onto her shoulders as she looked down into the case. He looked back and smiled at Marcus.

"I saw that," she said, looking at Jacob. "What does the marker say?"

"It's a story. A legend about the ring. Our country is full of storytellers," Jacob said evasively. "Come on now, there is plenty more to see and if we don't move along we'll be eating at midnight."

"We're not waiting that long, I'm hungry," Phillip complained.

"You ate your sandwich and half of mine before we left," Ostride said.

"I'm still hungry."

"Then let's move along," Jacob said.

The rest of the exhibit was filled with tapestries, ornately carved furniture, paintings, silver goblets and bowls, china, and unusual gifts bestowed to the king and queen, along with antiquities from the royal palace.

"We must have caught up to the tour group," Jacob said. Megan glanced out the doorway and saw a group of tourists being escorted to the exit. She looked again, noting a tall man dressed in a leather jacket at the end of the group.

Westin? It can't be, Megan thought.

"They have the right idea," Marcus said, glancing at the last of the visitors. "Let's go now."

CHAPTER 47

"What's your pleasure, Prince Charming?" Megan asked. Marcus raised one eyebrow and wore a crooked smile. "Coffee, tea, or hot chocolate?" The apartment was warm and looked like a holiday picture with its crackling fire and the starry lights on the Christmas tree. Marcus took hold of her hand and pulled her to him as he lay on the couch.

"Just you," he said, and kissed her. Lying next to him, Megan listened to the wind pounding against the walls of the apartment. A piece of ice broke away from the roof and tumbled down, skating noisily over the tiles. The fire whistled and snapped and Megan snuggled deeper into the couch and Marcus' chest. He kissed the top of her head and they lay quietly staring at the tiny white lights through the boughs of the Christmas tree.

"Megan, do you forgive me?" Marcus asked. Megan was silent and rubbed the top of his hand.

"I'm still angry and hurt but I wouldn't be lying here if hadn't," she said, hugging his arm. He nuzzled up to her face and kissed her cheek and then turned her to himself. "But don't do it again." Megan said, wagging a finger at him. He smiled broadly as he grabbed and kissed her finger and then the palm of her hand.

"You stop that." Megan said laughing. "I know where you're going and it's a dangerous place."

"No, an adventure," he said, as his body enveloped around hers and he kissed her passionately.

"An adventure," Megan mused. "Spoken like a true man." The telephone rang and as she got up to answer it Marcus pulled her back into his arms.

"It could be the King of Spotsylvania with a better offer," Megan joked.

PLANS · VICTORIA J.M. HOFFBECK

"Old and fat with seventeen wives," Marcus said, as Megan raced to the phone. She looked back at him, squinting her eyes. "And lots of cats," he added. Megan began to laugh out loud.

"Hello," Megan said as she answered the phone. "Excuse me for a moment." Megan held her hand over the receiver. "Marcus," she whispered, "did you tell anyone that you would be here?" She handed him the telephone.

"The hospital," Marcus said, and took the phone. His face became sullen. He walked over to the picture window and pulled back the curtains. The weather had changed. Underneath the streetlights Megan could see the falling snow swirling in gigantic whirlpools. The waves of snow twisted and hurled over rooftops and swept across the street until finally exploding with the next gust of wind. The flames in the fireplace began leaping furiously in every direction as the wind found an escape in Megan's chimney.

Marcus hung up the telephone and threw on his coat. "There has been an accident," he said. "Everyone else is either gone on holiday or can't make it in to the hospital. They need surgeons. Call Albert's Restaurant and tell Jacob to meet me at the hospital," Marcus said, opening the door. "I'll be back," he said, and kissed her.

"Call me or have someone call me to let me know that you made it there all right," she called as he ran down the stairway.

"I will," he yelled up the stairwell. Megan ran back to the picture window and watched Marcus struggle against the wind and snow toward his car. She picked up the phone hastily.

"Albert's, and please hurry, it is an emergency."

* * *

By the time Marcus reached the hospital, the most critical patients were already in surgery with Dr. Weisman's team. The others were being prepped and had been taken into the surgery suites. Marcus scrubbed his hands and arms furiously as Jacob ran into the room with a nurse following him, trying to hand him his surgical cap and gown.

"What happened?" he asked breathlessly.

"An accident on Petra Pass. A semi-truck and passenger cars, seven or eight of them."

"How many injured?" Jacob said as he scrubbed down.

"Fifteen. Your first one is a child," Marcus said. Jacob focused on the soapy water and threw his coat and sweater on the floor.

"Where is everybody?" Jacob said angrily. "Where are the on-call teams?"

"No one knows," Marcus said, turning off the water. "Doctors Weisman, Bruckner and Smith are with the worst. We're on our own."

Jacob stood paralyzed, looking at Marcus, the hot water running down his arms.

"We have no choice," Marcus said. "Besides, you're the one who wants to specialize in transplants. You can do this," he encouraged. The hot water began to burn and Jacob resumed scrubbing. The nurse who followed Jacob held out an open glove for Marcus to put his hand into. Marcus noticed the woman had been crying. "Lara, what is it?" Marcus asked.

"My father was in one of the cars." Her confession opened a floodgate of tears.

"Where is he?"

"He's your patient," she said with a cracked voice.

"You can't go in," Marcus said firmly, and looked around the room for an experienced nurse. "Marie, I need you," he called. The nurse nodded and opened the door of the surgical suite.

"I have to go in," Lara begged.

"You'll be no good to anyone," Marcus said, and then realized he had just made a bad situation worse. "Lara, please."

"Dr. Holcombe," Marie called. "Come quickly."

* * *

Hours later, the pale faces of the surgical teams emerged from the suites. Marcus threw his third set of blood-stained garments into the laundry hamper. Jacob leaned up against the room's wall and slid down to the floor closing his burning eyes. Matt Dutcher flung open the door with Josef Eckhart marching in behind him. "We came as soon as we could. The storm held us up," Dutcher said.

"What is the status...." Eckhart inquired. Dr. Weisman entered the room with his smock drenched in blood and his eyes tired, gray, and cold.

"Where have you been?" he bellowed, looking at the two young physicians.

"We were at Dutcher's cabin and we were trapped in by the storm," Eckhart said.

"I hope you enjoyed your vacation gentlemen. It will cost you two weeks' pay," Dr. Weisman roared. "Your teams were on-call. You are to be in town and no more than fifteen minutes away from the hospital." Dr. Weisman's face was red with white streaks darting from the folds of his neck.

"Two, of what should have been your patients, almost died eleven hours ago. You can thank these gentlemen for their lives and your skin. All of the patients' charts are in the electronic records. I expect you to memorize each one of them. Consider yourselves on duty."

Dutcher and Eckhart left and Dr. Weisman's lead nurse untied his smock and handed him a towel. "Carmen, what are we going to do with these children?"

She looked at Jacob sitting on the floor with his eyes closed and at the prince splashing cold water on his face. "There is hope, Abraham," she said cheerfully. "There is hope."

* * *

Marcus and Jacob walked down the hallway to the chapel. They opened the door and saw Lara still praying and waiting in front of the small altar. Marcus walked up beside her. She was clutching a wadded tissue when she looked up at the prince.

"He'll be fine Lara. No need to worry." Relief poured out in her tears.

"Thank you," she said to Marcus. She looked up at the cross at the front of the chapel. "Oh, thank you, God, thank you."

Marcus sat down next to her in the pew. Jacob sat in front of them and then turned around and patted Lara's hand.

"Your father is probably upstairs by now," Marcus said. "Why don't you go see him?"

Lara wiped away the tears, straightened her uniform and smiled. "Do I look all right?" the young woman asked. "My father hates it when I cry."

"You look fine," Marcus said, "but he is asleep and will be for hours."

"Yes, of course," Lara said with a nervous laugh. "Thank you," she said as she left.

The door swung closed and in the quiet of the chapel Jacob and Marcus looked at each other.

"It was a miracle we saved them all," Jacob said.

Marcus looked down at his hands. "I don't know how I did it," Marcus confessed. "Thank you," Marcus said, looking at the cross. "Thank you, Lord Jesus."

Dr. Weisman saw Jacob and Marcus coming out of the chapel and called to them from the hallway. "There is a hot meal waiting for everyone in the lounge. You had better get there before Smith does."

"What time is it?" Marcus asked.

Dr. Weisman looked at his watch, "Ten-thirty on December the fifteenth."

"The fifteenth?" Marcus mumbled. "Fifteenth! The senate! Are the roads clear?"

"I don't know. They are clear to the hospital," Dr. Weisman replied.

Just then, Broderick appeared at the opposite end of the hallway. "Prince Marcus," he called, holding a valise and a garment bag. "The Senate had postponed the hearings because of the weather but will now convene in less than one hour." Marcus grabbed the bags from Broderick and ran to the locker room.

"Broderick, have my car up front. I'll be there in twenty minutes."

CHAPTER 48

Only one road was plowed to the Senate building but the balcony was full of reporters and Dreiholmian citizens anxiously waiting to hear the prince speak. A loud thump in the back of the balcony caused Marcus to look up from his seat next to his father's throne. He saw a reporter's assistant, his shoulders loaded with bags, talking to one of the royal guards posted at the door. Another guard inspected a bag that he had dropped to the balcony floor. Prince Marcus looked to his side and surveyed the guests beside him. Peter, dressed in a black suit, looked pale. He was clutching a leather file in his hand and gulped hard as he watched Lord Greven standing beside his desk. Whether he could feel Marcus looking at him or not, Peter broke away from watching the formidable opponent on the senate floor. Marcus gave him a reassuring nod and Peter tightened his posture and laid the leather envelope on the plain wooden table in front of him. Ms. Olin was beside him along with a staff of contractors, development specialists and geological experts who were talking among themselves, waiting for the session to begin.

Marcus exhaled slowly and looked up again at the spectators. Payton was standing next to the balcony railing, looking down over the senate floor below. Broderick was seated in a row behind him and Sarah was beside Broderick with her eyes fixed on Peter. Marcus wanted to laugh when he spotted Jacob dressed in a white physician's jacket and jeans. He must not have been able to get back home in time to change, he thought, as his eyes wandered to Phillip and then to Dr. Weisman and his father's advisors. Marcus could feel the knot in his stomach tighten. He closed his stinging eyes and prayed silently the only two words that came to mind: Lord, help.

The gavel struck down sharply and the senate president called the session to order. Marcus took a deep breath and released it as he stood in front of the railing that separated him from the senate floor. The crowded room fell silent. Marcus looked across the room, recognizing each face, and then he began.

"By right, once each senatorial session, it is my privilege to bring an issue before the Senate for immediate debate, and conclude with a final and binding vote. To my regret, I have never once initiated my right, an error I intend to remedy from this day forward," Marcus said slowly. The walking sticks, an ancient tradition in the Dreiholm Senate, tapped modestly on the floor in support.

"I come before you today to begin a process and to offer one solution to resolve a crisis that has long plagued our nation. To our shame, we have neglected the dire need for housing, housing for our young people, married couples, families, and the elderly." The balcony came alive with tapping, clapping of hands, and cheers. "We have ignored the discontentment, discouragement and discomfort of our people and as a result, our greatest asset, our most cherished treasure, the citizens of Dreiholm, are leaving this nation for foreign lands in pursuit of a dream that should and can be a reality right here." The tapping turned to stomps in the balcony and the senators looked up at the faces above them.

"In the twenty-first century, we are the pioneers of medical and technological research, yet today we enforce antiquated lease agreements, hinder renovation to existing properties and discourage, and most often, block new development. A country such as ours, rich with ingenuity and innovation and blessed with resources and peace, has little excuse for our neglect. I take responsibility for my willing ignorance on this matter, and I beg for my people's forgiveness and pardon. I have no excuse. Now I look to you, members of the Senate, to rectify a wrong. I am bringing you a plan, a development for the Petra Mountains."

Lord Greven's eyes turned to slits of black as he glared at the Prince. "This project, in its first phase, will house three hundred and fifty families. It is a small start. It is a test of our creativity and a measurement of our commitment," Marcus continued. The stomping rose to a thunder above him but Marcus' eyes remained on the senate floor and the unflinching cold stare of Lord Greven. "The men and women beside me are the experts of the Westwind project. They will answer your questions," Marcus said. Lord Puttem stood to his feet, twisting his cane.

"You expect us to make a final decision on a matter of such magnitude and consequence before the session ends this afternoon?" he asked acidly.

Unaccustomed to abrupt interruptions, Marcus stepped forward to address Puttem directly, but then thought better of it and guarded his tongue by gritting his teeth.

"You are well acquainted with the information to be presented," Marcus said. "Similar projects have been introduced before. Westwind has addressed the prior concerns of the Senate and has incorporated the changes necessary to satisfy any skeptics."

"Your Highness understands we must conclude our session at three o'clock," Lord Puttem said sternly.

"I am quite familiar with the rules and procedures of the Senate, Lord Puttem. I strongly suggest that we dispense with any unnecessary discussion and begin debate on the issue at hand," Marcus said.

Lord Puttem turned to Lord Greven. The elder statesman spun the silver-topped cane in his hand and grinned at the prince.

"If this project is acceptable, when is it to commence?" Lord Schuler asked.

"I see no reason for delay. The project will start immediately," Marcus said. "And I see no need to delay this discussion any longer. I will have the chairman of the Westwind Housing Group, Peter Bach, introduce the panel and I now ask the aides to pass out copies of the project report to you."

The brightly dressed aides, holding armfuls of neatly-bound reports, began passing them out to the lords. The doors in the balcony opened and senate aides entered with copies in large sacks. The reporters scurried to the door, ripping copies out of the aides' hands, going out into the hallway and coming back in again as they reported their news. Marcus sat down before the Senate and Peter took his place at the podium. The fear that was so evident moments ago in the young man had disappeared. The panel presented their report and quickly the debate was underway.

As time passed, Marcus could see Lord Greven's lieutenants were losing the fight. Each ailing argument presented was rebutted by the panel with facts and studies to the contrary until the debate had diminished to awkward moments of silence. Lord Greven was curiously silent, Marcus thought. He had stopped every other building project proposed in the past, why not an attempt to stop this one?

The clock in the chamber struck two and Lord Greven rose from his seat. He brushed his full gray mustache and smiled broadly and chuckled as he leaned on his walking stick.

"All of this is amusing," Lord Greven began. "We have seen these proposals before. This one is not unlike the others," Lord Greven continued, spreading his arms to his fellow senators. "We have asked ourselves the same questions before, questions of cost, safety, security, and transportation. All have been answered admirably by the panel of experts the prince has provided to us, but we have not touched on one question that, in my humble opinion, is of the greatest concern to our nation. Should our pristine mountain slopes, the brightest jewel in his majesty's crown, and the fortress in which we have found refuge throughout the darkest hours of history be marred, disfigured, and surely spoiled by this destructive development? Surely not. And where would it end? Would one lead to another and then to another small but unsightly blemish?

"Gentlemen, we have discussed and debated this before and have concluded in unanimity for the Ecological Act that our king eagerly signed into law. We were praised by the international community for our efforts and now you want to revert back to this destructive and caustic practice and disregard the Act as if it does not even exist?" Lord Greven said smugly.

"Certainly, you are not suggesting that the Ecological Act prohibits all building in the mountain regions, Lord Greven," Earl Bowman countered.

"Absolutely not, Lord Bowman. It is just that the Petra Mountains are the nesting ground of the European Swainson's hawk, and to destroy its habitat would be contrary to the Act and forbidden by law."

"The European Swainson's hawk is not an endangered species," Peter blurted out from the podium.

"Who are you, boy, and do you also claim to be an expert on ornithology?" Lord Greven sputtered.

"I am a servant to His Majesty's son, the Prince of Dreiholm and no, I cannot claim to be an expert bird watcher," Peter said. Marcus snickered, watching the pompous lord flush. "But I am familiar with the subject. My mother, Camellia Bach, is the renowned illustrator and writer for *Europe's Field and Stream* magazine and is a consultant to His Majesty's wildlife service. She is present in the spectator's balcony," Peter said. "Would you like me to ask her to step down?"

"Mrs. Bach," Lord Bowman called out. A trim woman who had been sitting next to Sarah stood up. Her long black and gray hair was pulled up neatly in a barrette.

"Are you Mrs. Bach?" he asked.

"Yes, I am," she answered from the balcony.

"Is this true?"

"The European Swainson's Hawk is not endangered by any means," she said. The crowd laughed as Greven grunted and turned a ripe red.

"Tell me, Mrs. Bach," Lord Greven said, "would bulldozers, cranes, blasts of dynamite, the constant hammering, the literal destruction of its habitat have any effect or disrupt in any way the hawk's ability to reproduce?" Lord Greven thundered.

"The population..."

"Yes or no, Mrs. Bach," he interrupted.

"The extent of the disruption..."

"Mrs. Bach, surely we would all love to hear your full opinion on this matter, but since we are pressed for time and must make a hasty decision, I will ask you again to please answer yes or no."

"Yes," she said quietly, looking at her son.

"I don't think we heard you, Mrs. Bach."

"Yes," she said louder.

"Then building would negatively impact the hawk's ability to maintain its current healthy status in our ecosystem and could quite possibly cause the birds to be endangered in the future," Lord Greven pronounced. "A clear violation of the Ecological Act," he said, smiling at his fellow senators. Greven's lieutenants tapped their canes in support.

"You're grasping, Greven," Lord Baumann said.

"Grasping, grasping!" Lord Greven laughed. "Weren't you the one who introduced the bill that became the Ecological Act?"

"You're stretching well beyond its intended purpose to protect and plan for the future, which the Westwind plan has done; not to prevent progress or dream up possibilities that may or may not come true."

"I take offense, Lord Baumann," Greven said in a wounded voice. "This is not a dream. It is a reality. And one that is prohibited by law."

"That is a question of interpretation," Lord Baumann said. He stood and then pressed his knuckles into the desk. Peter's face began to turn white as he watched the lords conferring among themselves, siding with one or the other. Greven's lieutenants were dispersed on the floor, challenging and debating and gathering votes. Marcus stood and walked to the divide and the room fell silent.

"Perhaps I didn't make myself clear in this proposal. I thought I had," Marcus said regally. "Venue is of little consequence to me. We chose this parcel because it best accomplishes our goals and the wishes of the Senate. But I am open to your suggestions," he said, looking out onto the floor. "Lord Greven?"

"Your Highness knows my opinions on such matters."

"No suggestions then?" Marcus asked.

"None, Your Highness," Greven answered.

"Then I have one that might appease the Senate and the Swainson's Hawk," Marcus said, gripping the railing before him. "Lord Greven, were you not an advisor to my grandmother?"

"I was," Lord Greven said proudly.

"And as a reward for your services, she gifted to you Baumen Castle and its fifteen-hundred-acre estate, a property that you yourself have expanded and refurbished over the years. In fact, when I was so graciously invited to your home this past year, you boasted that you had just completed another fine home on that land, a mansion nonetheless, for one of your many grandchildren. Isn't that right?"

"As you know, Your Highness, that is within my right," Lord Greven said stuffily.

"A right you willingly deny my people!" Marcus shouted. "Now, since you have found the property suitable to build homes for your grandchildren, I would be willing to make arrangements to have Westwind purchase the adjacent lands to your estate for development." Marcus regained his composure and slightly adjusted the cuff on his sleeve. "It is choice land, close to existing rail lines, the business district and the capital. And, as you know, very conducive for building," he said evenly.

Lord Greven's eyes burned as he clenched his fist and clutched his cane. "The King would never approve of such a proposal."

"You dare to speculate on the King's intentions or have you forgotten to whom you are speaking," Marcus said, holding on to the railing and glaring down at Lord Greven. "My people congregate in hovels, cramped to capacity with nowhere to go except out beyond our mountain borders. Those of us born or blessed with means have become complacent, ignorant and foolish. I know my people, their strength, their ability, their endurance, and their faith. They have been tolerant beyond measure. And if their patience has not waned, mine has. I will not drive them out, I will not give them up, and I will not let them down," Marcus promised, glaring at Greven.

A wild cheer rang from the balcony and the bell rang, calling an end to the session and for a final vote. The balcony rumbled as the voices died down.

"You now have two proposals," Prince Marcus said, looking down at the senate floor. "The original before you and an alternative," he said, his eyes now focused on Lord Greven. "It is my prayer that you will choose wisely." Marcus retired to his seat and looked to the president of the senate.

"The Senate will now come to a vote," he ordered.

* * *

Peter ran out of the senate quarters, searching for Sarah among the many faces waiting in the grand foyer.

"We did it! Sarah, it passed! It passed!" he said, lifting her up into the air, spinning her around. A reporter took a shot and others followed in a glittering array of flashing lights. Marcus came out of the chambers surrounded by a mass of security, congratulatory senators, hungry reporters, and multitudes of excited and jubilant citizens. In the midst of questions and the echoing cheers, Marcus saw his father. He had not entered the chamber but was now behind the glass wall above him. Their eyes met and the King of Dreiholm smiled.

"Your Highness, Your Highness," a reporter called. "Now that you have championed one cause for the people, will there be others?"

"God willing," Marcus said in a determined voice, "many more."

CHAPTER 49

"No, we haven't had any sleep," Jacob said into his cell phone. "I'll be fine." He saw Marcus walking down the hospital hallway, no longer in formal attire from the senate meeting, but back in his scrubs. "I have to stay here. I'll grab something at the cafeteria. Really, I'll be fine," Jacob said.

"Are you talking to Ostride?" Marcus whispered as he approached. Jacob nodded. "Is Megan there?" Marcus asked.

"Ostride, is Megan there?" Jacob nodded again and turned away from Marcus who followed him down the hallway. "What is Phillip doing there?" Jacob asked. Marcus smiled and leaned against the wall. "Doesn't he ever have work to do?... No, I'm not jealous," Jacob said looking at Marcus, disgusted. "Yes, I am very tired. I love you too."

Marcus motioned to Jacob that he wanted to talk to Megan. "I know, I will," Jacob said. "Ostride, Marcus wants to talk to Megan. I'll call you when I'm ready to leave." Jacob handed his phone to Marcus. "We have to find a job for Phillip," Jacob whispered, and then headed to the nurses' station across the hall.

Hearing Megan's voice gave him the first sense of calm that he had known all day. "I'm fine," Marcus said, "they're doing as well as can be expected. I was thinking that I would stop by tonight after I get some sleep. Good. I'll come over then," he said, closing the phone and handing it back to Jacob.

"What are you doing back here at the hospital?" Jacob asked.

"The same thing you're doing here, looking after our patients," Marcus said. He sat down on top of the desk. "How are they now?"

"Everyone seems to be holding their own except Stewart. We may have to go in again," Jacob said, shaking his head as he looked at the computer screen. "We'll know one way or the other by this evening." He sat back in his chair. "By the way, good job," Jacob said with a sincere smile. "For a minute at the senate meeting, I remembered that my best friend was the Prince of Dreiholm."

"In training," Marcus said, smiling and looking down at his feet.

"What are you two doing here?" Dr. Weisman asked as he stepped out of a patient's room. Marcus and Jacob laughed, knowing their mentor had less sleep than they. "I know. It is addicting, is it not? But you will learn something when you get as old as I am. You need food and rest," he said, putting his hands inside his coat pockets. "The food service is treating us to a buffet in the doctors' lounge. Go, eat, and then get some rest," the elder physician said. "You will be called if you are needed."

Neither of the young men moved. "Go! Go on Jacob, Prince Marcus. I will be in to join you in a minute."

Marcus slid off the desk. Their adrenaline depleted, he and Jacob slowly walked down the hallway. They passed the elevators and followed the aroma to the lounge. "You know, he called you Prince Marcus," Jacob said, looking at his friend out of the corner of his eye. "I think that is the first time."

"The first," Marcus nodded.

* * *

The wind made a sad and lonely howl as it flooded the chimney of Megan's apartment, whistling as it pressed against the windows and pushed through the fine cracks of their frames. Megan could feel the cold draft as she stood in front of the picture window. The storm had subsided in the morning when she had trudged through the snow to see Ostride. But now in the dark of night the snow was blowing again, and from the light of the street lamp Megan could see that the roads were drifting over with snow and the bare spots had become black sheets of ice. She looked at the clock on the kitchen wall and then back out at the drifting snow.

Marc's probably sleeping right through the night, she thought. He deserves the rest and there's no sense in him coming out in this snow. She closed the heavy curtains and then picked up the telephone. After dialing the hospital to leave a message for Marcus to stay and avoid the storm, she changed her mind and quickly set the receiver back down on its cradle. She picked it up and set it back down once more before settling into her cocoon of blankets on the couch. Wrapped in her down comforter, she huddled down into the pillows and picked up a book. With her hands barely peeking outside the ripples of blankets, she opened the cover. "Glasses," she said in disgust. She wrenched her neck back and saw them on her nightstand by the bed. Instead of leaving her warm nest, she strained her eyes to read but her mind kept wandering back to Marcus. He's all right, she told herself. He's been at the hospital all day and most likely warmer than I am. She hooked a knitted loop of an afghan with her toe and wound it around her feet and tucked it underneath the down blanket. The feather pillows puffed out on either side of her face and she smiled secretly. In the recesses of her mind she could see Marcus sleeping on her couch and the flames of the fire reflecting on the gold strands of his hair.

Her smile faded as she examined the picture in her mind and saw what she knew now as Marcus's family ring shining on his hand. How will this ever work, she wondered helplessly, considering their many differences. "If you don't know what God wants you to do, ask Him and He will gladly tell you," Megan recalled from her Bible study. "Ask Him," Megan repeated aloud. "Lord, what is it that you want me to do?" she pleaded. "It would take a miracle to bridge this gap. I really don't know anything about this place or his family and I can't even speak the language! But what is your will, Lord? Is Marc the right one? You know, he's never even told me that he loves me, but you know Lord, I love him."

Another gust pounded against the window and Megan buried herself even deeper into the blankets. She stared at the ceiling and noticed a crack in the wall. Another job for poor Mr. Grutner, she thought. The telephone rang and she jumped to reach it before it rang again.

"Hello," Megan said.

"Megan, meet me at Summit and Fifth in ten minutes," the breathless voice said on the other end of the line.

"Westin?" Megan asked in surprise.

"Yes. Hurry."

"What's the matter?"

"Just meet me at Summit and Fifth in ten minutes. I need...." His voice trailed off and the phone went dead.

Megan ran to the window and pulled back the curtains. She looked down to see the wind pounding the building with gusts and small pellets of ice. The street was a dune of snow, deserted and dark. She grabbed a coat, slipped on the first pair of shoes she found, and ran out of her apartment and down the stairway, skipping steps as she fled. She opened the heavy front door to the outside and a blast of white icy pellets struck her face. She could see from the top of the outside steps that the sidewalks were also covered in ice. She held onto the railing as she slid down and jumped over the sidewalk and into the snow, running in the deep drifts until she had to stop to catch her breath. She looked up at a street sign. Her heart was pounding in her chest and a stream of frozen milky air flooded from her mouth. The houses and shops that lined the streets beside her were lifeless and encased in snow. Down the hill, in between the waves of white, she could see a large building decorated with Christmas lights. She rushed on and then stopped at Summit Avenue. The green street sign was glazed in an ice shell and the streetlight across the avenue was flocked with a thick layer of snow. Another violent wave of wind descended down upon her and she reached for the pole with her bare hands.

"Megan!" Westin called. She could see his arm reaching out to hers, and he pulled her toward the shadows of an alley. Westin put his arms around her and guided her through a fence door at the back of the alley. He locked the gate behind them, blocking out the ferocious wind. Dressed in black from head to foot, Megan could barely see him in the dark veil of the buildings beside them. The snow-covered streetlight exposed a faint image of his blackened face.

"What's this all about?" Megan asked in low voice. "Why are you here dressed up like that?" she asked. Westin pulled her into his arms and began kissing her before she could say another word. "Westin!" Megan said, struggling to get free.

"Megan, come away with me," he said, holding on to her. Megan stepped back into the light. Westin clung to her and in the dim glow she could see his face and his eyes searching hers.

"What's happened?" Megan asked, wide-eyed.

"Come away with me," he said clutching her arms. "I can take you to Hong Kong, the beaches of South America, the Greek Islands."

"No," Megan said. "You have a job. I have a job." We have an obligation. A commitment to finish what we started, Westin. What you're doing is important to me, to you, and so many others. We can't turn our backs on what we know is right."

"Megan, I'm offering you the world."

"The world?" Megan said, looking into his eyes. "Westin, I don't want the world."

"Whatever you do want, I'll get it for you," Westin said. "Please, Megan, come away with me now. You'll be safe with me."

Megan put her hand up to his face. "Westin, what's happened?" she asked. A crumpled up piece of newspaper tumbled in the alley, scraping against the wall of the brick building, doing cartwheels until it disappeared into the shadows. He continued to search her eyes.

"I have to do what is right," she said, "I can't run away."

"It really wasn't an act," he said softly, holding her hand to his lips. "Was it? You really are committed to your mission, your principles."

"An act? What do you mean?"

"I hoped, but I didn't believe," Westin said, fading back toward the shadows. "Megan, come with me," he pleaded.

"I can't," Megan said. She felt him kiss her hand as he blended into the night. The sound of police sirens pierced through the winds and the sound of an alarm clanging in the distance echoed in the streets.

"Come with me," he whispered from the shadows.

"Westin, what happened? Whatever it is it can be worked out. I'll help you," Megan said. He pulled her into the darkness and kissed her again with a fervor and intensity of a fated end. A police car sped by, its sirens blaring and its red and blue lights flashing as it raced down the road. Megan turned to see it and when she looked back Westin had vanished.

"Westin?" Megan called. She waited, but the only sound she could hear was the sound of the wind rattling the gate and the rush of snow and ice above her. "Westin!" Megan called out again. "Don't go!"

She went up and down the alley, feeling her way through the darkness. It was empty. She ran back to the gate but there were no tracks, no sounds, only the scream of more and more police cars gathering in the distance. She looked out at the street, anxious and puzzled.

Westin watched her as she stood beside the light post, wind

billowing around her in bright clouds of whirling ice and snow.

"Goodbye Megan," he said quietly from the deep shadows on the other side of the structure. "You will always have my heart."

CHAPTER 50

"Good evening," Dr. Weisman said.

"Good evening," Marcus returned.

"Couldn't you find a bed?" he asked, looking at Jacob asleep in a chair and Marcus sitting up from the couch.

"Convenient," Marcus said, his head still swimming with restful slumber. "What time is it?"

Dr. Weisman pushed up his sleeve to see his watch. "It is eleven-thirty exactly."

"It can't be!" Marcus said, springing to his feet.

"What's the hurry?" Dr. Weisman asked, opening a package of crackers and crumbling them into a cup of soup.

"I was supposed to stop by a friend's house tonight."

"You might as well take your time."

"Why?"

"Only emergency routes are plowed but it started to snow again an hour or two ago." He took a little of his soup and rested his elbows on the table. "As for the rest of the streets, they are blocked. The crews will wait until the snow stops to clear them again. Besides, your young lady would surely be asleep by now."

"How did you know I was going to see Megan?" Marcus asked.

"I am old, not dead," Dr. Weisman said, peering over his glasses. "Your valet called earlier and asked if he could bring you and Jacob a change of clothing. He offered to stop by my house so my wife would not have to venture out in this weather. I hope you do not mind?"

"No, certainly not."

"The clothes are in your locker."

"Thank you," Marcus said, as he was about to push open the door to leave.

"Marcus," Dr. Weisman said, stopping him at the door. "You and

Jacob did a fine job in surgery. I am proud of both of you. And at the Senate,..." Dr. Weisman stopped. "It was a very good day."

Marcus pushed the swinging door back and forth in his hand and then looked at the doctor.

"You're usually very frugal with your compliments," Marcus noted.

"You children rarely give me reason to do so," Weisman said, crumbling another cracker in his soup. "It is when the exceptional talent becomes art, or courage and wisdom advance to leadership, that accolades are worthy, but even then, sparingly."

"And that is why they are most cherished," Marcus said humbly.

"Good night, Prince Marcus. Give my greetings to the young lady."

After a shower, shave, and putting on the clothes that Broderick had brought to the hospital, Marcus was refreshed and ready to see Megan. It was shortly after midnight when he looked at his watch. He knew he should call her before he started to her apartment but that would give her an opportunity to say no. It's not like we haven't stayed up until three o'clock in the morning before, he thought as he drove down the road. Why do I like that place so much? he asked himself. He thought about their evening dinners, studying together and sitting in front of the fireplace, and he realized that they had spent more time at her apartment than at any of his homes.

In the rear-view mirror he could see his security guards trailing close behind him. The blowing squalls had subsided and the emergency thoroughfares were clear but still slick with ice. "Disc one," Marcus commanded, and the music began to play in his car. He had found the disc in his backpack after one of his late nights at Megan's apartment. He recognized the purple and blue label right away. It was his favorite, what Megan called a southern rock band. He turned up the volume and started tapping the steering wheel to the heavy bass beat. The streets were barren and the precious solitude gave Marcus a rare chance to test out the abilities of his new car. Venturing off the emergency route and turning onto the avenue, the low car began to drag until it came to a complete stop. Megan's side street was covered in dunes of drifted snow that covered the ice beneath. Backing up only made the situation worse. Marcus tried to rock the car but the wheels spun and packed the snow into ice craters. The security guards parked behind him on the cleared street and ran towards the car. Marcus sheepishly stepped out. "I never should have tried to go through this," he admitted.

"We'll call for help," the guard assured him.

"I'm going to Miss Buchanan's apartment," Marcus said, starting down the street past the guard. "Here." He tossed the guard his keys.

"Yes, Sir. I'll stay with the car and Karl will follow you."

"I'll be all right, Max," Marcus said in the still night. The guard ignored the prince's reassurance and waved Karl on to follow him to the apartment. With a bounce in his step, Marcus hopped onto the sidewalk, stomping his feet and shaking the snow free from his pants. He looked up with anticipation and could see Megan's light was still on in her apartment. He followed a narrow path down the sidewalk and began to pick up his pace as he went.

In the distance he could see a drift of snow piled oddly in the middle of the path. He got a sick feeling in his stomach and looked up again at the light in Megan's apartment and then back at the drift. He noticed a dark shadow beside it and began to run.

"Megan!" Marcus screamed. Max jumped over the wrought iron fence and ran after the prince, catching up to Karl as Marcus slid down to the ground beside the lifeless body lying in a pool of frozen blood.

Marcus felt for her pulse. "Thank God, thank God!" he whispered. His hands began to shake as he and Karl feverishly brushed away the mounded snow from her body. "Call the hospital!" Marcus shouted. But when he looked up, Max was already talking on the phone to the emergency team and running back to the car.

"Megan," Marcus said, hovering over her. "Megan, can you hear me? Wake up! Megan, please," he pleaded, putting the palm of his hand against her face. Her flesh was cold and ashen. Her eyes remained closed as Marcus carefully lifted her head from the frozen red pool that stretched out beneath her. He could see the deep cut on the side of her head and he yanked at the scarf around his neck and carefully wrapped the bloody wound.

"Ice," Karl said, pointing at the jagged red-stained spike on the sidewalk.

"Megan, Megan," Marcus coaxed as Karl draped his coat over her.

"She may have frostbite," Karl said, looking at her bare ankles. Still cradling her, Marcus took off his coat and covered her feet. Her breathing was slow and shallow and underneath her jacket Marcus felt under her arms and her abdomen. Her body was wet and cold. "We have to get her warm now!" Marcus said.

"Sir, the ambulance is coming," Max said, running toward them and carrying a black bag. They could hear the sirens of the ambulance in the distance and then saw its flashing lights on the hill. Max dropped the bag beside Marcus and ripped off his coat, exposing his gun in the shoulder holster, and gently laid the wool coat on top of Megan. Karl opened the emergency kit and Marcus snapped the heat packs and put them next to Megan's chest as he huddled over her.

"Here they are," Karl said, as the medical team came through the snow. One of the medics fell on the sidewalk as he was running with the gurney. Max helped him to his feet and grabbed the gurney.

"Careful!" Marcus shouted to one of the medics lifting Megan off the ground. Megan's eyes fluttered open. Her face wrinkled in pain as she tried to move her head. "Megan," Marcus said, stroking her face as he ran beside the men carrying her. "Megan, don't move," Marcus said in a soothing voice. "I'm bringing you to the hospital."

"Marc?" she said faintly.

"You're going to be all right," he promised.

"Cold," she barely whispered and then began to shake. She could hear Marcus yelling at the medics in his native tongue and then it all went black.

* * *

"She's awake," a medic said. Megan could feel the rumble of the road beneath her and she winced as she opened her eyes to the bright lights in the ambulance.

"Megan, I want you to talk and keep talking to me," Marcus pleaded. She started to shake violently. "Give me another blanket," he ordered, and the young medic reached above his head and pulled down another silver blanket and spread it over her.

"Two minutes to the hospital," the driver announced.

"Megan, do you remember going outside?" Marcus asked.

"Ummm," she mumbled, closing her eyes again. Her frozen body rattled and she tried to reach for the pain in her head. "My head," she shuddered. The medic held her arm to her side.

"I know," Marcus said softly, "we're giving you something for the pain."

"Call you," Megan said, in a trembling voice.

"I'm right here Megan, I won't leave you," Marcus said, kissing her fingers and warming them against his face. "I promise."

The doors to the ambulance flew open and the emergency staff pulled the gurney from the ambulance and wheeled Megan into a balmy emergency room used for hypothermia patients.

"She may have a concussion. Her temperature has fallen to ninety-three degrees," Marcus said, still holding Megan's hand. Dr. Weisman was waiting in the room with his team and he went to Megan's side.

"Can you tell me your name?" Dr. Weisman asked, looking into her eyes with his penlight.

"Megan... Buchanan," she said slowly. Megan's teeth chattered and then she coughed, making her head explode in pain. Marcus felt her hand wrench and grasp on to his.

"Good. Good," Dr. Weisman said as he carefully unwrapped the scarf from her head and handed it to Lara. "And where do you live?" Megan's back arched in pain.

"Home, Marc," she muttered and her body went limp.

"Megan!" Marcus shouted. "Megan, don't. Megan!"

"She's passed out," Dr. Weisman said listening to her heart. "We need her in X-ray, prepped for surgery if needed, and let's get her warmed up," Dr. Weisman ordered. "Hurry." A flurry of nurses rushed around Megan's bed peeling off the layers of blankets and cutting away her wet clothes. Jacob bolted into the emergency room as Dr. Weisman was trying to get Marcus away from Megan's bed.

"You must leave," Dr. Weisman said to Marcus.

"No."

"You will leave and you will leave now!" Dr. Weisman ordered. Jacob stepped beside Marcus. "We'll take care of her, Marcus," Jacob said calmly, taking Megan's hand away from his and rubbing Megan's arm. "We'll take care of her. Go on."

Marcus looked desperately at his friend and let go. Lara took the prince by the arm and walked out of the emergency room. "I came when I heard. We'll take care of her," she promised, leaving him at a bench outside the emergency room. "We'll take care of her," she repeated and then rushed back through the swinging doors. Marcus collapsed on a vinyl bench in the empty hallway. Jacob came out and sat next to him.

"They're doing everything they can. She's in X-ray. We'll know in a minute," he said.

Marcus clasped his hands and rested his elbows on his knees and bowed his head. Jacob saw his tears falling to the floor.

"I thought she was dead," Marcus said. Jacob put his hand on his friend's back.

"Dr. Weisman's with her," Jacob said. "That's the best care a person can get."

Marcus nodded his head silently.

"I checked on Lara's father when I woke up," Jacob offered.

"How is he?"

"Good, good. You did a good job," Jacob said.

Marcus could feel his heart pounding in his chest and a swollen lump throbbing in his throat.

"Let me see how she's doing, and I'll be right back," Jacob said.

For the first time in his life the antiseptic smell of the hospital nauseated Marcus and he rushed to the bathroom and hung over the sink. "Lord God, help," he said as he took deep breaths and felt his stomach contract. "God, please help Megan," he prayed. He rinsed out his mouth and looked into the bathroom mirror. In the recesses of his mind he could see Megan lying on the sidewalk, her body still and lifeless and her face void of color. He watched as he examined the gouge in her head and saw the blood on his hands. He felt the cold of her body and could see his tears falling as he looked in the mirror. He took a towel and covered his face, wiping off his perspiration. He hung on to the sink and ran the water. He could feel his stomach lurch and then release. He splashed cold water on his face and held his face into a towel.

"Marcus!" Jacob called as he swung the door open.

"I'm in here," Marcus said.

"It looked worse than it is," Jacob said, looking at his friend in the reflection of the mirror. "No brain injury, mild concussion, and her temperature is rising," Jacob said. "If we watch her carefully, she'll be fine."

"Where is she?" Marcus asked, wiping his face again and then throwing the towel in the wastebasket.

"You won't be able to see her for awhile."

"Watch me," Marcus said sharply.

"Dr. Weisman just finished stitching up the wound to her head and has ordered a hydrobath to bring up her body temperature and relax her muscles. Lara has her in there now. She's nauseated and awake but she won't be for very long. They'll clean her up and bring her to her room shortly." Marcus' stomach was still cramped in a knot. He reached for another towel. "What room will she be in?"

"285," Jacob said. Marcus stood over the sink looking into the mirror at Jacob.

"No, send her to the suite," Marcus said.

"The suite?"

"Yes, tell them. I'll be out in a minute."

"I will," Jacob said. Marcus heard the door close and he buried his face into his towel. Thank you, Lord Jesus. Again, thank you, Marcus prayed silently.

CHAPTER 51

"It's done," Jacob said, "I changed Megan's room."

"Good," Marcus said. He turned to his locker, pulled out a clean shirt and threw the soiled one into his bag. As Marcus tucked in his shirt, Jacob noticed a slight tremor in his hand.

"I checked with Lara. Megan's doing fine and will be in your room in few minutes."

"Thanks."

"By the way, Payton's here," Jacob added.

"Why?" Marcus asked, facing him again.

"With no relatives here, he's her first call for emergencies, I guess," Jacob said. "Her uncle and aunt have been contacted in the States."

Just then Phillip stormed into the locker room. "I've been looking all over this place for you," he said. "Where have you been?"

"Megan's been hurt," Jacob said.

"Megan?" Phillip asked. "What happened? Is she all right?"

"When I found her she was hypothermic, knocked out in front of her apartment," Marcus said.

"This doesn't make sense," Phillip said, his forehead furrowed in puzzlement. "Something's not right in all of this."

"What are you talking about?" Marcus demanded. "All of what?"

"The jewels have been stolen," Phillip said carefully.

"The jewels? When?" Marcus asked.

"As far as we can tell, somewhere around eleven," Phillip said. "Whoever did it knew exactly what they were doing. He or she or they took only the best and never tripped one alarm or alerted one guard."

"How could this have happened?" Marcus questioned. "With all the security...."

"No one knows. The only reason they found out anything at all was because one of the guards likes to look at the jewels in between his usual rounds and he saw they were missing."

"That's strange," Jacob said, "when Megan woke up in X-ray she was agitated. They calmed her down but the nurses kept saying that she wanted you and then asked them to call Payton."

"Why was she outside?" Phillip asked. "I walked her home from Ostride's and she knew you were coming to meet her at her apartment. Why would she leave? It doesn't make sense."

Marcus thought back to the moment he found her on the sidewalk. Her ankles were bare, her jacket was open, and she didn't have any gloves or a hat on.

"She was running to tell me something," Marcus said rushing out of the room.

Marcus reached the suite as the king and Chuck Payton were walking out. The king's bodyguards encircled them and lined the hall.

"A beautiful girl," the king said to Payton.

"Father!" Marcus called out from the elevator.

"Your Highness," Jacob and Phillip both said in surprise. The king looked at them and motioned to them to come closer as he continued to talk to Payton.

"I'll talk to her again in the morning," Chuck said to the king. "I don't know if she can give us much more but maybe there'll be a detail or two we can glean after the fog of the sedatives pass."

"Keep me informed," the king said.

"Father?" Marcus said, reaching his side. The king put his hand on his son's shoulder. "Post guards at the door and cover the hospital," the King said to the guard beside him.

"Done, Your Highness." The gray-haired leader of the guard looked at two of his men across the hallway, and with a nod of his head they stood in front of Megan's door.

"She has told us everything she knows," the king said to Marcus. "I will call for you tomorrow." Marcus looked into his father's eyes and knew not to question him further. "The child needs her rest. You take care of her. I will take care of everything else tonight," he said, walking with Marcus down the hallway.

"Did they take everything?" Marcus asked.

"No, not everything," the king said as he studied his son. Marcus glanced back at the suite and then at the elevator. "I will call for you tomorrow," he reassured Marcus and then stepped into the elevator with his bodyguards and Payton.

"Phillip, Jacob, come with me," the King commanded. Dutifully the men stepped in, shuffling around the guards. Before the doors closed, the King saw his son bound for Megan's room. He snickered, looking down at the floor and holding his finger to his lips. Ida might be right about this one after all, he thought.

* * *

Marcus stood at the end of Megan's bed. She was asleep with the white sheet and blankets tucked snugly around her. He sat down beside her and touched her hand. It was warm and flush with life. He smiled and let out a sigh of relief.

"I gave her a sedative to help her rest," a voice from across the room said. Marcus jumped and saw Dr. Weisman standing in a corner by the light. "I assume that Jacob briefed you on her condition."

"Yes," Marcus said. Lara came in and put some ice water on the nightstand and checked Megan's intravenous fluids and her temperature. She turned out the small light above her bed, smiled at the prince and left the room.

"How is her temperature?" Marcus asked.

"A little below normal but nothing to be concerned about now," Dr. Weisman said. "She gave us a scare, but she is resilient. I want her to rest. She will not be feeling well in the morning."

"Her head?" Marcus asked.

"Yes, that and her hip and the upset from the hypothermia. She must have fallen on her right side. The tissue is severely bruised. I will watch her tonight."

"I'll stay," Marcus said quietly. He looked at Megan's face. Her lips and cheeks were a soft petal pink and her dark hair was loosely braided and resting against her shoulder. A lazy renegade curl hung on her forehead and another next to her cheek. He brushed the curl on her cheek aside.

"I will be downstairs if you need me," Dr. Weisman said. He left Megan's chart on the desk and turned the desk light down low. "Otherwise, I will be back for my regular visits."

"I'm sorry," Marcus said, as the doctor was about to leave the room. "I should have left when you asked, but I didn't want to leave her," Marcus said. The old doctor looked at the young woman lying in the bed and then at Marcus.

"No apologies are necessary," the doctor said.

* * *

Jacob walked into the suite holding a large cup of hot coffee. "I thought you might like some," he said, handing it to Marcus.

"Thanks. Where's Phillip?"

"He went to get Ostride."

"Ostride?"

"I told them there was nothing either of them could do, but they insisted on being here when Megan wakes up," Jacob said. "Ostride seems to be of the opinion that doctors only make you worse, not better. I don't think she trusts us," Jacob said whimsically, making Marcus smile. "Has she awakened at all?" Jacob asked, glancing at her chart.

"Once. I gave her some water and she went right back to sleep," Marcus said. "I don't think she will even remember."

"Oh, before I forget, Phillip brought this by," Jacob said, and dug into his pocket. He pulled out the small but exquisite diamond ring that was at the museum and dropped it into Marcus' hand.

"I asked him to get it for me," Marcus said.

"I think the king had some inclination," Jacob said, leaning against the wall.

"He did?" Marcus asked.

"When Phillip went to the museum to get it, the King was there inspecting the damage. When he saw Phillip enter, he handed him the ring and said, 'You would be looking for this,' and sent him on his way."

"What did Father want to ask you and Phillip earlier?"

"The usual," Jacob said. "Honestly, I think he just wanted you to have some time alone with Megan." Jacob watched Megan sleeping peacefully. Without any makeup on her face she looked younger, Jacob thought, almost childlike in her slumber. "Are you ready?" Jacob asked.

"I'm ready," Marcus said.

"I wonder if the old fable will come true?"

"It's just a story," Marcus chided, looking at the ring and then flipping it onto the top of his little finger. "I will pick the woman I will marry. Not one from a spun tale."

"Still I wonder," Jacob said, looking at Megan's finger.

"And not a word to Ostride," Marcus warned.

"I'm not the one you should be telling. Have a chat with your cousin. He spends more time with these two than we do."

"He's already been warned," Marcus replied.

"We've got to find him a job," Jacob said, holding on to the edge of Megan's bed. "Remember that man in Bogotá we met, the one with seven daughters? I bet he could use a photographer."

"Are you trying to get him a job or married?" Marcus asked.

"Both," Jacob said dryly. The gleam of the diamond ring on Marcus' finger caught the light and Jacob's eye. "The ring was almost lost."

"Stolen, you mean," Marcus said.

"Whoever committed the crime tried to get it. The security around the case was disabled but the ring was left intact. The thief must have run out of time and left it," Jacob said. "It's strange though, and I'm not trying to be critical, but why would anyone want to take the time to steal that ring when more precious gems from the crown jewel collection were left behind?"

CHAPTER 52

When Megan awoke the sun's red and orange glow was about to crest over the horizon. She usually enjoyed watching the deep blue melt away to the dawning of the new day, but today the beams of light pierced her eyes and made the ringing in her head feel worse. She turned from the window and saw Marcus sleeping on a chair pulled close to her bed. Jacob and Ostride were sharing a couch and Phillip had joined two chairs and an ottoman together to make himself a cot. With another throb of pain, she closed her eyes again and reached for her head. Hearing the rustle of the stiffly starched sheets woke Marcus.

"Megan," he said in a hushed voice. He reached for her hand that was reaching to her head and gently set it back down at her side. "You have a deep cut and bruise on your head. You're going to experience some pain," he said in his doctorly voice. Megan tried to speak but began to cough. Marcus held a glass of water up to her and put the straw to her mouth.

"Now I get to take care of you." He smiled as she drank the water. She held on to his hand and closed her eyes.

"I have a pounding headache," Megan whispered.

"We can up the meds," Marcus said calmly.

"No," she whispered, "I don't want to fall asleep again."

"Good morning," Ostride said softly, coming to Megan's bedside with Jacob. Ostride's hair was in a ponytail and the bright striped turtleneck she was wearing matched her smile. "I came as soon as I heard. They told me you were going to be just fine but I had to see for myself. Who can trust what these two say?" Ostride jested.

"Hi Meg!" Phillip said from across the room. His voice boomed in Megan's ears and she winced in pain.

"Shh!" Marcus scowled.

"Sorry, Meg," Phillip whispered.

"I see you're not lacking for medical attention," Dr. Weisman said, as he entered the room. "Could you all step out into the hall please?" Marcus made no effort to move with the others as Dr. Weisman came to Megan's bedside. "Marcus, would you go find Lara for me?"

"Can't we buzz her?" Marcus asked, as the old doctor listened to Megan's heart.

"Ask her to bring in fresh linens and a new gown for Miss Buchanan. I think this young lady would like to freshen up, don't you?"

"Yes, of course," Marcus said, looking at Megan. "I'll be back."

"A bit of privacy would be welcomed around here," Dr. Weisman said to Megan as Marcus left. Megan smiled and closed her eyes.

"It's nice to have friends, but thank you," she said softly. Dr. Weisman quickly examined her and sat down next to her bed.

"You'll be fine in a few days but until then, and sometime after, you will have headaches, experience stiffness, pain from the bruises and perhaps even some nausea and dizziness. That is why I am going to recommend that you stay in the hospital for one or two more days." Megan tried propping herself up in the bed.

"I'm sure if you can just give me something for my headache, I can manage at home."

"I am sorry, Miss Buchanan, I refuse to budge on my decision." Megan slumped down into the warm bed. "Don't look so sad. It's not so bad here. I've been told our food is far superior to most hospitals."

Megan looked around the room at the carpeted floors, billowing curtains, satin settee, elegant coffee tables and wet bar. "Are all your rooms like this one?" she asked.

"No, no," Dr. Weisman laughed. "I wish they all were like this one but no, this room is reserved for Prince Marcus and his family."

"Oh," Megan said quietly. Lara came into the room carrying sheets and a new gown.

"You rest and I'll see what I can do to keep the peace in here," Dr. Weisman said, patting her hand. "I will check on you later."

"Thank you," Megan said. Lara's experienced hands painlessly bathed her, administered her drugs, and slipped her back into a fresh bed within a matter of minutes.

"Much better," Lara said looking at Megan propped up by pillows.

"Are you hungry at all, Miss Buchanan?"

"No," Megan said, "I feel a little queasy."

"That's from getting up and down and moving around, but I would like to see you try to eat something to replenish your energy," she said, tidying up the room. "We're lucky we have a cloudy day. It's easier on the eyes and the head," Lara said. She noticed that Megan was still squinting even in the dull light of the gray day. "Is that better?" she asked as she closed the blinds and turned on a small lamp by the desk.

"Better," Megan said.

"What if I brought you a pot of tea, a bit of toast and some broth. Do you think you could try?"

"That would be fine," Megan said.

"Then I'll be back in two shakes of a lamb's tail," Lara said with a hint of Irish as she left and Marcus quietly entered the room.

"Where is everybody?" Megan asked.

"Dr. Weisman told them to leave. He wants you to rest," Marcus said. He watched her for a long moment. Her vibrant blue eyes were quieter, deeper, and darker than before, but the shine and brightness of life had returned. Marcus bent over and gripped the metal frame at the end of the bed. His face was pale.

"What's wrong?" Megan asked.

"Megan, if I hadn't gone to your apartment last night, or if I were delayed any longer you probably would have died," Marcus said solemnly. "I found you on the ground, in the middle of the sidewalk, bloody and nearly frozen."

"You came," Megan said with a clear but soft voice.

"But Megan,..." he protested, coming to her bed side.

"Marcus," Megan said, with a hint of a smile on her lips, "I'm fine." He held on to the chrome guard attached to the bed, tapping it with the palm of his hand. He looked down and Megan put her hand on top of his. Her hand was soft and warm as he cupped it into his own hand and looked into her eyes.

"Don't ever do anything like this to me again," he said and bent over and kissed her. "I don't think I could take it." Megan reached for his face and stroked his bristled cheek. "I haven't had time to shave," he apologized.

"You look wonderful to me," Megan said. He kissed her again and unfastened the guard lock, dropped it down below the bed and sat down next to her.

"Megan, what happened last night?" Marcus asked. "You knew I was coming to your apartment, so why did you leave?"

"Westin called," Megan said.

"Westin?" Marcus said gruffly. "The ambassador? What does he have to do with this? Did he do this to you?" Marcus' jaw tightened and his eyes burned coldly.

"No," Megan said, adjusting to sit up in the bed. "I slipped and fell. It was an accident. You haven't spoken to your father?"

"I am going to see Father today," Marcus said. "I have been with you since your accident."

"You have?"

"Yes, I have," Marcus said, picking up her hand and resting it in his.

"Westin isn't the English ambassador," Megan confessed.

"Then who is he?" Marcus asked.

"Sort of a detective," Megan said. "An independent contractor of sorts, for governments and highly connected individuals."

"A mercenary," Marcus snapped.

"Not quite...," Megan began. Lara interrupted as she walked into the room with tea, toast and broth on a small wheeled cart.

"Try to eat something. If you need anything at all just press the red button," she said and left the room. Megan tugged at the top of the sheet and blanket and pulled them to her chest, then reached for the tea.

"Megan, I don't understand. What did he want?" Marcus asked.

"Marcus, Westin told me he has a job to do here, an important job. Your father knows about it and he probably can tell you more but I thought he needed my help in some sort of emergency."

"Did he?"

"No," Megan said, taking a sip of the tea.

"Then what did he want?" Marcus asked. Megan looked into her cup and took another sip.

"Megan?"

"He wanted me to go away with him."

"He wanted you to go away with him! Where?" Marcus demanded as he got up and stood beside her bed.

"I don't know," Megan said, "I remember something about Hong Kong."

"Why didn't you go?" he asked distantly. Megan's eyes narrowed.

"Why? How could you ask why? Why do you think?"

"Do you love me, Megan?" he asked, looking down at her.

"Yes, I love you," she said with a scowl on her face.

"Are you sure?"

"Now that was the wrong response," Megan fumed.

"Are you sure?" Marcus repeated.

"Of course, I'm sure."

"How do you know for sure?" he asked.

"Because I'm not in Hong Kong," she said. Her eyes darkened to a brilliant blue.

Marcus brushed back his mane of blond hair with his fingers, his eyes searching hers. He took the cup of tea from her hand, set it on the table, and sat down next to her. He took hold of her hand and Megan noticed how hot his hands were. She could see tiny beads of perspiration on his brow.

"Marcus, what is it?" Megan asked. "You know, you drive me crazy."

"I know," Marcus said. He took a deep breath and slowly released it. He looked down, shook his head and then looked up at her. "Megan, I'm not a romantic. I don't write poems or sing songs, and I have a hard time remembering birthdays, but I remember every moment we have spent together. I remember the first time I saw you. I remember how your skirt was caught in the top of your boot and how you steadied yourself, leaning on my shoulder. Even then I think I knew." His voice filled with emotion. "Megan, you are beautiful. You are warm, unafraid and faithful. You challenge my heart and my mind. When we are separated, I long to be with you and when we are together I feel complete. I love you and I can't imagine spending one more minute without you in my life. Please, marry me." Marcus pulled the ring out of his pocket and slipped it on her finger. "Will you marry me?"

Megan looked at the sparkling ring and recognized it as the band that sat alone in its case at the museum.

"But Marc, there are other considerations. I don't know if..."

"No," Marcus stopped her. "The only thing that can keep us apart is your decision."

"Yes, I will," she said in a steady voice.

Marcus shot up and stood for a moment looking at her lying in the bed. "Megan, I promise... I promise to you and to God that I will love you and be faithful to you for the rest of my life. You are happy, aren't you?"

"Very," Megan said, smiling.

CHAPTER 53

"I got the ring." Megan mused, watching the diamonds sparkle in a rainbow of colors against her pillow.

"Was there any doubt?" Marcus asked, happily watching her play with it. He closed the journal he had been tacitly reading and put his hand to her face, stroking her cheek and brushing back a curl of her hair. "How was your nap?"

"Good, I was worried I was having a dream," Megan said, still looking at her glittering finger. "Oh, my IV is gone!" she said, noticing the bandage on her hand.

"I took it out while you were sleeping. There is no need for it any longer," Marcus said and sat down next to her. "Megan," he started. "We have to tell people about our engagement, I've already told my parents."

"When did you tell your parents?" Megan asked.

"They stopped by this afternoon while you were sleeping."

"You didn't," Megan anxiously said. "Tell me your mother didn't see me like this."

"Yes, why?"

"Marc."

"Mother insisted. She wanted to see who would be wearing the ring," he said.

Jacob walked into the room holding an electronic patient chart.

"Megan, you look as good as new. Almost better," Jacob said suspiciously, and then noticed the ring on her finger. "You did it!" he exclaimed, grinning at Marcus. "And to think we almost lost hope entirely. Congratulations!" Jacob said and kissed Megan.

"Thank you," Megan said, with a broad smile.

"Look at that, it's a perfect fit," Jacob said, glancing at Marcus. Marcus shrugged his shoulders and then smiled.

"What's going on?" Megan asked suspiciously.

"Hasn't Marcus told you?" Jacob said, pulling up a chair.

"Told me what?"

"About the legend, more or less a tradition here in Dreiholm."

"No," Megan said, glancing at Marcus.

"When the king's first son is born, the mother, the queen, picks out a ring for the infant's someday bride, asking God to bless their marriage and their life together," Jacob said. "It has been said among the people that there is only one perfect match for the ring, and evidently, it's your finger."

"And what will they think of a common foreigner marrying their prince?" Megan asked.

"You're not common in any stretch of the imagination, Megan. I think even Phillip told you that. And the populous will be overjoyed, considering what they thought were their choices," he said, getting up from his chair. "Well, I have to call Ostride and tell her the good news. She would rather see me stretched out than to miss a piece of news like this."

"You see, Megan, we can't keep this a secret. People will be wondering and asking questions," Marcus said.

"I know they have been trying to keep it quiet, but the fact that you're in this room has everyone in the hospital guessing," Jacob said. "And it won't be long before the hounds smell a story."

"I wasn't planning on keeping it a secret. I'm happy about it," Megan said, wondering why they were so concerned. "I suppose I'll have to make some adjustments but it can't be that monumental that we all have to worry about it. We went out all that time without too much fuss. I don't know why it would be any different now," Megan said, looking at the two sharing uneasy glances at one another.

"There will be adjustments," Jacob agreed.

"How much could really change?" Megan asked.

"I think we should pick a date for the wedding," Marcus interrupted. "When would you like to get married?" It was evening again and Lara had opened the shades to the window. Megan could see dreamy bundles of lace snowflakes falling from the velvet blue sky.

"I've always wanted a Christmas wedding," Megan said, "with candles and green garland, holly bouquets with white roses and red and green velvet ribbons."

"A small ceremony. Just our family and close friends," Marcus added, kissing her hand. "Nothing overly elaborate."

"Something simple and reverent," Megan said.

"And how are you going to manage that?" Jacob asked Marcus.

"Simple, I'll call Mother and have her make all the arrangements," Marcus said as he flipped his phone open.

"For what?" Megan asked.

"The wedding," Marcus answered.

"Marc, put that thing down, we have plenty of time," Megan laughed. "We can make our own plans." Jacob looked down at the patient chart and opened it to a random file, pretending not to listen. "Marc, you're not thinking about *this* Christmas?"

"Of course. You weren't thinking about next year?"

"Marc, it's next week! Have you lost your senses?"

"It's not a problem," Marcus said.

"Marcus! You put that thing down."

"Mother, could you hold for a minute," Marcus said, as he covered his phone.

"What do you mean it's not a problem?" Megan shouted in a rapid whisper. "I don't have a dress, we haven't sent out invitations, and what about my family? How are they going to get here with such short notice? They don't even know that I'm engaged."

"We'll have the dress made, the invitations will go out overnight and I'll get your family here, not to worry," Marcus said and walked into the sitting room. "Mother, we are getting married on Christmas."

"No, no, no, no, no!" Megan begged as Marcus went into a closet and closed the door.

CHAPTER 54

Ostride embraced Megan and then handed her a cascading bouquet of holly and a dozen perfect white roses. Megan held her breath and looked up at the ceiling of the narthex to the gold chandelier above her. It was reminiscent of everything she had seen in the past week. The grand home where Marcus lived, and the palace. It was radiant, spotless, gold, shining and beautiful. And it was so far away from the simplicity of home, from her past, now foreign to her present.

"You're just beautiful," Ostride said. Megan's face felt flush and her hands were ice cold. Her eyes brimmed with tears. "Knock, knock," Ostride joked with her usual sunshine smile.

"Who's there?" Megan replied, taking short deep breaths.

"Boo."

"Boo who?" Megan said, playing along.

"Boo hoo! This is no time to cry," Ostride said, with her bouquet in one hand and extending the other. "You have a man to marry and he's a real prince," she giggled. Megan laughed uneasily as the palace coordinator approached them, stopping once to give directions to the guards at the door.

"It's time," the coordinator said. "The King and Queen have taken their places, your aunt has been seated and your uncle will be here momentarily. As soon as the music starts, the doors will open and Ostride, just as we rehearsed, you will slowly walk down the aisle. Now both of you take a deep breath," she said, inhaling with them. "Now release and relax. Everything is going smoothly." Megan looked at the side door, unguarded and open. She looked up past the chandelier. Lord, God is this right? Am I doing the right thing? Megan prayed.

Her uncle Joseph emerged from the small door of the chapel and stood gazing at Megan. The white satin gown and the ripples of an almost translucent veil trailed the length of the room. On top of her

PLANS · VICTORIA J.M. HOFFBECK

head was a small tiara glittering in the dim evening light. Their eyes met and Megan began to see through a watery haze. He came over to her side and put her arm in his. His lip quivered and they both looked straight ahead.

"I'm sure your parents are very proud, as proud as I am," Joe said, and covered her hand with his.

The coordinator stood in front of Ostride and Megan and her uncle. "Breathe in, breathe out. Good. Relax. Ostride, step forward. One, two."

The organ pipes thundered and filled the room. With one sweep the two guards opened the double doors to the sanctuary. The sweet fragrance of fir and cloves billowed out into the narthex, and like the stars in the sky, burning candles fluttered and reflected their light on the gold and stained glass windows that covered the walls of the sanctuary. Holly and pine bow garlands with bits of gold and red climbed the marble pillars until they reached the gold-covered ceiling with sculpted portrayals of Cherubim and Seraphim praising God. Ostride, dressed in white with red and green ribbons woven into her blonde hair, stepped out into the sanctuary.

"It's like watching a dream," Megan said to her uncle. The coordinator smiled and motioned for them to step forward as Ostride reached the altar. Megan looked again to the unguarded door.

"Miss Buchanan," a voice whispered. The coordinator motioned for her from behind the door to take a deep breath and exhale and then smiled. "Now," she mouthed.

The music thundered between the walls of the church and the hundreds of guests stood as the bride stepped out onto the red carpet. She hesitated at the doorway, looking at the cross ahead of her.

"Just like a walk by the river," her uncle whispered, and together they went forward. The guests were captivated by the flickering candlelight that illuminated the gold embroidered edges of Megan's veil. The diamonds she wore ignited into a display of faceted brilliance as they walked down the long aisle. Megan spotted Chuck and Annie Payton standing together at the end of a pew. Annie was smiling, almost laughing with excitement. Chuck, dressed in his finest tuxedo, winked as she passed by. At the front she could see her aunt weeping quietly into her handkerchief. Megan could feel her heart flutter.

O Lord is this right! her heart cried out at the altar. There, for the first time this night, she looked at Marcus. He was perfectly tailored and groomed, and his eyes were as vibrant as the blue sash across his chest. The organ fell silent.

The bride looked to her uncle. "Trust God," he whispered. Megan looked up at Marcus and her uncle placed her hand in his. The couple walked together and stood before the cross. And there, in the safety and comfort of his hand, Megan felt the undeniable presence of God's peace that erased any doubt in her heart. Beside her husband she had found her new home.

* * *

"How does it feel to be a married man?" Megan asked Marcus as they danced among the guests on the ballroom floor. Marcus looked down at her with a mischievous smile.

"Hold that thought," Megan said.

"How does it feel to be a married woman?" Marcus asked in return.

"Ask me tomorrow morning," she teased.

"You won't have to wait that long." Marcus slowed their dance to reach for a glass of champagne and held her close as he drank from it. "Darling?" he asked and put the glass to her lips. A ravenous fire burned in his eyes that made Megan smile sweetly as she looked up at him.

"Tired, old man?" Phillip asked Marcus, but was looking at Megan. "Is it finally my turn to dance with the bride?"

"Where have you been?" Megan asked. Marcus noticed Jacob standing alone on the edge of the ballroom floor with a glass of punch in his hand. He motioned to Jacob to join them.

"Well, now that Marcus has voluntarily given up his bachelorhood, I've become, how can I say, more attractive," Phillip said. "In fact, I can't find a moment's peace." A group of young women standing near Lord and Lady Baumann began giggling as they ogled Phillip from across the room. "But the pandemonium has been invigorating," Phillip said, while he watched the women from the corner of his eye.

"I gladly bequest my eligibility to you, cousin. Good luck," Marcus said.

"I don't think I will be giving it up anytime soon. There is only one Megan," he said kissing her. "I know I have been difficult, Megan, and I do regret it."

"It's all forgotten, we're family now," she assured him.

"Yes, we are," Phillip said, "and I plan on visiting often."

"Where is that man from Bogotá when you need him," Jacob said into his glass. Marcus grinned as he watched Phillip scan the floor of beautiful women.

"With whom is Ostride dancing?" Marcus asked.

"Your uncle, Prince Phillip," Jacob said, watching Ostride between the couples crowding the floor.

"Father?" Phillip asked. "Huh. He must be in a good mood," Phillip said as he watched an attractive woman in a green dress and deep red lips parade past him.

"Meg," Ostride called from the floor. "Pictures." Prince Phillip was leading her to the stairway where the photographer was trying to gather the wedding party together.

"Duty calls," Marcus said. Phillip began to drift off to the provocative woman in the green dress. "And where are you going?" he asked his cousin.

"That man has taken plenty of pictures and I have a pressing engagement."

"Family," Marcus reminded him. "Duty."

"Why does it always have to interfere with my love life?"

"Your love life can wait," Marcus said, glancing at the alluring creature still eyeing Phillip. "Believe me, she won't go away," he said as he drew Megan up the stairway to the dais where the royal family and their honored guests were seated. The photographer positioned the wedding party in front of the towering Christmas tree, laden with crystal ornaments, white lights and holly bouquets with bright red ribbons. The photographer's assistant busily adjusted bow ties, straightened jackets and displayed the ornate bead work of the women's dresses. "This will be the last one together," the woman said as she snapped the shot.

"Meg, you still haven't thrown your bouquet!" Ostride cried.

"I nearly forgot," Megan said. The king and queen looked at her inquisitively. "At home," Megan explained, "when a bride marries, she throws her bouquet out to all the unmarried women at the wedding party. Folklore has it that the woman who catches the bouquet will be the next bride."

"And Marcus, you are to take off Megan's garter and throw it out to all the eligible men, in the hope that they might be the next groom," Megan's aunt explained.

"Her garter?" Marcus asked.

"It's a charming custom," Phillip's mother said. "Phillip, catch it," she demanded.

"Mother!" Phillip protested.

"Go on," she said. The king snickered and the queen pinched his arm.

"Are you sure you want to do this?" Marcus asked Megan.

"Of course." Megan said, lifting up the yards of satin to reveal a white lace garter at her thigh. She balanced her jeweled slipper on Marcus' knee and the photographer, with a smile on her face, snapped a picture. Phillip whistled from the bottom of the steps, calling attention to the event. In a moment, all the eligible men had gathered around to catch the bit of lace.

"Fill your eyes, gentlemen," Marcus said, "it will be your only satisfaction." A roar of laughter came from the crowd as he slid the garter from her leg. He noticed that Megan's initials had been sewn on to the lace with gold thread. Young women gathered beside the men, and Megan turned around and threw her bouquet over her head to the screaming girls. Before she could turn around she could hear the king laughing and the queen shriek in delight.

"That girl can jump!" Uncle Joe exclaimed. Ostride triumphantly raised the bouquet above her head, laughing as she came up the stairway.

"But you're already going to be a bride," Jacob said to her as he put his arms around her.

"Not yet." Ostride said, kissing him. "Now you can't get out of it!"

"Your turn," Megan said to Marcus.

Marcus pointed the garter at the men and let it fly from his fingers. It deflected off the tip of Sir Keaton's hand and fell in the sea of black and white tuxedo tails. After a moment a victorious arm held up the garter. Phillip looked up at his mother from the outer boundaries of the anxious men and shrugged his shoulders. The king and Prince Phillip laughed aloud and with a snap of the king's fingers the orchestra began to play. The guests twirled onto the floor, still amused by the game.

"That boy," Phillip's mother said, shaking her head. The queen took her by the arm and led her back to their table.

"Elizabeth, he's still young," she said.

"And he's making me old," Elizabeth said, watching her son flutter among the guests.

Marcus put his arm around Megan's waist and began dancing with her at the top of the steps.

"I'm ready to leave," Marcus said. Megan bowed her head and then turned to look out at the dance floor. Jacob was kissing Ostride as she held on to her won bouquet. Across the room Phillip was dancing with a young woman, and her aunt and uncle had joined Chuck and Annie at the king and queen's table.

"Marc, it's so beautiful. I just don't want it to end," Megan said. She could feel his chest grow as they danced and when she looked up at him his eyes had turned from that of an adoring husband to an impatient and starved man.

"You win," she said. "But somehow I don't think I'm going to lose."

Marcus took her by the hand and presented her before the king and queen to bid the family a good night. As they approached, a member of the royal guard, in his dress uniform of blue and gold, came before the king, holding a large box.

"Yes?" the King asked.

"Forgive me Your Highness, but the man who caught the garter left this gift. It is for the new princess, Your Majesty."

"Put it with the other gifts," the king commanded.

"I beg your pardon, Your Highness, but the gift has been scanned and it may be in Your Highness' best interest if the princess were to open the package as soon as possible."

The king nodded his head and the guard set it on their table. Marcus looked at the gold box and then at Megan who was inspecting the lavishly wrapped package for a card. Finding none, she tugged at the red and gold bow.

"It's an awfully big package," Megan said in the midst of the silent table. "Who was the gentleman who left it?"

"We do not know," the guard said apologetically.

"Get Phillip," the king ordered to an aide. Phillip, who was dancing close by, bounded up the stairs to the king and stood next to Marcus.

"Phillip, did you see who caught the garter?" the king asked.

"No, not clearly. I just noticed that he was a tall man with dark hair," he said. "Did he leave this gift?" Phillip asked, watching Megan unwrap the package.

"Yes," Marcus said, clenching his fist. Underneath the wrapping was a plain cardboard box, closed with a gold foil seal. Megan peeled the seal back and found inside a large piece of green velvet cinched together by a gold cord.

"It's heavy," Megan said, trying to lift it. Marcus took it from her hands and lifted it out of the box and set it on the table before the king. Megan untied the cord and the bag unfolded before them.

"The jewels!" the queen exclaimed as she stood up next to the king. The wedding guests, who heard the queen and could see the package, murmured frantically among themselves as other guests tried to look on. Marcus' eyes burned and Megan could see Chuck talking privately to Prince Phillip.

"Everything is here," the queen said. Megan picked up the priceless jewel from the queen's crown that filled the palm of her hand. "Even the diamond," she said softly.

The king snapped his fingers again and a company of guards encircled them. Marcus looked around the room and then at the guard who brought the gift. "Where is this man?" Marcus demanded.

"He left as soon as he gave the north gate sentry the package," the guard said.

"Find him!" the king bellowed sternly and then glanced at Prince Phillip. The guard and two others ran out the doorway as two more came into the ballroom to replace them and stood guard around the king and the jewels. Phillip watched his father gently touch his mother's gloved hand and then quickly vanish from the room.

"William," the queen rebuked, "we should be thankful for whoever has returned the jewels. Look! They are all here." She sorted through the tangled jewels, chains, rings and bracelets. Megan put the matchless diamond into Marcus's hand. Marcus rubbed the stone's smooth face between his fingers, looking into its many facets and then tossed it onto the green velvet.

"I've never seen this one before," the queen said curiously, pulling at a fine gold rope. She carefully slipped it through a knotted bracelet and looked at the unusual gold tag attached to the necklace. On it was engraved a message. "To Megan, from A Changed Heart," the queen read aloud. She handed the necklace to Megan who carefully examined it. At the bottom of the sparkling rope was a gold filigree heart. It was a delicate scrolled cage and inside was another heart, a brilliant ruby like she had never seen before, suspended from a tiny chain. Below it was a pool of glittering unset diamonds.

"*A Changed Heart,*" her uncle said. "Of course!" He closed his eyes and recited:

"*As I looked within my heart and only found darkness and despair,*
I turned to a stranger who let me in and did not deny me his hope or care.
And through his kindness he melted my heart, once filled with evil deeds,
And led me to a light I had not known, one that fulfills all my needs."

"The poem, *A Changed Heart*," Ostride said. "But there's more."

"Yes," Uncle Joe said.

"Joseph, who wrote that?" Annie asked. "The name of the author is at the tip of my tongue."

"I know, I know. I'm struggling too," he said stroking his chin. "I want to say it was a British fellow."

Marcus glared at the jewels. His dark blue eyes became almost as black as the flawless onyx on the green velvet and as still and cold as the brightest diamond in the queen's crown. Megan set the necklace down among the rest of the jewels.

"Please, put this with the others," Megan said to the king and queen. "I'm so thankful they have been returned to you."

"Mother, Father, I think it is time we said good night," Marcus said, taking Megan's hand. Phillip cringed and glanced at Jacob who was watching his friend.

"Marcus," Jacob called out. "Merry Christmas." Marcus looked down at the jewels and then at his friend.

"Merry Christmas," Marcus said. "And God's blessing upon you and your family."

"And you and your family, Your Highness," Jacob said.

CHAPTER 55

Megan looked at Marcus who held out his hand, waiting for her on the first step of the vast staircase. She picked up the lengths of her skirt and together they walked silently to the room that had been prepared for them. He rubbed one of her almond-shaped nails between his fingers as they walked down the guarded hallway. When his hand ran across her wedding ring, he stopped and looked at the diamonds.

"Regrets?" Megan asked. Marcus threw open the doors in front of them and inside, standing at attention, was a staff of three maids and Broderick.

"Broderick," Megan said in surprise. Her friend did not look at her but stared straight ahead at the blank wall.

"Good Evening, Your Highness," Broderick said. Marcus remained silent.

"Good evening," Megan said and then looked at the company of maids in starched white blouses with blue ribbon collars. Megan noticed that the younger maids wore blue and white striped pinafores over their full skirts. The eldest maid, with striking white hair, wore only the full skirt and blouse with an embroidered royal crest stitched onto its one pocket. Marcus picked Megan up off the floor and carried her over the threshold and set her down on the thick white carpet in front of her maids who curtseyed before her. The powder-blue room was lined with gold and trimmed with pure white. The dark furniture gleamed in the tempered light of crystal lamps and the largest bed Megan had ever seen faced a wall of beveled windows and a balcony that looked over the ice-covered St. John River.

"We are here to assist you, Your Highness," the eldest maid said to Megan, as another maid opened the adjoining door to a sitting room and bath.

"You can call me Megan," Megan said as she kicked off her shoes.

She squished her toes into the deep carpet, relishing the soft wool under her feet. "Better," she said, and bent down to pick up the jeweled slippers. Another maid rushed to her feet and picked up the shoes from the floor.

"Thank you," Megan said.

"If Your Highness is ready, we will assist you with your gown," the older maid said as she stood by the door to Megan's private quarters.

"Megan, please," Megan said again. She had saved a rose from her bouquet and gently stroked the creamy white petals and then set it down onto the blue satin bed. When she looked up, she saw the young maids curiously watching Marcus. The eldest maid stood to the side of the door and looked straight ahead.

"I'll feel ridiculous with people calling me Your Highness all the time," Megan said to Marcus. Broderick was helping Marcus with his coat, pretending not to even notice Megan as he brushed the jacket and hung it on a wooden hanger.

"As she wishes," Marcus said quietly, barely acknowledging the maids. He turned away and gave his cufflinks to Broderick who watched the wide-eyed expressions of the young maids. The senior maid bowed and directed Megan to the next room and closed the door behind her. Marcus rubbed his brow.

"She will come to understand, Sir," Broderick said.

"Adjustments," Marcus said to himself.

The maids hurriedly undressed Megan and carefully carried her wedding gown out of the room. "It will be sent to Jenkin, madam, who will refresh and preserve it," the elderly maid said as she watched Megan's eyes follow the dress out the door.

"Yes, of course," Megan said, standing on a platform surrounded by full-length mirrors. The maid unfastened the white crinoline at her waist, folded it in thirds and hung it on a pink satin hanger. "I am sorry, what is your name?" Megan asked.

"Adeline, madam. This is Greta," she said of the maid busily tidying and boxing her shoes, "And this is Emma." She nodded toward another maid putting her jewelry into burgundy velvet cases. "We are your personal servants. If you need anything, at any time, all you must do is pick up any one of the telephones in the palace and the house staff will connect us to you."

Emma closed the velvet cases in front of Megan and placed them into an open safe on the far wall. Greta went into one of the closets and came out carrying a long ivory gown.

"Your friend, Miss Ostride, sent this to you," the young maid said. Megan recognized the negligee as one they had envied in a store window. It flowed down her body, caressing every curve and dipped generously down to the small of her back.

"Your Highness,... Megan," Adeline corrected herself. "Would you like your hair up or down?" she asked. Megan pulled the comb from her hair. In the mirror she could see her dark curls fall over her shoulders. "Down, thank you," Megan said and handed the maid the jeweled comb from the family's treasury. Adeline gave the comb to Emma, and then sent the younger maids out of the room. "Will there be anything else, madam?" the maid asked.

"No, I don't think so," Megan said. The maid opened the door to leave, carrying the few remaining garments left in the room.

"Adeline," Megan called out. "Is it wrong to want the staff to call me by my given name?"

The senior maid hesitated and then closed the door again. "It is not wrong madam, but it is not our custom and may show a lack of respect for the position that you now hold," Adeline said. Megan's eyes shifted to the floor.

"I want to feel at home," Megan sighed, "but perhaps it would be better if informality were limited to our private rooms," she said. The maid bowed her head and Megan thought for a moment that the experienced maid might have grimaced a smile.

"I will direct the staff as to your wishes, Megan. Good night and may God bless you and Prince Marcus." Adeline closed the door as she went out.

Megan stood alone in the dressing room. She held on to the handle of the bedroom door, listening to the silence on the other side. It was cold at her feet and she could feel the passing flow of a winter wind. She took a deep breath and opened the door to the bedroom. It was dark and cold. The balcony doors were open and the moon flooded the darkness with its blue light. From the doorway she could see a dark figure looking out over the frozen river. Megan took Marcus' coat and covered her shoulders. She stood inside the open doorway, watching him, his hands clenching the railing as he searched the still landscape. She stepped out into the night and a wisp of her hair brushed to the side of her face. She stood behind him and put her arms around his waist and felt the warmth of his body.

"Where is he, Megan?" Marcus asked. "Where is this man that can walk past our guards and in and out of my home as he pleases?" Megan looked down at the gardens below and the vacant, snow-covered benches.

"I don't know," she said, "whoever it was, I am glad he brought back the jewels."

"Westin," Marcus said, tightening his grip on the railing.

"Maybe," Megan said.

She stepped back and into the warmth of the bedroom, removed the coat from her shoulders, and draped it over her arm. Marcus followed her, closing the balcony doors, and turned slowly to face her. Streams of light beamed through the windows refracting in the beveled panes, splashing patches of blue across the room and casting a grid of shadows on the bedroom floor and ceiling.

"He loves you, you know," Marcus said from the end of the room.

"Hum," Megan sighed as she put his coat aside. Her hair cascaded down in dark waves, ending at the almost bare curves of her body. Marcus stayed at the end of the room, wrapped in the blue light, watching as she gripped the top of a soft cushion on the chair beside her and then stood behind it, leaning over it as she watched him.

"Do you know what I was thinking this past week while I was being fitted for dresses, having catered lunches and touring your many properties?" Megan asked. "What am I doing here?" she said softly, and ran her fingers through her hair, brushing it back. "I know who I am, Marcus. I'm a small-town girl with small-town dreams and I'm miles away from home in a thousand ways, lost in the beauty and grandeur of your life but lost nonetheless." She paused. "Tonight, while I waited for the chapel doors to open and walk down the aisle I saw an unguarded door and I thought I should run as fast and as far as I can," she said, looking into his stormy eyes. "Then I saw you, and I took your hand and I looked into your eyes, and all of my doubts and fears vanished. Nothing else mattered, not my work or my dreams or any other man. I knew together, with God's help, we would overcome all that life puts before us." she said. "I love you and Marcus you are and will always be my best friend, my husband and my one true love."

His eyes were shining like pools of ink hidden in the dark shadows. "Megan, have I told you how much I love you today?"

"Yes, you have," Megan said, stepping into a ribbon of light. "And I never tire of hearing it."

"I'll never stop," he said, moving closer to her.

"No regrets?" Megan asked, as the diamonds on her hand flashed in the moonlight.

"None," he said, taking her into his arms. He lifted her hand to his lips and kissed it, looking at the diamonds. "But does a ring really make you mine?" he asked.

"No, it doesn't," Megan said, "but a promise does. I made that promise to you." He drew her closer and the straps of her gown fell down her shoulders.

"Love me?" Megan said. "Show me."

Marcus' ravenous eyes pierced the night and Megan felt the shimmering negligee slide down to her feet.

"With pleasure," Marcus said.

"The pleasure is all mine," Megan said.

CHAPTER 56

Nestled snugly between the soft down bed and a plump white down comforter, Megan awoke and smiled as she watched Marcus sleeping, his head above hers and his arm wrapped around her in the bundle of warmth. She inched up to his cheek and kissed him but his eyes didn't flinch. He lay peacefully asleep not making a sound.

"Hum," Megan sighed. "Tired? I think you need more exercise," she whispered. In one sudden leap, Marcus was on top of her. "Ah!" she screamed, covering her mouth as she laughed aloud. Marcus had picked her up and had her cradled beneath him, his eyes still burning an electric blue.

"Tired?" He said laying her gently on the billowy softness of the bed. "I was just waiting for you."

"Me?" Megan laughed. "You were sound asleep."

"You're mistaken," Marcus said, kissing her. "Did I tell you I love you today?"

"Yes, you did."

"I did?"

"Yes," Megan said, "at midnight, one o'clock, two-fifteen, four-thirty, and what time is it now?"

Marcus looked at the clock to his side.

"Seven-twenty-two."

"And seven-twenty-two," she said. "And if I didn't tell you, which I'm sure I did, I love you more."

"Not possible," Marcus said kissing her again.

"Marcus?" Megan said. "What time did you say it is?"

"Seven-twenty-five now," Marcus said shifting his eyes to the clock.

"Aren't we supposed to have breakfast with your parents at nine o'clock before we leave?"

"Yes," Marcus said kissing her neck and shoulder.

"We have to get moving," Megan said, slipping between the sheets and Marcus.

"It's just my parents," Marcus said, holding on to her.

"Maybe I'll get used to having them see me in my night shirt but right now the King and Queen of Dreiholm are going to see me clean and with pants on," Megan said as she slid out of bed.

"Megan!" Marcus cried, as she hurried into the next room and blew him a kiss from the doorway.

"Get up. Up, up, up," Megan said, going into the bathroom. "We don't have much time."

* * *

She smiled, stepping out of the shower onto warm marble, and a seeing a long, white robe waiting for her on a brass hanger. On the robe was an emblem, a small shadow of the family crest of blue and gold with her initials monogrammed over it in gold thread. She paused as she looked at it. "Megan Holcombe," she said aloud, reaching for the robe. The metal hanger had warmed it from top to bottom. "This is heaven," Megan murmured, bundling the fluffy robe collar to her neck. She opened the door to the bedroom and saw Marcus in a matching robe by the windows shaking his wet hair. Beside him on a small table were papers scattered across its top. He picked up a plain white sheet and smiled triumphantly.

"And what are those?" Megan asked, holding her comb in her hand.

"Our honeymoon plans," Marcus said.

"Where are we going?" Megan asked, slowly stroking her long tresses. "I don't know why you wanted to keep it a secret."

"Because I want to surprise you," Marcus said. "I've been planning this since the day we met."

"Since the day we met?" Megan asked. Her black eyelashes knitted together causing her eyes to turn a seductive shade of ocean blue.

"I'm taking you on a tour of Europe," Marcus said, taking her in his arms, "to every place that has ever meant anything to me so that not one will be without a memory of you in it," Marcus said, tightening his hold on her. "I want you to see everything I've seen, and together we'll see more.

"But we will start our trip off the coast of Africa on a yacht, in the warmth of the sun," he said, flexing his broad chest and lifting his head as if he was already soaking up the sun's rays. Megan was lifted into the air as he pressed her to him. She laughed in delight and reached up on her toes and kissed him. When she regained her footing she reached up and combed the side of his hair with her fingers and then touched his face.

"It sounds wonderful, but I was just starting to feel at home in this room," she said, glancing at the bed and then up at Marcus. Her fresh smile brightened her suggestive eyes.

"I never would have guessed," Marcus said with a crooked smile.

"What? That I'm so affectionate?" Megan said stepping back.

"I can think of other words," Marcus said.

"And you? Who would have known?" Megan said, sizing him up as she reached down for a grape piled high on a silver tray and popped one into her mouth. "It's just too bad you need so much sleep," she said and turned around to comb out her hair. Marcus took the towel off his shoulder and snapped her on the backside. Megan laughed and ate another grape.

When they had finished dressing, she looked at the papers on the marble table and picked up the page Marcus had been holding in his hand.

"You know, they do expect me back at work after break," Megan said seriously. Marcus stood behind her, slipping his hands around her waist and leaning his head on her shoulder.

"I've made arrangements," he said and kissed her neck.

"Arrangements?" Megan asked, leaning back on his chest. "What arrangements?"

Marcus turned quickly as he heard the sound of heavy footsteps echoing beyond their bedroom doors. Muffled voices called out orders and the rapid march drew nearer to their room. A loud banging at the door shook it on its hinges and Marcus pushed Megan back behind him.

"Code red!" the royal guardsman yelled in a booming voice. The doors crashed open and a company of men dressed in sealed suits and black gas masks ran toward them. The officer, carrying two black jumpsuits, dropped them at the feet of Marcus and Megan, and then went to the balcony doors with his weapon.

"What is going on?" Marcus demanded, as the guards placed the couple's feet into each of their suits, then pulled them up, sealing the suits tightly, and shoving hooded gas masks toward their faces.

"A bomb, Your Highnesses," the officer said from the balcony. The sound of helicopters thundered overhead. "Move out!" he ordered and a guard on each side of Marcus and Megan lifted them up by the arms and rushed them out of the bedroom. Marcus reached for Megan but in the bulky suit he was unable to hold on to her.

"Go, go, go!" The officer yelled to the guards. The guards holding onto Megan grabbed on to the back of her suit and lifted her up off the ground and ran down the hallway. The halls were empty. The palace guards had vanished and not one servant was in sight.

"What bomb?" Marcus yelled angrily, struggling as he was being carried away. They reached the back stairway and the officer had still not answered him. "What bomb?" Marcus yelled again, breaking free from the guards. He reached for Megan and stopped her guards before they could enter the winding stairwell. The guards looked at the officer, who nodded for them to stop.

"Chemical, Sir." the officer said.

"Chemical?" Megan asked. Through the black goggles, the young officer looked directly into Megan eyes.

"Preliminary status, Quickclean," he said. "We don't have much time."

"God, no," Megan prayed. "Please God, no!" She grabbed Marcus by the hand and pulled him down the narrow stairway. Even in the thick suit Marcus could feel her hand dig into his flesh and pull him as she ran faster down into the tunnel.

"Megan, what is it?" Marcus asked.

"Are we going underground?" she asked the officer.

"No. You and Prince Marcus are going up."

"Where?" she asked.

"From here to the port and up," the officer said as he opened the hidden door to the heliport. The whirling blades blasting ice and snow threw Megan back into the guard behind her. The guard pushed Megan and Marcus ahead and onto the helicopter.

"Where are my parents?" Marcus asked the officer.

"Underground, Sir," the officer yelled above the blades' thrusting thunder.

"How much time?" Megan asked. The officer shook his head. "Not much," he replied, and banged on the side of the helicopter with his open hand. The helicopter ascended into the air and the pilot called back to them through the speakers. "Ready to evacuate in ninety, eighty, seventy...." In the distance, Megan could see they were heading toward a Gulfstream jet waiting on a runway. She saw the American flag on its tail fin and military personnel on the ground.

The chopper barely touched ground when the pilot yelled, "Evacuate! Evacuate!" A door in the floor of the helicopter opened to a chute. Marcus dropped Megan into it and jumped after her to a tent-like quarantine room. An American soldier waiting, dressed in the same black bio-terrorist gear, pushed them into a scanner as he kept his eyes on another soldier who gave him an all-clear sign from beyond a glass wall.

"You're clean," he said, and directed them across the room to the ladder going up into the plane. Megan's foot slipped off a rung and she slid, catching herself before she fell into Marcus. A lieutenant in the plane reached down and lifted her inside, pushing her to a tight corner, and then extended his hand to Marcus.

"Loaded. Candy loaded," the lieutenant said into his wire headset.

"Waiting for K2. Repeat. Waiting for K2."

"Minus thirty and counting," the pilot returned.

"Go to the back, get seated, and buckle up," the lieutenant ordered. Megan stumbled through the narrow aisle until she reached the middle of the airplane. It opened to a communication center with booths and small tables on either side. On the other side of the center she could see Chuck Payton seated across from Ostride and Jacob at the back of the plane. Ostride was sobbing heavily into Jacob's chest, and silent tears fell from Jacob's face. He saw Marcus and managed to lift his fingers in a hopeless acknowledgment. Payton twirled around in his seat to see Megan and Marcus coming down the aisle.

"You can take off your gas masks in here. It's secure," he said, standing up to help Megan.

"What is all this all about?" Marcus demanded, ripping off the mask.

From behind a door, Westin appeared and came toward them with an automatic weapon tucked in the crook of his left arm. He looked at Marcus with disdain and then at Megan.

"You! What are you doing here?" Marcus roared.

Payton got between the two men. "Marcus, there are a few things that need to be explained."

"Then explain!" Marcus said through gritted teeth.

"K2 loaded," the lieutenant called. "K2 loaded." The engines of the plane began to whine as Phillip burst through the communications center. He tripped on an exposed cord that ran across the aisle and grabbed onto a seat to steady himself. He took off his gas mask and saw Marcus and Westin glaring at each other. Westin headed to the front of the plane and bumped into Megan as he passed her. Marcus charged after him.

"You nearly killed her," he said, pushing Westin up against the plane's wall. Westin broke free from Marcus' grasp and pulled a combat knife from a pocket of his jacket. He held it to Marcus' throat.

"Don't!" Megan screamed. Westin glanced back at Megan's tear-filled eyes.

"I nearly killed her? You can take credit for that, and a thousand more, Your Highness," Westin sneered. Marcus' military training kicked in. He grabbed Westin's wrist, twisting and crushing it until the knife dropped to the floor. Westin's gun lurched forward.

"Stand down!" Payton commanded. Westin's eyes were wild with rage and then simmered as Chuck put his arm on Marcus' shoulder and pulled him back. Westin scooped up the knife on the floor and slid it back into the sleeve of his jacket.

"Welcome, Prince Marcus, to your world," he said sarcastically, "or what's left of it." Westin looked back at Megan with a bitter smile and then he hurried down the steps outside the plane.

"Minus ten, nine, eight," the pilot called out. The lieutenant sealed the hatch. "Get back, get back!" he yelled as the jet engines thundered louder and the plane rumbled down the runway. It arched up into the sky, with the lieutenant straddling between a doorway and Marcus clutching a railing. His knuckles turned white as the jet climbed with rocketing speed into the clear sky. Megan fell back into a seat and watched as Marcus braced himself. High above the clouds, the plane leveled out and the intense pressure subsided. An officer in the communication booth was speaking in Dreiholmian and then English, calling for Chuck before she closed her door.

"Are you all right, sir?" the lieutenant asked.

"Yes, I'm fine," Marcus said, still hanging onto the railing. He walked back unsteadily toward Megan, grabbing onto the tops of chairs. Phillip sat across from them and turned when he heard the communications door open and saw Chuck Payton coming out. Chuck sat down next to Marcus and pushed a button that elevated a narrow table from the floor.

"What is this all about? And what did he mean, my world?" Marcus demanded. "What am I doing in an American aircraft? Why are you here? And..."

"Hold on Marcus," Chuck said in a calm voice. "I can answer some of your questions, others you'll have to ask your father, and Megan can answer a few."

"What does Megan have to do with any of this?" Marcus asked.

Chuck looked at Megan. She was staring out the window, down at Dreiholm. Her gloved fingertips were at her lips and tears glazed her eyes.

"They agree with me. The cat's out of the bag. They have to know," Chuck said to Megan. "They'll be on the team from now on."

Megan glanced at Phillip.

"Him too," Chuck added.

"Megan? What is he talking about?" Marcus demanded.

Tears streamed down her face. She looked down at the rubbery black gloves sealing her hands and let out a deep sigh. A tear dropped and rippled onto the table.

"Years ago," Megan began, "my mother and father did research together. They did independent studies, some for the government, others on their own," she said, blinking the tears from her eyes. "During one of their private studies, they found something. At the time it didn't seem like much so they put it away. After they died I found it among their papers and decided to pursue it, taking over where they left off. It was a long shot, but I made a discovery. People became interested – my government, your government, your father. I thought I could just hand it over to them and be rid of it. But when I won the scholarship, I was asked to carry on until all the tests were completed. I didn't want to, but I was convinced I had to," she said, letting out a deep sigh. "It had become too important to ignore any longer," she said. Tears were dripping down her face. She took a deep breath and exhaled.

"Your government is working in cooperation with mine to further the research. Your university and Mr. Payton had the equipment in place, and I--my parents, that is--provided the formula," Megan said, looking at the blanket of white clouds from her window. "But now it's too late." She felt a sharp pain in her heart and reached for her chest. She tried to brush away a tear from her face but the black gloves pinched her skin and she began to cry.

"I should have worked harder. I should have worked harder," she sobbed. "I should have tested it."

"Megan, what were you doing?" Marcus asked. He took her by her shoulders and turned her to him. "What were you developing?" he asked as the tears streamed down her face.

"A neutralizer," she whispered.

"For what?"

"For the AQ2 nerve agent."

"AQ2," Marcus muttered and then looked at Payton. His eyes burned and blurred with tears. "Is this what happened? Was AQ2 released?"

"We're not certain of anything yet," Payton said. "We'll know shortly."

"How many are dead?" Marcus asked.

"Five that we know for sure."

"Five?" Marcus said, wiping his face. "A dram of AQ2 will kill thousands."

"It happened in a cave inside Mount Petra. But as you both know, it creeps and spreads at a rapid rate," Chuck said. He looked at his watch and then at Marcus. "If it escaped, it would have suffocated the whole Petra Mountain Valley by now, and will make its way into Hebl within minutes."

"No," Marcus whispered. "No."

"We couldn't take any chances," Chuck said. "We had to get you out of there."

"Why?" Phillip asked in a tear-choked voice. "Why? We should have stayed with our people."

"No," Chuck said. "Marcus is heir to the throne, you're second, and Megan, well Megan is the closest thing we have to an answer right now."

"What about Ostride and Jacob?" Phillip asked, wiping away his tears.

"Ostride is Megan's second, her right-hand associate. She checks and duplicates Megan's work. As for Jacob, Ostride wouldn't leave without him. The reverend was about to be evacuated but he spared a few moments to marry them so we could work around the rules."

"Uncle Joe, Aunt Julie?" Megan gasped.

"We moved them to London for now," Chuck said, resting his hand on the table. "We did what we could for as many as we could," he said solemnly.

"What do we do now?" Phillip asked.

"We'll wait until we get word," Payton said. "The king will contact us when he knows."

Marcus could hear Jacob comforting Ostride and saying a prayer for the people in the mountain valley. He could feel his eyes sting and burn as he closed them while he squeezed Megan's hand.

Dear God, oh dear God. I beg of you to spare these innocent people, Marcus prayed. When he opened his eyes he saw the American officer in the front of the plane silently praying and holding the cross that hung around his neck. For a moment their eyes met and Marcus shared his peace. The officer smiled, nodded and then walked into the cockpit.

"How did this happen?" Marcus asked. Chuck's eyebrow peaked as he looked down and brushed his hand over the table.

"It's been brewing for a long time," Chuck said. Beads of perspiration were forming on the faces of Marcus, Megan and Phillip, still dressed in their airtight suits. Chuck pressed another button and cool air began to circulate above them.

"I don't understand," Marcus said. "How was I responsible for any of this?"

Payton knew he was referring to the comment Westin made before he left the plane. "Nicole de Sonnete," Chuck said flatly. Megan broke away from the window when she heard mention of Nicole's name.

"The property she sold to you for Westwind, it was adjacent to Petra Mountain?"

"Yes," Marcus said, "but what does that have to do with this?"

"Well, before she sold it to you she must have discovered Greven's secret," Chuck said. "On Mount Petra and on her father's property was a cave. That cave holds the mother lode of military-grade biological and chemical weapons."

"Greven," Marcus repeated.

"Greven has long been suspected of being sympathetic to terrorist groups, and it's not surprising when you consider his past affiliations," Chuck said. "Your uncle, Prince Phillip, suspected that he had been supplying chemical weapons to radical terrorist groups around the world for some time, but he could never find the evidence or the cache of weapons he knew existed in order to arrest him. Marcus, when you chose Petra Mountain for Westwind, Greven became agitated. He was confident he would succeed at the Senate and block the development, but to protect his interests he called for reinforcements to speed up his dealings."

"Westin," Megan said.

"Westin Parker is his real name, Chuck said. He was already here on another assignment but when he found out what Greven had and what he was planning to do with it, he contacted us. Greven wanted Westin to deliver the goods to a purchaser in Turkey, and of course we wanted to relieve Westin of the goods, but Greven didn't trust him with all the details. He told him to be in Turkey on January first to make the deal, but Westin hedged and convinced Greven that he had to be close to the situation. That's when something unusual happened."

"The engineers on Petra," Marcus said, "the shootings."

"Exactly," Chuck said. "Greven's men made a mistake. Westin, on our dime, was sent to investigate and found the cave and the weapons. Greven had AQ2, VX, UX, as well as bombs, missiles, and components to make nuclear weapons. You name it, it was in there. Because of the magnitude, we no longer were just interested in the weapons, we wanted to know more about the buyers and their intentions."

"Why didn't the king just arrest Greven then, and get the information out of him?" Phillip asked.

"Lord Greven is a powerful and very dangerous man," Chuck said. "The king knew Greven would deny knowing anything about the weapons on Petra Mountain. Westin didn't know if the weapons were Greven's or someone else's. At the time, we didn't know about Nicole or the group that shot at the engineers. All we had were cryptic messages from people we suspected were linked to Greven. We were concerned if we took a chance that he would have fled or worse."

"Like detonating a bomb," Marcus said. Chuck looked down at the table.

"Then there are more dealers?" Phillip asked.

"Greven isn't alone," Chuck said quietly.

"How did Nicole know and why didn't she say something?" Marcus asked bitterly. Chuck looked at Megan. Her face was pale and her lips a blush of pink. Her long eyelashes were shining with droplets of tears.

"She came across information about the cache – she has her ways to get information as we all know – and was worried her father was involved with Greven. When she found out that you wanted the property, she asked her father for it and sold it to you," Chuck said to Marcus. "Her father's willingness to give it to her eliminated her fears that he was involved, but she saw another opportunity."

"What benefit could she see in this?" Marcus asked.

"She guessed that Greven was behind the weapons and on that guess she decided to blackmail him. She found her intuition was right. Greven agreed to give her allotments of money for silence. Unfortunately, that wasn't what she really wanted."

"Nicole was never denied anything," Marcus said. "She didn't need the money. What did she want so badly that she was willing to deal with a devil for it?"

"You," Chuck said.

"Me!" Marcus choked.

"She decided when she sold the property to you, that if you agreed to marry her, she would make you a hero. Her plan was that after the nuptials, she would tell you about the weapons and Greven. You, in turn, would break up a terrorist syndicate and receive the accolades from around the world. But if you didn't ask her to marry you, she planned to testify that you were conspiring with Greven to distribute the goods." Chuck said.

Marcus leaned back in his seat and closed his eyes.

"At some point she decided that you weren't going to ask for her hand and she put her plan into action."

"At the ball," Phillip interjected.

"Most likely," Chuck agreed. "The trouble was, she didn't know who she was dealing with. Greven got word, and at their regular exchange of blackmail money, he had her killed."

"How? How did he get word of her plan?" Megan asked in a shaking voice.

"Westin had to tell him," Chuck said. "Greven had a contingency plan. He was willing to play along with Nicole and even share some of his money, a small sum compared to what he was making, but he was not willing to take a fall. He told Westin that if word ever got out, he was going to blow up the cache of weapons to wipe out any evidence, along with anyone and everyone else who could accuse him of the crime."

"Is that what happened?" Marcus asked. Chuck nodded his head.

"Yes, but not because of Nicole. Greven has been shipping out weapons ahead of schedule ever since the senate hearing on Westwind. Westin and our group took care of those but the deadlier ones on Petra Mountain remained. Westin tried to export them with the others but Greven resisted. Westin finally forced his hand and the shipment was bumped up to the same night Marcus found you on the sidewalk," Chuck said, looking at Megan. Megan thought of Westin's black face and black clothing the night she saw him in the alley.

"I thought he..." Marcus began.

"Stole the jewels?" Chuck finished. "He did. Greven needed a distraction to move the goods, so he sent Westin to steal the jewels and then go to meet the buyers in Turkey to collect the money."

"So the king knew they were going to be stolen?" Phillip asked, stunned.

"No, Westin kept that from us until the end," Chuck said. "At that time we were only aware of the weapons movement, but it turns out that Westin's elaborate distraction was in vain. The buyer of the weapons got word to Greven that he was delayed in Hungary and at the last minute Greven canceled the move and decided to revert back to his original plan to move the goods on January first."

"You knew all this was going on. You knew about Nicole and Greven, about the weapons, so why didn't you get Greven then?" Phillip complained.

"Did you see Greven at the wedding?" Chuck asked. "Ever since the senate hearing he has been out of the country or underground, we don't know. He literally disappeared. Westin is the only one who has seen him since, and then only once. We didn't dare go after him, not knowing if his hand was on the trigger."

"Then why this and today?" Marcus asked.

"An envelope," Chuck said. "Late last night the king received an envelope with no address, no markings on it at all. Inside was a thumb drive containing the records of Greven's transactions. We don't know why or where it came from, all we know is that when the program file was accessed, a timer was activated."

"To the bomb?" Marcus asked.

"Yes."

"Sir," the communications officer called to Payton. "You have a call." Payton unlatched his seat belt, walked to the booth and closed the door. Phillip helplessly lifted his gas mask and dropped it again in his lap. He looked out the window.

"I'm so sorry," Megan said in despair, "I'm so sorry."

"I wonder how many are gone?" Phillip asked. "Albert's must be gone by now." Megan thought of the little restaurant that overlooked the valley, the young girl that checked their coats, the waiter and Albert... all gone. Streams of tears flowed from her eyes again and Marcus held onto her hand. When she turned to him, his eyes were fixed on the communication room's door.

The sudden jarring of the opening door made everyone jump. "It was the Sarin gas. The bomb didn't go off on the AQ2! It was Sarin! I can't believe it," Chuck said, shaking his head. "I can't believe it. It didn't blow up."

"What does that mean?" Phillip asked Megan.

"It's a miracle," Megan said quietly, feeling lightheaded.

PLANS · VICTORIA J.M. HOFFBECK

CHAPTER 57

After their prayers of gratitude, Megan took the clothing that Chuck had given her and went into the small airplane restroom to change. The airtight suit was like an encapsulated sauna and she was covered with dripping sweat. She ripped open the front and was unzipping the lining when she noticed a small piece of paper stuck to her skin. It was damp and limp and had a message written on it in black ink that had smeared when she touched it. She picked it up by its corner.

If you ever need me, ask Broderick, it read. Megan remembered Westin bumping into her on his way out of the plane. Broderick? Was he in on this too, an agent perhaps?

"Megan, do you need help with the suit?" Ostride asked through the door, her voice still shaking.

"No, I'll be out in a minute," Megan said. She rinsed the scrap of paper in water, tore the note into pieces, and flushed it down the toilet. When she came out of the lavatory, everyone except Marcus was seated around a larger table. The small booths had been collapsed and the crew was at the front of the plane behind a sealed door. Payton was seated at the head of the table behind his laptop and had several file folders in a stack beside him. They were waiting for Marcus.

When he came out of the communications booth, Marcus was wearing blue jeans and a plaid flannel shirt. Megan looked twice and thought the simple clothing didn't detract from his striking features, but it did soften his character in a way that she hadn't seen before. She reached for his hand and they both sat down at the conference table across from Payton.

"What did you find out?" Phillip asked Marcus.

"Greven was found dead in his home, along with his son," Marcus answered gravely.

"Kurt?" Jacob asked.

"No, Erich," Marcus said.

"Erich?" Jacob questioned. "He was the only person I would have trusted in that family."

"They don't think he had anything to do with it," Marcus said, resting his elbows on the table and folding Megan's hand between his. "He must have stumbled onto his father's dealings and made a copy of the file and sent it to the king," Marcus continued. "He must not have known that Greven had attached a virus that activated the timer and then detonated the bomb," he said and closed his eyes. "They think Greven found out and killed Erich, and then himself."

"We played hockey together," Phillip said sadly. "I liked him. He wasn't anything like Greven."

"What about the dead?" Jacob asked.

"They were Greven's people. The gas didn't escape beyond the boundaries of the cave," Marcus said. Above the sound of the plane they could hear the communication officer signing off to Dreiholm.

"What are we supposed to do now?" Jacob said.

"We are to take our instructions from Chuck until we hear otherwise," Marcus said.

"Why?" Phillip asked. "If the danger is over, why can't we just go back home?"

"The danger is not over," Payton said. "The AQ2 didn't blow but the containers were damaged. This is an incredibly unstable chemical. Every conceivable precaution will have to be taken to remove and dispose of it. We will have to evacuate the whole Petra Mountain community before any work can be done. It might take weeks or even months before it will be completed."

"So, what now?" Marcus asked.

"You can't go back until it's safe," Chuck said, looking around the table. "So you'll be relocated to the United States for now. Megan, your lab has been duplicated and your files have been transferred to your new site. Because of the time crunch, we've brought in a few more assistants to help you and Ostride along with your work."

"Who?" Megan asked.

"Your uncle Joe, for one. He was the first to sign up," Chuck said with a smile.

"I'm glad to have him," Megan smiled, but her eyes had filled with tears again.

"I'll help," Marcus said.

"Not with this," Chuck said. "This isn't your field. It would take you too long to ramp up to speed for the final stages of testing. For now, you and Jacob will be going back to school. You're both excellent surgeons, so you're both going to be busy learning the art of transplant surgery," he said, handing them each a packet and their file. "Your names and identities have been changed. Memorize them."

"Why? Why have our names been changed?" Phillip protested. "Is this like witness protection?"

"There are two missions here," Chuck said. "First, to keep you all alive. Second, to have the uninterrupted time needed to get the job done. There are still too many loose ends. Megan and Ostride know how to keep their mouths shut about their work, and it saved their lives and the lives of their staff. And because of that, we now have the hope of saving many more. If Greven would have found out about their research, he would have had them killed and anyone associated with them. So, from now on until you return home, you will live a quiet and simple life," Chuck said.

"I graduated?" Jacob said, looking over the paperwork.

"You and Marcus only had four months left of residency. Dr. Weisman agreed you're both ready. You will receive your real diplomas when you get home, but for now you will be working at a university hospital near Megan and Ostrid.

"What if someone checks up on our records?" Marcus asked.

"We add a few names to every graduating class for this purpose and your other records have been dealt with."

"I'm German," Marcus said, scanning the papers.

"So am I," Jacob said.

"Because of your accent and physical appearance, people will assume you're German, especially where you're going," Chuck said.

"Where are we going?" Marcus asked.

"To Minnesota," Chuck said and looked at Megan. "There have been a lot of changes of late and we thought some familiarity would be helpful. You might have to travel from time to time, but in Minnesota we can get access to just about anything we need."

PLANS · VICTORIA J.M. HOFFBECK

Chuck slapped both hands on the table as he stood up. "So, here's the drill." He handed Megan and Ostride their files. "Megan, you left for Dreiholm with the scholarship program. You met a German doctor while you were there, Dr. Marc Kohler. You fell in love, got married and decided to come back home to work for the University with your uncle. It shouldn't be hard to remember."

He turned to face Ostride. "Your friend and lab partner, Megan, introduced you to Jacob Heppner. You fell in love instantly and eloped. You will be working for Brier Pharmaceuticals and the university on a joint project."

"Sort of backwards but close to reality anyway," Ostride said. "Ostride Heppner, O.H. Oh!" she laughed, trying to sound positive.

"And what about me?" Phillip asked.

Chuck slid the last file over to him. "Your parents thought it would be best if you enrolled at the university. You are no longer a cousin to Marcus. You're now brothers," Chuck said, glancing between the two. "You look enough alike to pull it off, Phillip, and your parents were hoping that until you get acclimated to your new surroundings, you could live with Marcus and Megan." Chuck looked at the couple for an answer.

"Sure," Megan said.

"I don't need babysitting," Phillip grumbled.

"It was that or you meet up with your old military unit in Uruguay," Chuck said. Marcus glanced at Phillip who remained silent. "All right then," Chuck said.

"How did you get to head up all of this?" Phillip asked.

"I work with the Pentagon," Chuck said.

"What?" they all asked in unison.

"You own Brier's and work for the United States government?"

"I can't believe any of this," Phillip asked.

"I can walk and chew gum at the same time, as well," Chuck said. "Memorize your files and let me know if you have any questions. Everything you need is in your packets."

"People will be inquiring about our absence. How have you made an account for that?" Marcus asked.

"Everyone knows by now what has happened, and the king has issued an order that you and the new princess remain in isolation and in the government's protection until the danger passes. Standard procedure."

"I should be at home with my people," Marcus protested.

"We'll try to get you back on occasion, but not without the king's explicit and unequivocal permission." Marcus bowed his head. "I know you want to be there, Marcus, but being a father and knowing the ramifications of this situation, I understand and agree with the king's position. You'll just have to adjust to your new life for the time being."

"Uruguay," Phillip said, staring blankly out the window.

"Oh, and by the way, you won't be able to access any of your funds while you're in the United States," Chuck said to Phillip. "You're now Phillip Kohler. None of you boys will. It would be too easy to trace to your new location."

"How will we buy what we need?" Phillip asked. "Clothes," he said, pulling at the plain sweatshirt Chuck had given him to wear. "How about food and other things?"

"You're enrolled at the university with a scholarship to study photojournalism. That will provide a small allowance as long as you are enrolled in school and meet the academic standard. Perhaps you can occupy your extra time with gainful employment."

Chuck turned slightly. "As for you and Jacob," he said to Marcus, "you two will have to live on what you earn. The university hospital pays a fair salary, but it won't be enough to spend willy-nilly. You'll have to budget."

"It doesn't matter," Marcus said, "we'll make do."

"Yes, we will, and we have so much to be thankful for," Jacob said. He could see Ostride was tired and anxious and scared. Her long, thick braid hung over her shoulder and Jacob nudged it as he touched her face. "I knew life was going to be an adventure with you. And look," he said pointing to his file. "I'm going to be studying my life's dream. I'll be doing transplants and I'll be with you, and we're on our honeymoon," Jacob said, wiping away her tears. "It's going to be just fine."

"Of course it is," she said, laughing between her tears. "I have you."

CHAPTER 58

When Megan came back from the restroom of the plane, she noticed Phillip asleep, reclined in one of the large chairs by the communications booth. His tousled blond hair, almost white from the brilliant sun, was matted against his furrowed brows and locked jaw. A stack of blankets sat on a chair next to him across the aisle. Megan unfolded one and put it on top of him. He groaned and pulled it closer to his face and then fell back to sleep.

Megan thought about home in Minnesota as she looked down at Phillip. This is going to be a shock, she thought. There will need to be adjustments. Then she looked at Marcus sitting by the window. He hadn't slept since they'd left Dreiholm and had been silent for hours. Weaving between equipment and the seats, she made her way back to him. She pushed up the armrest between them and curled up beside him, putting her head on his shoulder and tucking her feet up underneath her on the chair. He kissed the top of her head and then returned to his watch of the black night. They sat listening to the constant rumble of the plane.

"I walked on the very precipice of my own destruction, completely ignorant of the peril of my choices," he said. "How could I have been so blind?"

Megan held on to his arm and then began to rub his hand. He took hold of her fingers and began to stroke the smooth surface of one of her fingernails as he stared out the window. "All those people, in my care, they could have died. My family could have been destroyed," he said with a quiet sadness in his voice.

"God loves, God leads, God protects, and God is in control," Megan said. Marcus turned away from the window and looked into her sure and steady eyes. "We all make choices, Marcus. Greven made his, Nicole hers, you made yours, and I made mine. Those choices affected many people but God is still in control, beyond our choices and our regrets."

"But, if only I had been a different person from the start," Marcus said, "perhaps I could have prevented this from happening."

"If only," Megan said. "Let go of this burden Marcus. You turned your back on a way of life. You've asked and God has forgiven you. Now it's time to forgive yourself."

"How can I?"

"Because God is in control. You must believe that," Megan said. "There isn't an intentional evil, a reckless act or a foolish blunder that He can't overcome. This event was the culmination of not one, but a thousand bad choices by a multitude of people, but still He had the last word. You must trust God. We make mistakes. We learn, commit ourselves to change, and pray that the next time we run up against a challenge we will do better than we did before. That's all we can do."

"I wouldn't have done it without you," Marcus said.

"I don't know about that. God usually has a few backup plans," Megan said.

"I can't imagine not being married to you."

"Not married?" Megan asked. "What do you mean?"

"You could have just as easily gone away so many times. You had every reason," Marcus said.

"Without you?" Megan laughed. "You think so? I would have dragged you on to this plane kicking and screaming if you hadn't come to your senses earlier," Megan said. "Leave you behind? Not married?" Megan mumbled to herself. "How ridiculous! "

"Have I told you today that I love you?" Marcus asked. Megan looked at her watch. It was late but just before midnight.

"Yes, you have, but you can say it again," she said with a smile.

"I love you," he whispered and kissed her.

"I love you, too," she said and kept her eyes on his chest.

"What is it?" Marcus asked.

"I've never seen you in a plaid flannel shirt," Megan said. Marcus brushed the flannel shirt.

"It is comfortable," Marcus said with a measure of surprise.

"And the jeans don't look bad on you either," Megan said. Marcus noticed a glint in her eye and laughed. "But I don't know if plaid is your thing. We'll have to go shopping when we get settled."

"You mean when I get my first paycheck," Marcus said.

"Chuck said you couldn't access your accounts but he didn't say I couldn't access mine. I'm not wealthy but I do have what my parents left me and that will be enough to get us started."

"That is your money," Marcus said.

"Now, it's our money," Megan said, looking down at her hands. Her rings glittered on her finger under the small reading light above their seat.

"Megan, I had so many splendid plans. I was going to take you to Greece and Italy, to the coast of Spain, to my apartment in London, a castle in Ireland, and to my land in Scotland. Then I wanted to take you home and teach you everything about Dreiholm and have you get to know my family and why I love them so much."

"Plans," Megan said. She thought of her arrival in Dreiholm and how her trust in God's plan brought so much change to her life. "God's plan" she whispered, "for all of us."

Jacob's arm dropped to the floor and stirred his deep slumber. Marcus watched as his friend looked at Ostride in his arms, kissed her and then fell back to sleep. "In the midst of this turmoil and chaos, he is content and happy," Marcus said. Megan looked at the couple sleeping peacefully.

"So, we're on an adventure then?" Marcus asked, looking down at Megan. Megan turned and looked into his shining blue eyes.

"For a lifetime," Megan said and smiled.

The intercom crackled. "This is Captain Davidson. Crew and passengers prepare for landing." When Payton came out of the communications booth he saw Phillip dozing in his seat, Jacob and Ostride slowly stirring, and Megan and Marcus sharing a kiss before they looked up at him standing at the front of the plane. From the windows they could see the glittering lights of the massive freeway system encircling the international airport in Minnesota.

"Heads up!" Chuck said, kicking Phillip's seat. "Boys, welcome to your new world."

A Changed Heart

As I looked within my heart and only found darkness and despair,
I turned to a stranger who let me in and did not deny me his hope and care.

And through his kindness he melted my heart, once filled with evil deeds,
And led me to a light I had not known, one that fills my every need.

In that moment I could clearly see
The difference between the Lord Jesus, the Christ, and me,
As if I stood before a mirror, I wanted to turn away —
Seeing before my eyes my ravaged heart of death and decay.

I fell to my knees and cried bitter tears,
Remembering the pain I had caused throughout my years.
Every unkind word, every good deed left undone,
When I lacked the strength and courage, when I said I was just having fun.

When I discouraged others,
When I demanded my own way,
When I walked out the door
When I was expected to stay.

I did not look up nor could I turn away
Instead from my knees, I asked the Lord to hear me pray.

In that moment, basking in a warmth I had never known,
I felt His peace and heard His voice calling my heart home.

Now, my days are not done, and in the time I have left,
It was my responsibility, I was told, to keep my heart well kept

I must fight off my foes, wearing the armor of salvation,
Exuding God's love and resisting temptation

I am not alone in the battle already won
I can trust the Holy Spirit and God's righteous Son
So, I will have no fear as I forge ahead
My debt has been paid, and I will live a life worth being led.

Author's Note

We all have plans, dreams for the next five or ten years, or even a lifetime, but plans change. Diversions take us down another path, underlying currents drift us off in a new direction, tragedy pulls us away, and true love can set us sailing. Plans are our attempt at direction, but God has a purpose for each life, and often it seems what we thought was the best plan for our life was just a starting point for His purpose.

I wrote the first draft of this book over 25 years ago, the first of a trilogy of books about Megan. I had just graduated from law school and Megan came to mind. Like her I had plans, but mine were meant to change, and it was my time to trust God to set the course.

Where Megan submits to God, Marcus and I share resistance and frustration; wrestling with God with questions: why isn't the world fair? Why doesn't He intervene in our pain? Why isn't God evident?

I have found that God is willing to answer if we are willing to listen, but first we must invite God's Son, Jesus Christ, into our heart. Faith, like love, is a commitment. And once made it can grow, as does our understanding and peace that is found only in God.

My hope and prayer is that you know, or will come to know Christ, and that this simple story might draw you nearer to Him who loves you; that you will seek God, have many daily conversations and ask a thousand questions of Him, and have the willingness of heart to listen for His answers. The stronger your relationship with Christ, the greater blessings will be upon you, and the gift of your life will be to this world.

Are you seeking Christ or are you a veteran Christian wanting to dive into Scripture? Are you searching for an answer to a difficult life question? Might I suggest visiting BillyGraham.org, Harvest.org, RZIM.org, and Insight.org. Each of these biblically-based ministries offer resources for a Christian walk.

Thank you for reading *Plans*. May God bless you.

– VJM Hoffbeck

Made in the USA
Columbia, SC
25 November 2017